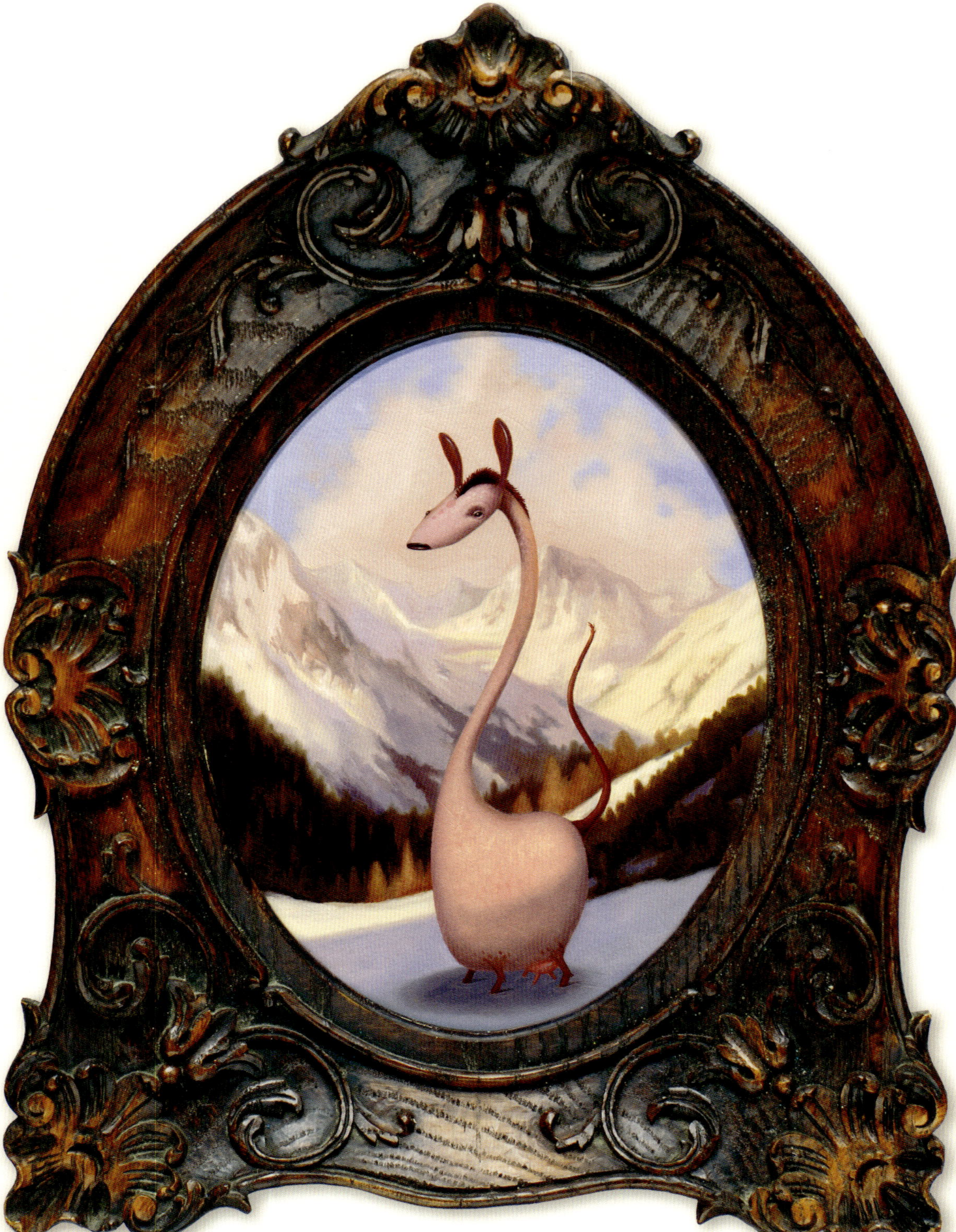

" Whatever was possible for Nature to produce,
has actually been produced." —*Buffon*

Scott Musgrove

THE LATE FAUNA OF EARLY NORTH AMERICA

Comprehensive, Scientific, and Popular

Featuring many Depictions

of

HITHERTO UNDISCOVERED AND NOW EXTINCT ANIMALS, CREATURES, AND OTHER BEASTS

Including

Some Explanations

Depictions, Diagrams, Recipes, and Charts

Relating to the Habits, Structure, and Classification of these

ANIMALS

Over Eighty Full-Color Plates

by

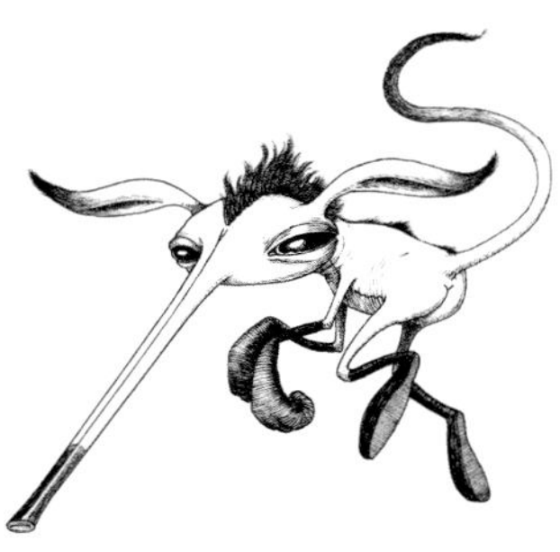

SCOTT MUSGROVE

Author of "The Accidental Taxidermist,"

"The Secret Life of Leftovers,"

and "The Natural History of Suburbia"

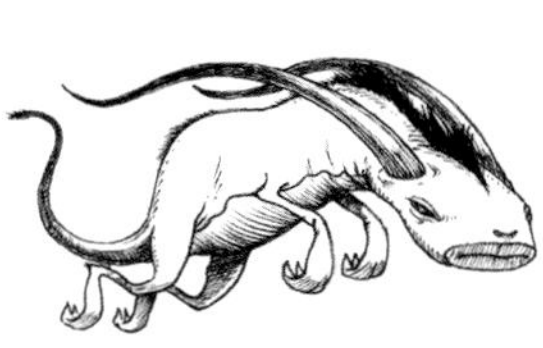

also

Co-Executive Director of

THE NATIONAL INSTITUTE OF CREATIVE BIOLOGY

Published by

BILLY SHIRE FINE ARTS

and

LAST GASP

2009

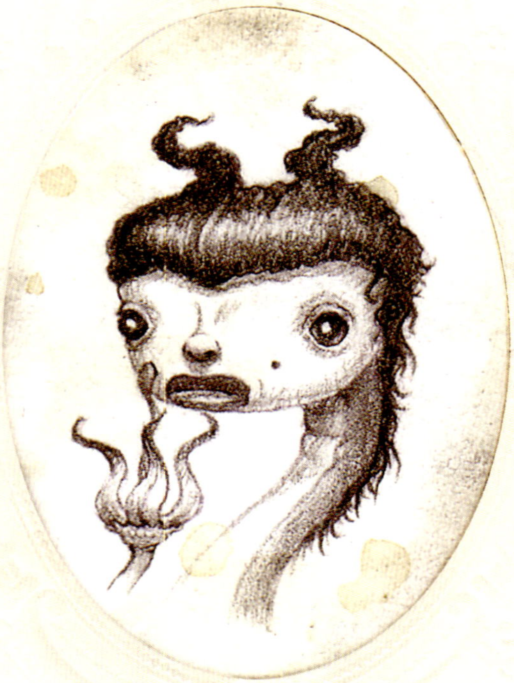

SPECIOUS BEASTS

an Introduction

I never intended to discover numerous heretofore unidentified animal species and, thereby, turn the scientific community on its ear. These discoveries, and my theories of how they came to be, have won me few friends and many enemies among experts in the fields of History, Biology, Zoology, and the Culinary Arts. . . . I don't have many friends in Mathematics either. When one reports honestly from the front lines of Evolutionary Biology, one should be prepared to ruffle a few feathers.

In challenging beloved scientific assumptions and throwing a Rhesus monkey wrench into the grinding machinery of the status quo, I have sparked a powder keg of reflexive anger from legions of zoological theorists whose scientific essays and thesis papers now appear, if not merely wide of the mark, patently absurd in the revelatory glare of my newly introduced fauna. They can no better account for the Salvelinus Fontinalis Hirsutus (Hairy Brook Trout) than they can the Elliptical Equine, or any of my newly discovered animal species lodged so high in the tree of life. No matter what your local zookeeper says, these are no mere evolutionary weeds - they are leaves on the Tree of life (Life Tree Leaves) that, sadly, have fallen before their time in the cruel summer of our fertile planet.

I am Scott Musgrove. I read these tree leaves.

ORIGINS (OF ME)

People always ask me: how does a guy go from being on a chain gang in rural Mississippi to being the Honorary Chairman of the National Institute of Creative Zoology? Well, I don't know, but it happened to a friend of mine. I'll have to ask him about it. As for my particular story, it is as tangled as the DNA Helix of an extinct Siamese Albinus Ambystoma. To some I am a paradigm-shifting zoologist; to others I am an American Dr. Frankenstein without the Ph.D., fancy castle or moral fiber.

As a child, I remember well the first time I saw the famous Patterson film of Bigfoot. While the rest of the world was focusing on watching Sasquatch, trying to determine his authenticity (except Aunt Barbara, who was focusing on her Gin and Tonic), I found myself marveling at all the strange fauna in the scene; the dodo-type birds scattering across the creek-bed to the safety of the bushes, the small, unfamiliar insects and amphibians falling from his fur as he lumbered towards the dark woods and the unnamed mammals leaping from rock to tree in the background. Here was a churning cesspool of fauna that was being ignored. Upstaged, as it were, by a preening exhibitionist Man Ape. Ultimately, this now famous film footage (and some unpaid speeding tickets) had much to do with my decision, years later, to move West to the relative wilds of the Pacific Northwest. I wanted to get a closer look.

One wonders, how could Science and History have given up on and forgotten these splendid and awkward creatures? Should these species have lived and died in vain? Well?? Did they pass the ruthless test of evolution throughout numberless millennia and struggle against the harshness and brutality of Nature only to die and lie buried beneath Interstate 90 outside of Bend, Oregon? That seems to be the case. In the instance of the Hairy Brook Trout, it doesn't help that he was so delicious.

The scientific community seems to have almost willfully ignored this domestic and, frankly, less-than-glamorous area of study, perhaps afraid of what they'd find, or maybe just kinda grossed out by the sheer fecundity, if not the queer moribundity, of the North American wilderness. Indeed, science had failed to milk this field of study, leaving it unmilked until the Zoological Udder became clogged. Well, I plan to keep tugging and squeezing until the world is verily flooded with the milk of forgotten knowledge! So to speak.

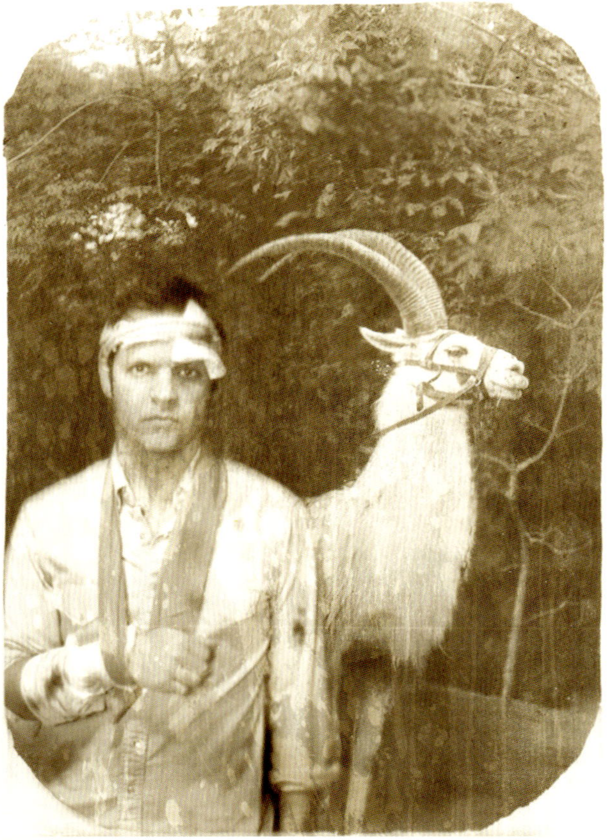

Perils in the field of research: Allergic reaction to partially-untamed llama escort (Louisianna Long-Horned Rental Llama.)

After college, with a few trips to South America under my belt, I began my research in earnest. While all the handsome, credentialed paleontologists with graying manes of hair, pointy English boots and khaki outfits were combing such glamorous locations as the Gobi Desert and the Great Rift Valley looking for high-ticket items like the very macho (and probably imaginary) "Tyrannosaurus Rex," I was clawing my way through the underbrush behind mini malls and under freeway overpasses in search of the forgotten cousins of the Calvus Mogera Terra (Bald Surface Mole). I unearthed nests of petrified "dog eggs" while being bitten and stung by relatives of the Palorus Subdepressus (Depressed Dinner Beetle) and the Cimex Nigrocinctus! A thankless task? Yes. Oh, hell yes. But one that, soon enough, was to bear unlikely, and revolutionary, fruit.

Let's look at the case of the Dwarf Basket Horse: it was during a routine excavation at the State Penitentiary in West Texas that I first discovered this charming creature. What I initially took to be a peculiar bird skeleton tangled in its own nest turned out to be, in fact, a curious mammal, which would later be known, mostly by me, as the Dwarf Basket Horse.

Early American pioneers encountered these creatures back in the 1800s, describing them in letters sent back East as "horse-seeds"; that is, they apparently thought these were horses growing on trees. Good guess. Unfortunately, the majority of settlers arrived from the South and mistook these things suspended in the trees for piñatas. As a result, the Basket Horses were whacked mercilessly with sticks, the settlers apparently expecting candy.

Due to poor communication, and ignorance of science, word never spread very far that these were not, in fact, piñatas. So, wave after wave of stick-wielding revelers moved across the land, beating the adorable Basket Horse deep into the blood-splattered pages of history. Only a few crude drawings survive to this day. Obviously, these were of little help in my research. However, thanks to my vast knowledge of biology, taxidermy, mammal anatomy, zoology, and...um...horseology, I think it's probably called, I was able to reconstruct the

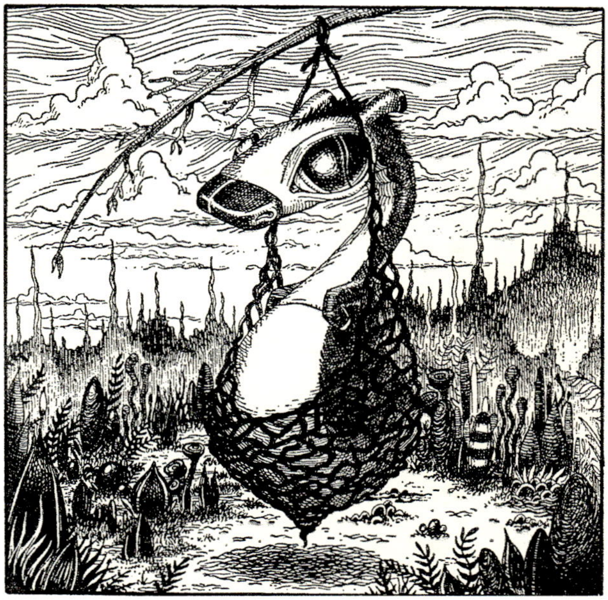

Early Late-Afternoon of the so-called Dwarf Basket Horse.

probable appearance of this animal. Owing to my rather large collection of various bones, sticks, fabrics, and furs, I am able to build pretty much any animal I need to. This drawing shows the Basket Horse in its native habitat, safely ensconced in its basket.

As a result of over-hunting and man-made environmental changes, most of these creatures were driven to extinction before they could be properly documented, let alone be bred into commercially available housepets. Who knows how many medical secrets, links in the food chain, and lip-smacking hors d'œuvres have been lost forever as a result of Man's reckless and wanton recklessness?

Let's take another example, that of the beautiful Booted Glamour Cat: The Booted Glamour Cat was always a rare creature. It never thundered across the plains in enormous herds like the American Buffalo or Harea Narcoleptus (Mild Prairie Rabbit), but mostly lived in pairs hereabouts and thereabouts. Like many animals discovered in the American West, it was first trapped and shipped to Europe to be displayed in private and pubic menageries. Eventually it was hunted to extinction for its exotic and quite fluffy fuzzy fur collar. It was a sign of status for a man to be seen about town

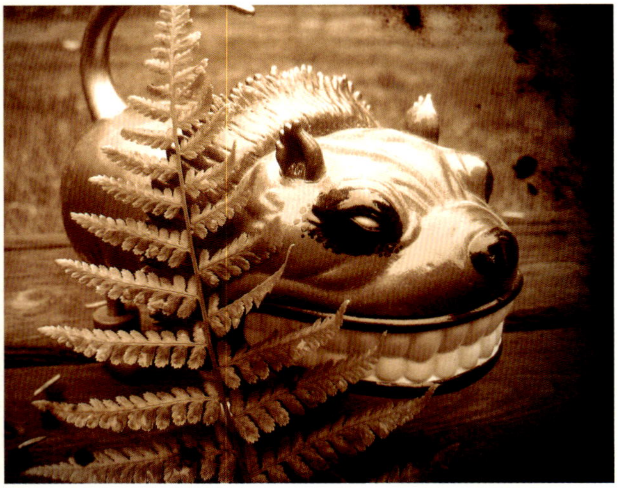

Genuine Booted Glamour Cat replica.

wearing the Glamour Cat's shimmering fluff around his own neck. Women were forbidden to wear them. In addition, the Glamour Cat's large, super-hard teeth were fashioned into tools for use in the mining industry. Fortunately, I was able to locate some 19th century amateur renderings of this animal, and I also unearthed some Glamour Cat skeletons when they were doing construction on a new mini-mall near my house. From all of this, I have been able to recreate what the Glamour Cat must have looked like before this vain creature was lured to extinction using compliments and mirrors.

Nearly everywhere we look in this modern world we see buildings, vehicles, and paving stones. But what came before? What used to trot, squat, or stalk on the very spot of your local hair salon, your favorite restaurant, or your very own home? What is that sound that wakes you in the night? Is it the ghost of the Great Prairie Squid who once preambulated silently in the stream that used to run beneath your bed? Perhaps that sound is just the millions of spiders and scorpions that fill the space between your walls, or the parasites that fill your belly. But maybe, just maybe, it's something talking to you from the past, from History itself. Maybe?

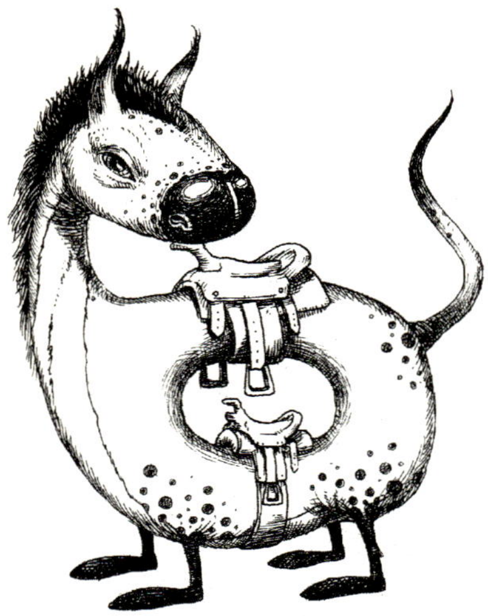

Elliptical Equine (dual-occupancy transport, artist depiction)

It is impossible that the mighty leviathan we call the Whale should be able to survive on nearly microscopic prey, yet it does. So why couldn't the Elliptical Equine have galloped and frolicked freely across the heights of the Sierra? And what a shame it was never domesticated. What a joy it would have been to ride a Double-Deckered Horse!

But for the Microscope, we would have no idea of the myriad of life living around, upon, and inside us. And if not for my courage, goggles, gloves, and shovel, the world may never have known of the Extinct Beasts contained within these pages.

Indeed, many people ask me (not the same folks that ask me about prison) about my research techniques. They are fairly basic and simple. You see: I'm no busybody. I'm frankly often a little surprised that I've been the first one to identify some of these species. Generally, after finding bones near the highway or in the abandoned housing development, I just start gluing them together according to my knowledge of anatomy. Once I end up with the proper structure, I drape different kinds of fabric or carpet over the bones to simulate the appropriate texture of the fur, as it must have looked long, long ago.

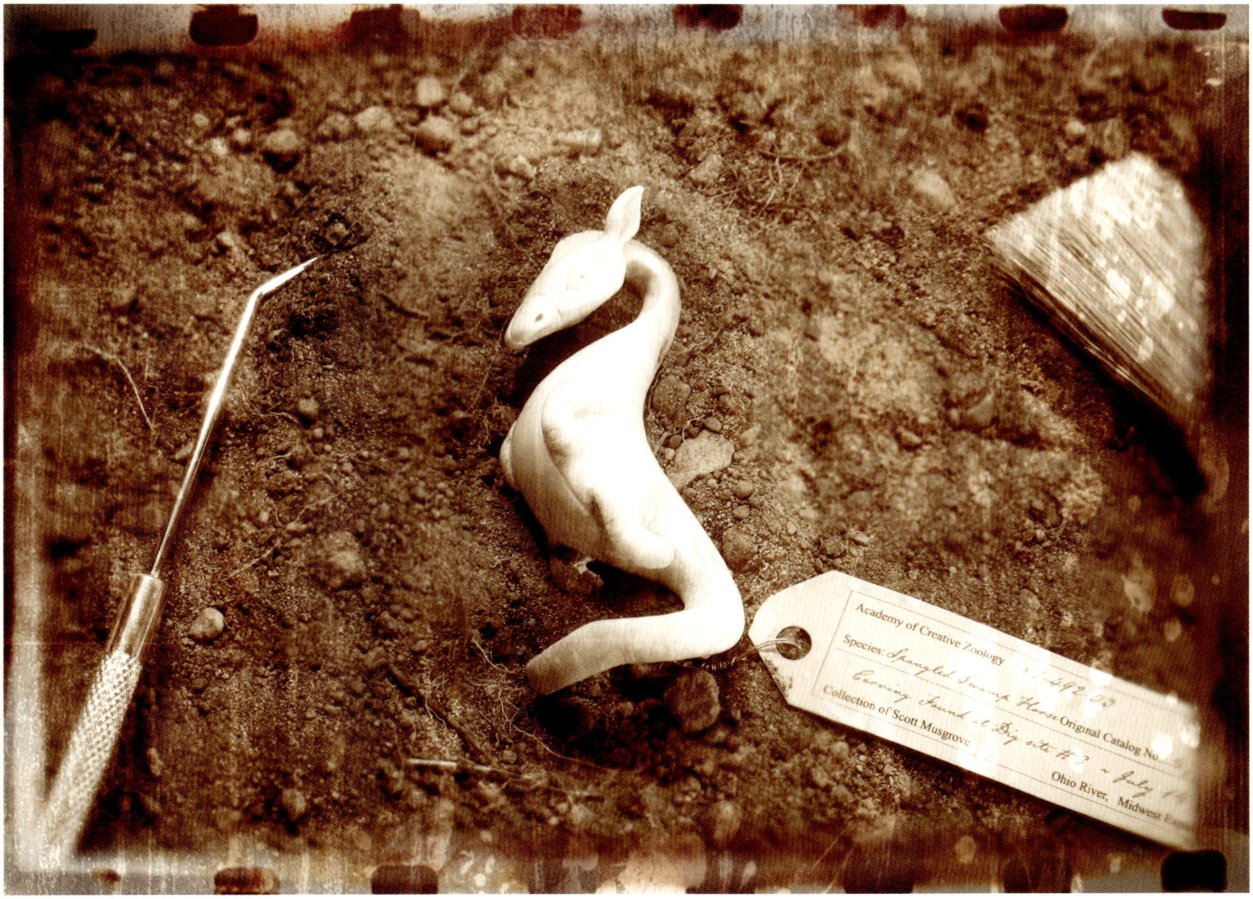

Discovery of Dwarf Swamp Horse, annual excavation expedition behind mini-mall near author's Summer house in Double Pines, OH.

Then I start taking notes and begin painting. Then, lunch.

BALANCING ACT

The Balance of Power in the Animal Kingdom has been upset. As we all remember from grade school, the number of eggs in the roe of the humble Mackerel is 546,680. Nature requires this number exactly, for a baby Mackerel can meet its end a multitude of ways. But Mackerel survive because of this balance.

Nature, for all its intrinsic balance, moves too slowly to oppose Man's sheer brute force and ingenuity. She visits upon us small indignities to avenge these crimes, but the porcupine's quill and the skunk's spray are but temporary slights. The bite of the Horse Fly is a painful nuisance, and the Crocodile's bite is surely unforgettable. However, they do little to quell Man's cross-eyed desire for destruction. In fact, these insults spur Man on to greater mayhem. How do we kill the pesky mosquito? We drain the swamps and lakes and blanket the forests with a poisonous fog. But what else do we lose when we do this? What happens to the Junior Swamp Horse? The Hydrophiidus Mare Maris? The Lesser Blackmouth Catfish?

Look around your house. Lift your eyes from this volume right now. Look there beneath your desk: observe your African Elephant Leg trash can, in which you so absently discard chewed chicken bones. Look there, dear reader, at the Gorilla Hand Ashtray in which you tap out the ashes from your Ostrich LegBone pipe. There on the bed: your snuggly Bald Eagle Feather-Filled comforter. These objects fill all of our homes. But did you ever consider from whence they came? And at what cost? To whom? Or What? Well? Did you?

Of course not, because then you'd have to give up the Ring-Tailed Lemur Skull Shift-Knob in your Bio Diesel VW. And how many of us are really prepared to do that?

WHAT HAVE WE HERE?

Each painting in this volume depicts not so much an individual animal as it strives to present an example of the

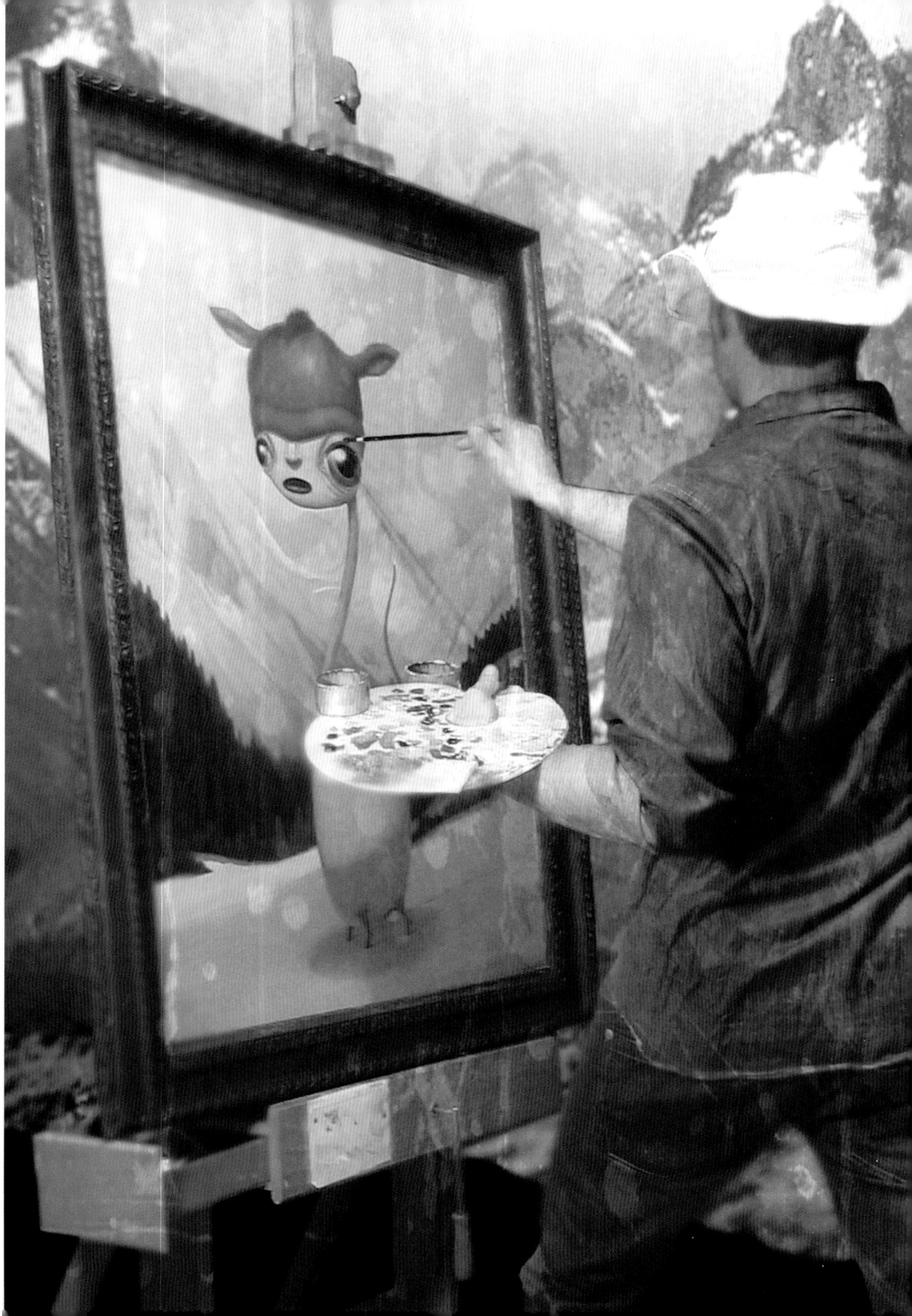

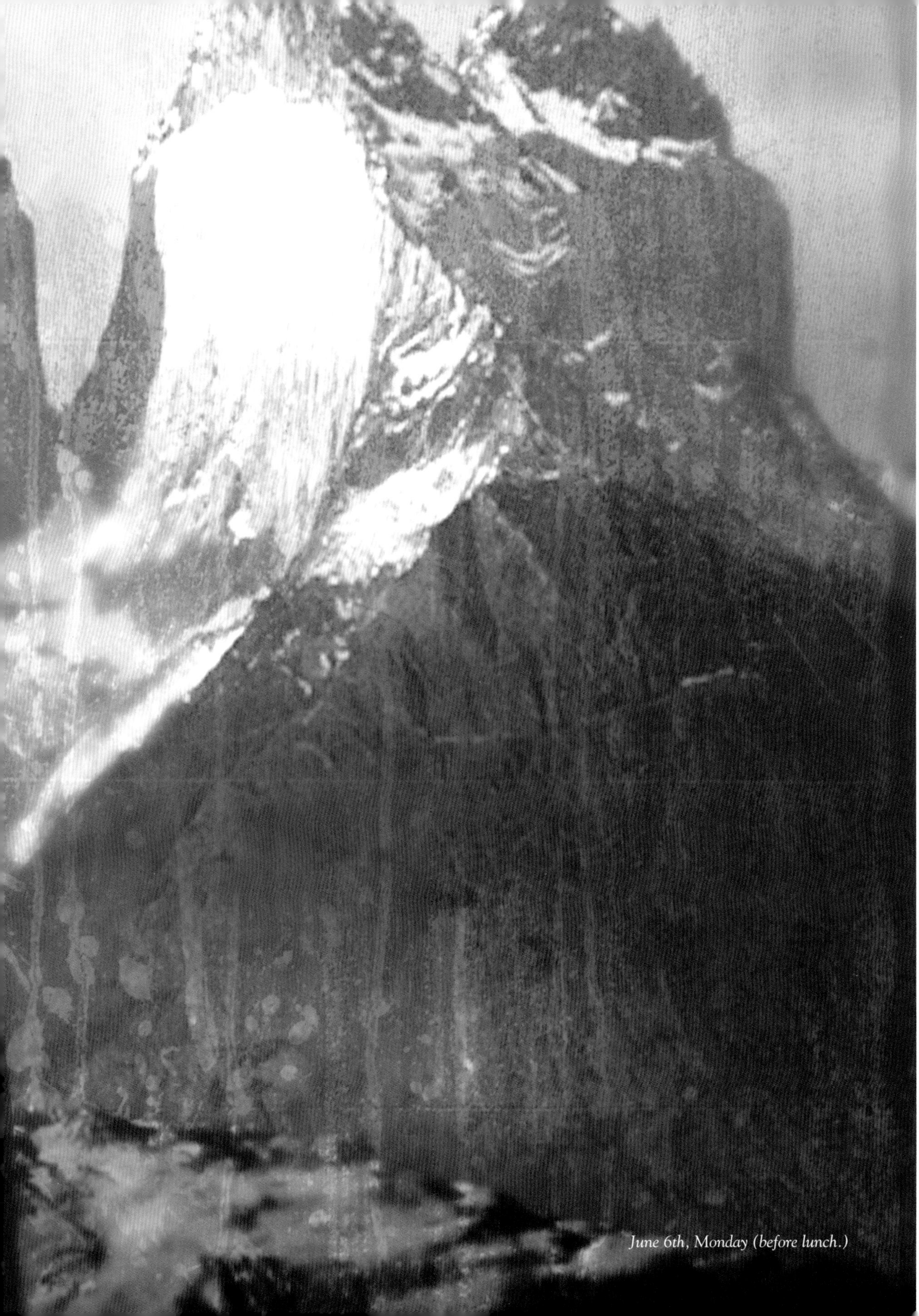

June 6th, Monday (before lunch.)

A TELLING STORY

I am now reminded of an adventure in Sumatra I undertook as a younger man. Along with a few unimpressive and forgettable companions, I hired a local Sumatran man to guide us into the jungly interior. We walked for several days through the humid, fetid air of the swampy forest. We trudged through mud, hacked through vegetation and washed ourselves as we forded through waist-deep streams. Finally, we reached our destination, a small village of about six huts built upon stilts to raise them above the mud floor of the jungle. We stayed in the hut of the village shaman, who, like the other men, wore only a loincloth made from a softened inner-tree bark.

As it happened, there were a few other shamans visiting from nearby villages, so a minor feast was prepared. Prior to cooking, a ceremony was necessary. The four shamans sat in a circle and killed a chicken so that they could read its entrails by firelight. From these chicken guts they could divine the future. Sadly for the village (and especially sad for the remaining village chickens), the intestines bore bad news. So, they killed another and another chicken until they got the answer they wanted. They just wouldn't take "no" for an answer. The dead chickens were whisked away to the back room of the hut, where the women had the cooking fire going.

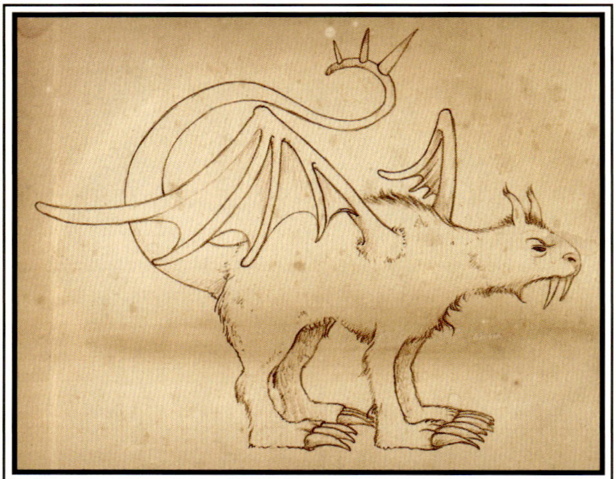

Shortly, I was summoned into the very dimly lit cooking area, where a wooden cup containing a warm dark liquid was put to my lips. Was this chicken blood? The international gesture for "chug this" was made. I took as small a sip as I could manage without offending. I nodded approvingly as I tried not to gag. I hurried out of the cooking area and back to the main room to find my canteen. I chugged the whole thing, trying to wash the bloody taste from my mouth. It wasn't enough. My companions, being otherwise occupied, had left their canteens unattended. So I chugged both of those, too.

Our meal of sagu and chicken went down fairly uneventfully. As the evening wore down, I felt the need to relieve myself of the burden of three canteens of water. So then, I...uh, where was I going with all of this?

Oh, right...

Obviously in such a rustic setting there were no facilities in the hut; trotting out into the jungle was the only option. Luckily it was a clear night, brightened by a nearly full moon. I wandered down to an empty streambed. I had a feeling of contentment as I stood in the moonlit jungle. I could hear the muffled chatter from the nearby village and an occasional grunt from the pigs that lived beneath the huts. Then, out of the corner of my eye, I saw some movement. Something was coming towards me in the streambed. It strode slowly but with confidence. It looked to be furry and about three feet high at the shoulder. It walked on four legs. It seemed to have feet instead of paws or hooves. I would guess a size 5 pair of women's shoes would have fit about right. The fur was short, but frankly, a bit unkempt looking. It looked somewhat like an anteater, but with a much shorter snout. Had I been in North America, I would have assumed it to be a bear and might have fought it, or killed it with my hands so I could study and paint it. However, this was unfamiliar territory and an unfamiliar animal. So instead, I ran like hell. I sprinted through the mud towards the safety of the huts. I vaulted over a couple of downed trees and used a pig as a step and leapt towards the nearest hut. Mid-leap, I remembered to zip up my fly and landed, presentable and breathless, in the shaman's hut.

"What happened?" the villagers probably asked in their obscure dialect. After a few deep breaths, I told my story. With our guide as the translator, I described the animal that had nearly killed me. I gave my best description and pantomime, but to no avail. The locals didn't know this creature. So I grabbed a pencil and paper from my porter's bag and commenced drawing.

While I drew the beast from memory, a small crowd of villagers surrounded me. As a trained wildlife artist, I must say I totally nailed the likeness. Yet the villagers looked puzzled. They chattered with each other, trying to identify the animal, or perhaps they were just discussing how awesome my drawing was. Regardless, no positive identification was forthcoming. At this point, I began to notice the appearance of some village children who had woken up from all the commotion. Over shoulders and between knees, they peered wide-eyed at my drawing. Since my hope of identifying the animal was quickly fading, I decided to entertain the kids a little. So I began drawing wings on the animal. And then I added huge claws. Then, fangs and a spiked tail. Silently, I congratulated myself for being so clever. By the time bloody horns protruded from the creature's back, I heard gasps from the villagers.

When I looked up from my drawing, everyone, especially the children, was shrinking back in horror. Immediately I regretted everything (including the incident with Mrs. Weinberg). I realized that I had made these kind villagers afraid of their friendly, peaceful jungle home. They really believed that I had seen such an awful creature outside of their hut. Where they were once in harmony with their environment, they now lived in fear.

I learned later that all the villagers abandoned their village and their loincloths and moved to the city, where they must wear pants at all hours, and shirts. But the real lesson I learned is that reports from Explorers like me are not always reliable. It seems that sometimes people exaggerate or perhaps just don't see things as they truly are. Since that event, I have vowed to draw, paint and describe everything as it really exists or existed. So, as a result, everything you see and read in this book is a Fact. So I destroyed an entire village with my lies and exaggerations...but that's no reason to judge me. I am not a bad person. I don't have huge claws or a spiked tail.

—— S.M.

species in its natural habitat. However, even by depicting a "generic" representative of the species, we can't help but see in it a singular animal with a singular personality.

Is that personality really there, or do we imagine it? Are we incapable of turning off the part of us that wants to see familiarity in even the most alien of species? Again, take the Booted Glamour Cat as an example. When we look at this painting, we don't just see a type of animal, we see an individual who, if alive today, would certainly enjoy long walks on the beach, horseback riding, a fine Cabernet, and eating toothpaste. We can't assume that all Glamour Cats would enjoy such things, but we know that this particular Glamour Cat would. So we can't merely think in scientific terms about these animals. They were individuals with their own hopes and dreams, just like you and me. My dream was to be a dancer, but like the Glamour Cat, my dreams were dashed with a few crushing blows...in my case by Glenda Weinberg.

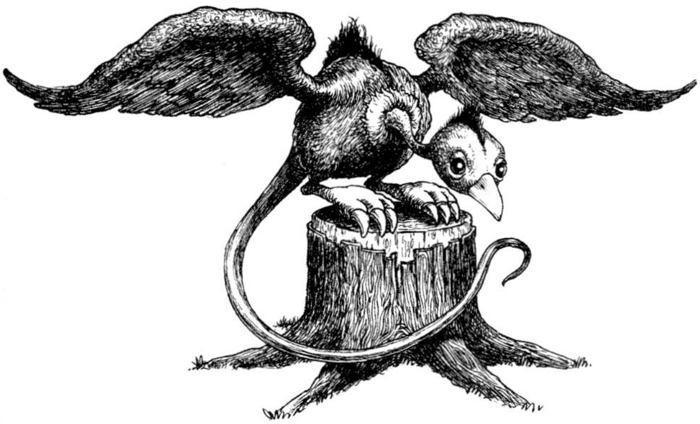

UNEXTINCTION?

Since all we may have left of some of these animals are partial physical remains, we must do our best with what we have. We have Science and we have Art. And from this, we must bring these beasts back to life.

Life. So, what is it then? What is it when, say, a Pelagus Bellua Bardus stamps at fish in the shallows and tosses his lustrous mane in the breeze of an approaching storm one moment, and then, an instant later, after being struck down by the hunter's bullet, he is an altogether different thing? Where once was "life" and motion is now but a lump of flesh and fur. It weighs the same, takes up the same volume of space, but yet, something is missing. It is less, much less than it once was. But what exactly has disappeared? And why won't it come back?

This is my mission; to bring them back, if only in paint.

A DAY IN THE LIFE

A man whose name is now synonymous with conservation, John James Audubon, was in his day a great murderer of beasts. An average day for him went something like this: he'd rise before dawn for a breakfast of dog eggs and whiskey. Then he'd grab his gun and set out to kill as many birds and beasts as possible before 10am. Then he'd head home for a nap. After lunch, he'd pose the dead things in as lifelike a manner as possible and paint them back to life in a scene as pristine as the one he'd yanked the animal from that very morning. Morbid? Yes. Practical? Again, yes. And so it goes with my endeavor, except that I attempt to bring these animals back, not just from death, but from Extinction itself.

"What is a normal day like for me?" you'd surely ask upon making my acquaintance. Well, like Audubon, I'm up early, but I prefer coffee and a Danish. Then off to the living room for a nap until midmorning. So I am very careful in this manner to cut out the whole entire killing part of my day. Then I don my dungarees and fold up my living room sofa and head out to dig: beneath a freeway underpass, on a golf course, beneath a municipal pool. Wherever my research leads me. My assistants and I work with no regard for the weather, no regard for our own safety, and very little regard for city ordinances. Back at the lab, we carefully catalog the day's discoveries. After countless hours spent recreating the newly excavated animals, I begin painting.

BUT A DAY TOO LATE?

Unfortunately, it's too late for these once proud creatures. They are gone, and we shall never see the likes of them again. Let us take care with what we have left...and make sure we don't repeat the mistakes of the past.

So, I now carry on in the tradition of Albertus Seba, John James Audubon, Edward O. Wilson, and Gary Hoeffelfinger to document that which we must not lose to the ages. But make no mistake, this is no easy business; one must have the mind of a detective, the eyes of a Casus Pelicanus, the patience of a right-fielder, the forearms of a sailor, a sturdy hat, some brushes, paints, and maybe a stapler. It is a difficult life, replete with poison ivy, poison nettles, rug burns, poison grass stains, restless leg, and ridicule...but don't pity me. I've gotten used to it all. It is a life consciously chosen, and by this point I have grown to like it. Indeed, a path necessary to follow. History plods forward, trampling those who pause. It's far too late to turn back now.

Now that these species are extinct, the best they can hope for is to be recognized posthumously by the very species that most certainly caused their extinction: MINE!

Let them now be celebrated by those who despised them most: US!

Let us now honor the creatures we didn't care enough about to save: THESE ONES!

Behold, already:
The Late Fauna of Early North America!

— Scott Musgrove
Seattle, Washington
January 2009

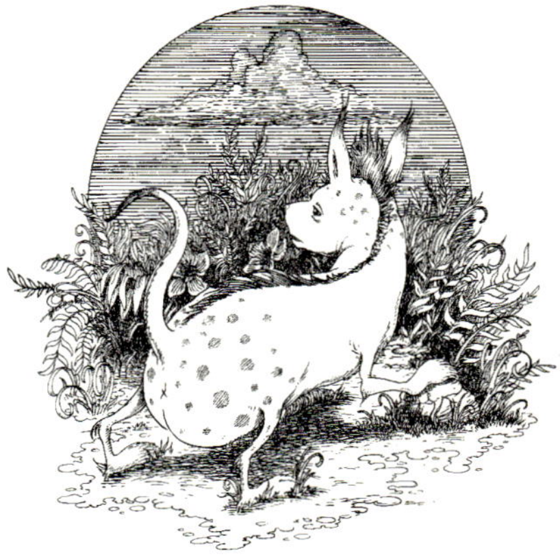

AUTHOR'S NOTE

While this volume is primarily intended for popular reading, it may also be used by the Scientific Community to supplement their work in this ever-expanding field.

I personally have discovered over 8,500 new and now-extinct species in the Animal Kingdom and, as might be expected, I have had to make a very narrow selection for this first volume.

In North America there are thousands of species of fish and hundreds of species of mammals. Heck, there are about a hundred poisonous toads just living in my attic. So the choices of what to depict are multitudinous. It is my expectation that you will enjoy, benefit from, and approve of my selections here. I have endeavored to select the most remarkable and formerly awesome species we have lost.

As to the inconsistencies in the naming of these animals: In some cases I have included the Scientific name of the species. With others I have only included the common name. This was done for no particular reason I can recall.

I have found it to be more economical, informative and certainly more accessible to the non-scientist to exhibit here my paintings of these animals rather than to compile a complete catalog of my writings, research, and photographs of my physical reconstructions.

Booted Glamour Cat

Extinct ~ ca. 1855

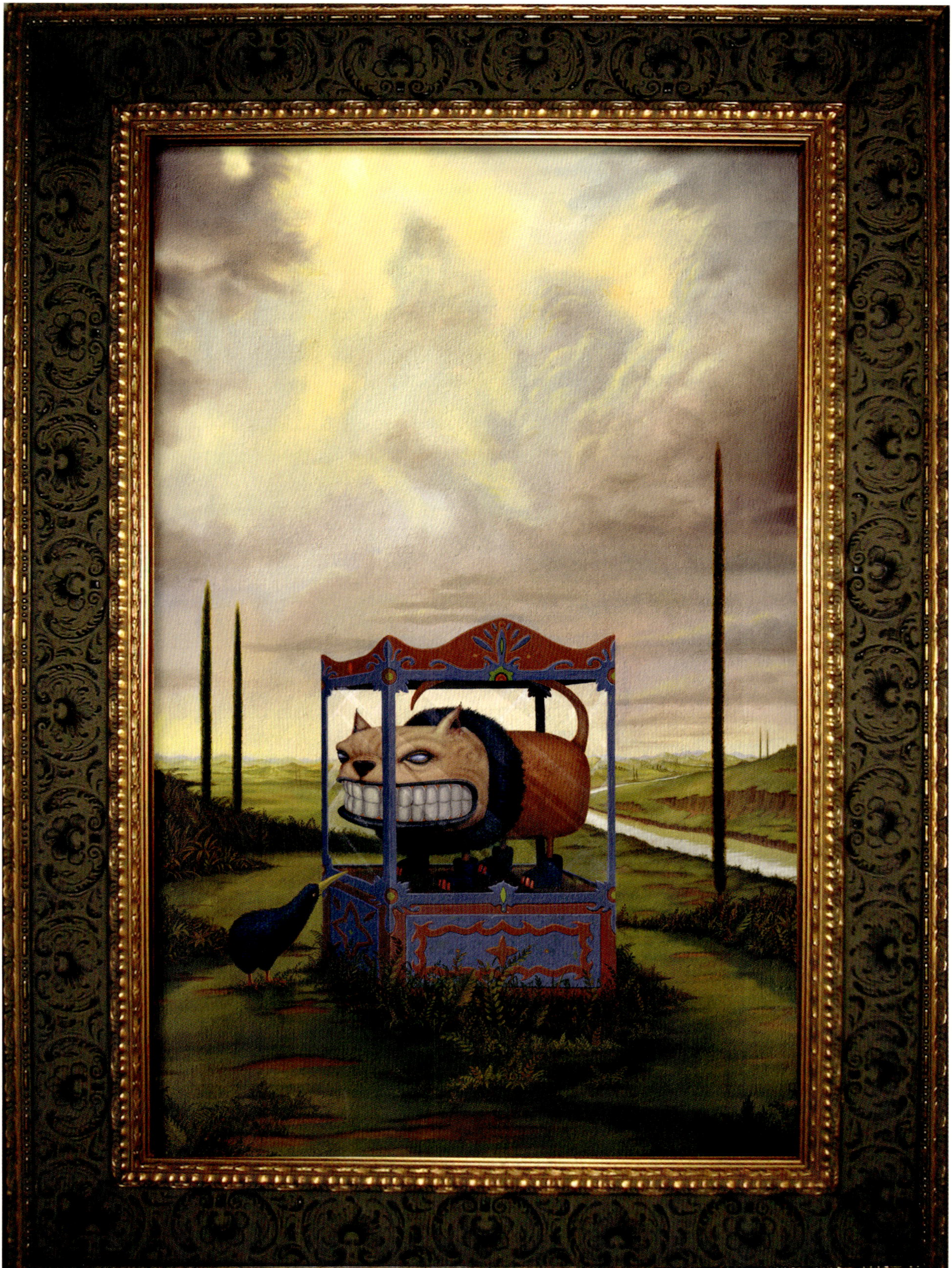

Long Necked Lotus Loris

Extinct ~ ca. 1901

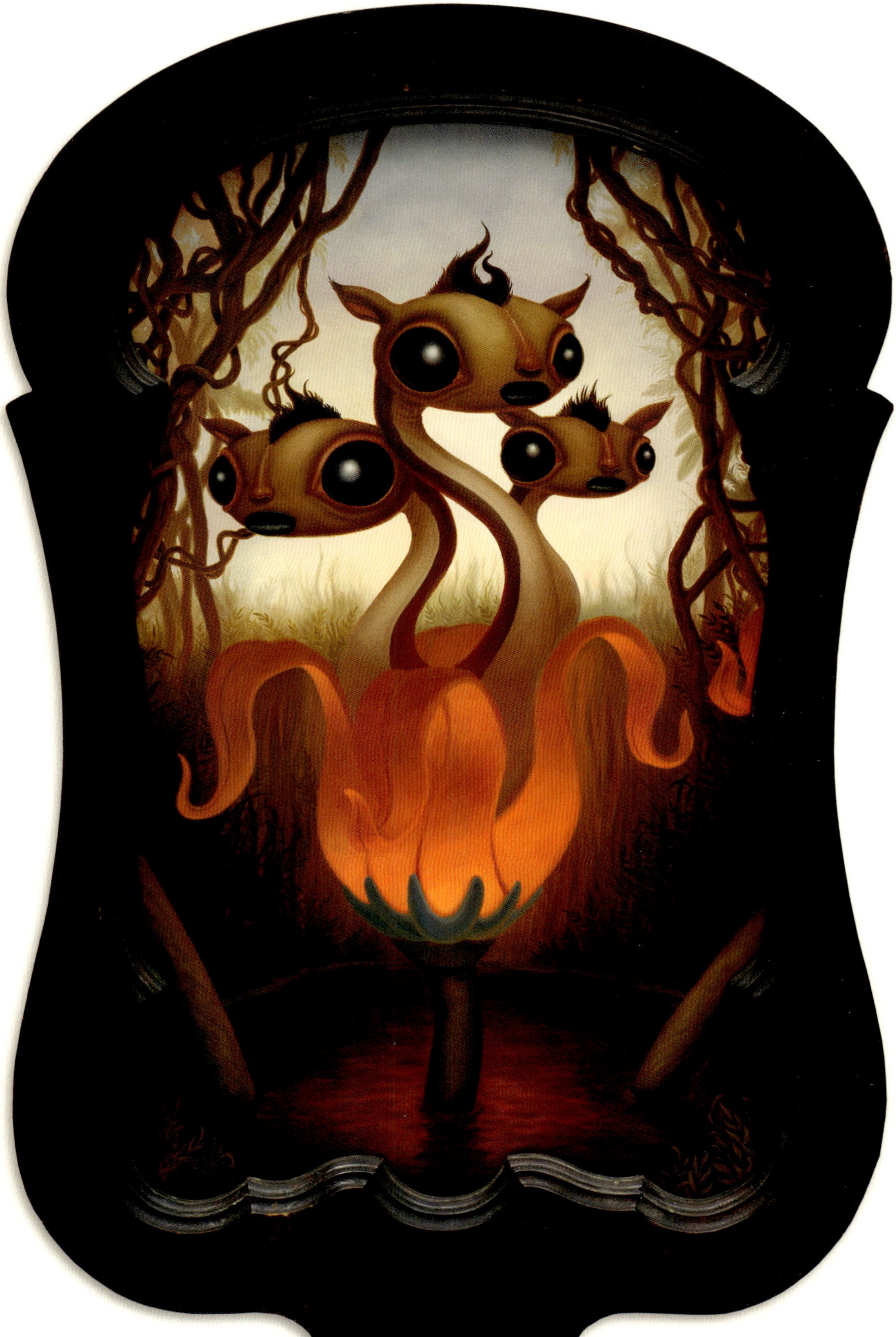

Northern BaronBeest
Extinct ~ ca. 1813

GATEFOLD:

Pelagus Bellua Bardus
Extinct ~ ca. 1822

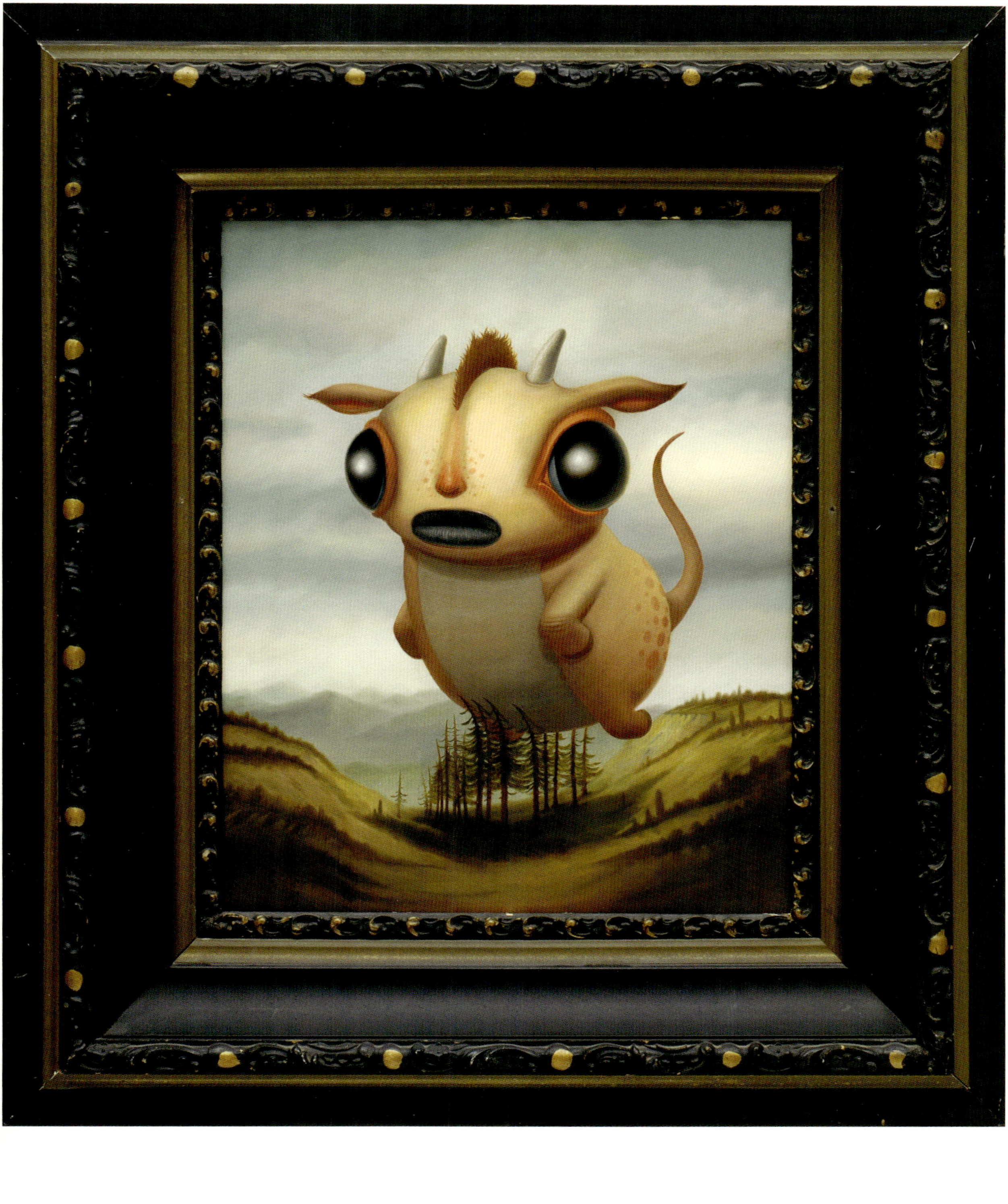

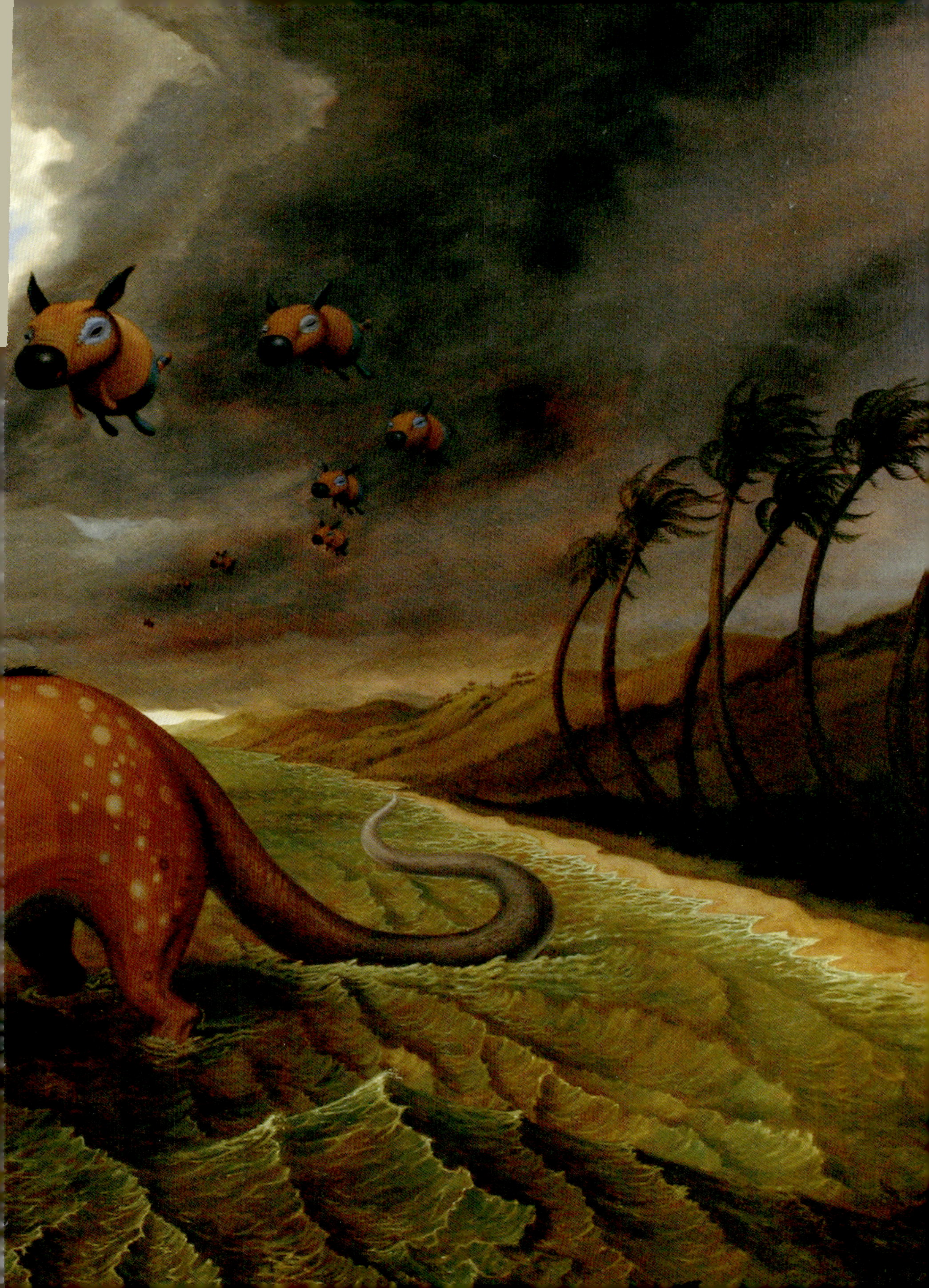

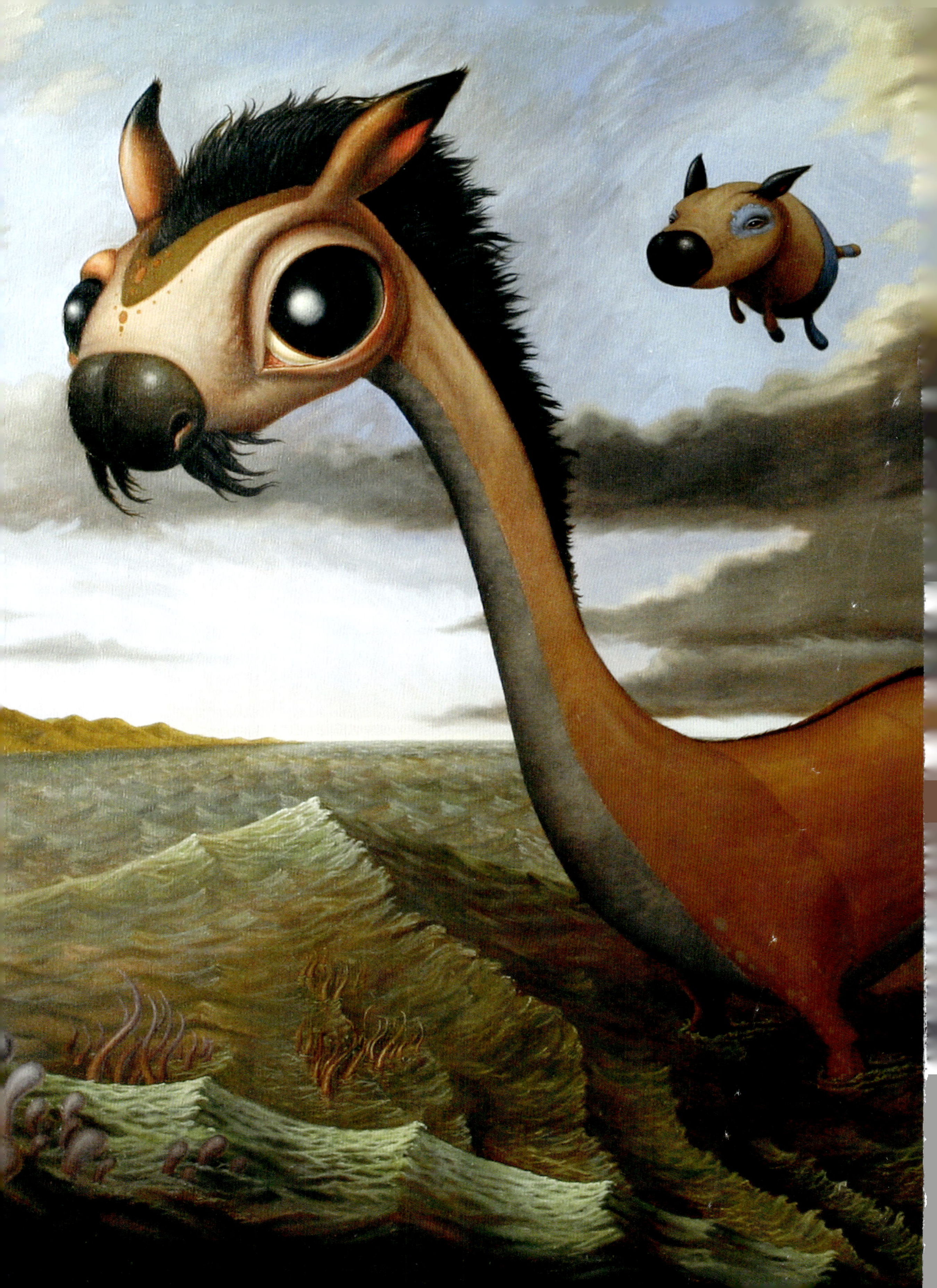

Delphic Okapi

Extinct ~ ca. 1825

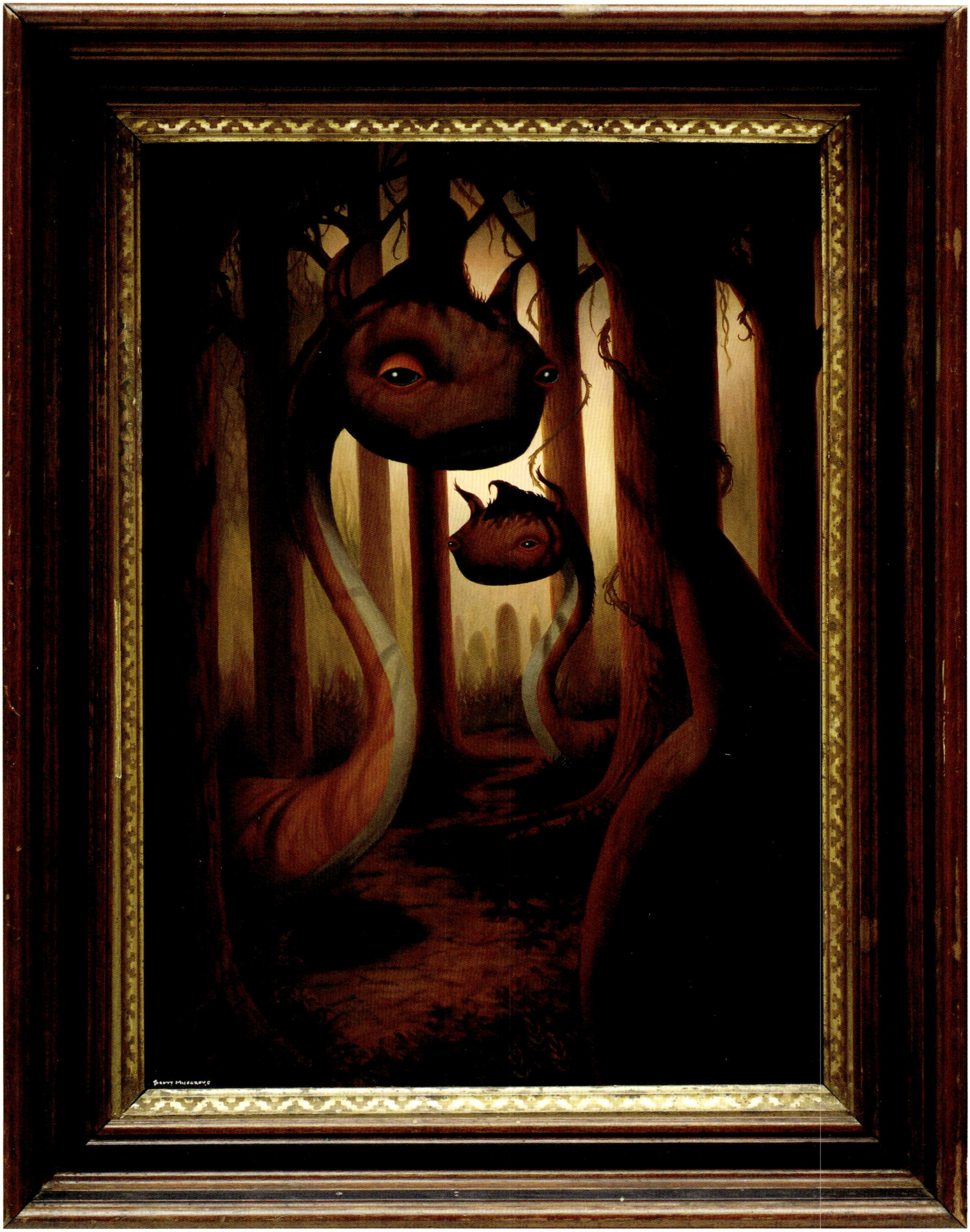

Dwarf Basket Horse

Extinct ~ ca. 1832

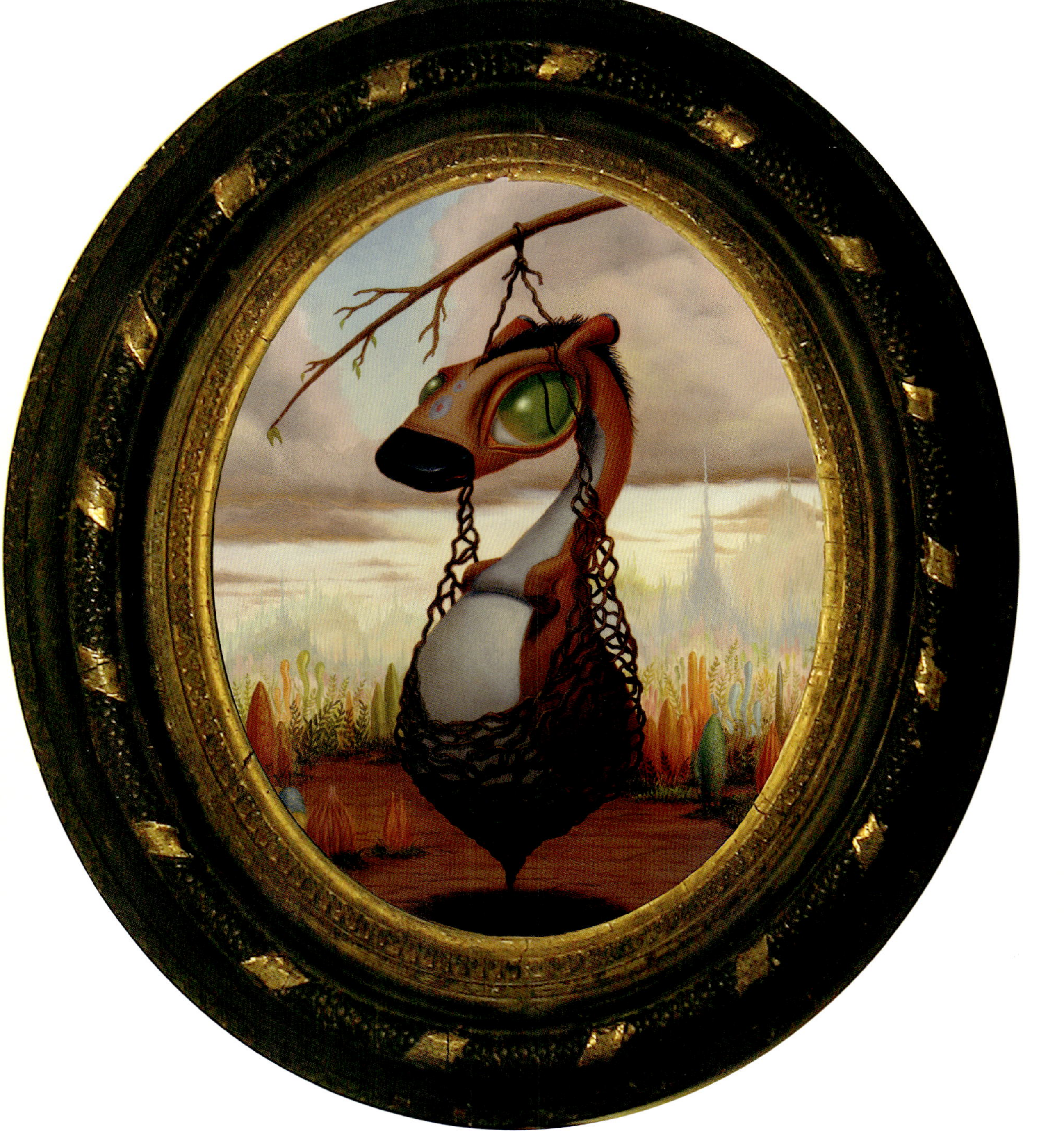

The Humble Bighorn Blackfoot

Extinct ~ ca. 1864

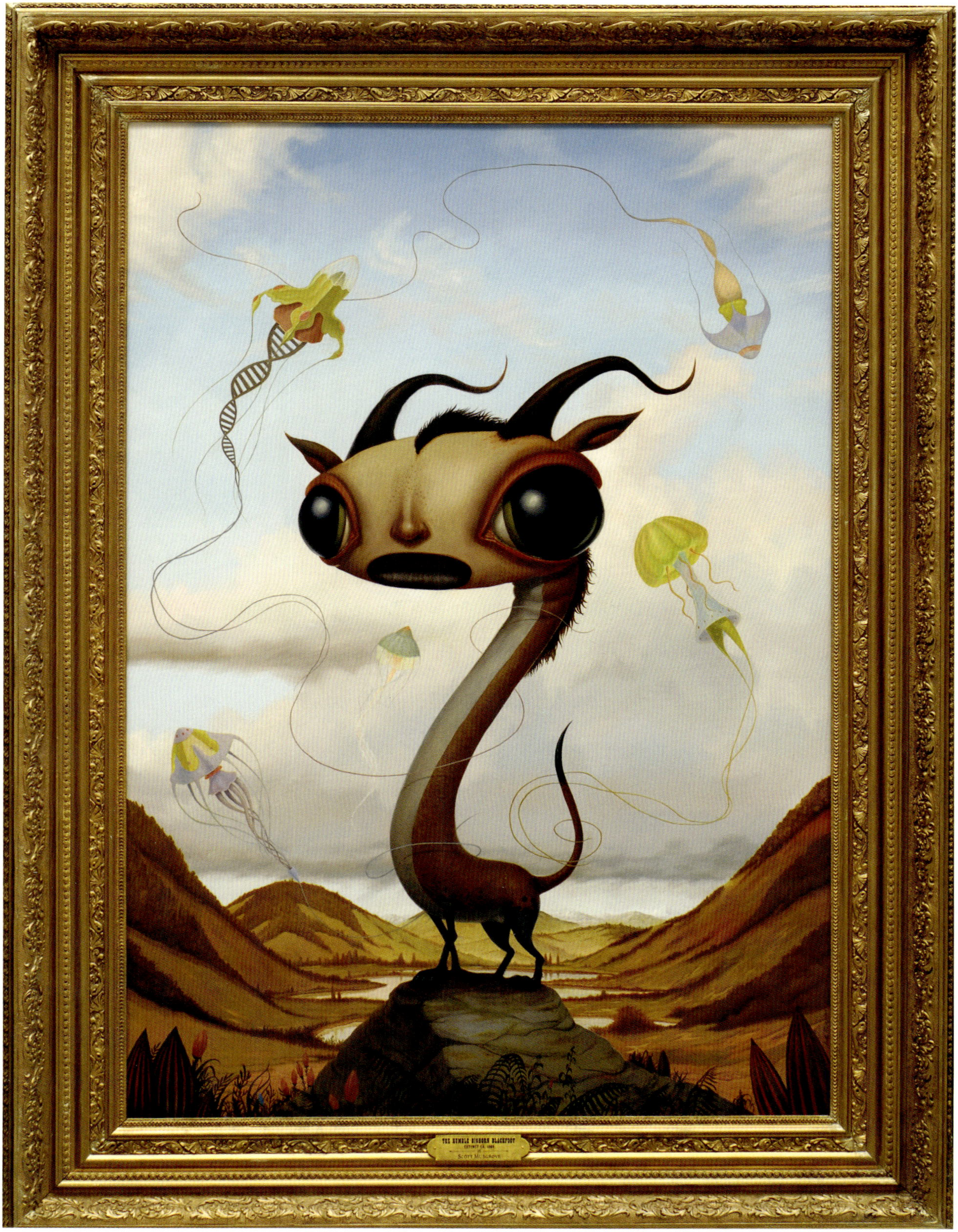
THE HUMBLE BIGHORN BLACKFOOT

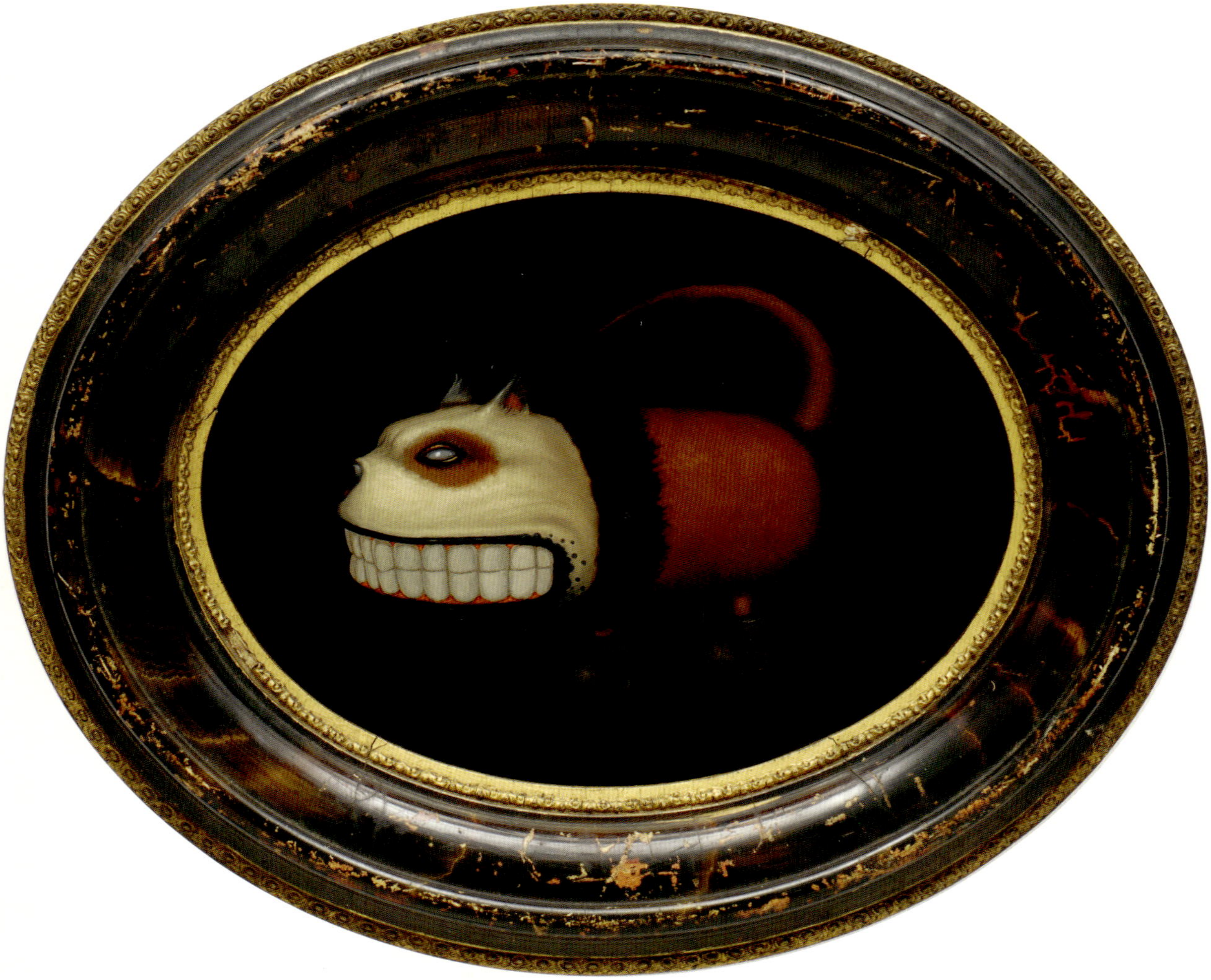

Booted Glamour Cat
Extinct ~ ca. 1855

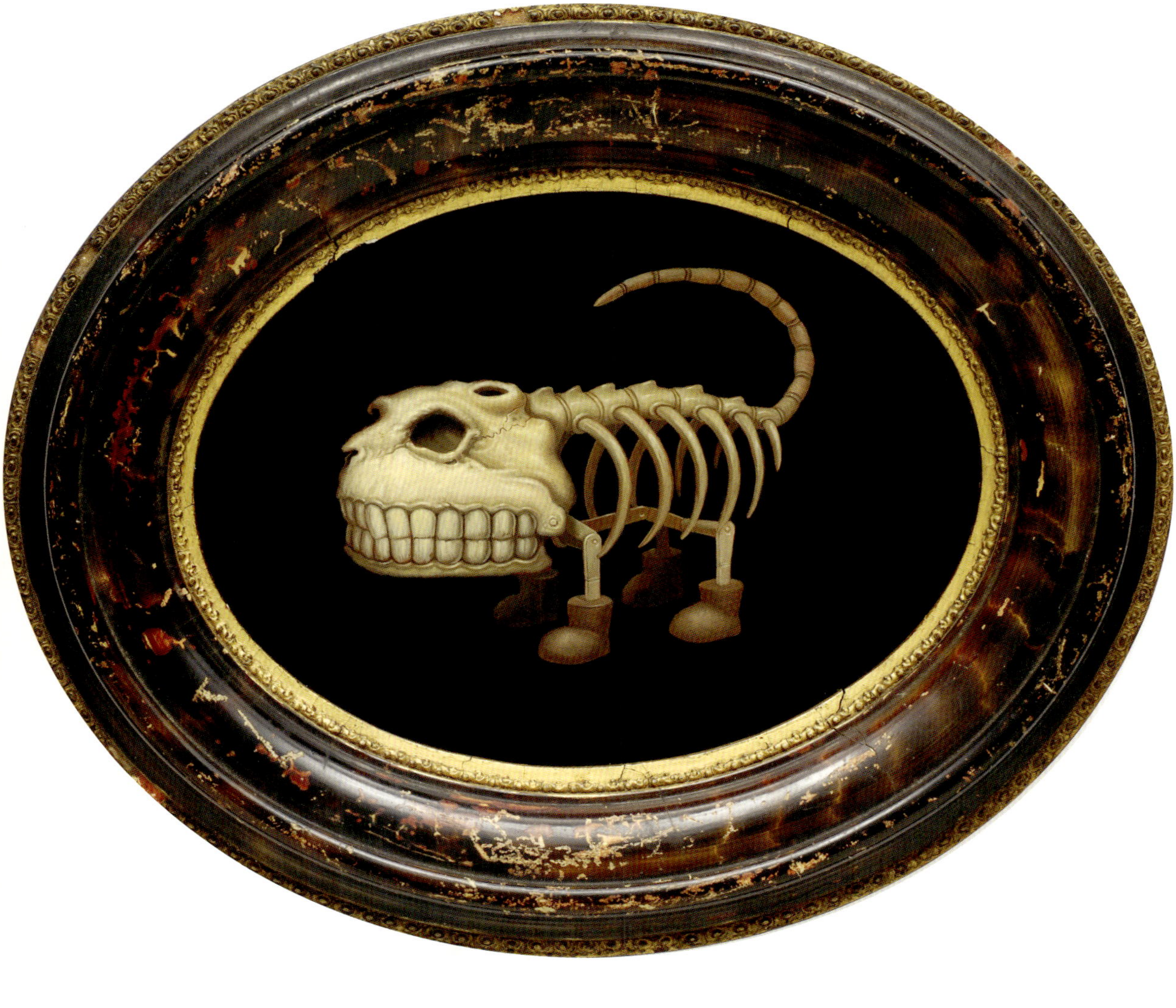

Soul of the Booted Glamour Cat
Extinct ~ ca. 1855

Spangled Swamp Horse
Extinct ca. 1805

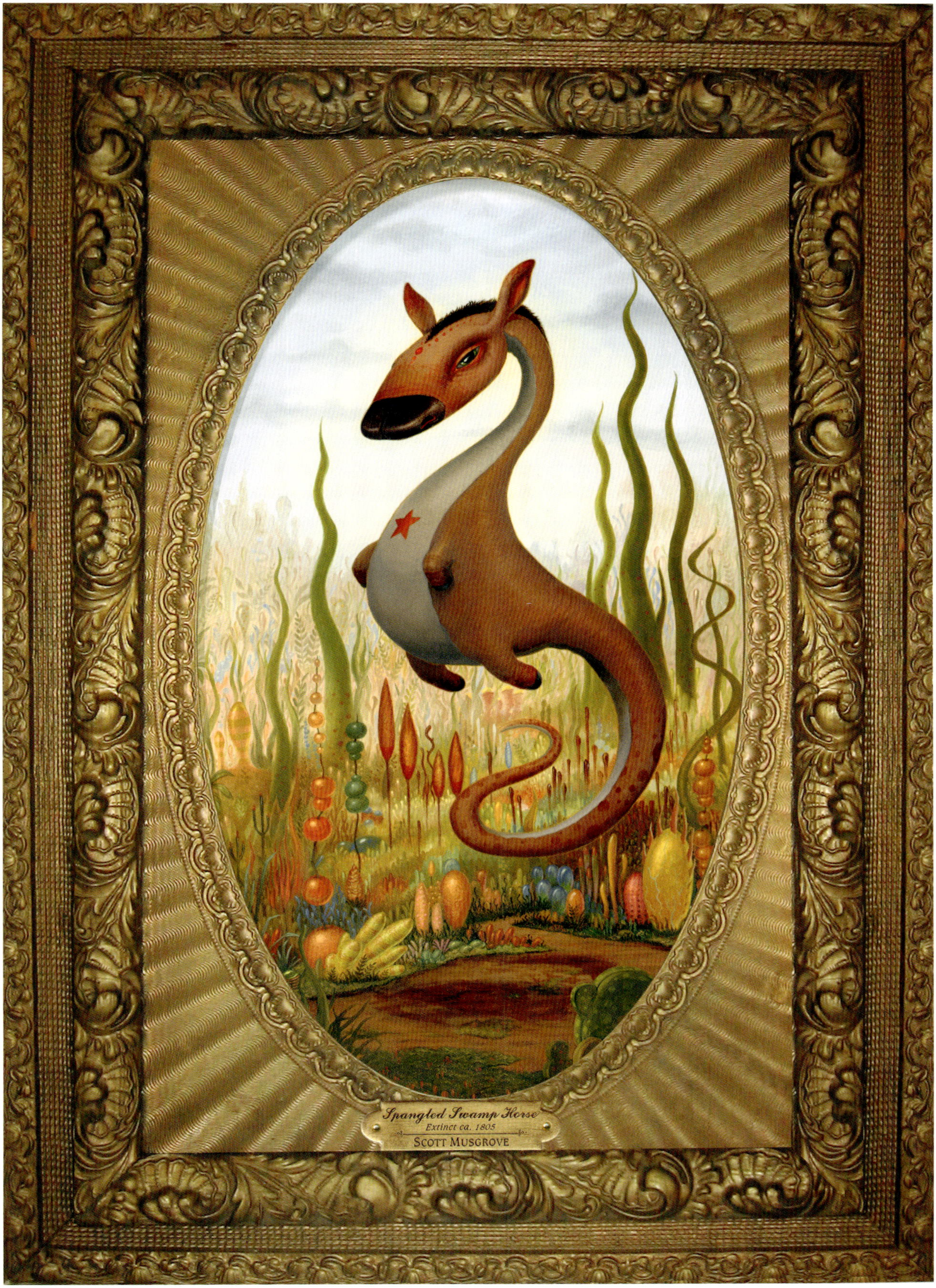

Spangled Swamp Horse
Extinct ca. 1805
SCOTT MUSGROVE

Bug-Eyed Marsh Fly
Extinct ca. 1805

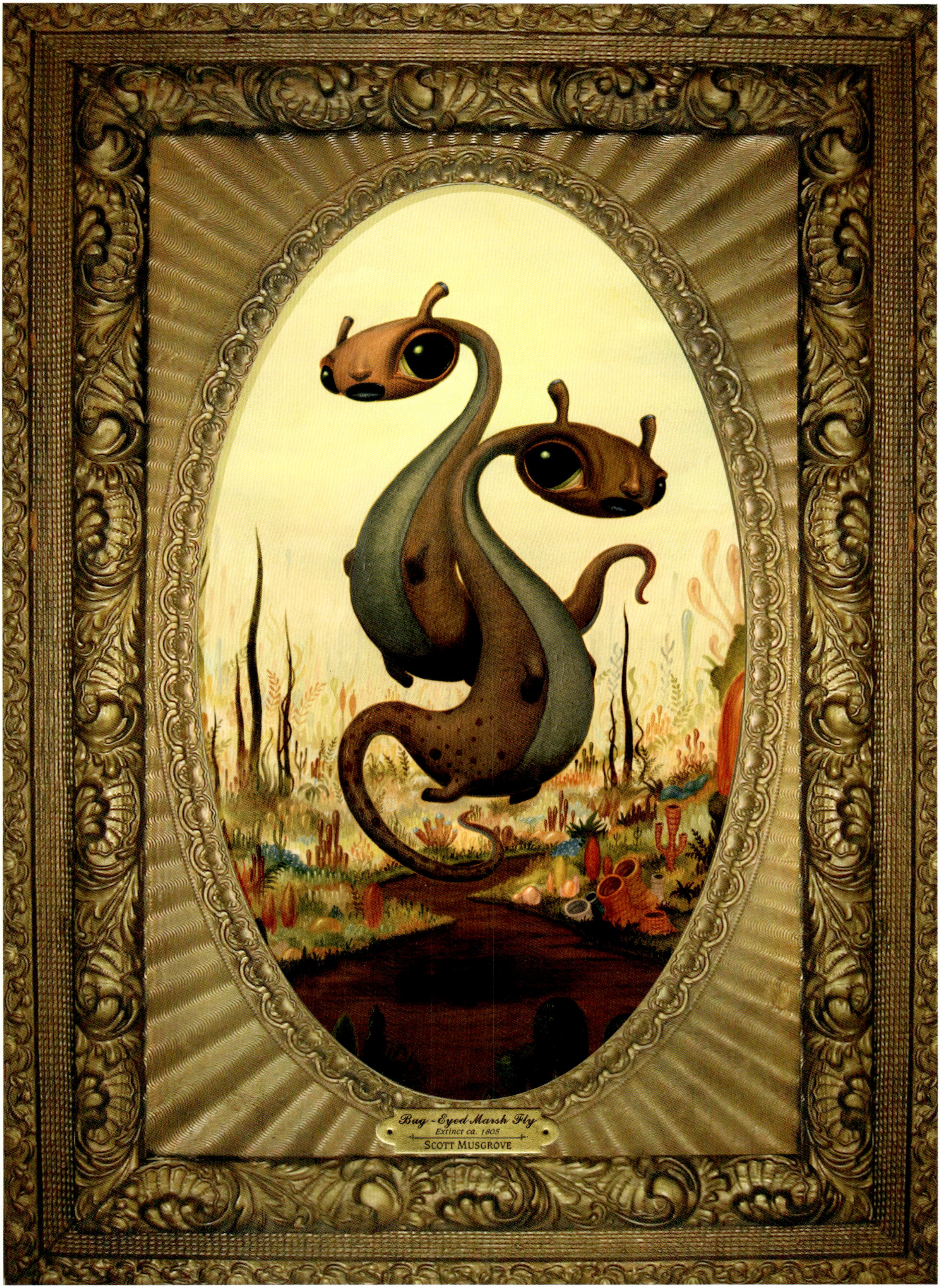
Bug-Eyed Marsh Fly
Extinct ca. 1805
Scott Musgrove

The Humble Bighorn Blackfoot

Extinct ~ ca. 1864

WOOD CARVING

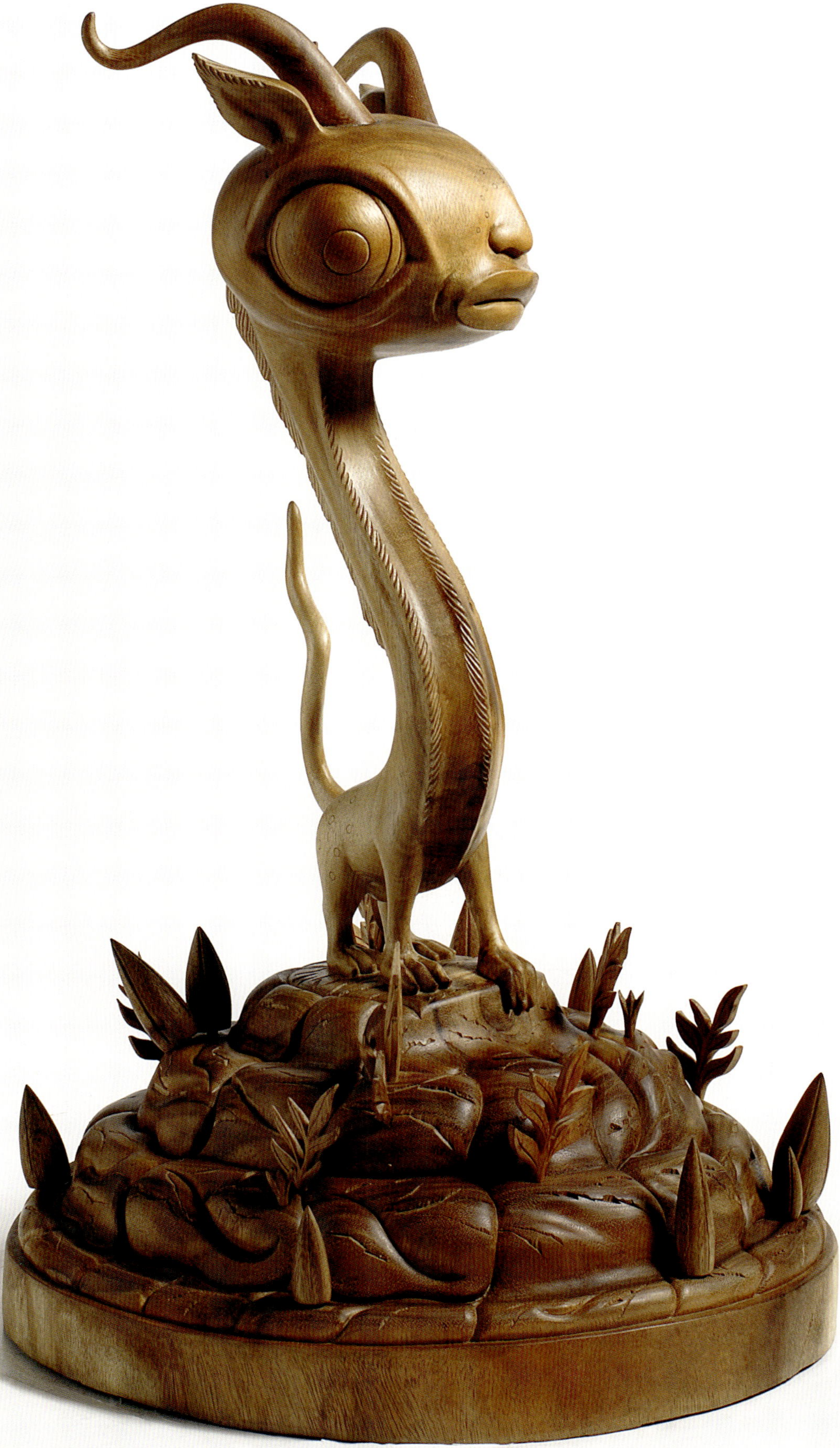

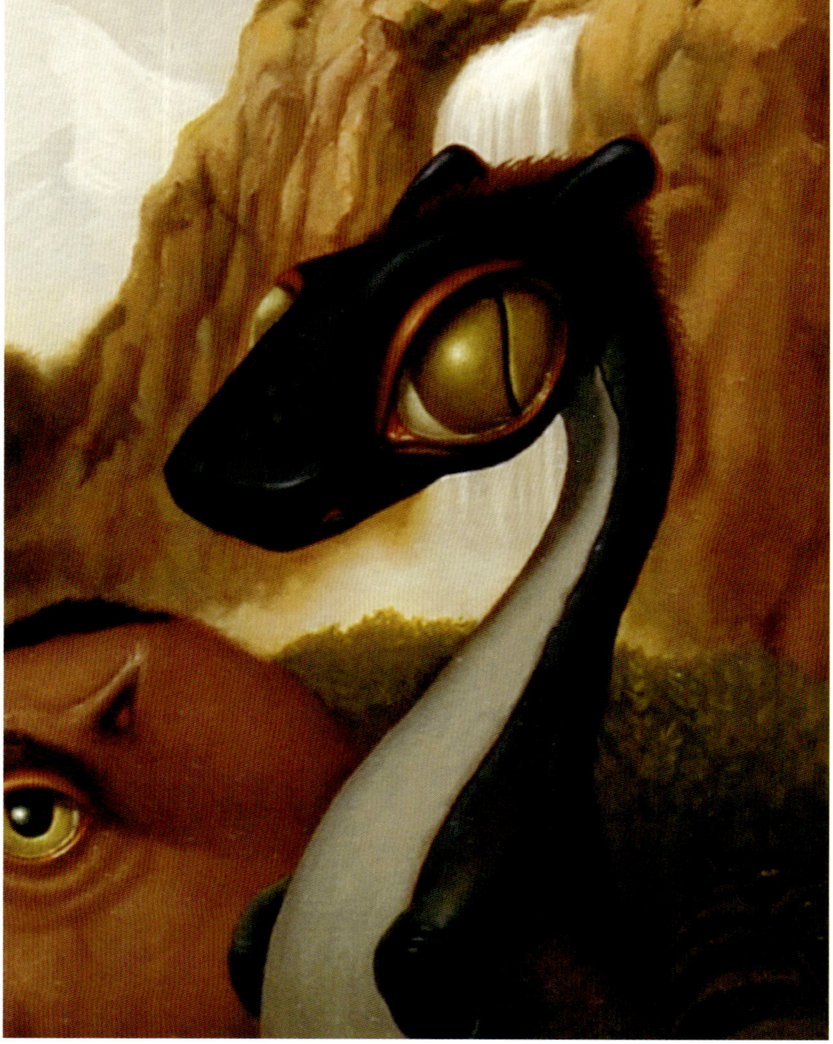

The Resting Place
ca. 1812
THIS PAGE: DETAIL

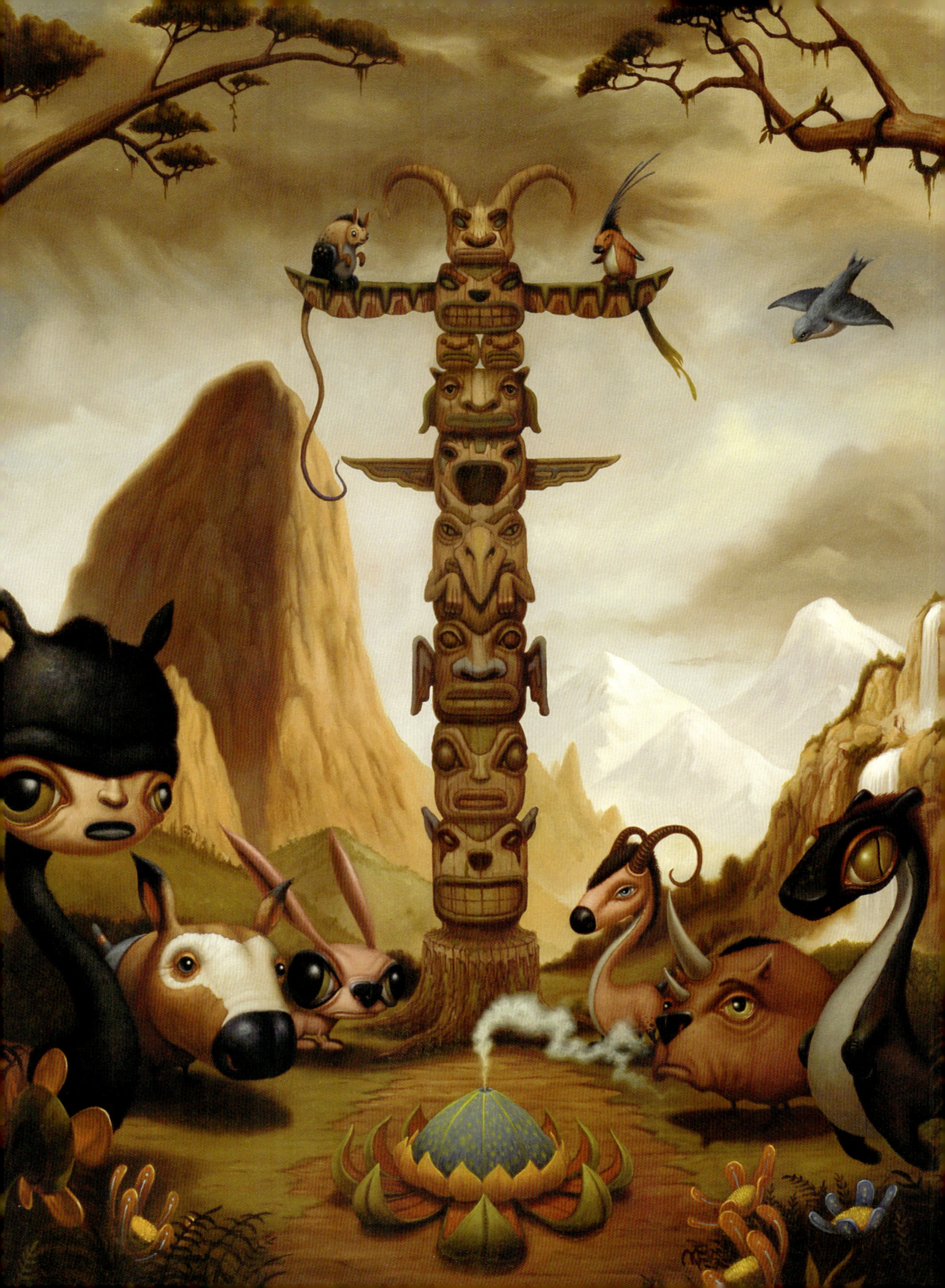

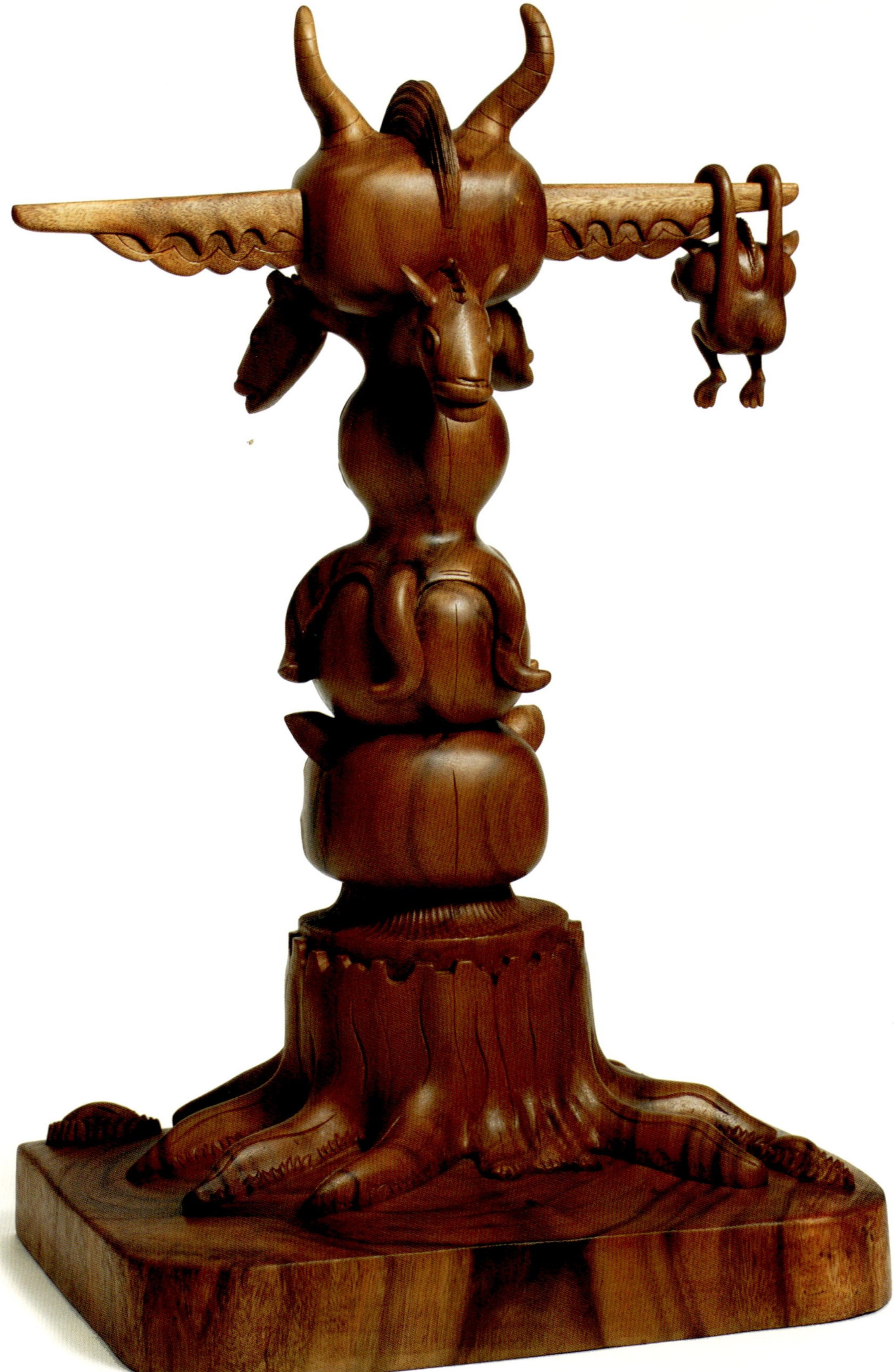

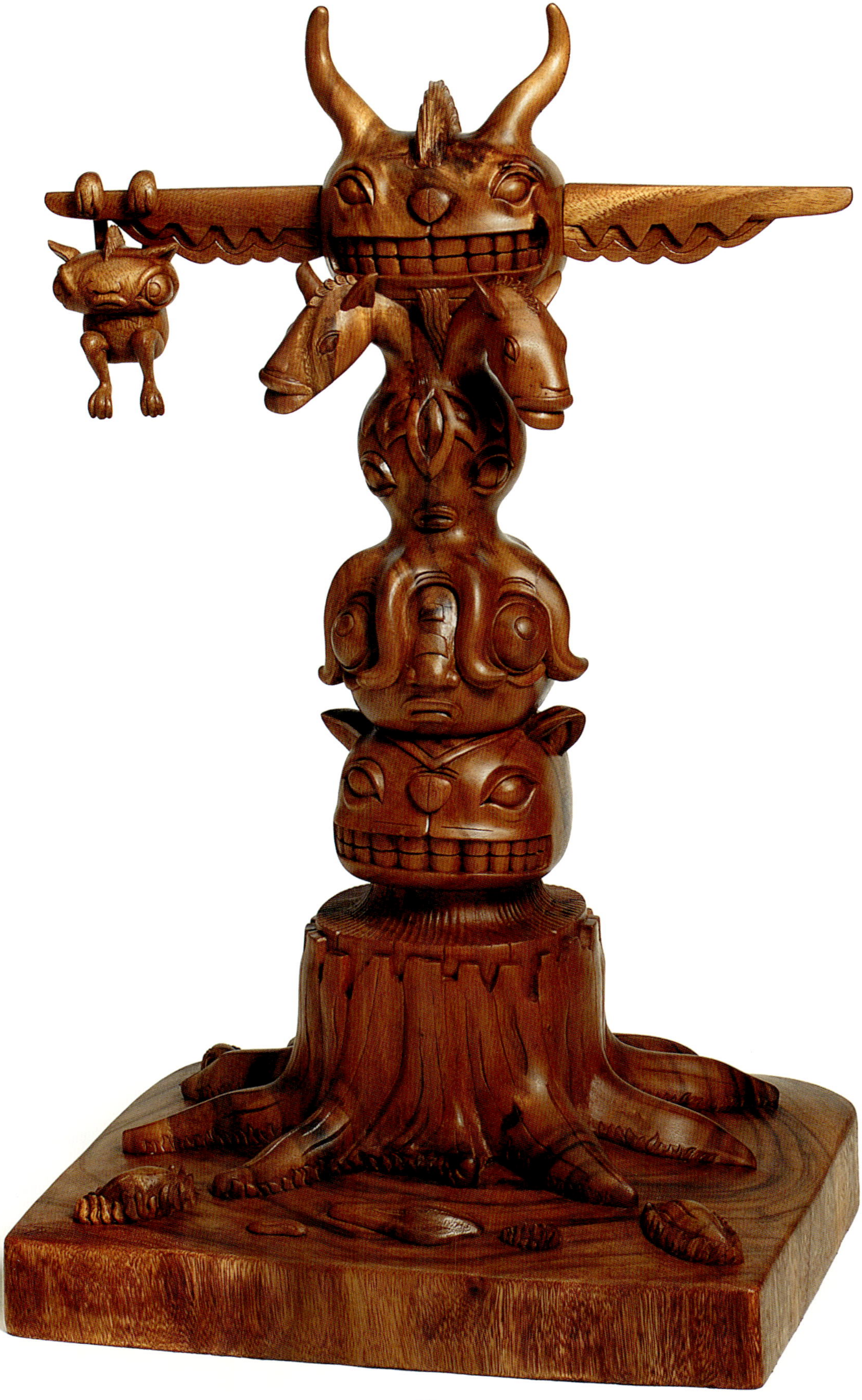

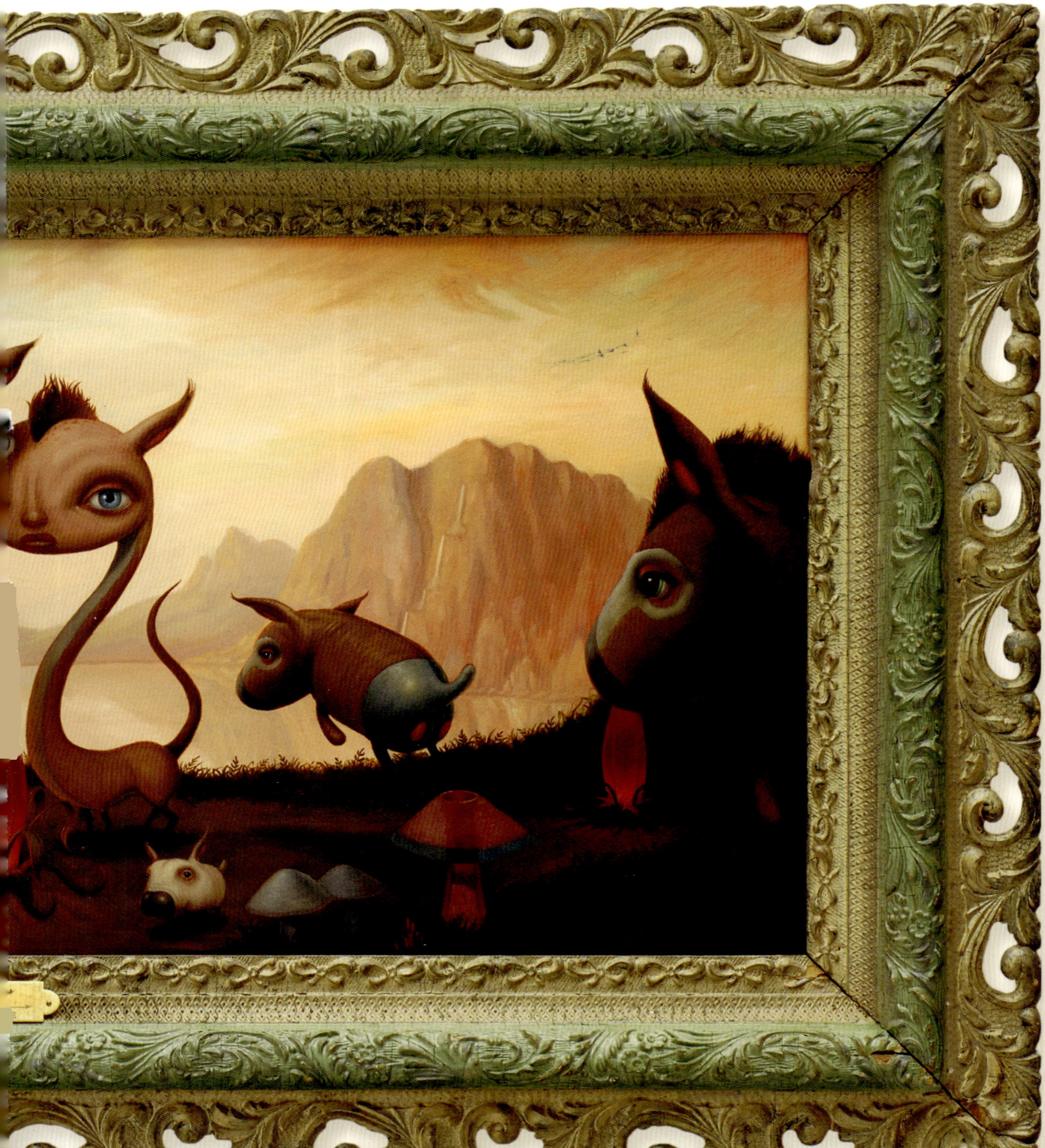

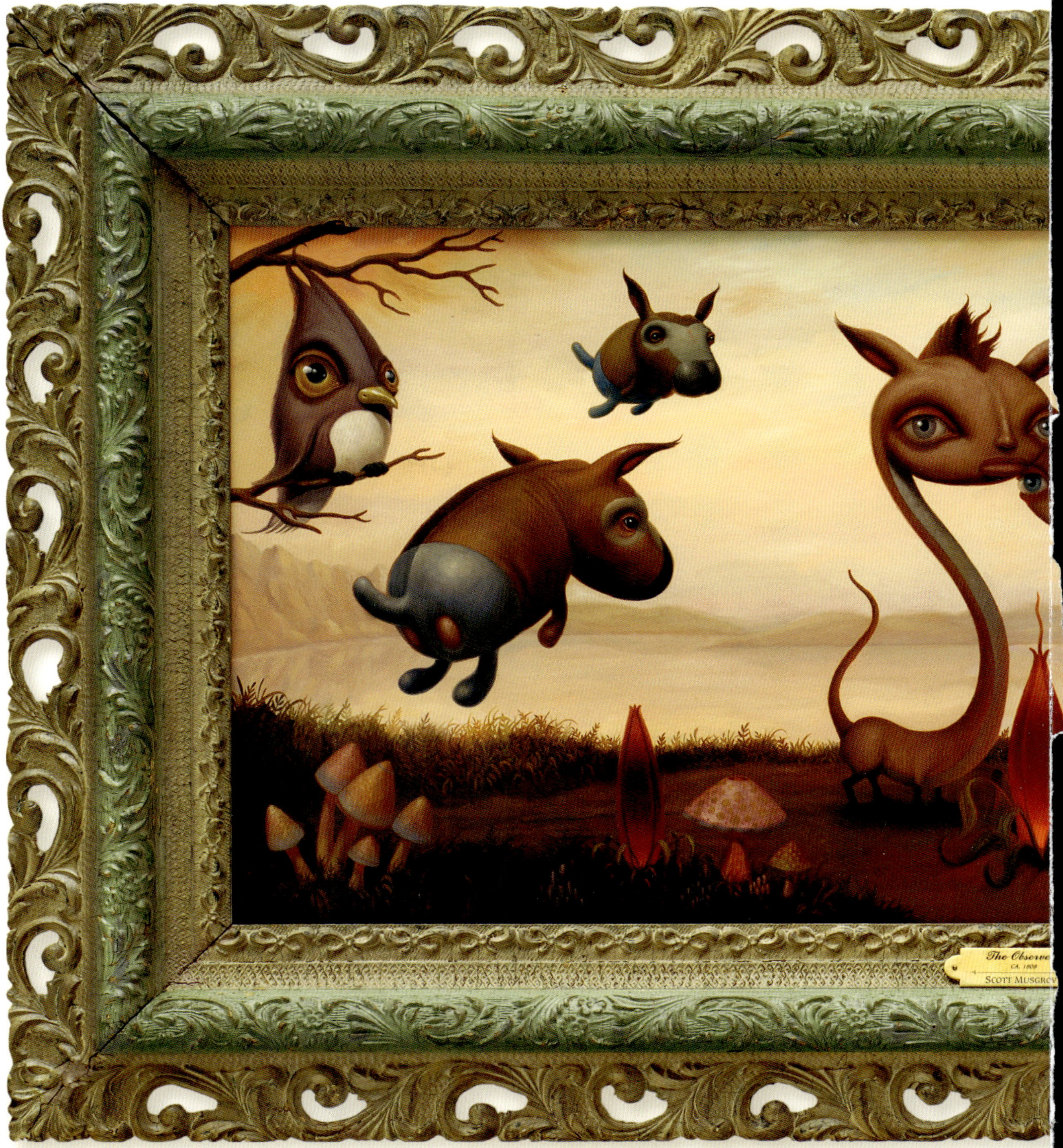

The Brethren
ca. 1880

PAGE 35 & 36
The Resting Place
ca. 1812
WOOD CARVING

GATEFOLD
The Observers
ca. 1808

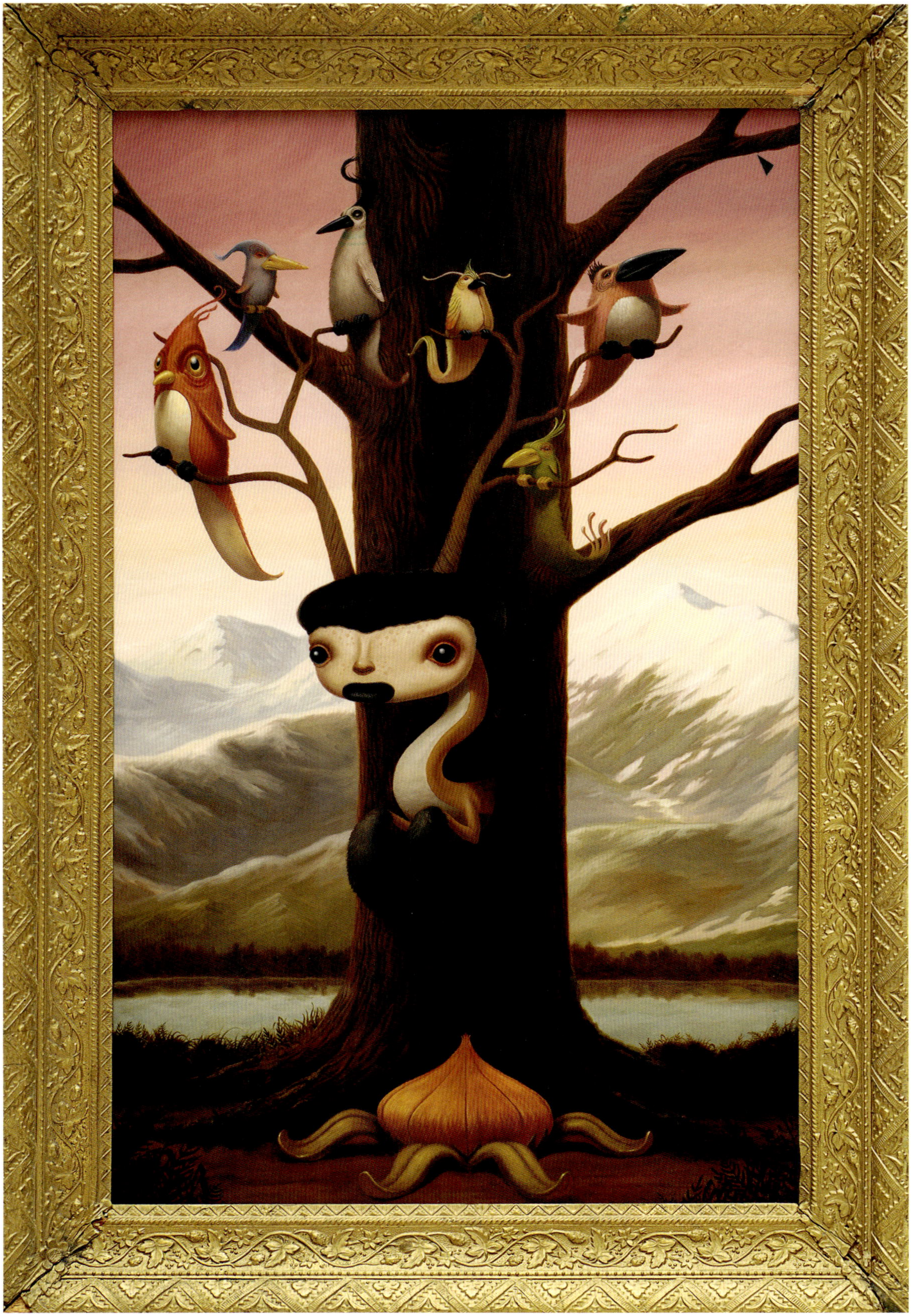

Elliptical Equine
Elliptical Equine Skeleton
Extinct ~ ca. 1864
WOOD CARVINGS

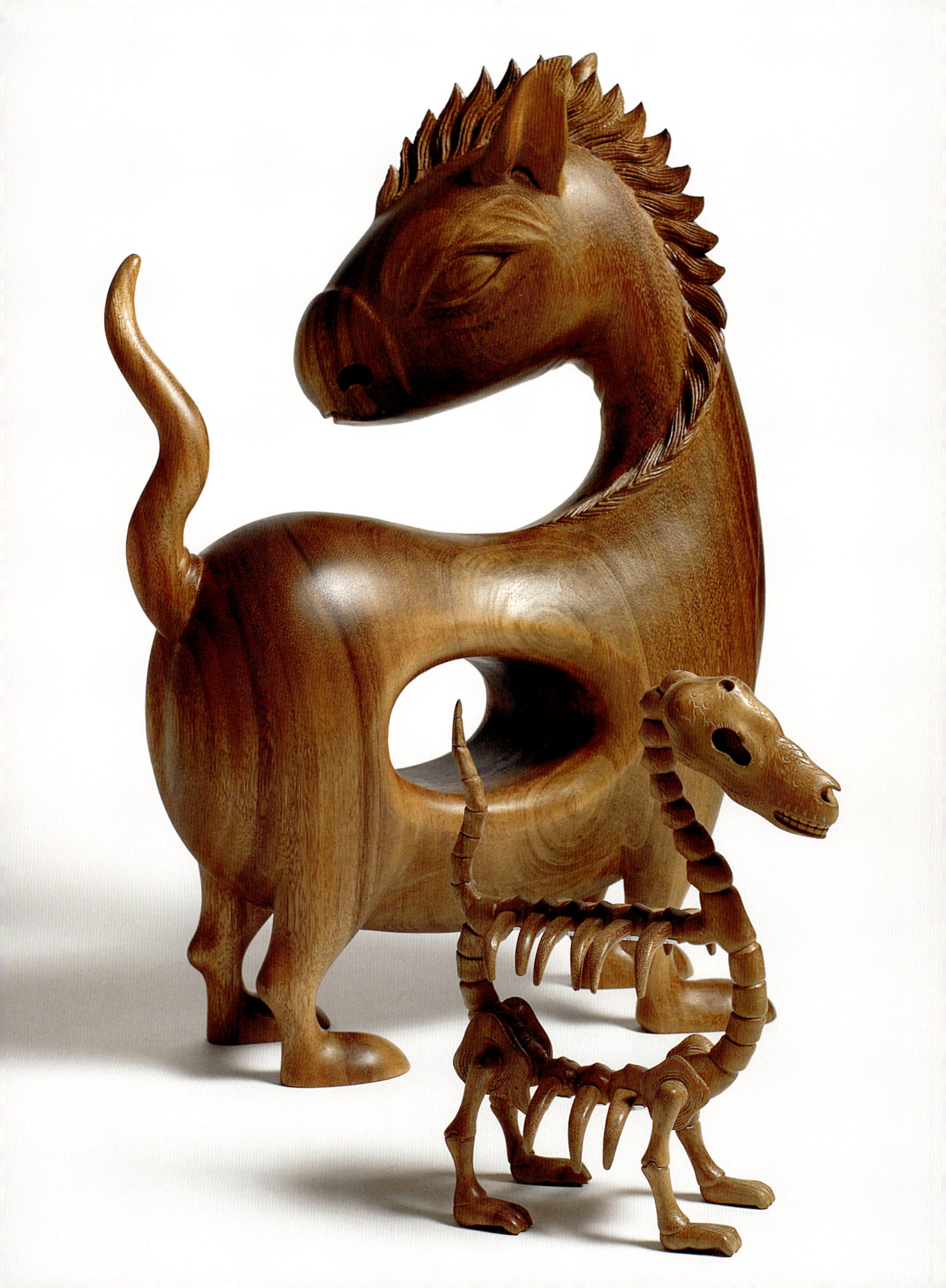

Sentries

Extinct ~ ca. 1879

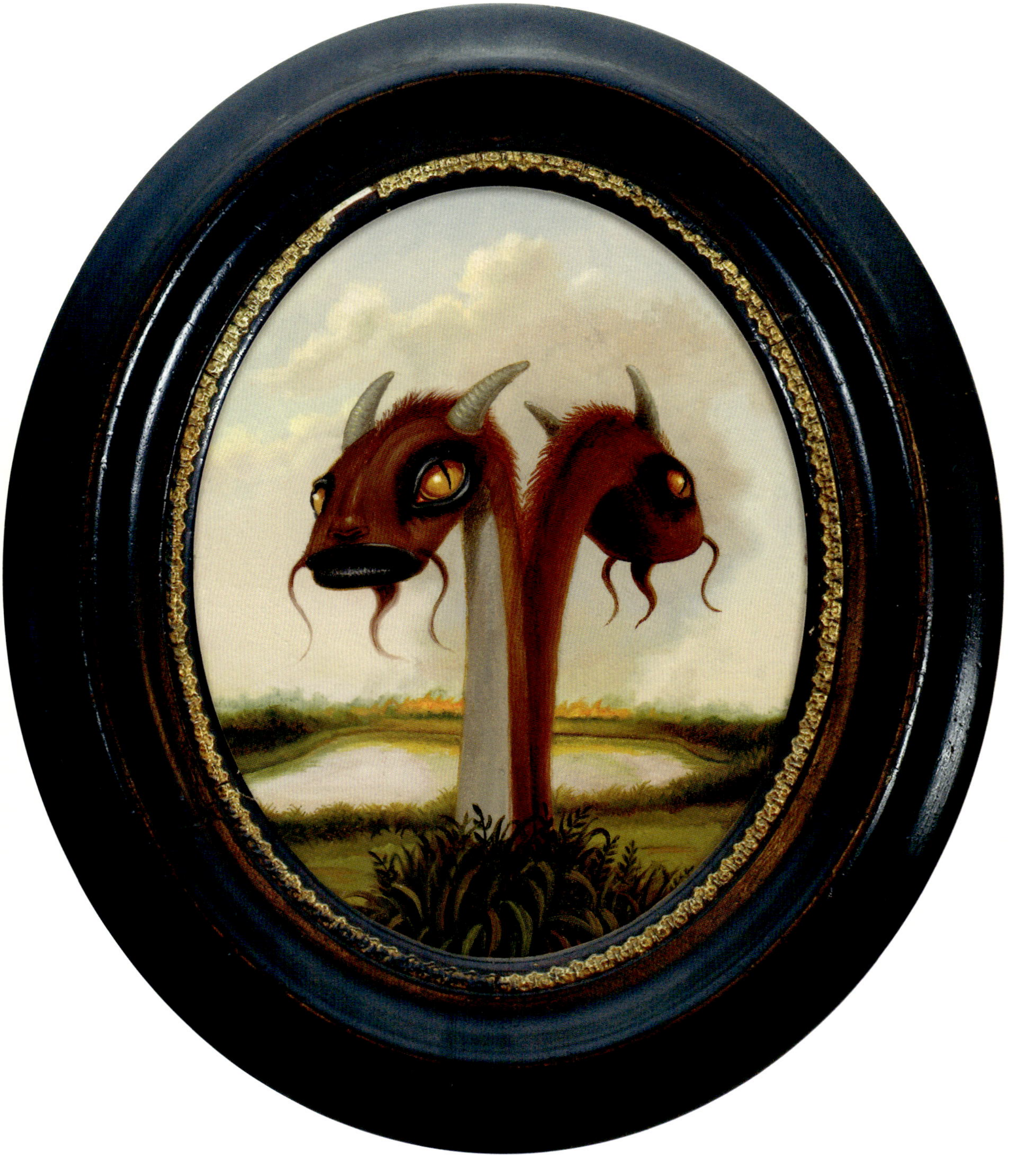

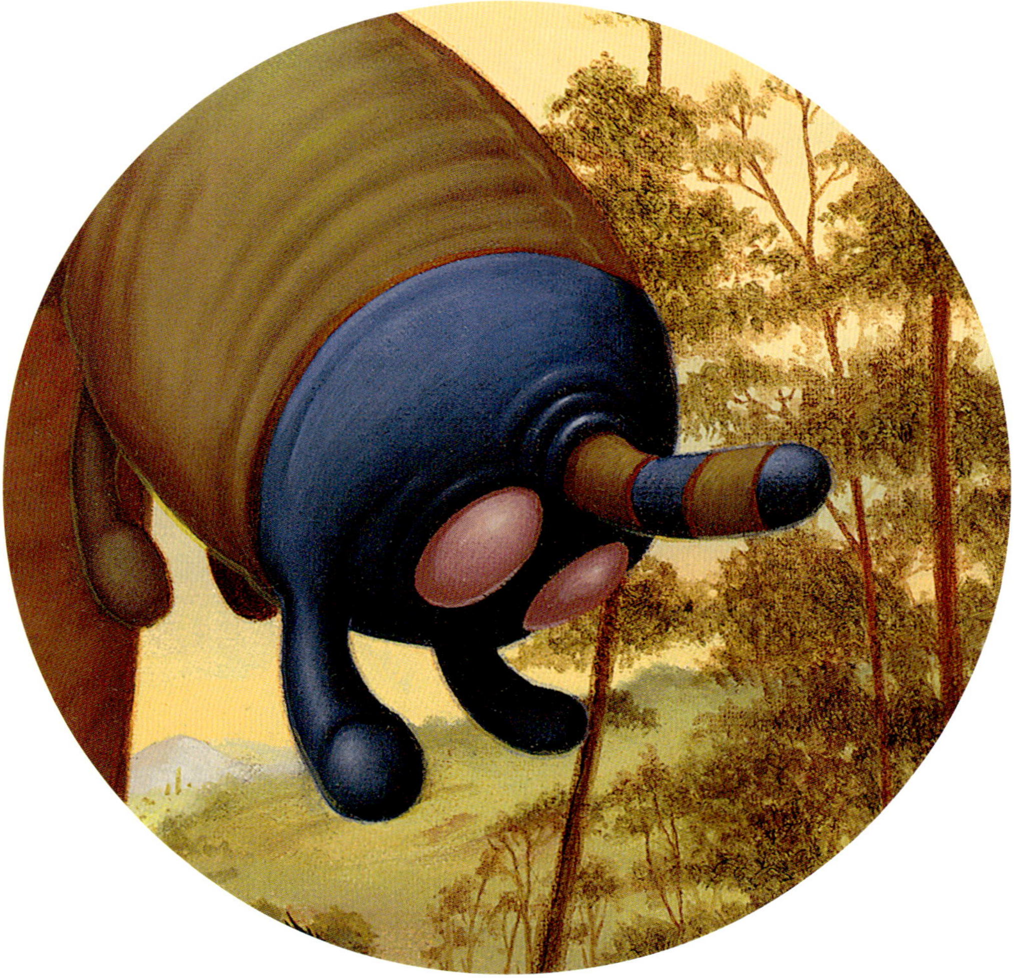

Nimbus
Extinct ~ ca. 1853

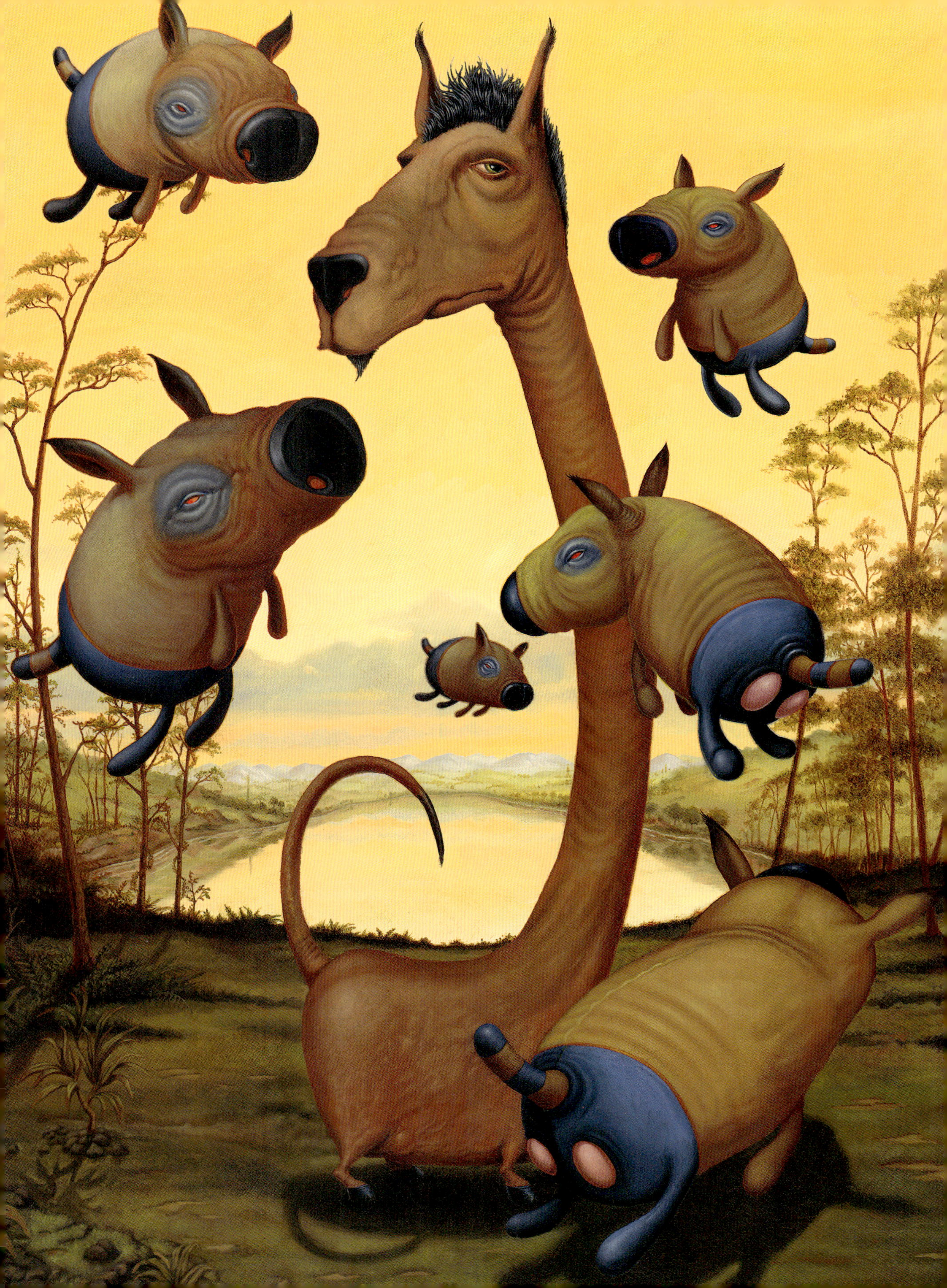

Vicunus Occultus

Extinct ~ ca. 1859

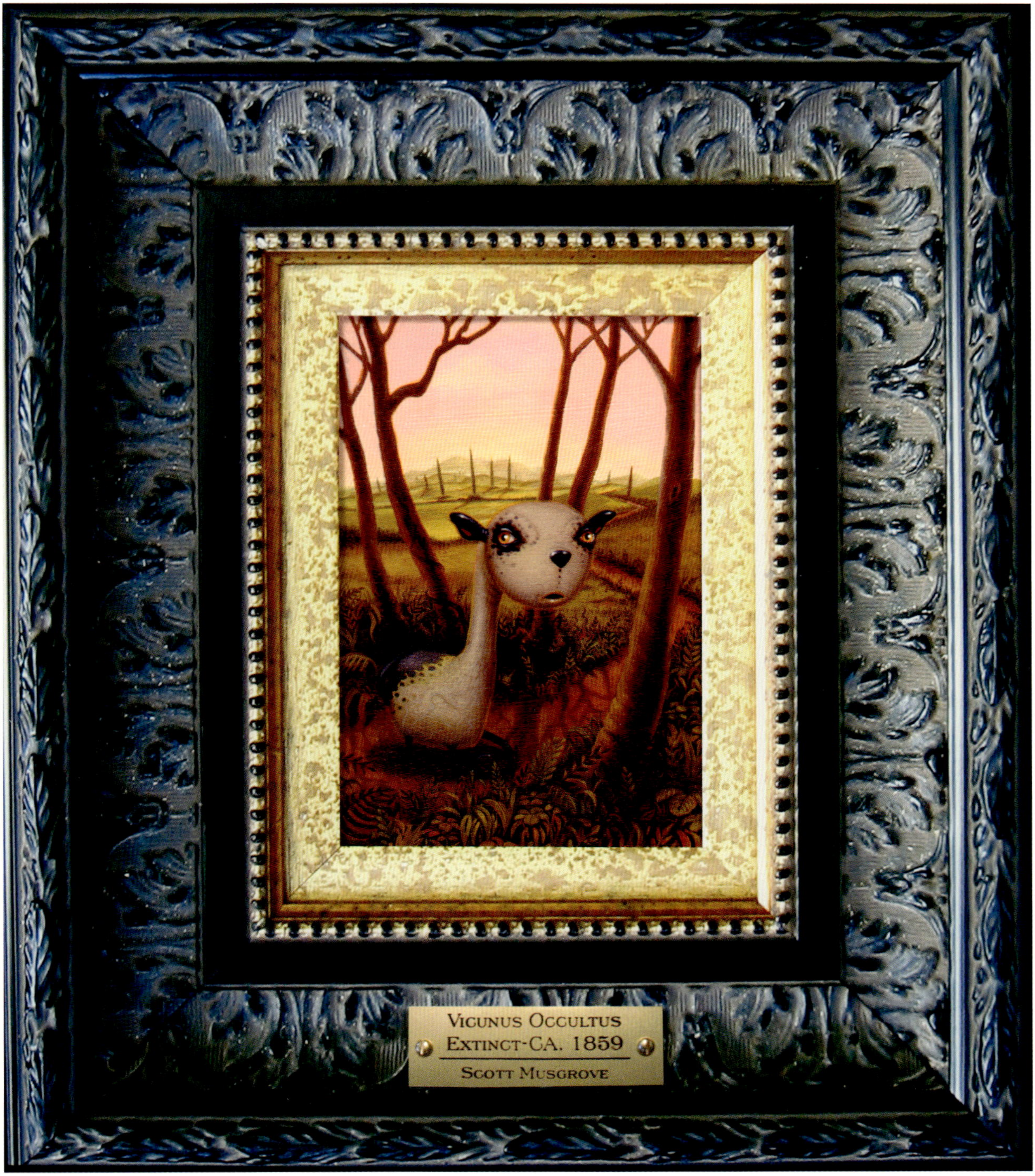
VIGUNUS OCCULTUS
EXTINCT-CA. 1859
SCOTT MUSGROVE

Enormous Lotus Larva

Extinct ~ ca. 1842

WOOD CARVING

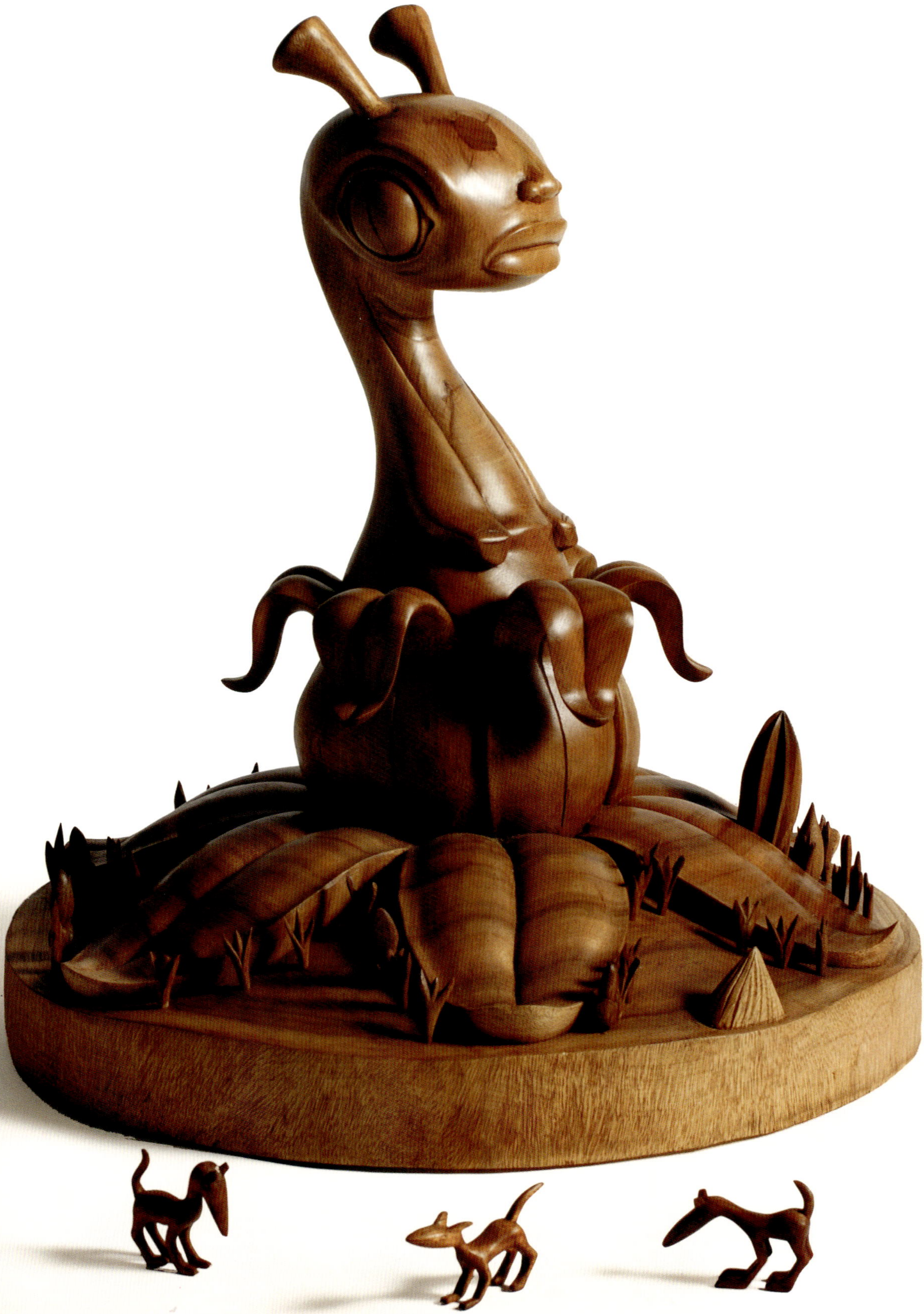

Enormous Lotus Larva

Extinct ~ ca. 1842

Now, if I may take another moment of your time, dear reader, let us pursue the subject of the Enormous Lotus Larva. Although called a "larva," this drawing depicts a full-grown Lotus Fly. And although called a "fly," it is actually a mammal. Even then, "mammal" is a bit misleading as this creature lays eggs but is not a normal "monotreme" such as the Platypus. Luckily, the Enormous Lotus Fly is extinct, so we needn't waste more of our afternoon quibbling about it.

The Lotus Fly is thought to have gone extinct in the 1840s, just before the dawn of photography. And as a result, no photographs were ever taken of this enormous beauty. Thanks to my tremendous knowledge of architecture, anatomy, crane operations, and a collection of surplus Army tent poles, burlap and fur, I was able to recreate a life-size reproduction of how this majestic, fuzzy, egg-laying giant must have looked to the indigenous people of North America. However, my neighbors were not impressed, and an injunction forced me to dismantle this impressive beast; otherwise, I'd show it to you.

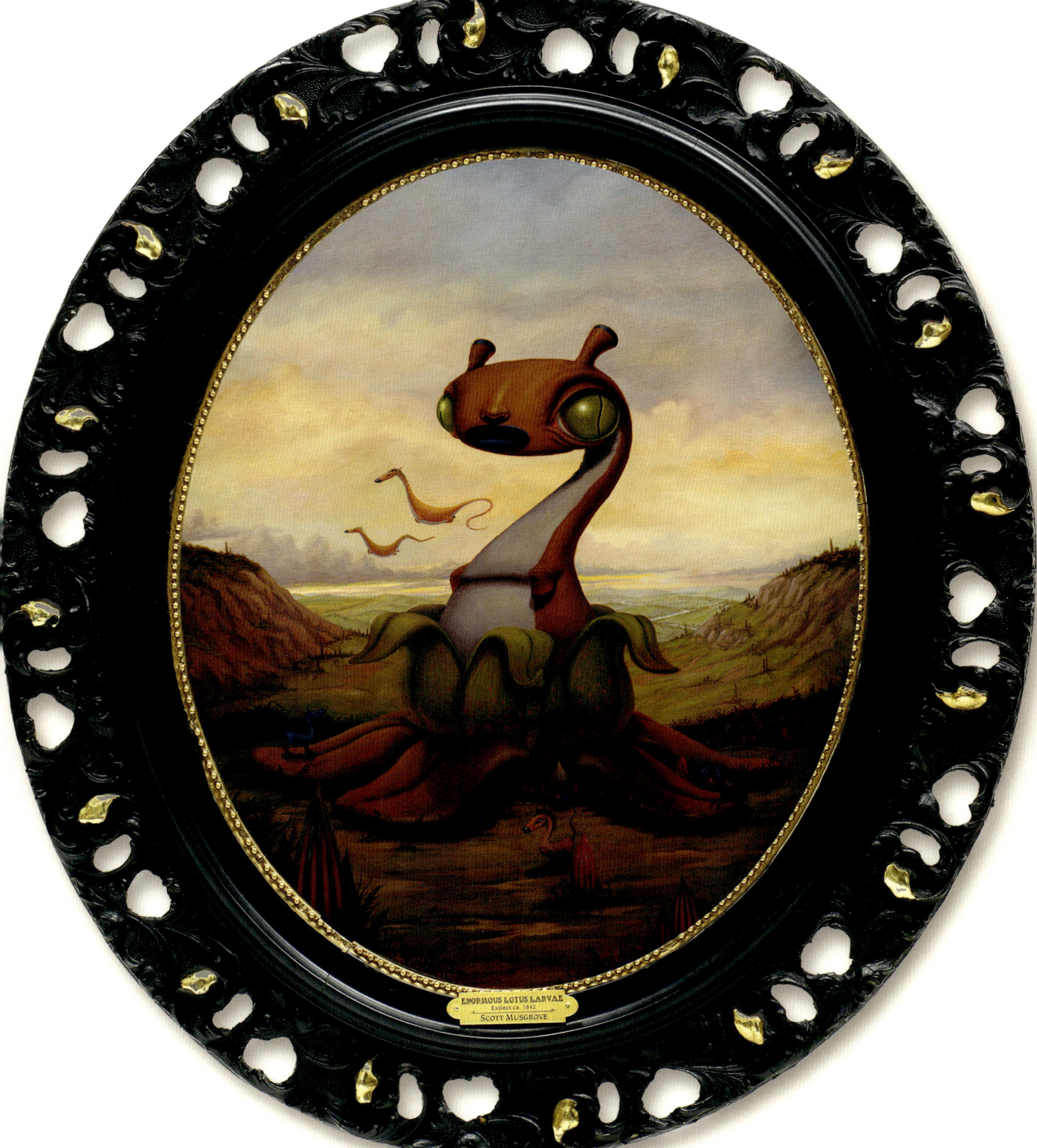
ENORMOUS LOTUS LARVAE
Extinct ca. 1842
SCOTT MUSGROVE

Blackmouth Catfish

Extinct ~ ca. 1825

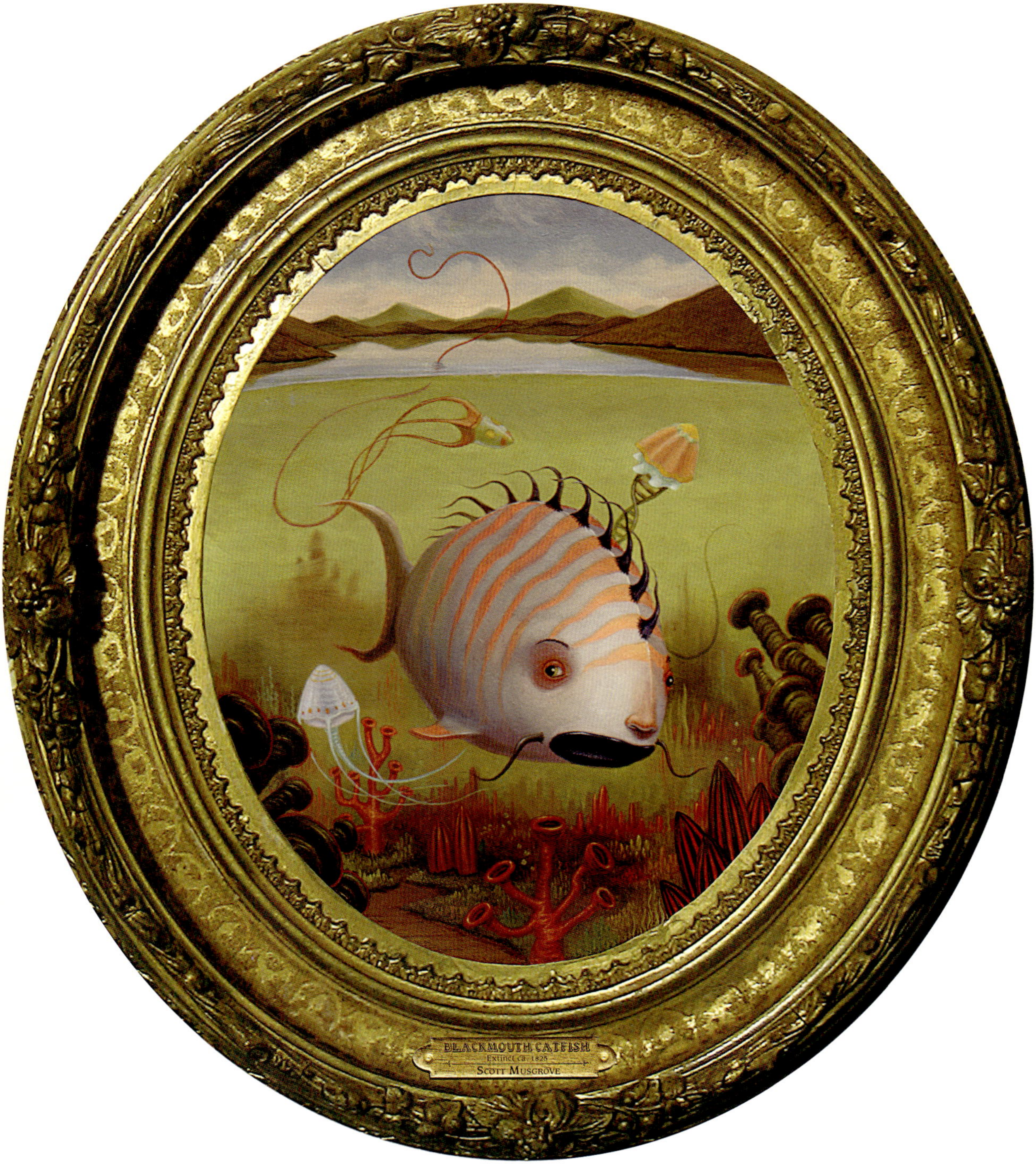
BLACKMOUTH CATFISH
Extinct ca. 1825
SCOTT MUSGROVE

Eventide Assembly
ca. 1842

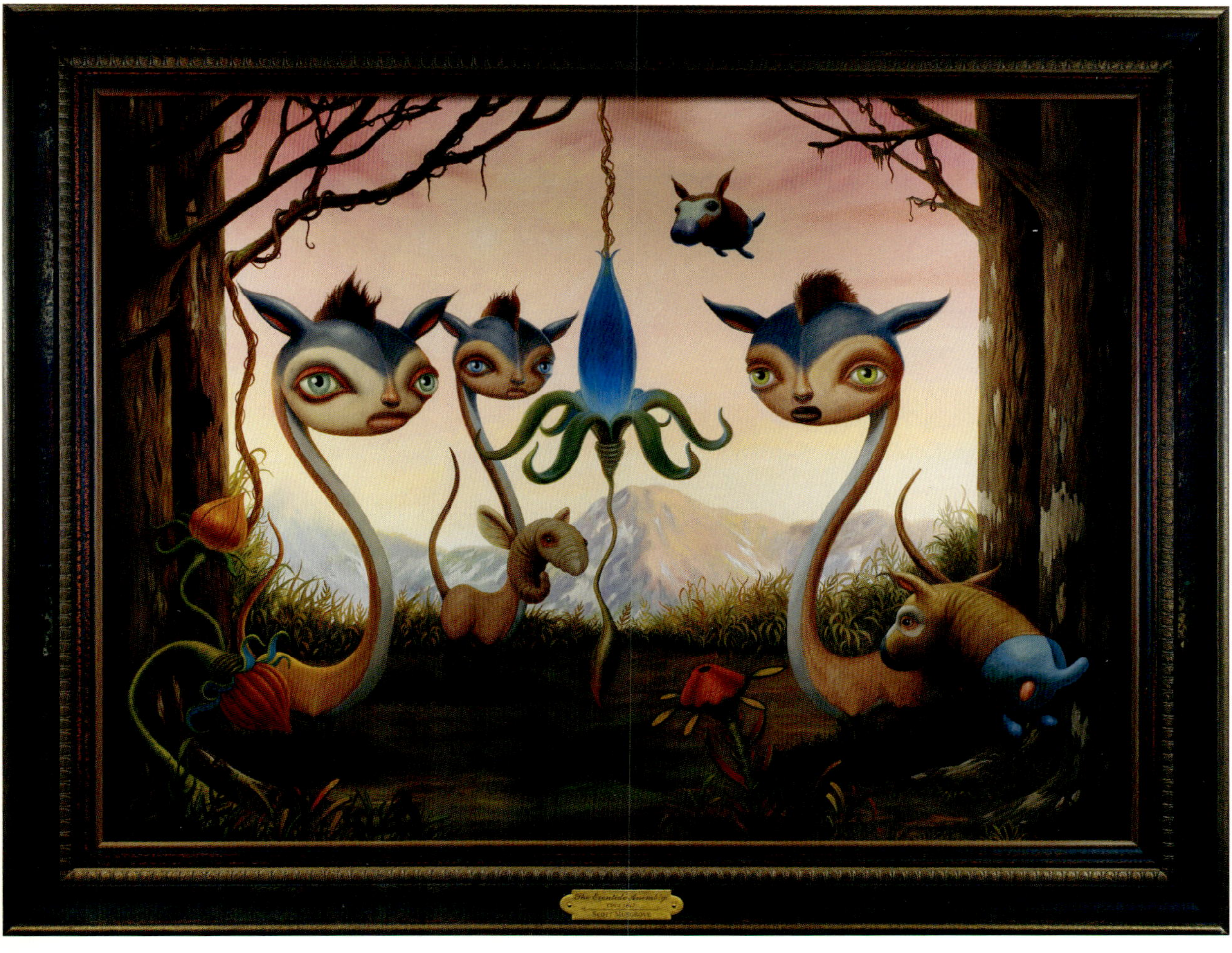
The Eventide Assembly
SCOTT MUSGROVE

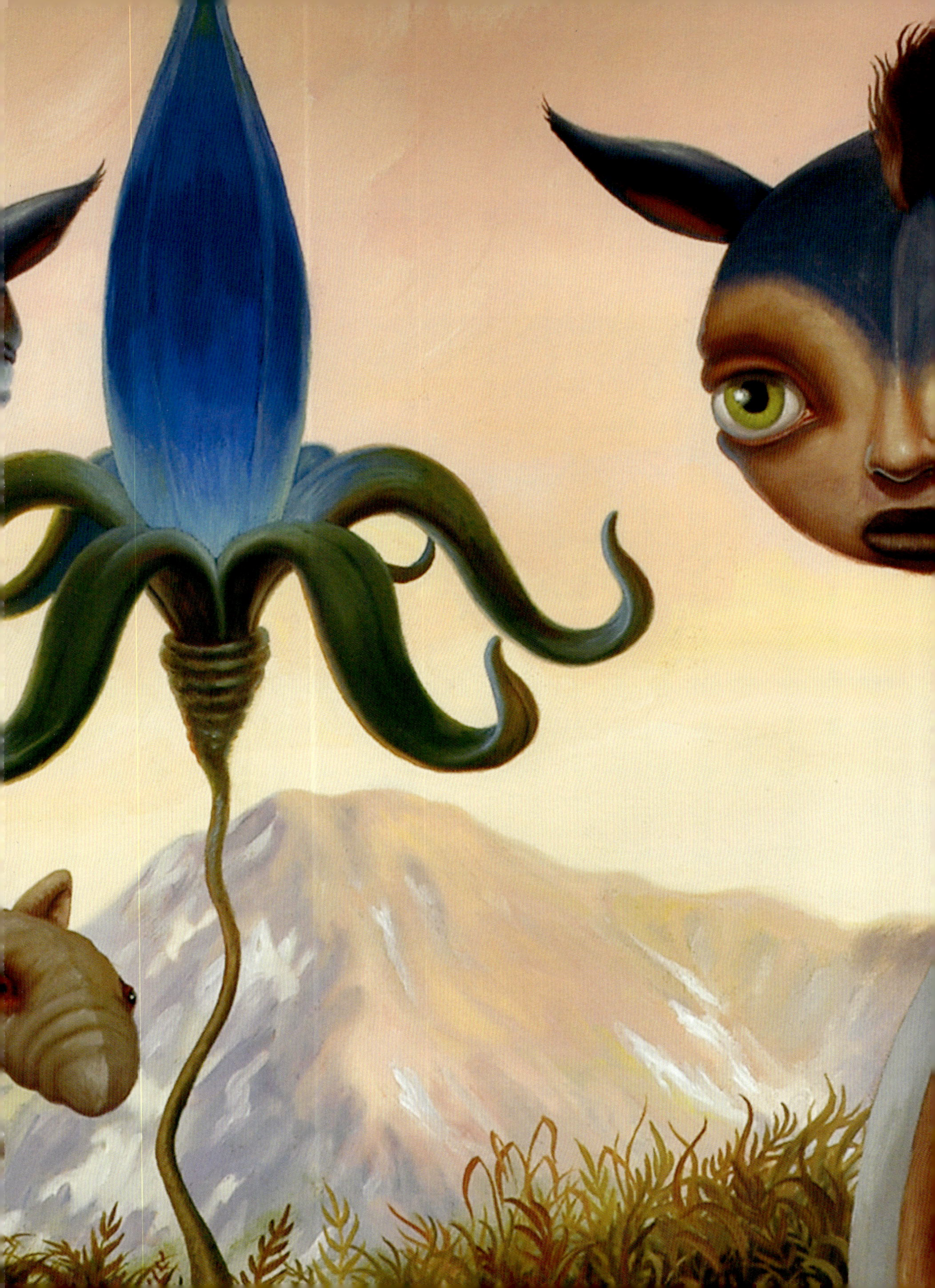

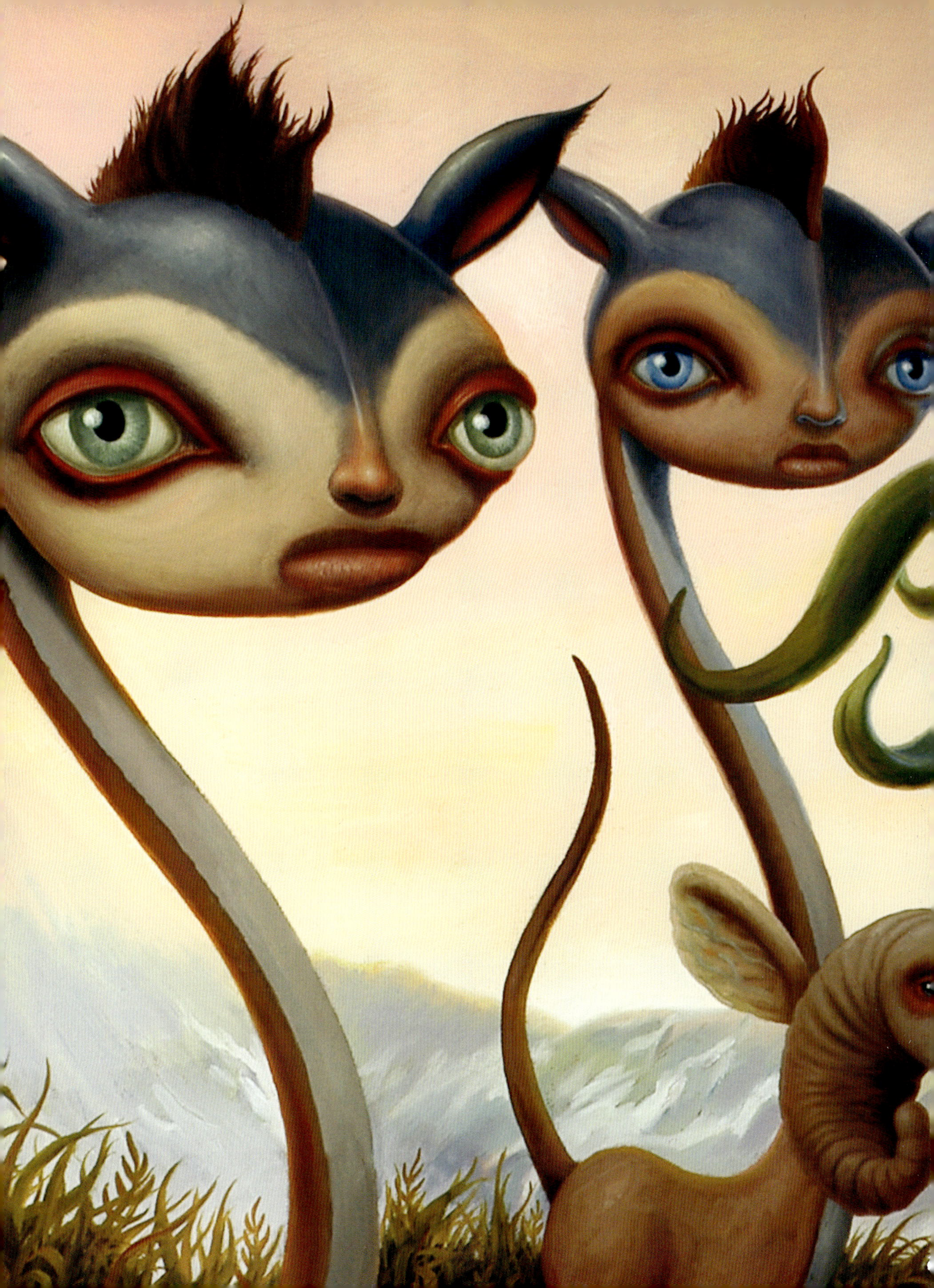

An Inland Empire

Extinct ~ ca. 1872

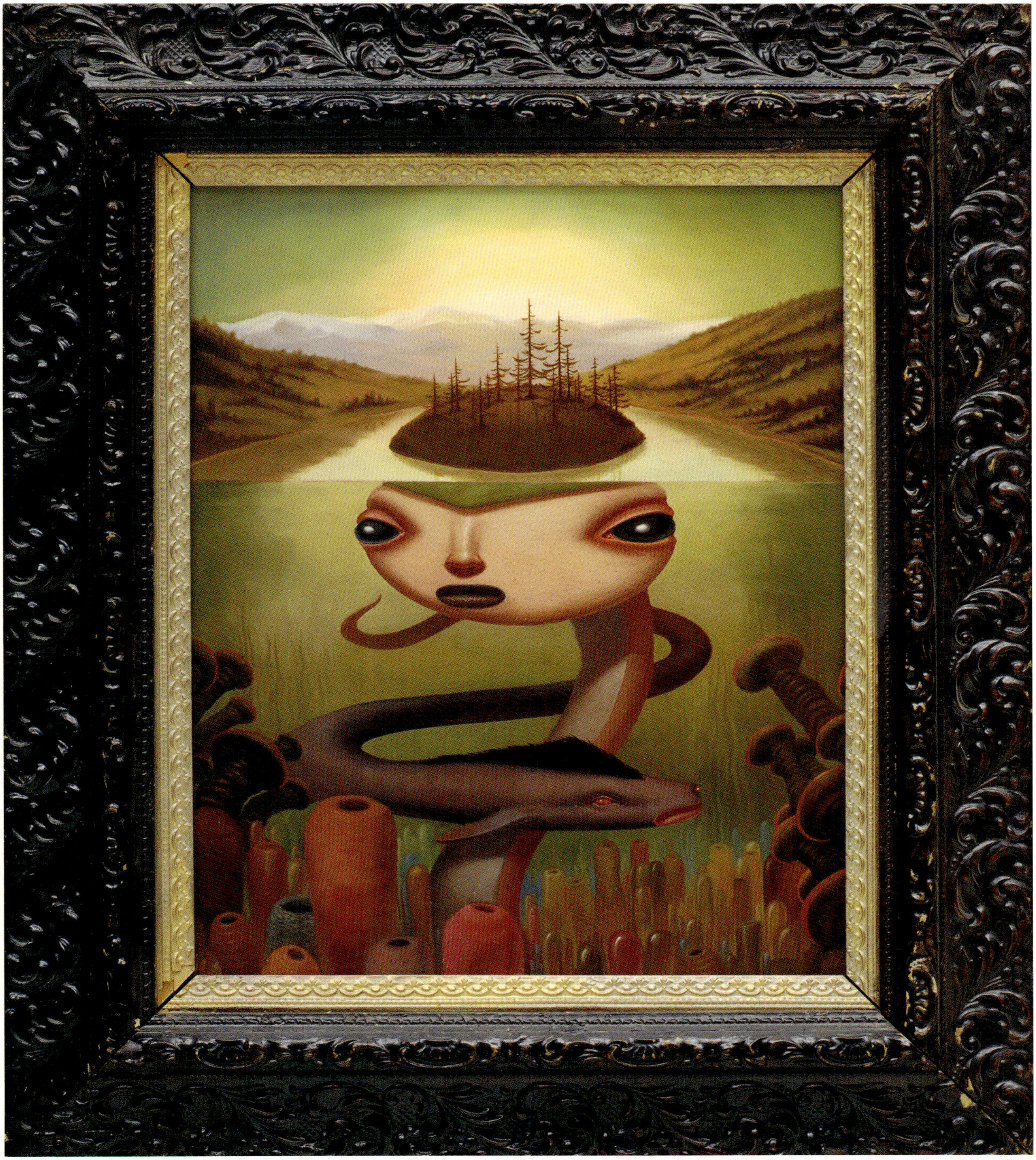

The Last Rhino

Extinct ~ ca. 1802

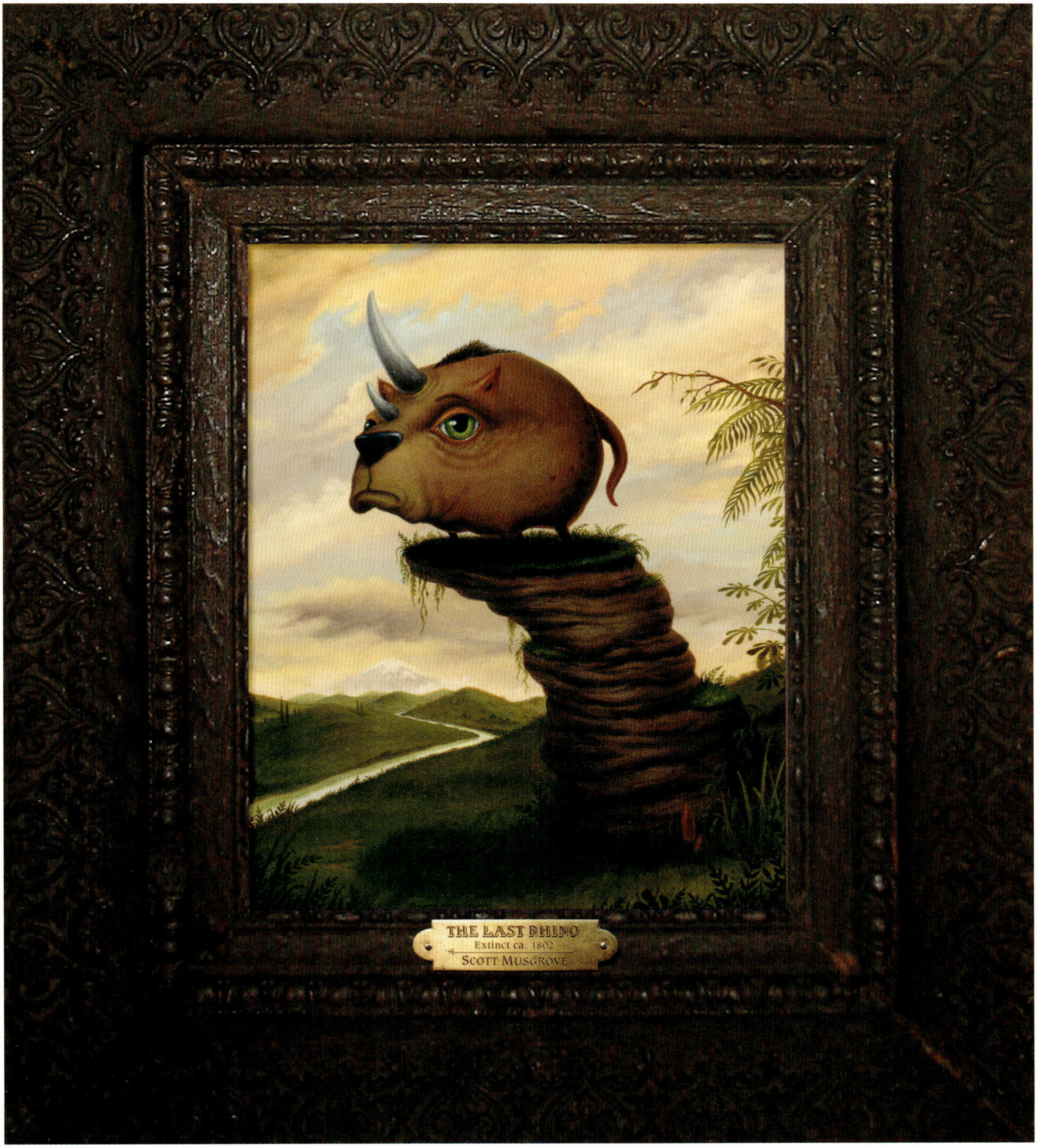
THE LAST RHINO
Extinct ca. 1802
SCOTT MUSGROVE

Alpacus Leviculus Maximus

Extinct ~ ca. 1800

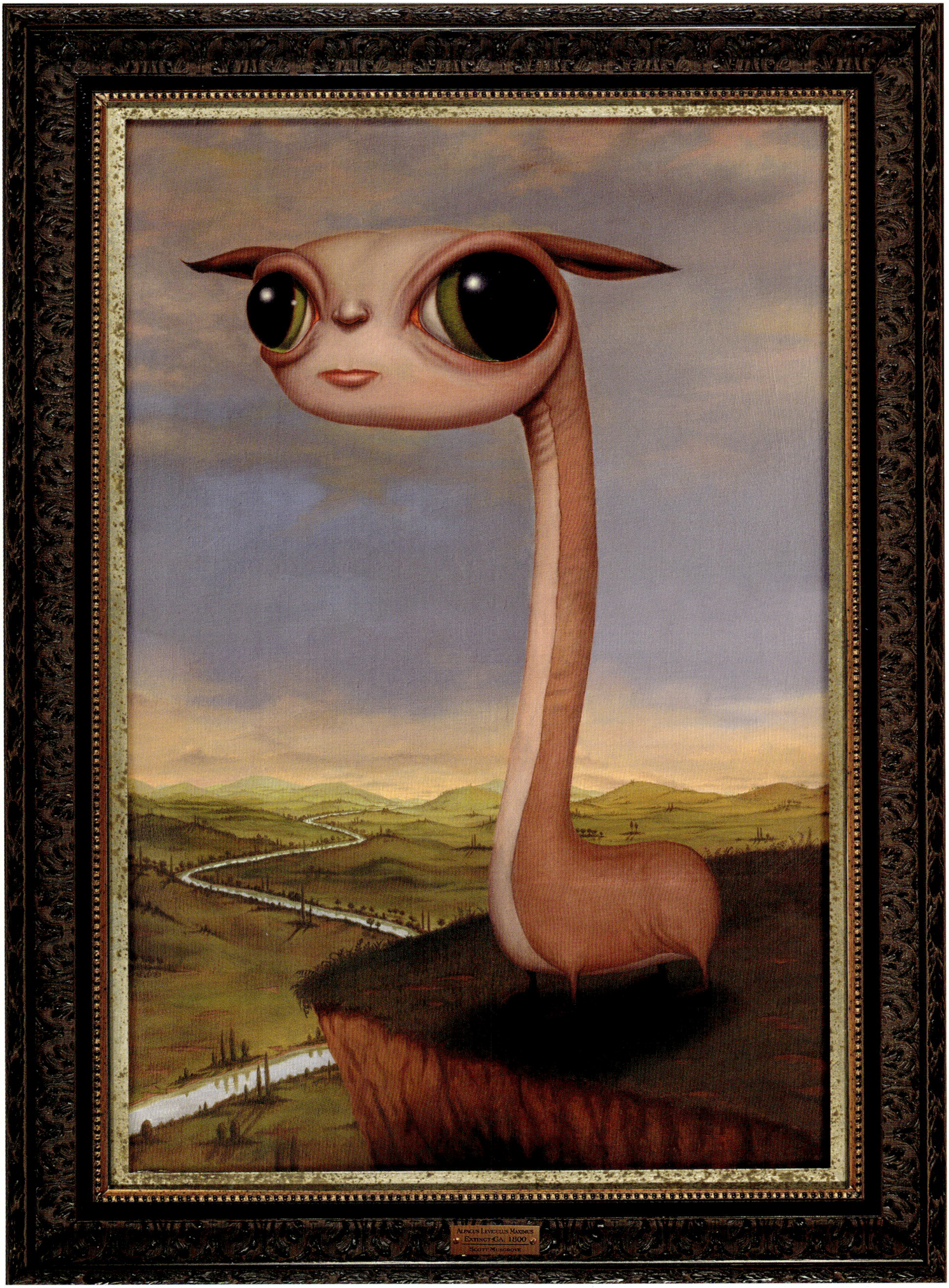
EXTINCT CA. 1800

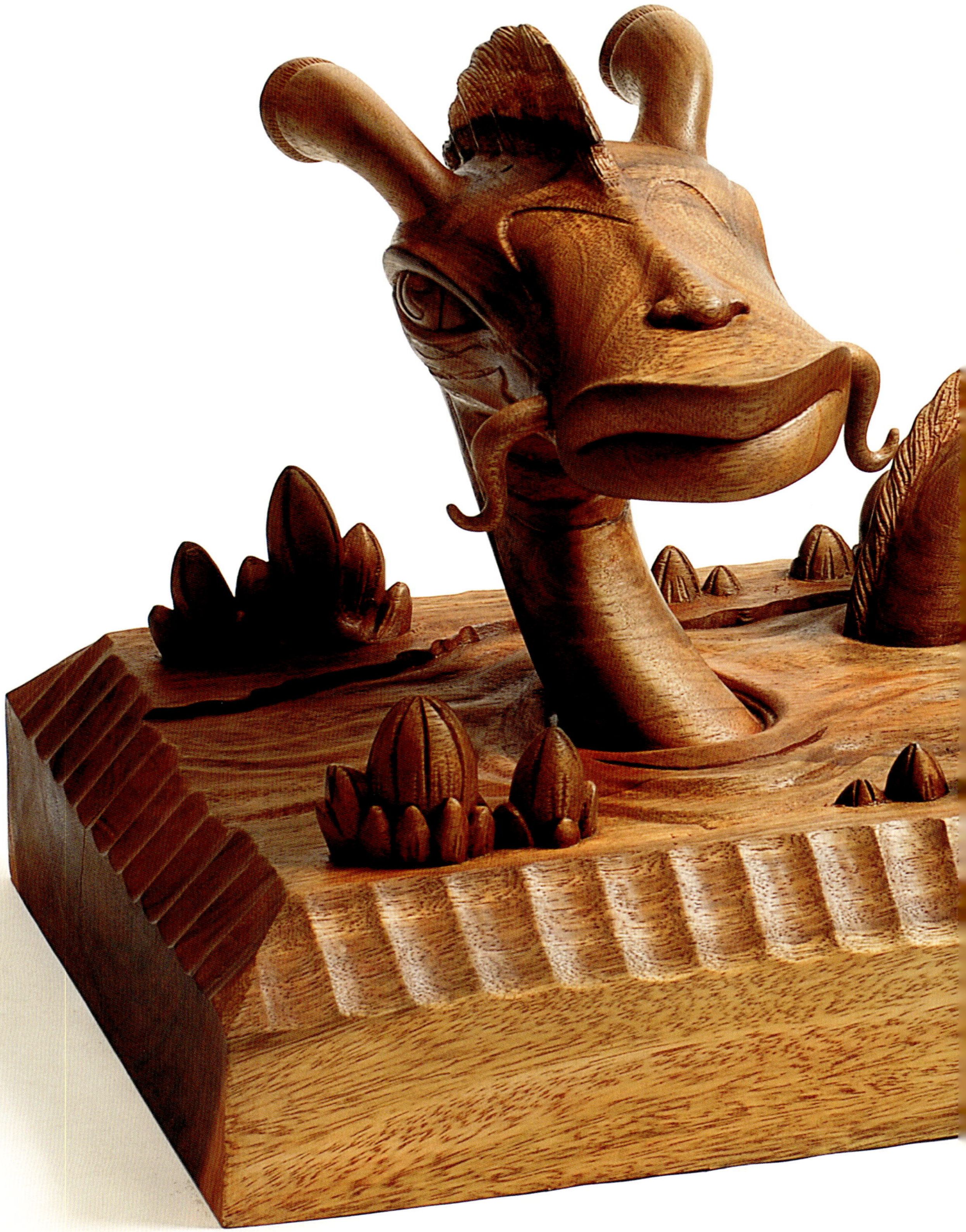

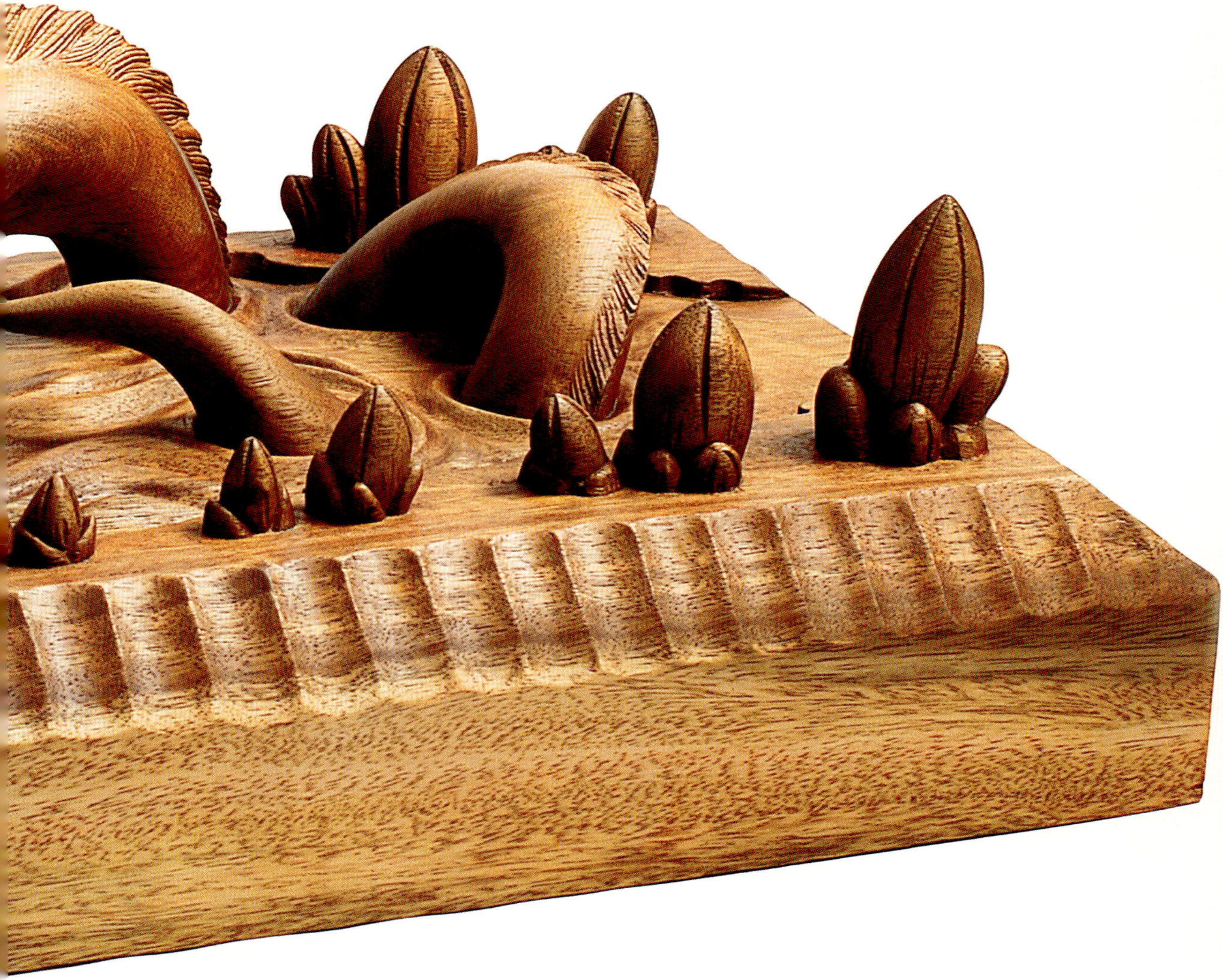

Hydrophiidus Alveus

Extinct ~ ca. 1820

PREVIOUS SPREAD

Hydrophiidus Alveus

WOOD CARVING

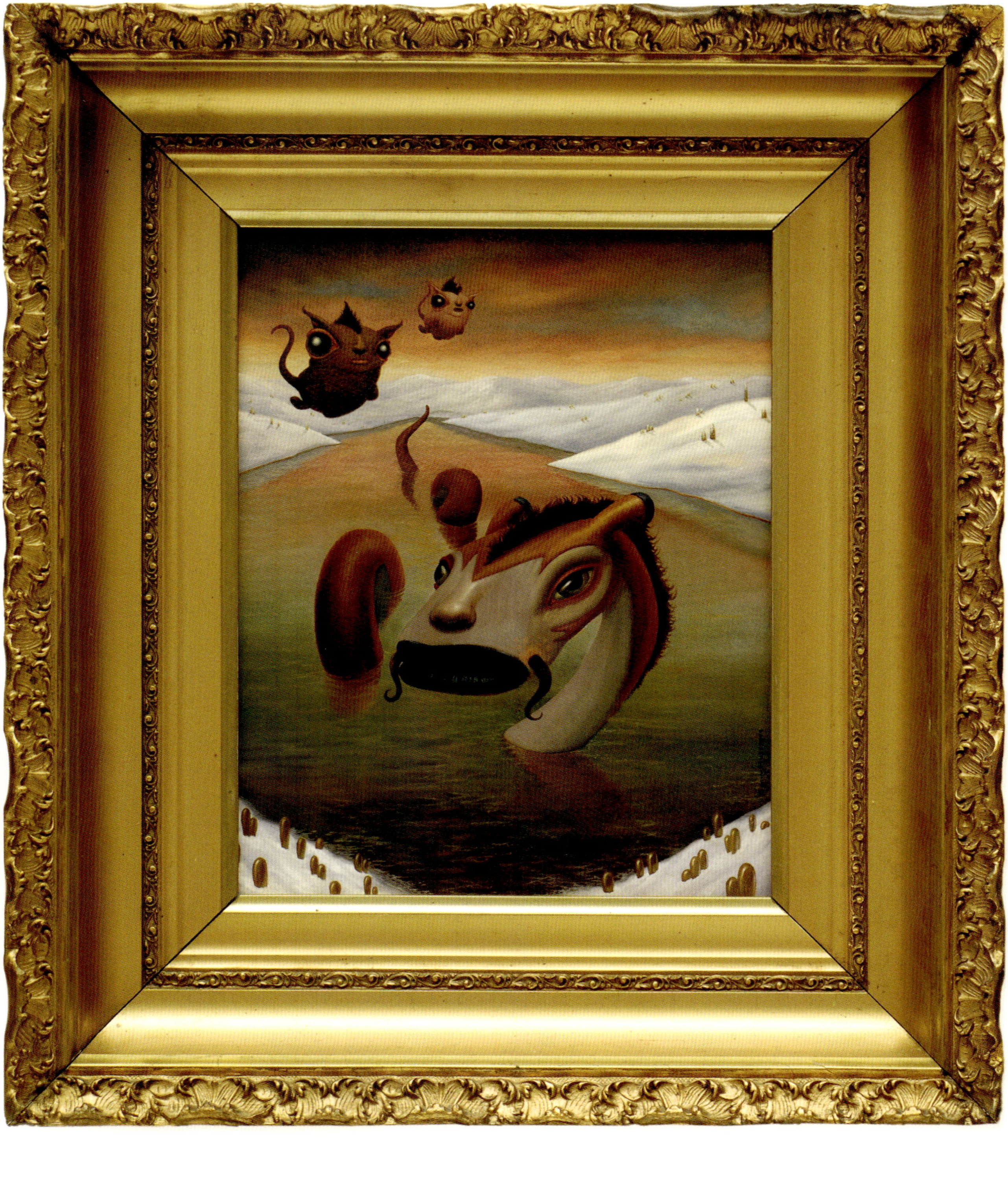

Albino Walktopus
Extinct ~ ca. 1877

NEXT SPREAD

Pastoralia Americana
ca. 1857

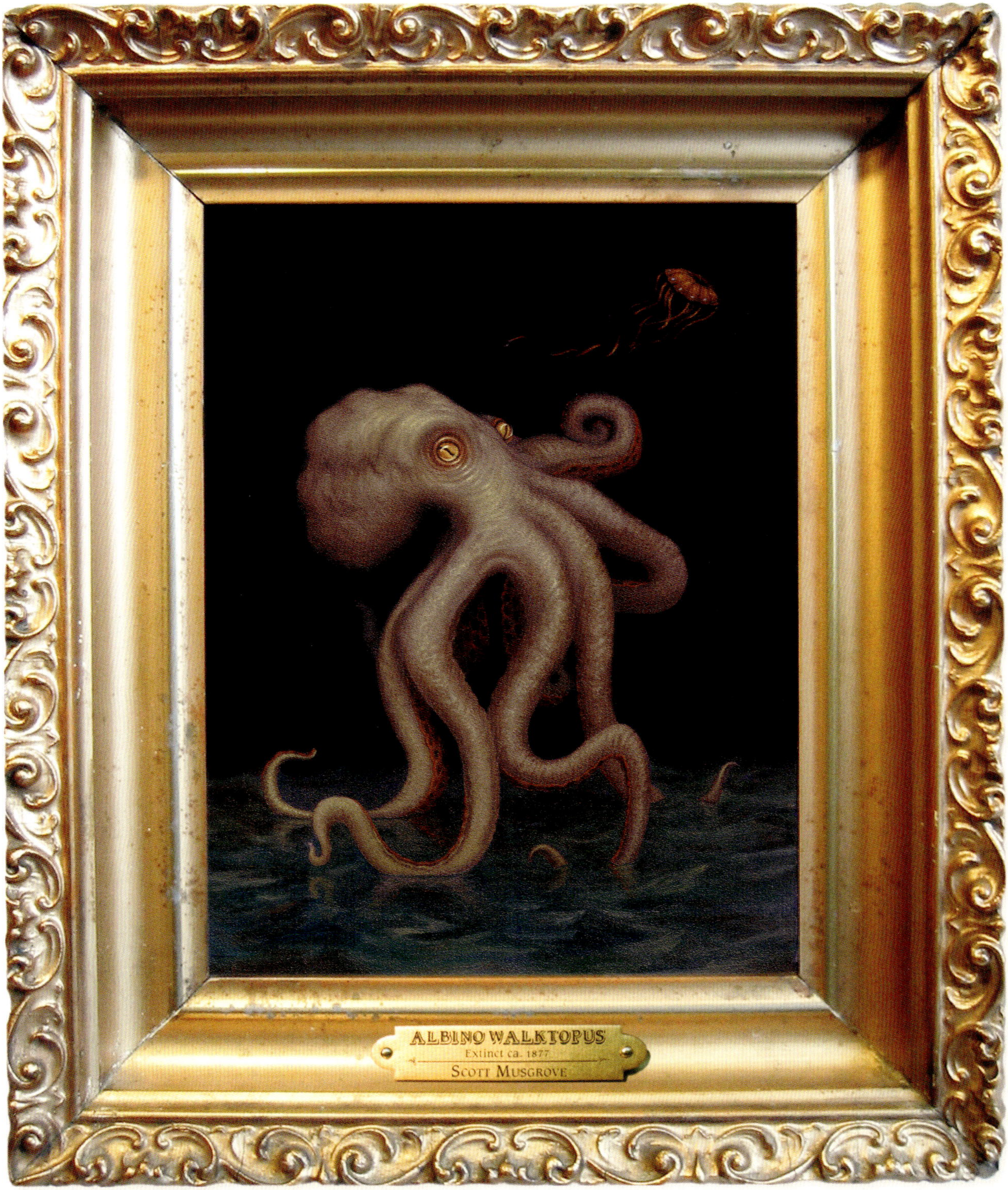
ALBINO WALKTOPUS
Extinct ca. 1877
SCOTT MUSGROVE

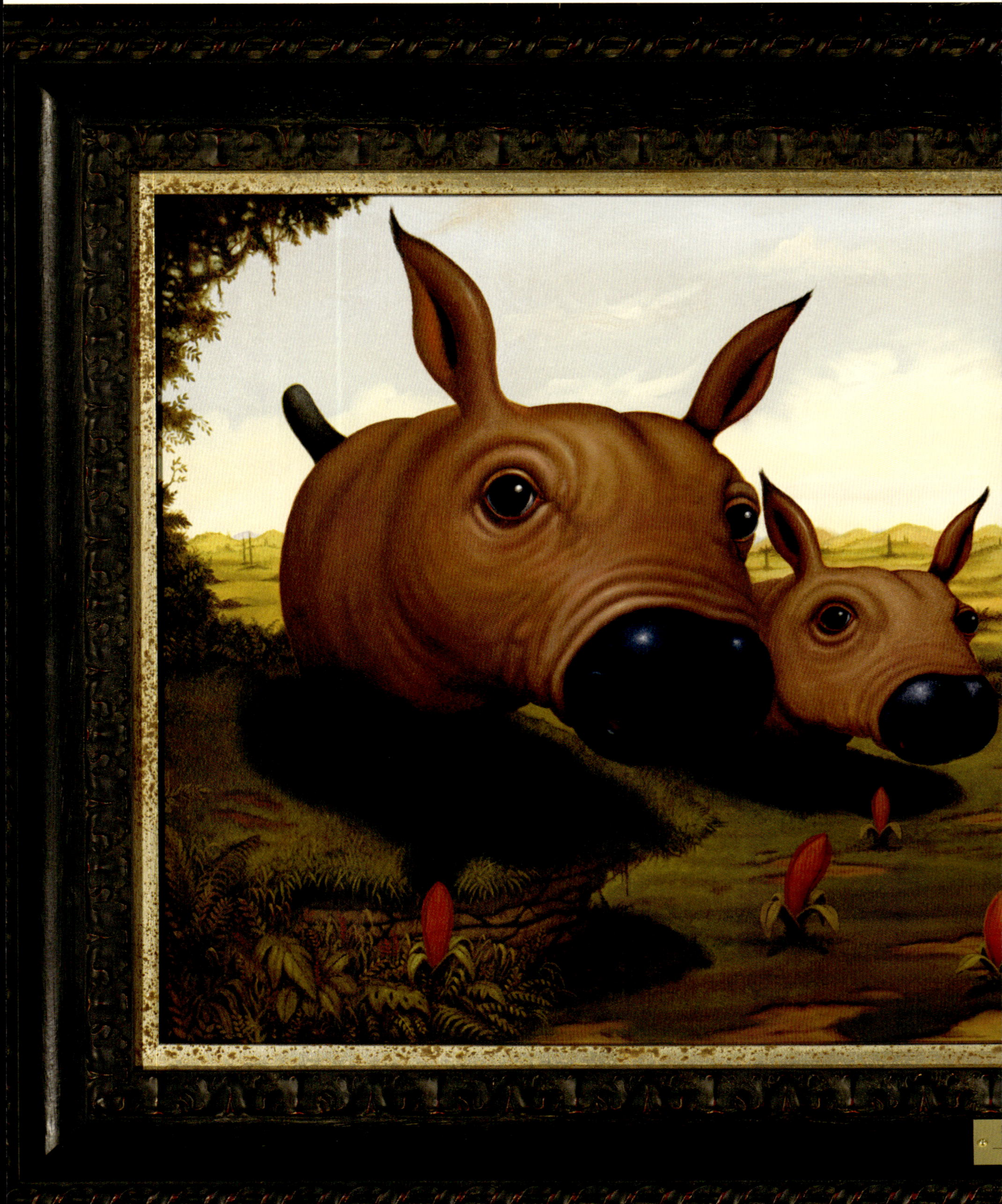

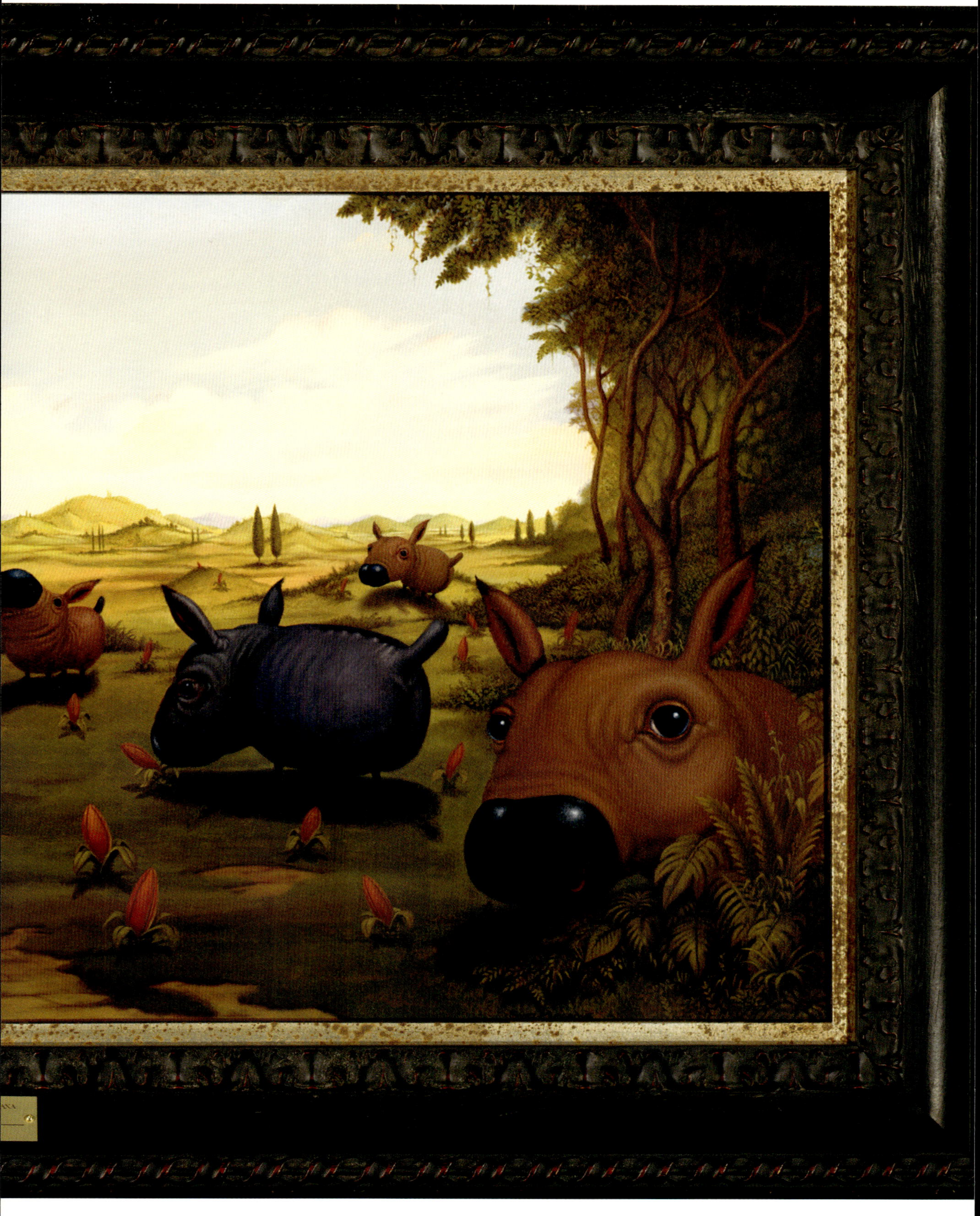

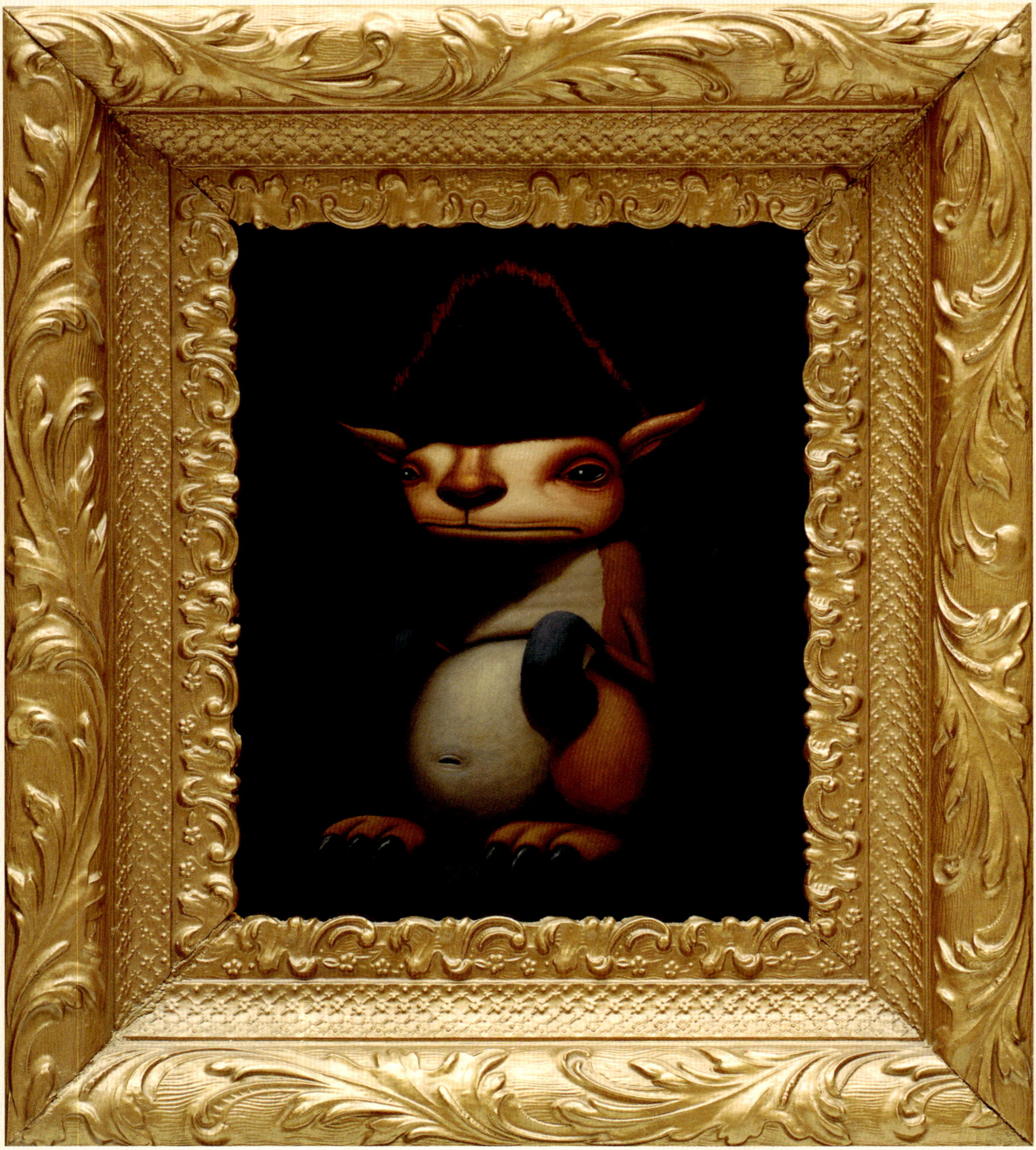

CLOCKWISE FROM LEFT:

Lepus Pilosus
Extinct ca. 1866

Deluxe Dromedary
Extinct ca. 1852

Glamour Llama
Extinct ca. 1882

Vicunus Comptus
Extinct ca. 1810

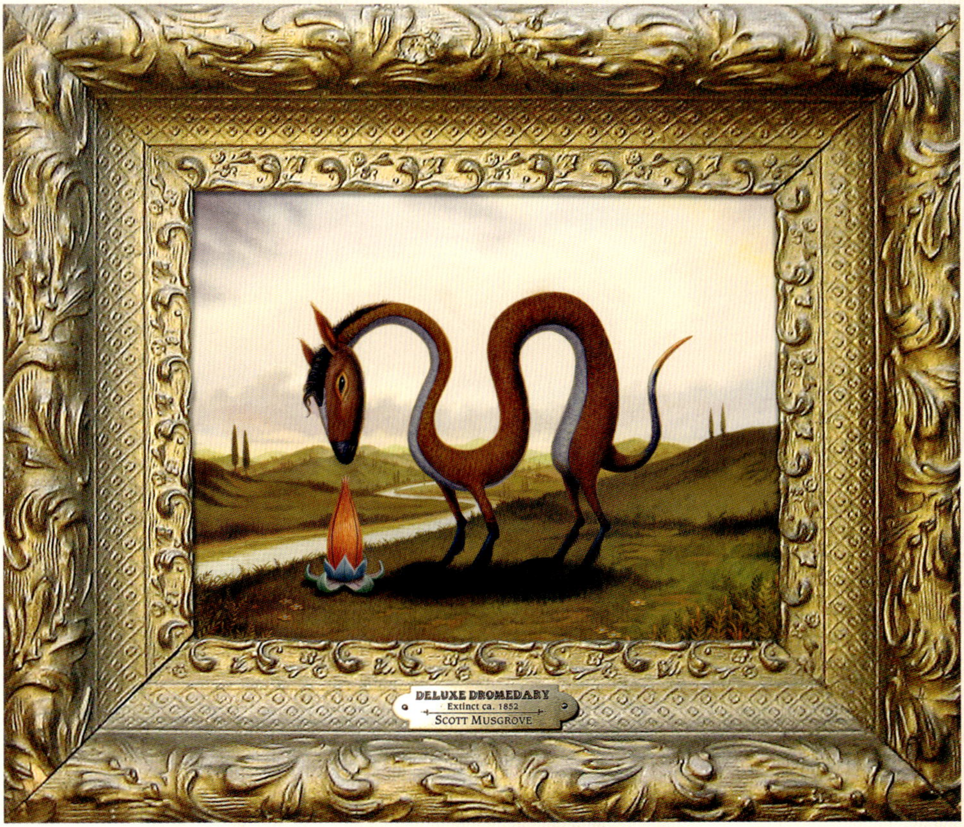
DELUXE DROMEDARY
Extinct ca. 1852
SCOTT MUSGROVE

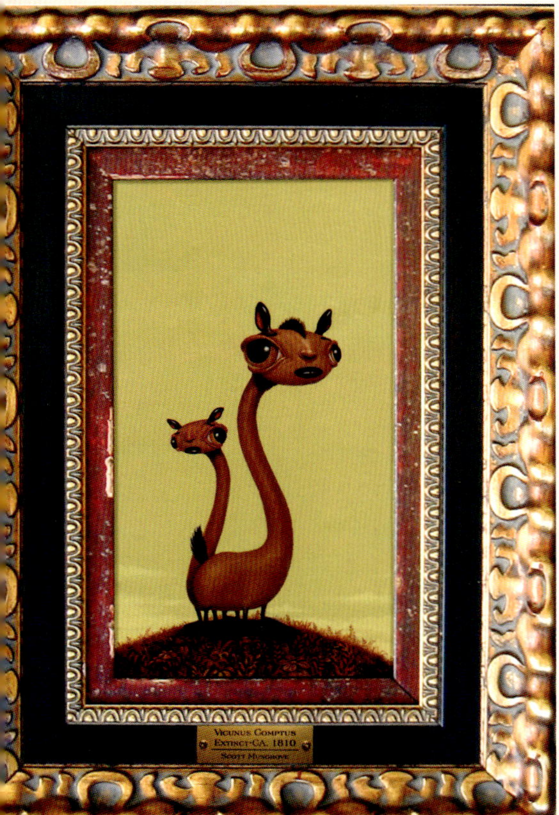
VICUNUS COMPTUS
EXTINCT-CA. 1810

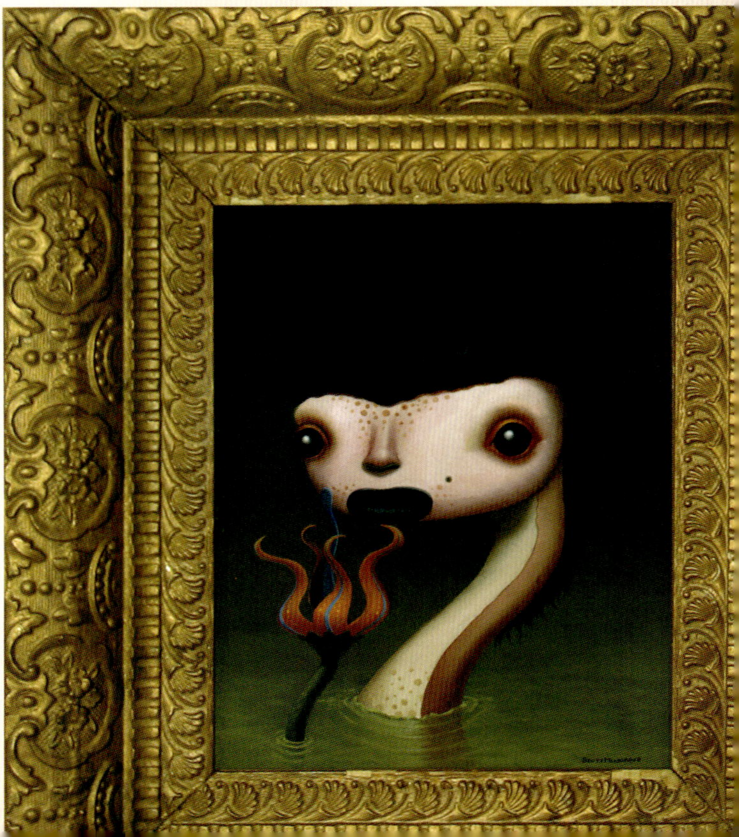

Ophidius Delphicus
Extinct ~ ca. 1933

GATEFOLD

Great Naked GlamourPuss
Extinct ~ ca. 1853

PAGE 79

Ophidius Delphicus
DETAIL

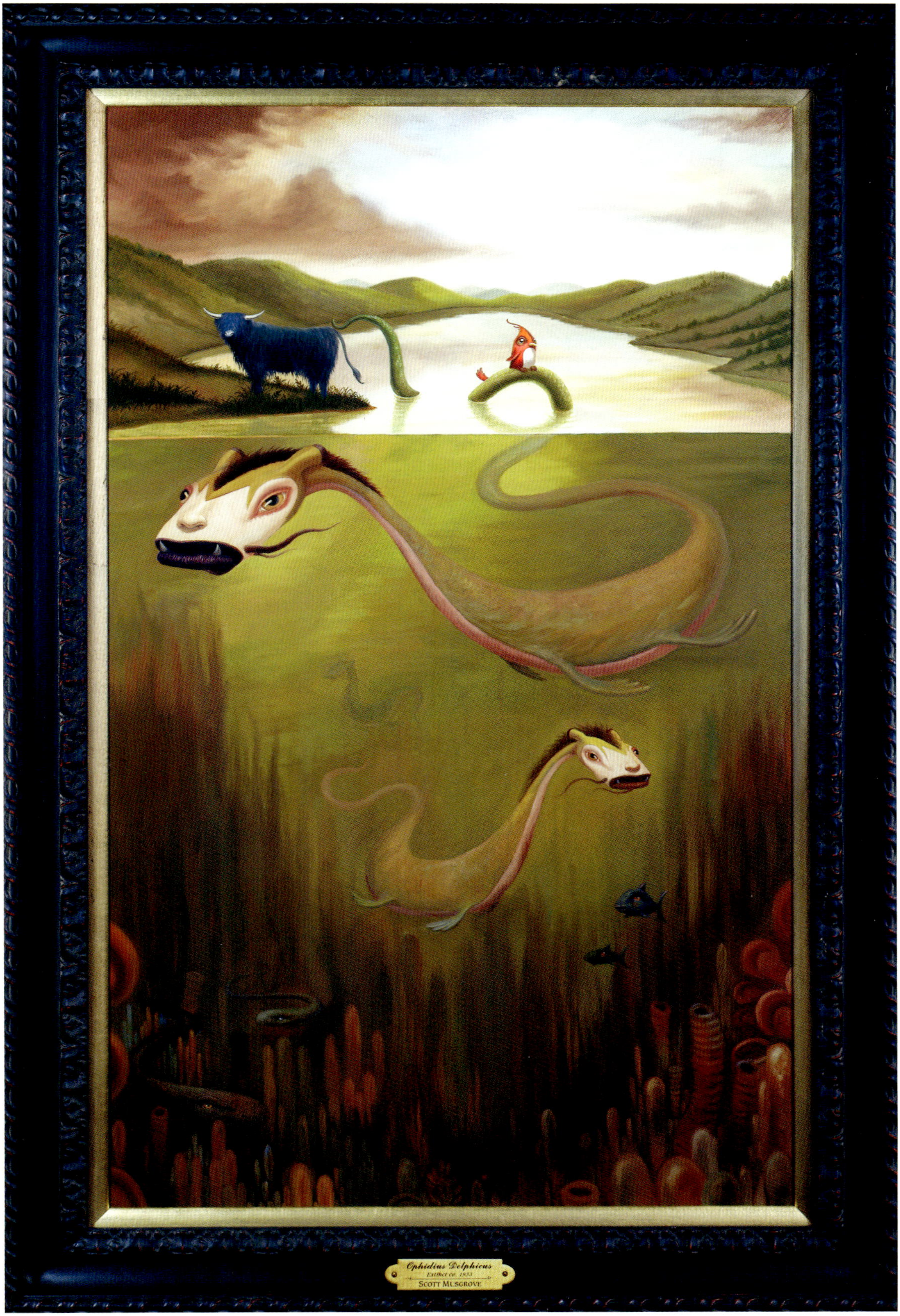
Ophidius Delphicus
Extinct ce. 1933
SCOTT MUSGROVE

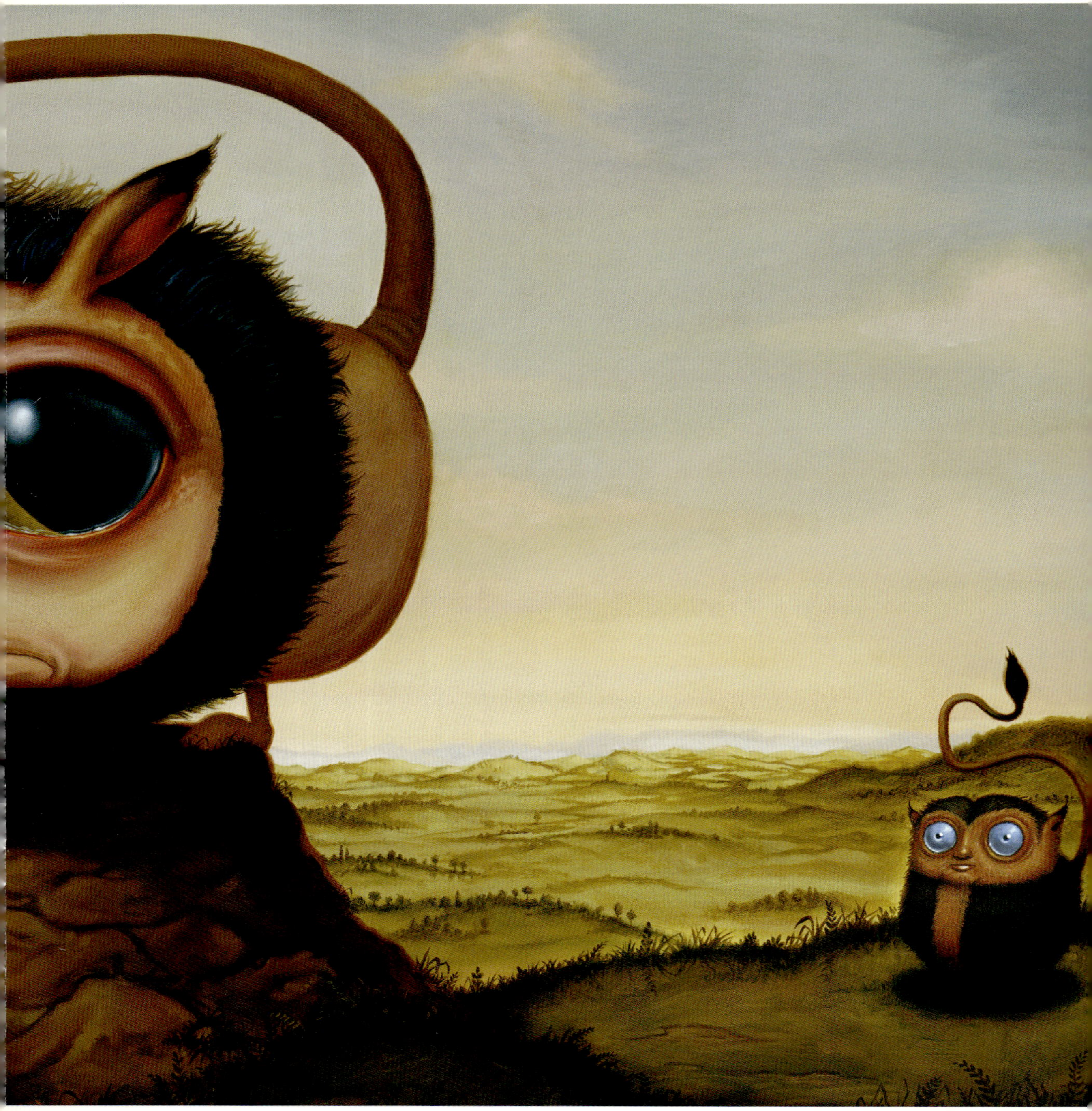

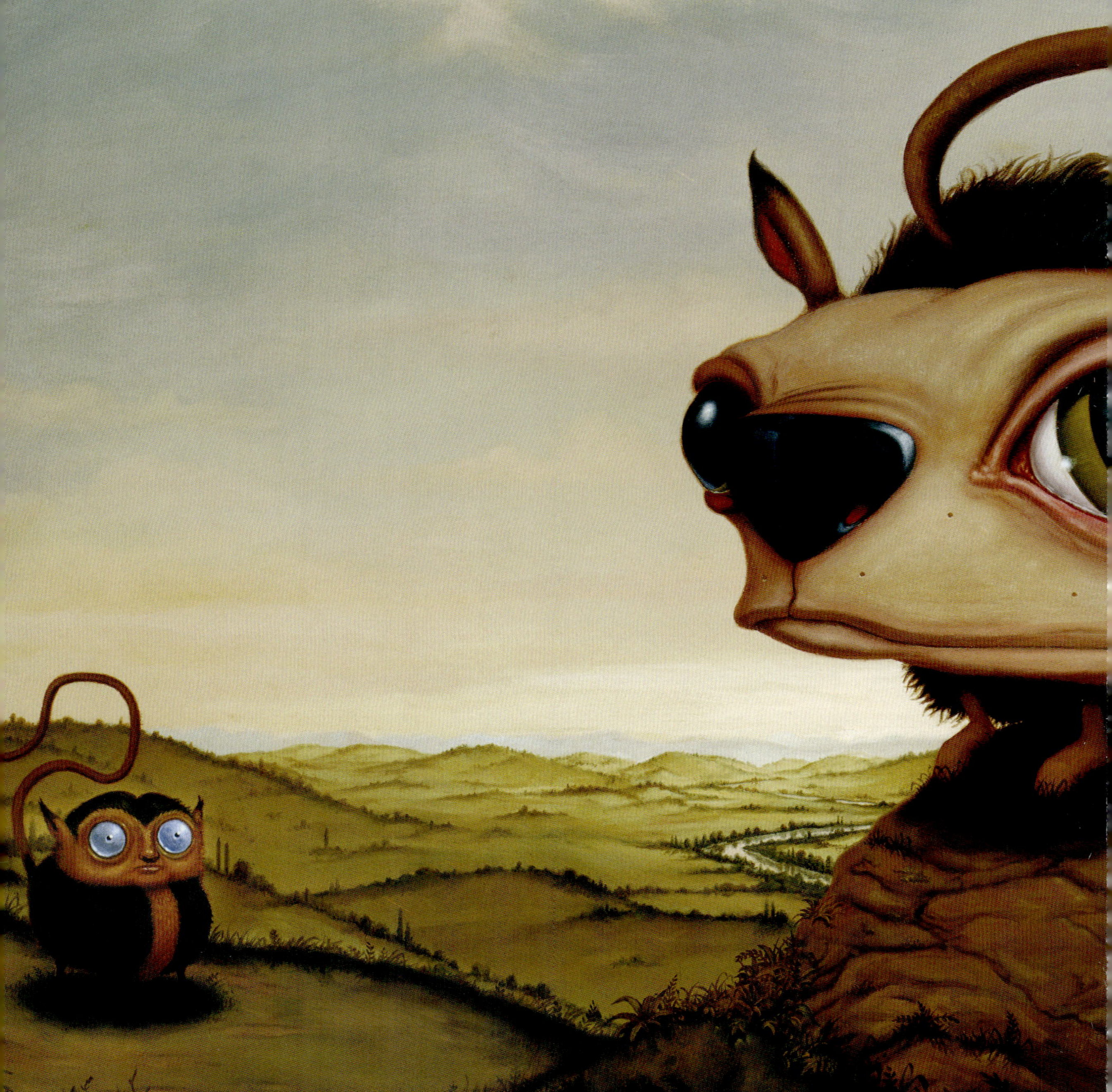

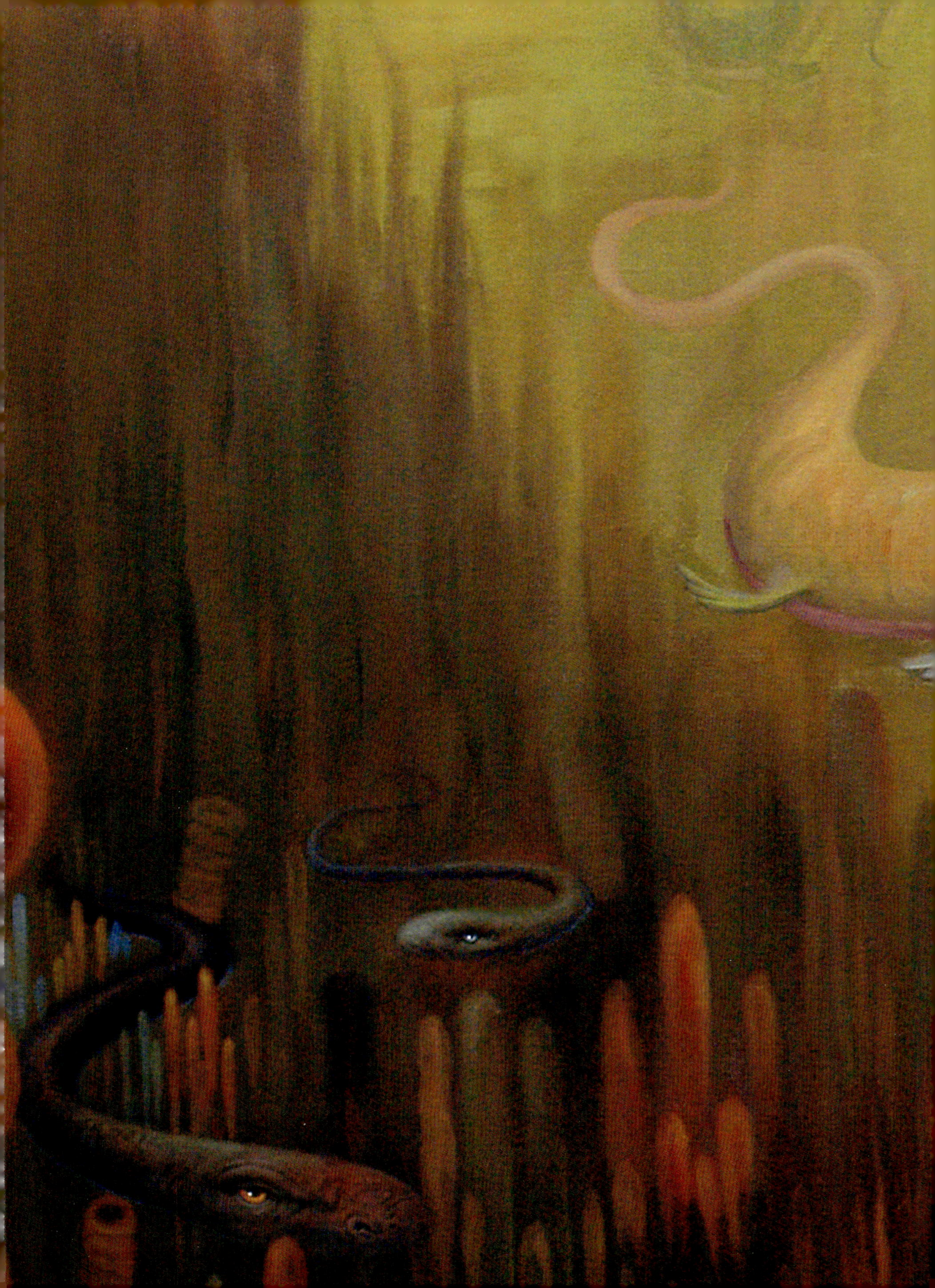

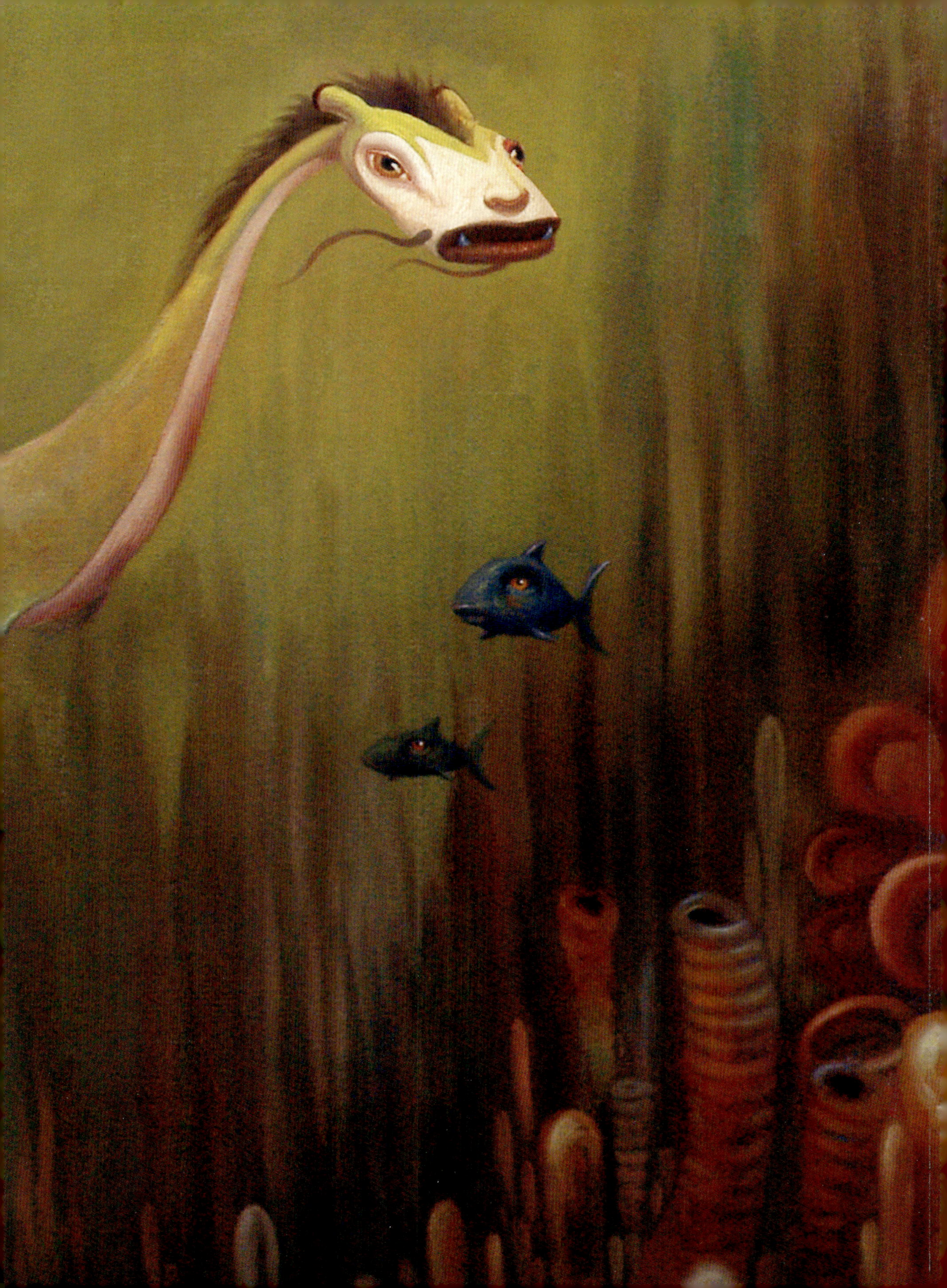

Lepus Perilous
Extinct ca. 1876

TROPHY MOUNT · WOOD CARVING

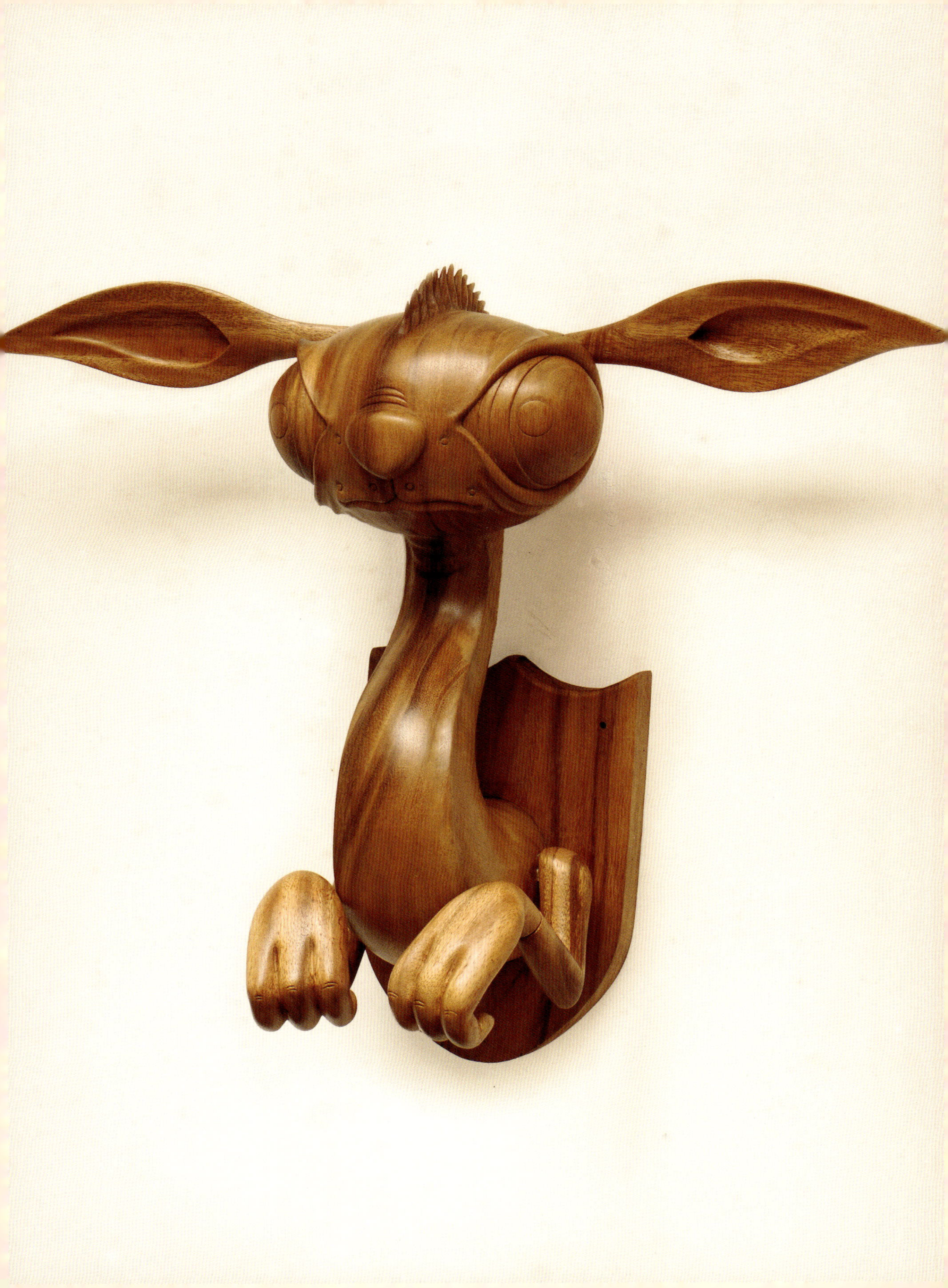

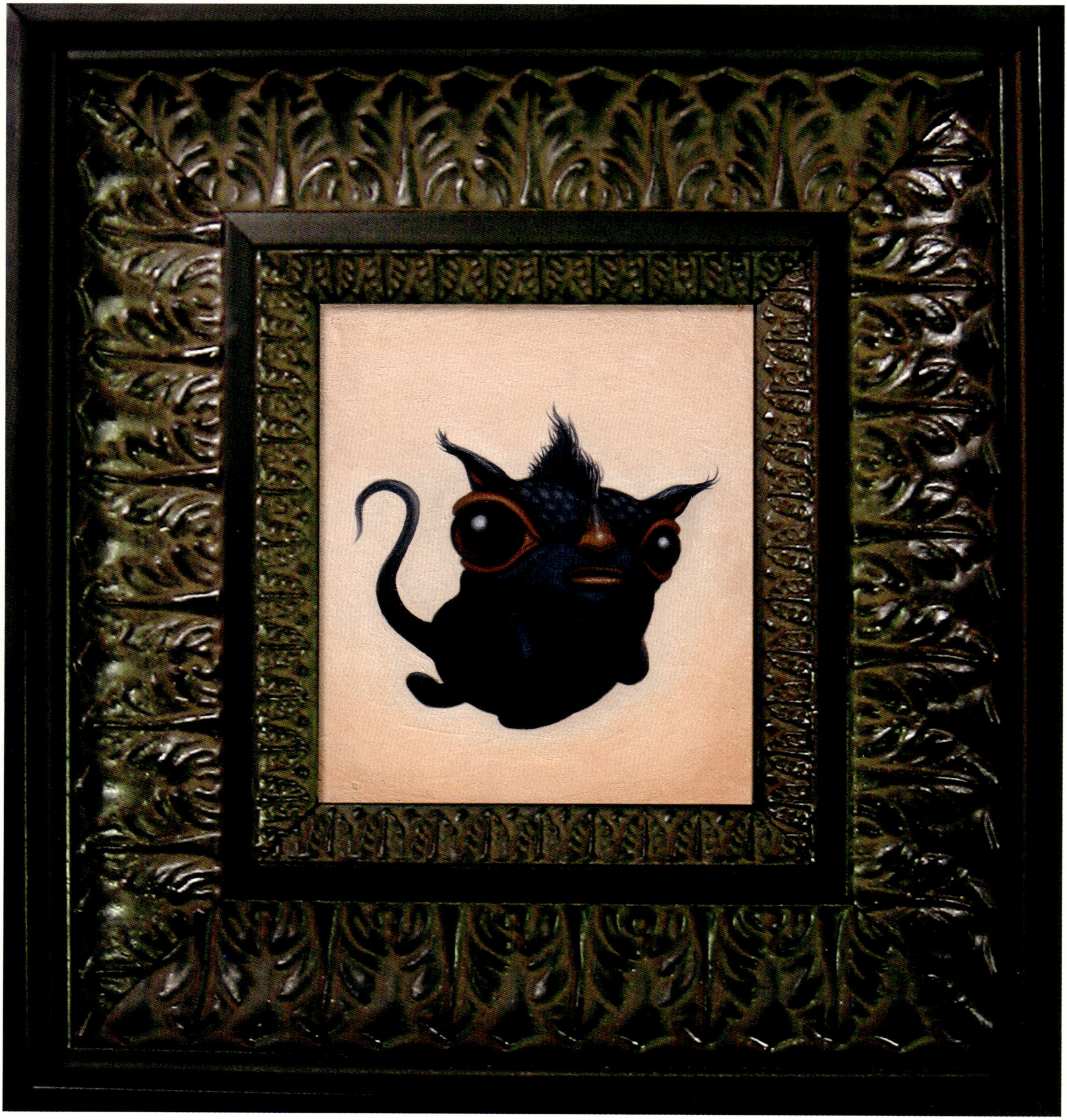

Chubbus Noir
Extinct ~ ca. 1877

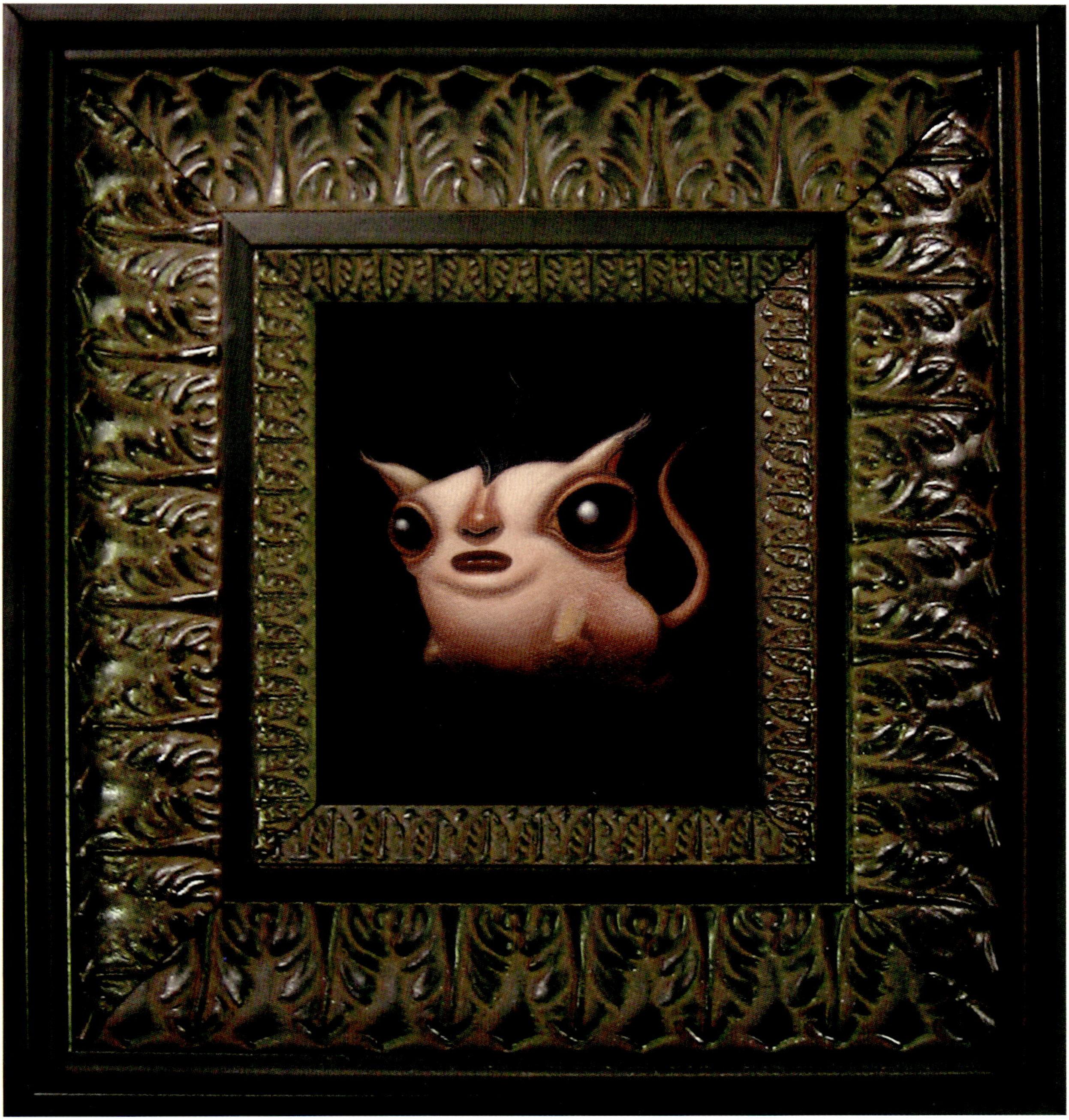

Chubbus Blanc
Extinct ~ ca. 1877

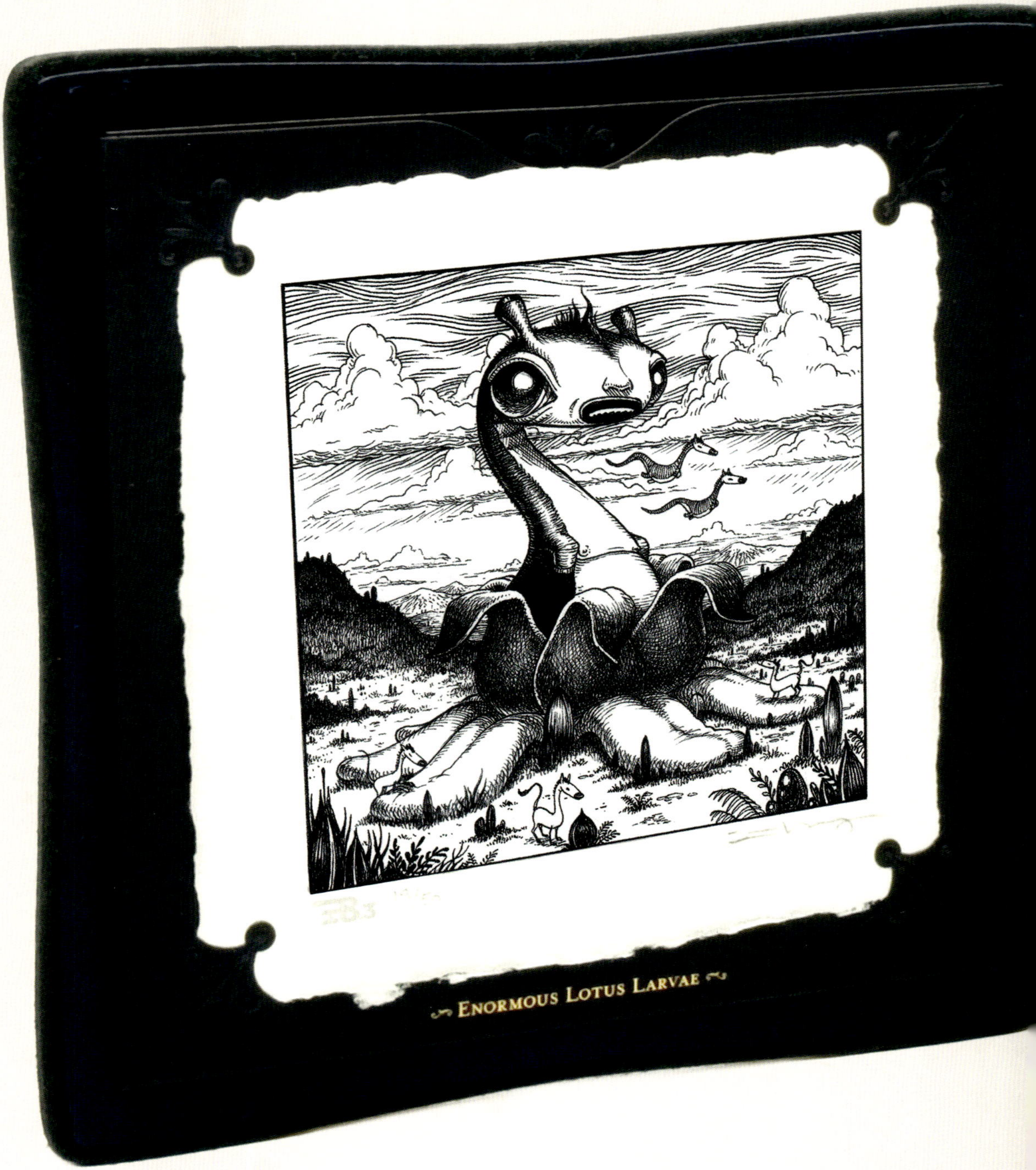
Enormous Lotus Larvae

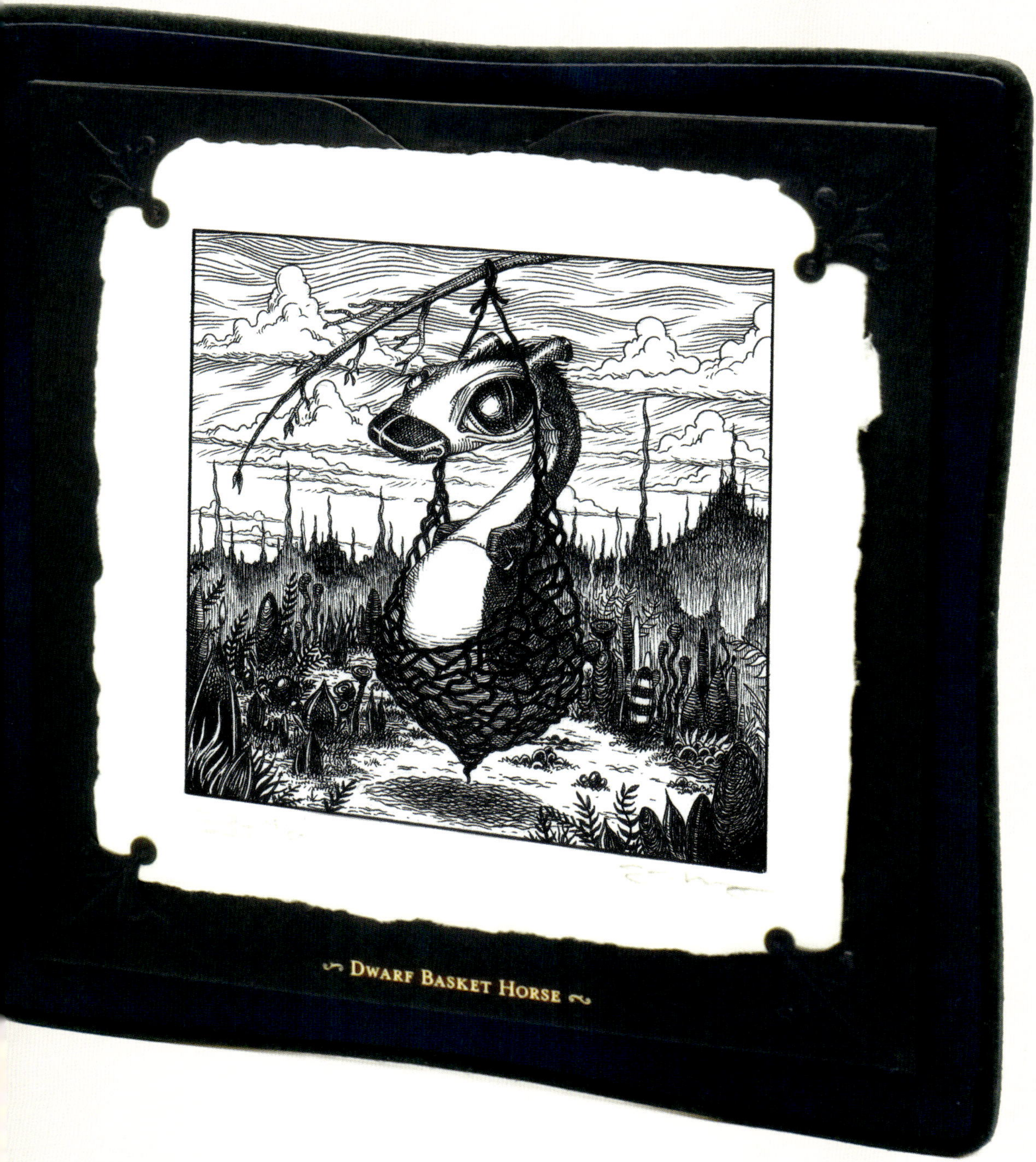
Dwarf Basket Horse

Chinese-American Llama

Extinct ~ ca. 1879

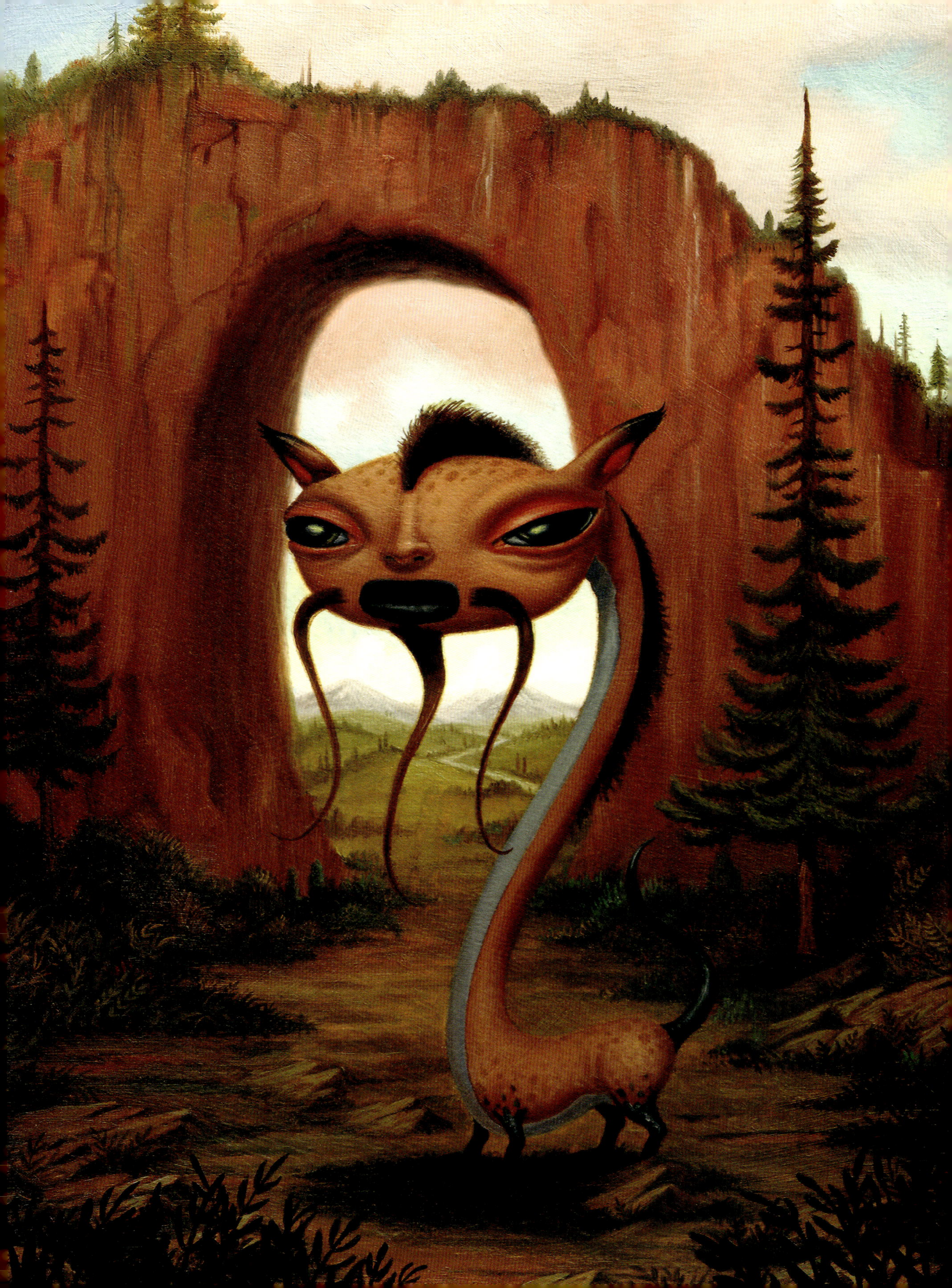

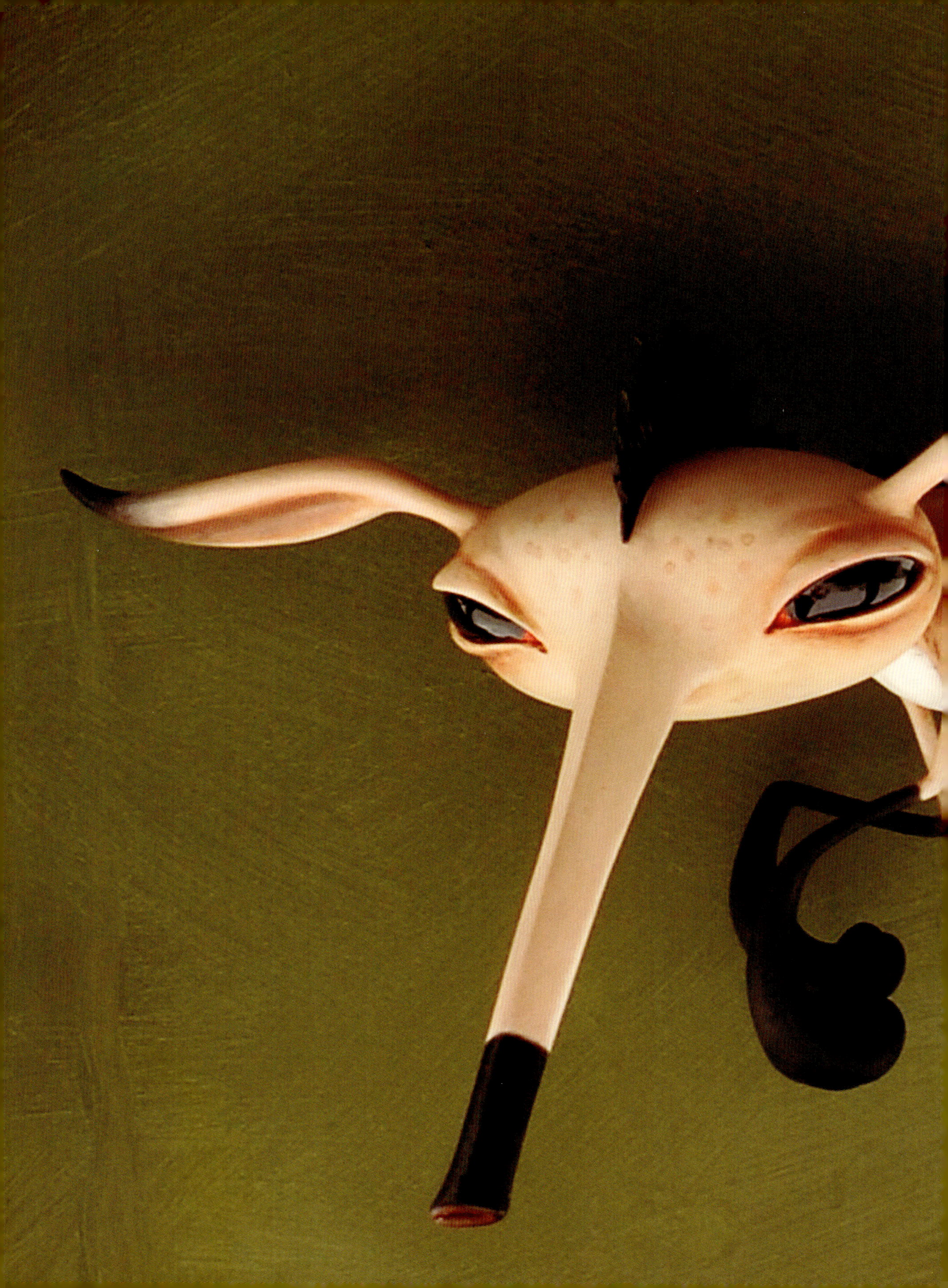

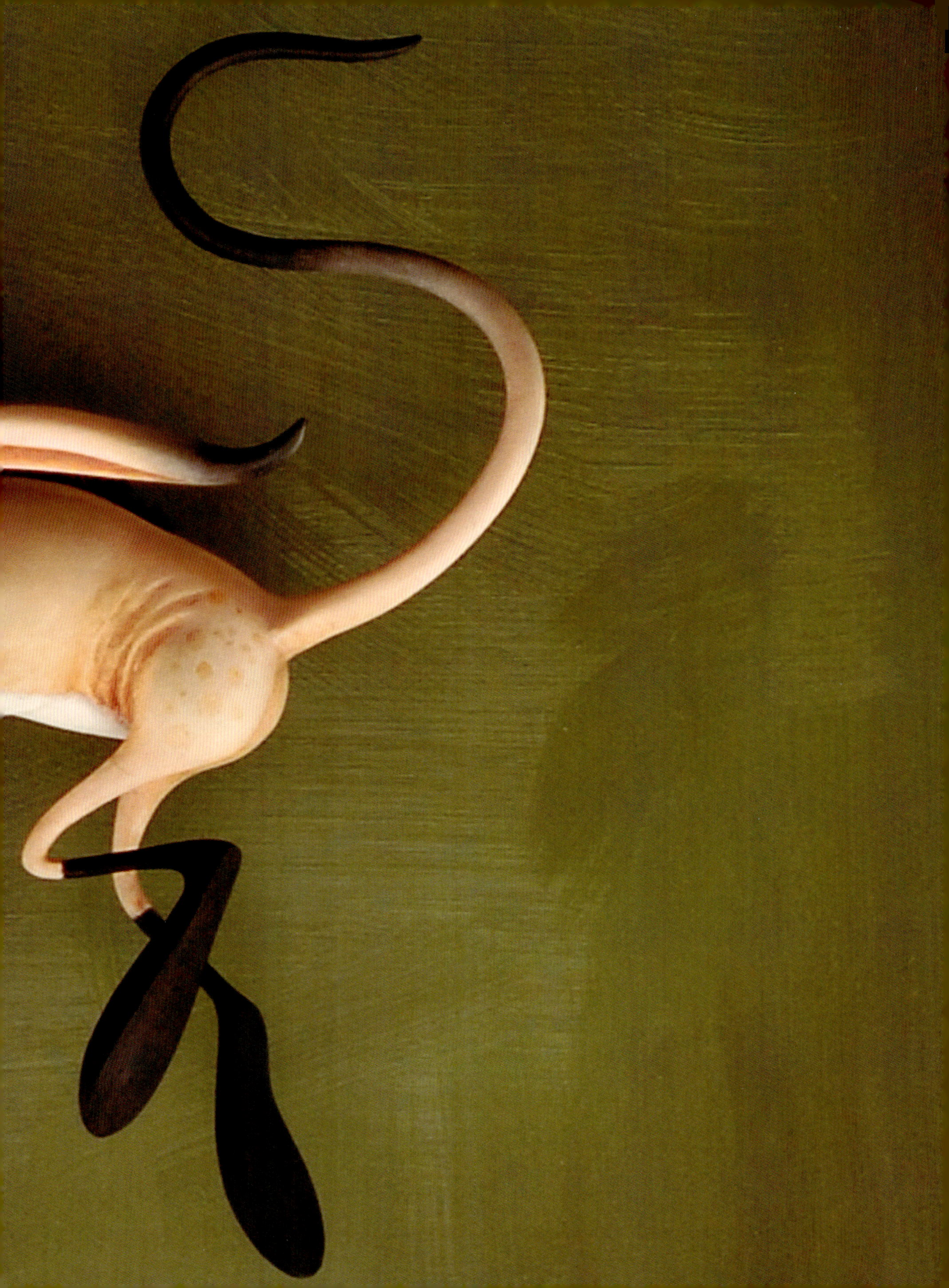

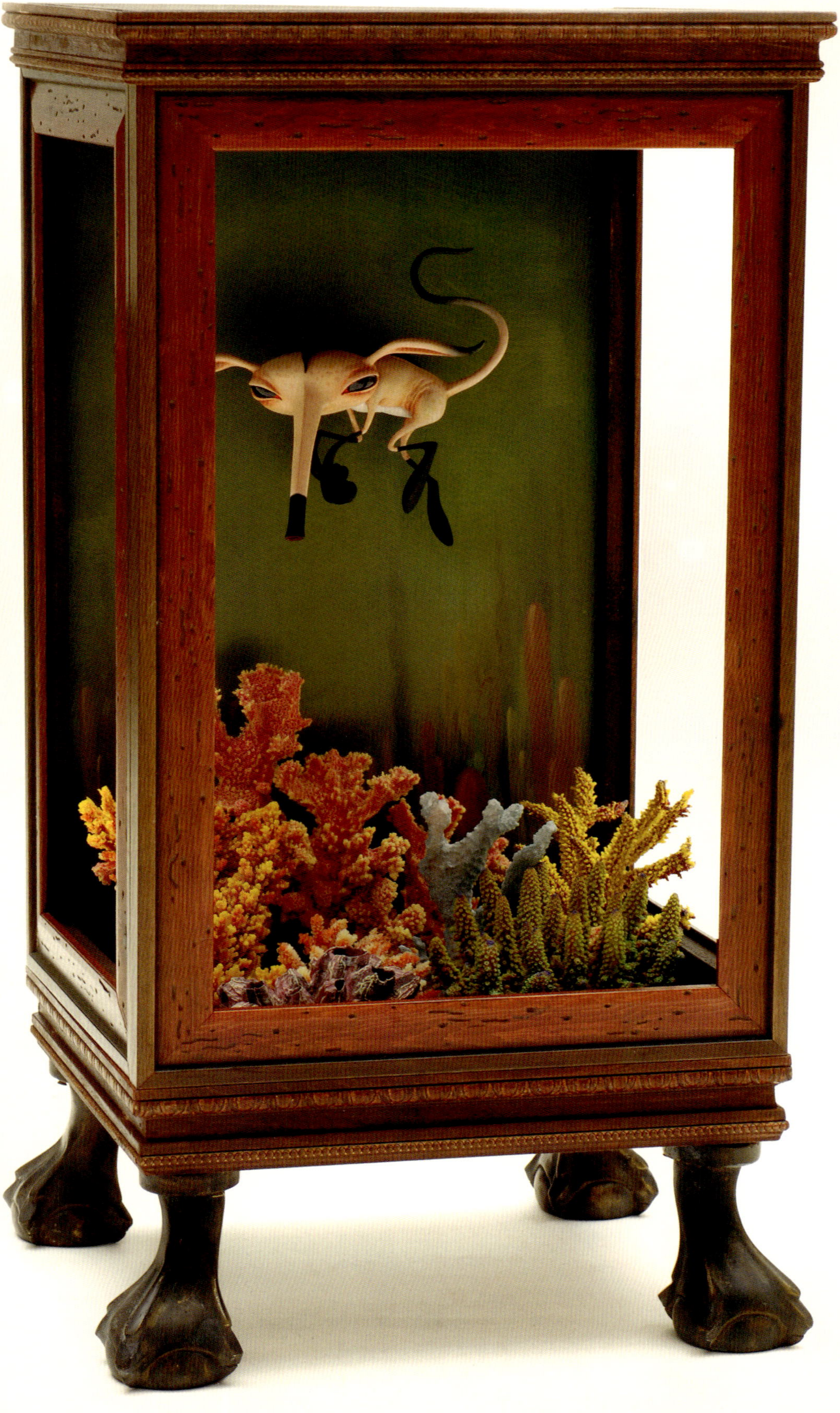

DIORAMA

Great Lesser Plant Sampler

Extinct ~ ca. 1877

mixed media collaboration with Mike Leavitt

Horned Sea Swan

Extinct ~ ca. 1819

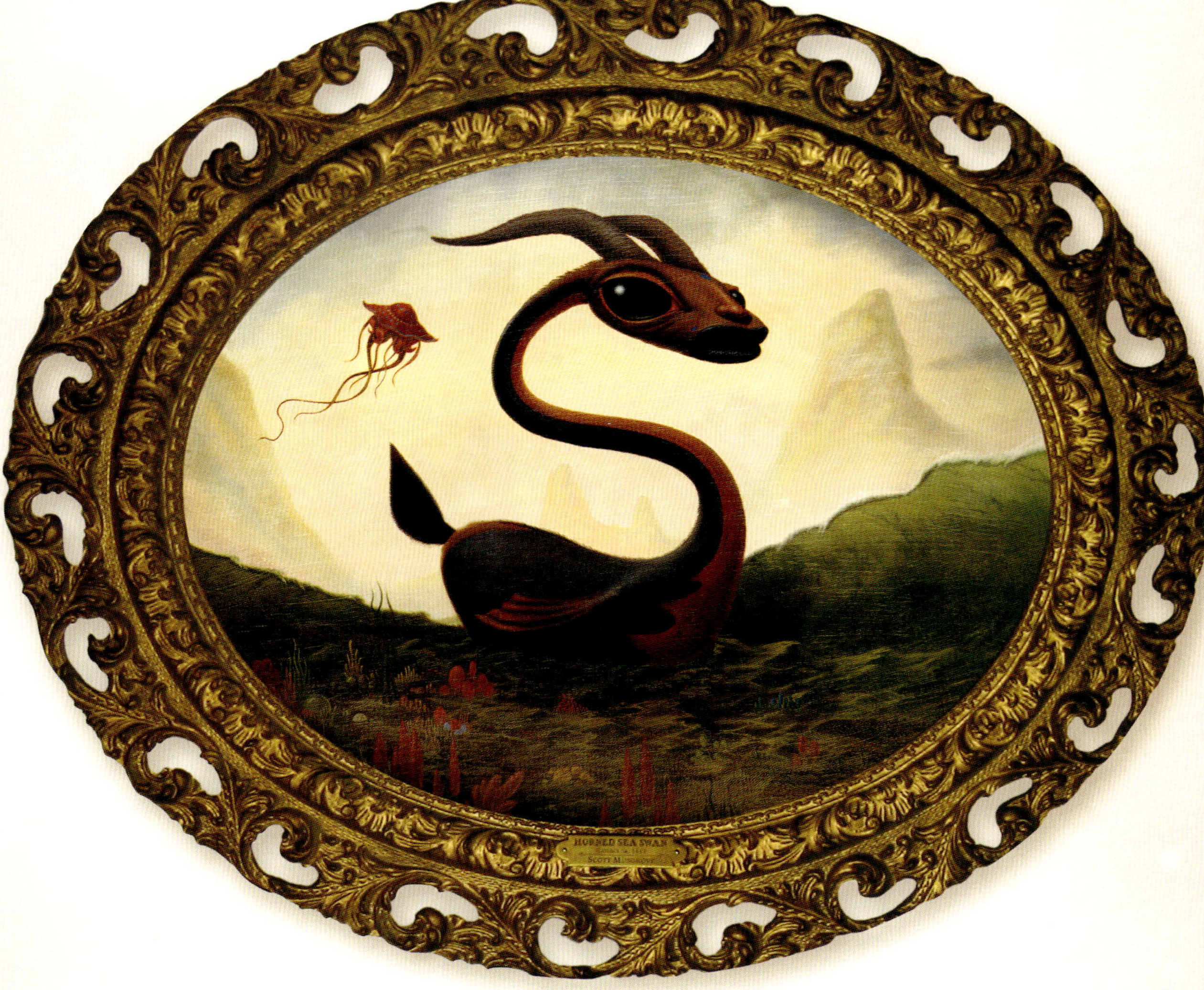
HORNED SEA SWAN

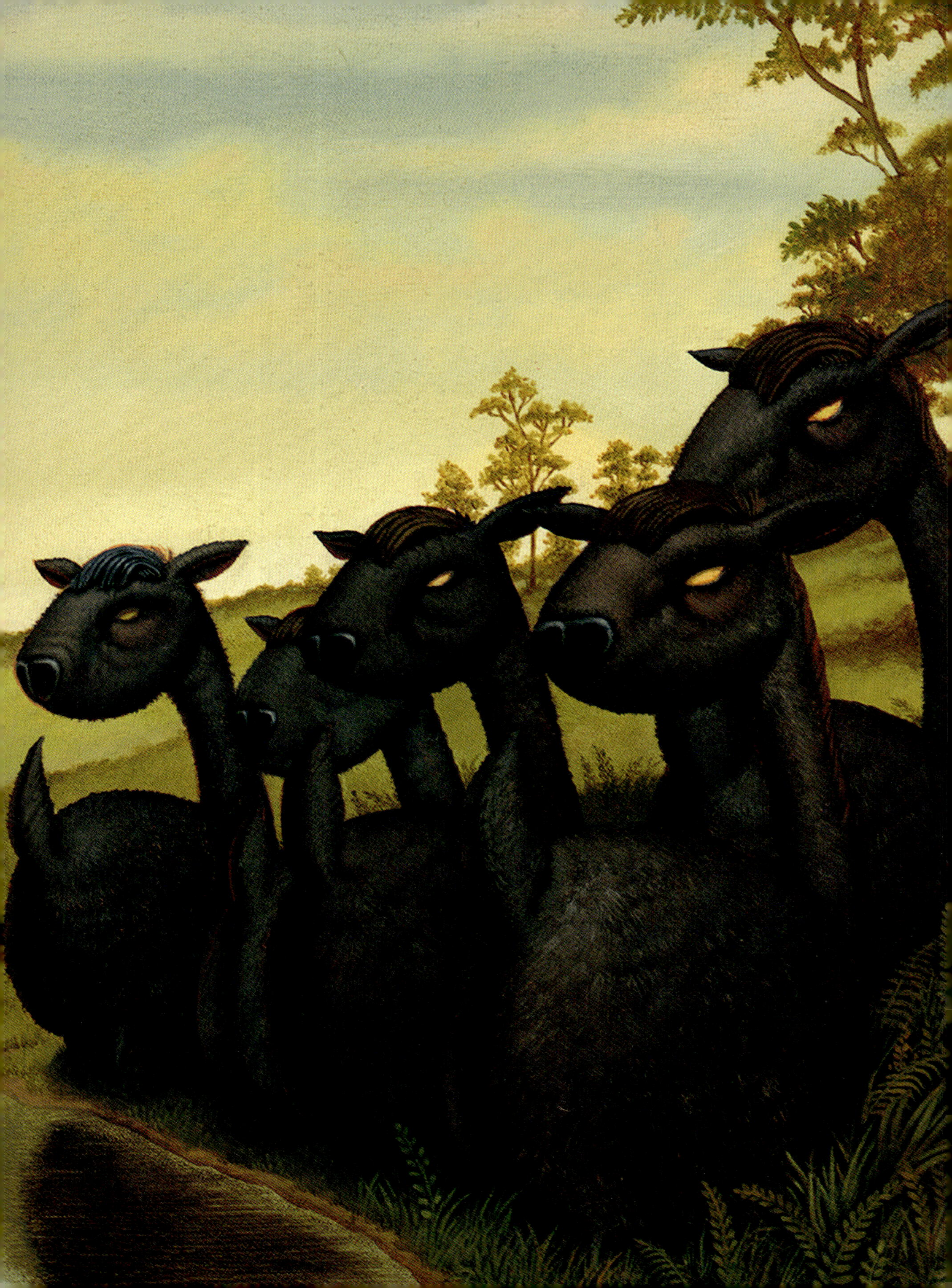

Bête Noire

ca. 1873

DETAIL

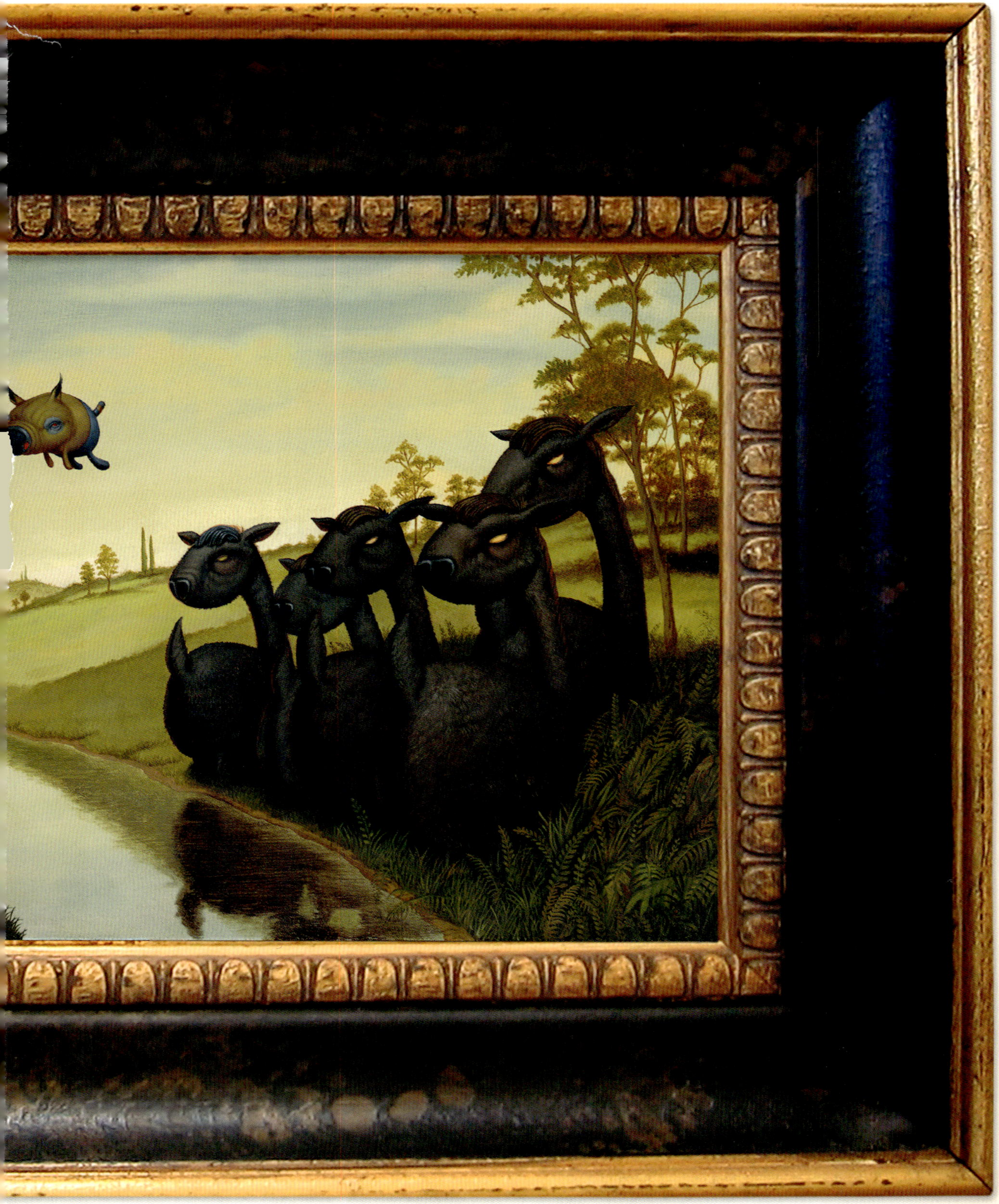

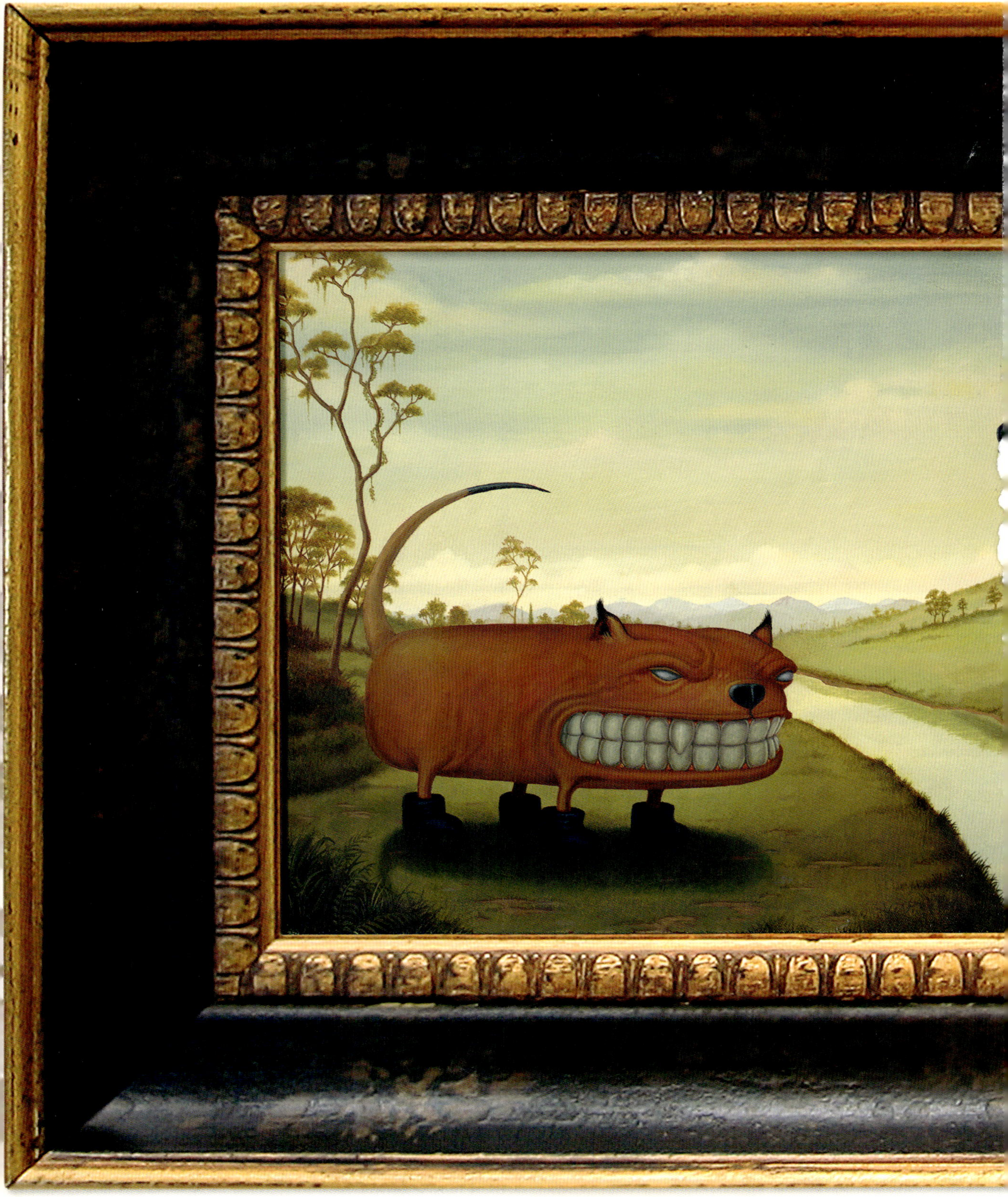

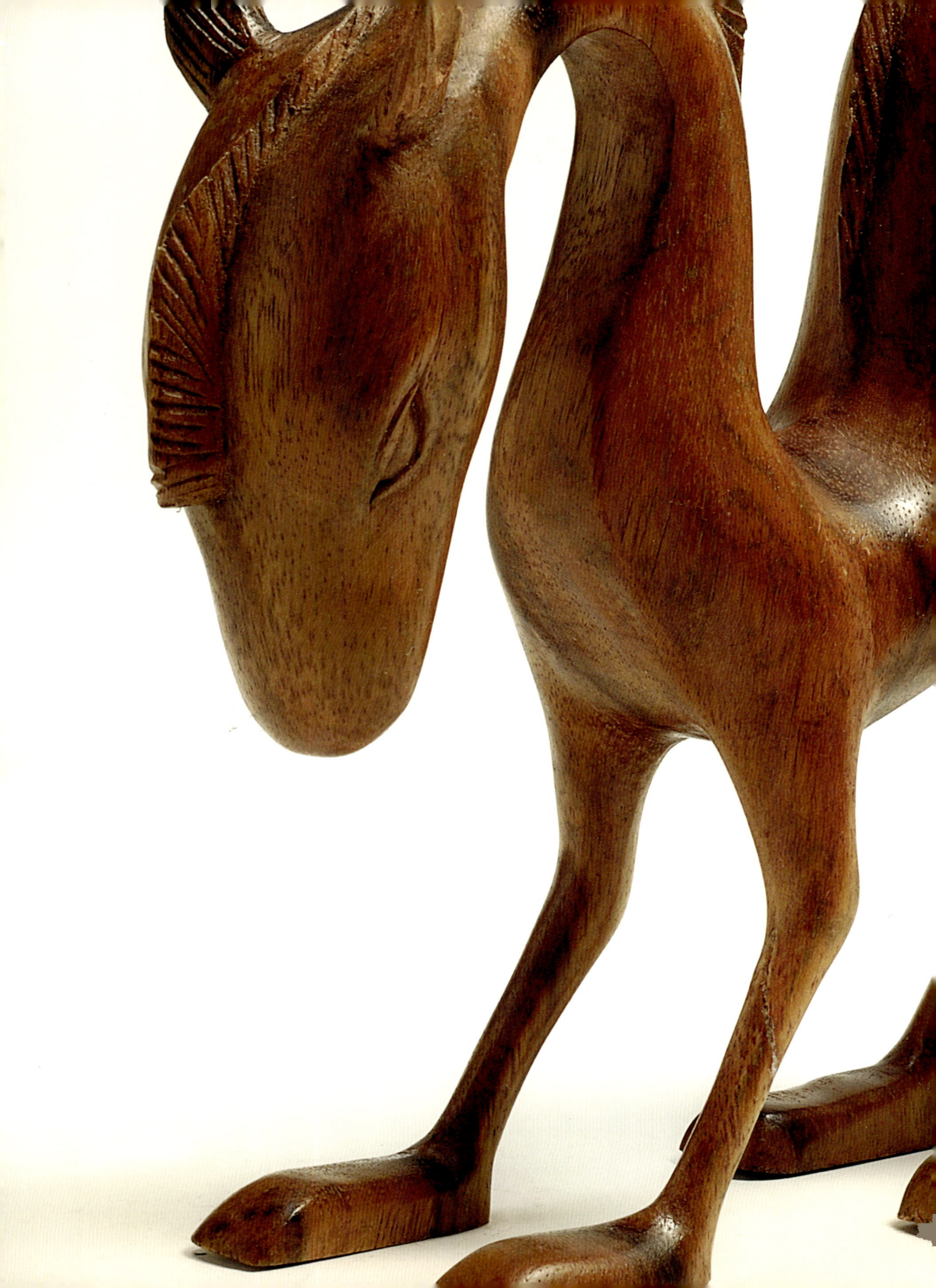

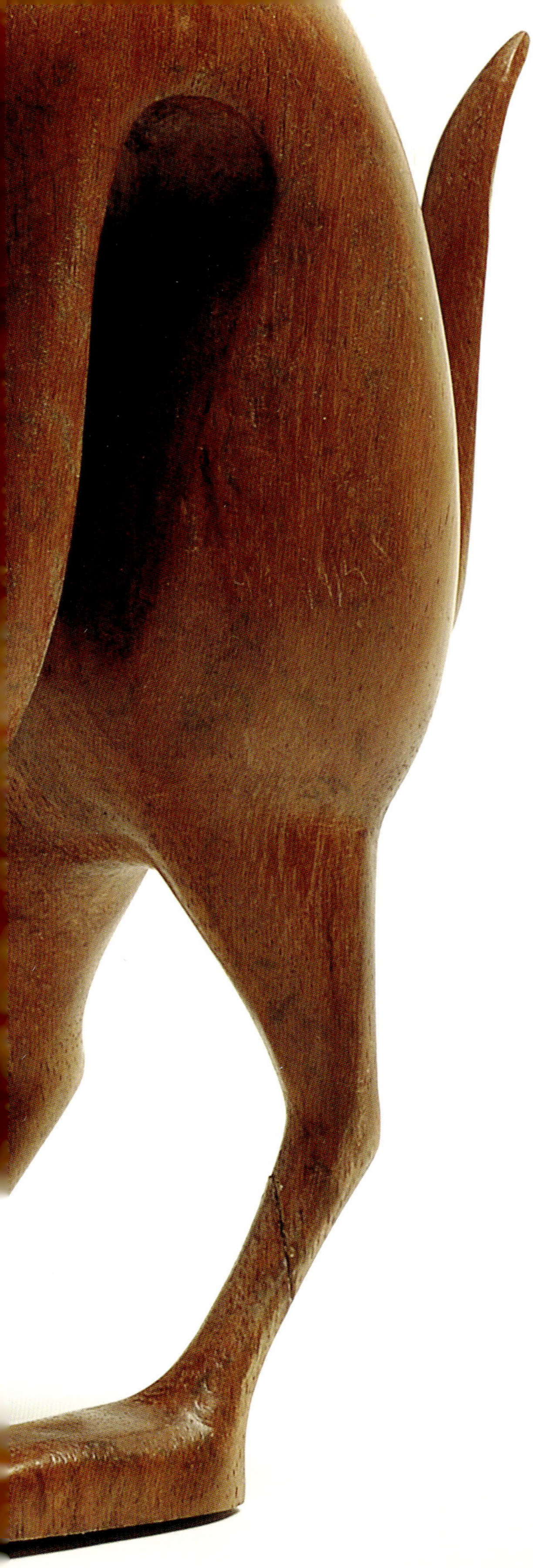

Deluxe Dromedary
Extinct ~ ca. 1852
WOOD CARVING

Maorius Equus

Extinct ~ ca. 1858

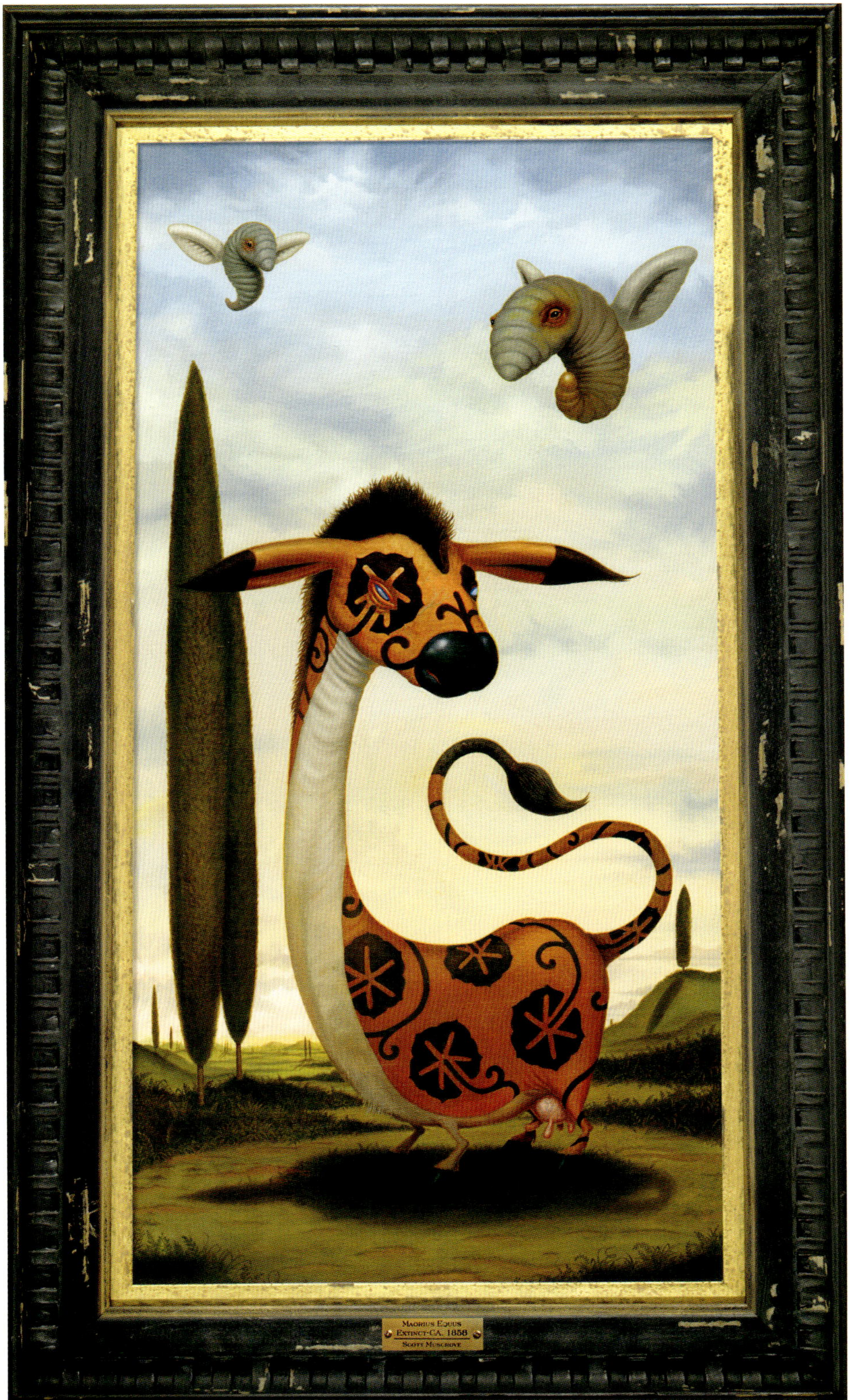
MAORIUS EQUUS
EXTINCT-CA. 1858
SCOTT MUSGROVE

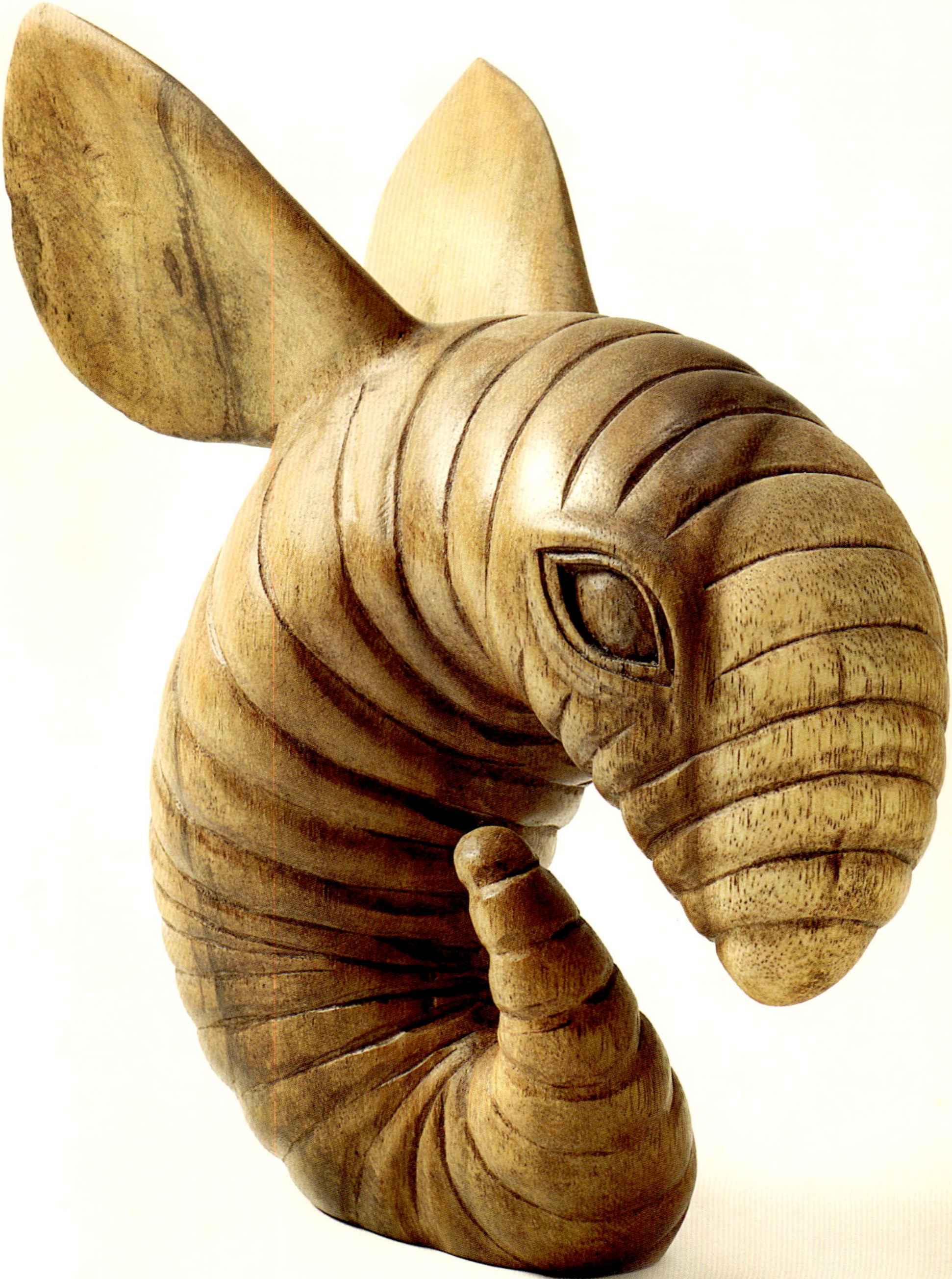

Canis Larvae
Extinct ~ ca. 1855
WOOD CARVING

FACING PAGE
Canis Larvae
Extinct ~ ca. 1855

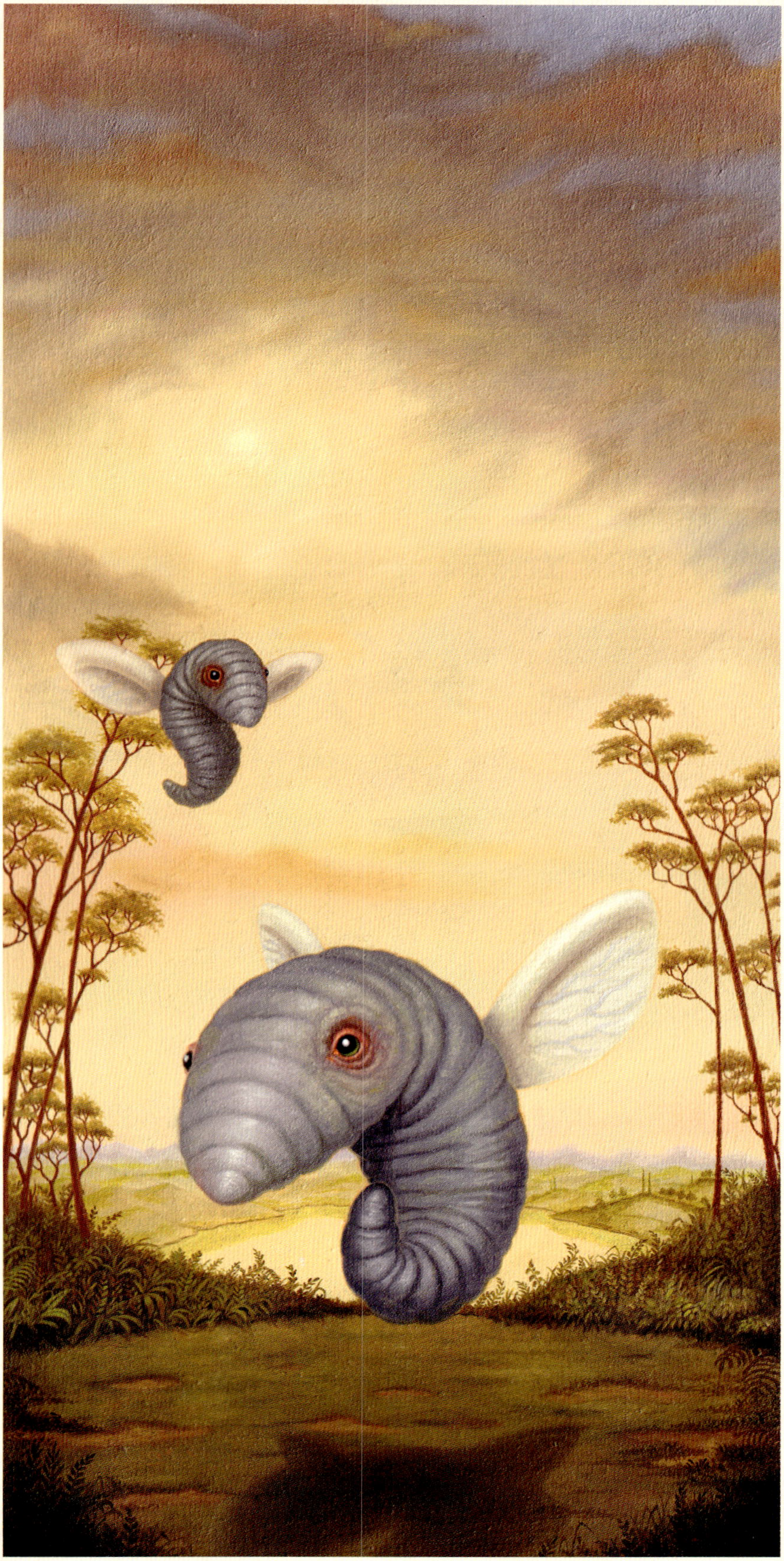

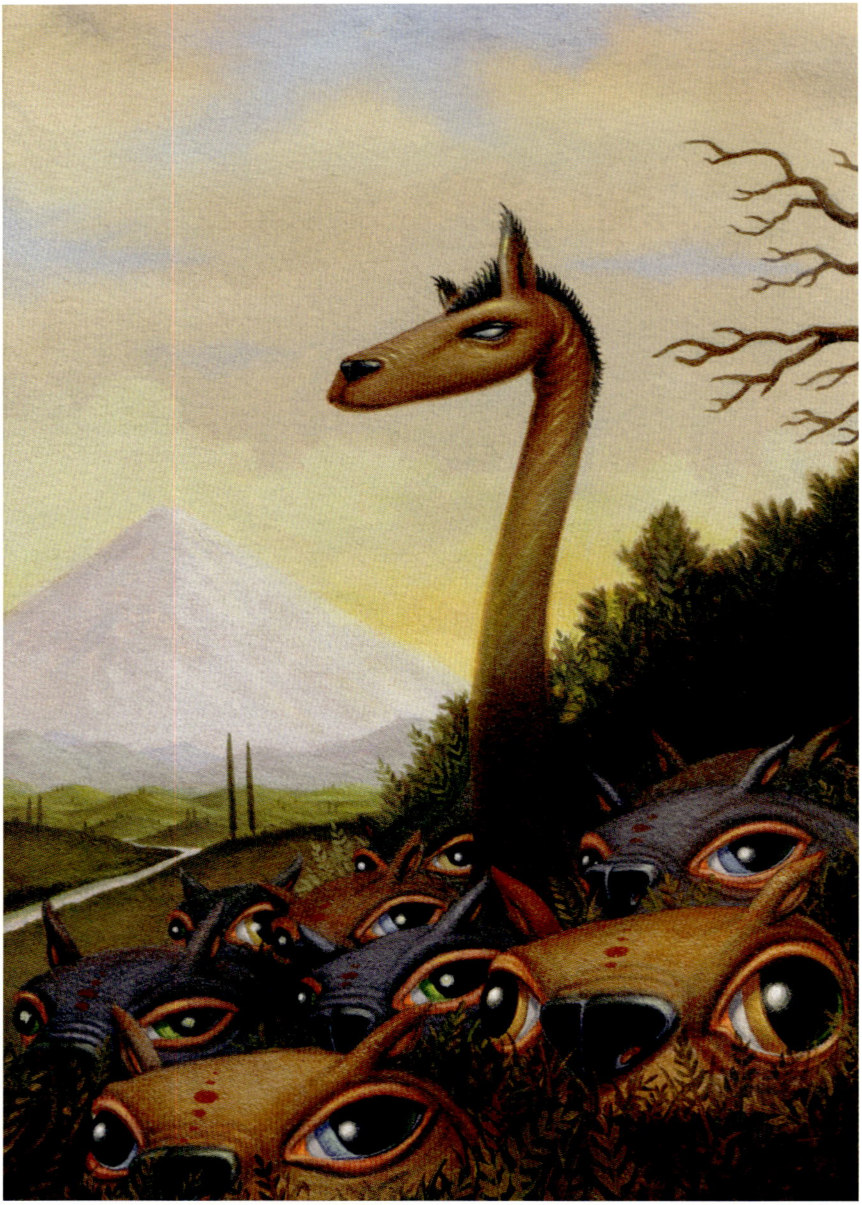

The Sentinel
Extinct ~ ca. 1899

FACING PAGE
Canis Odorus
Extinct ~ ca. 1866

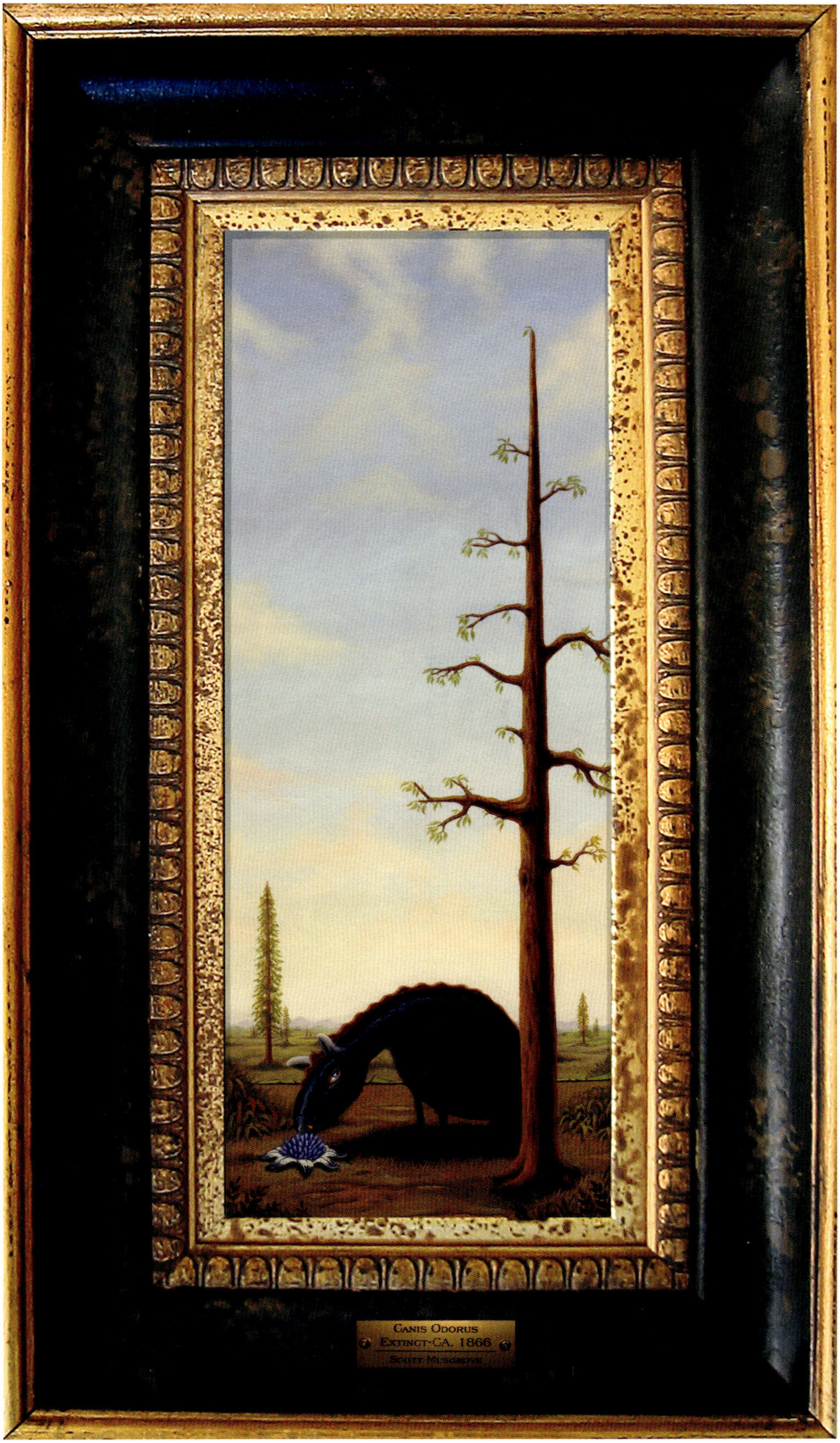
Canis Odorus
Extinct-Ca. 1866

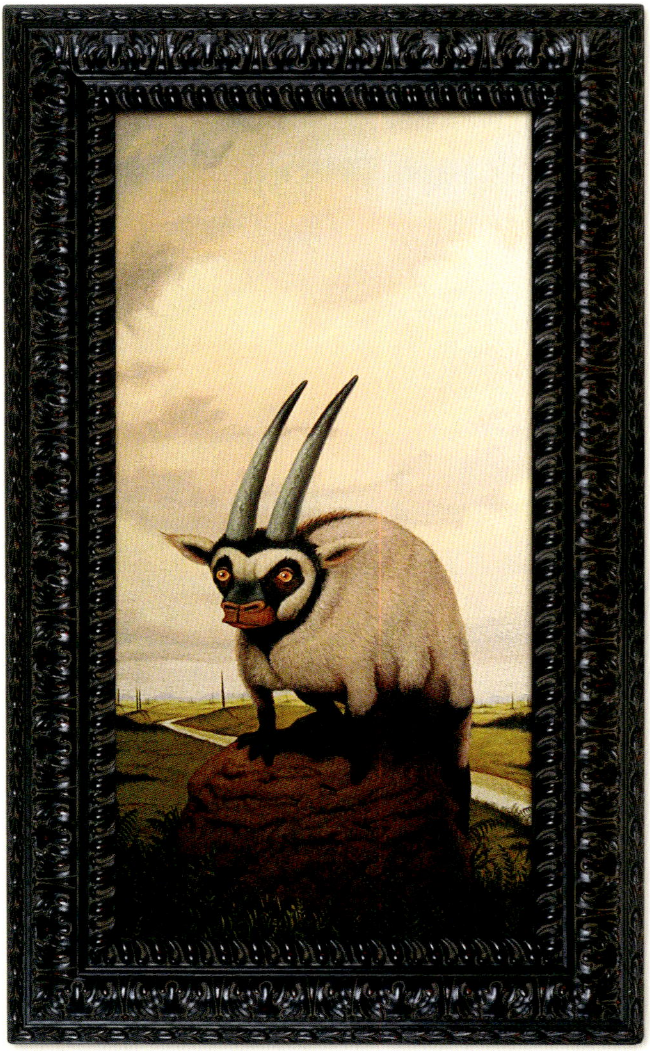

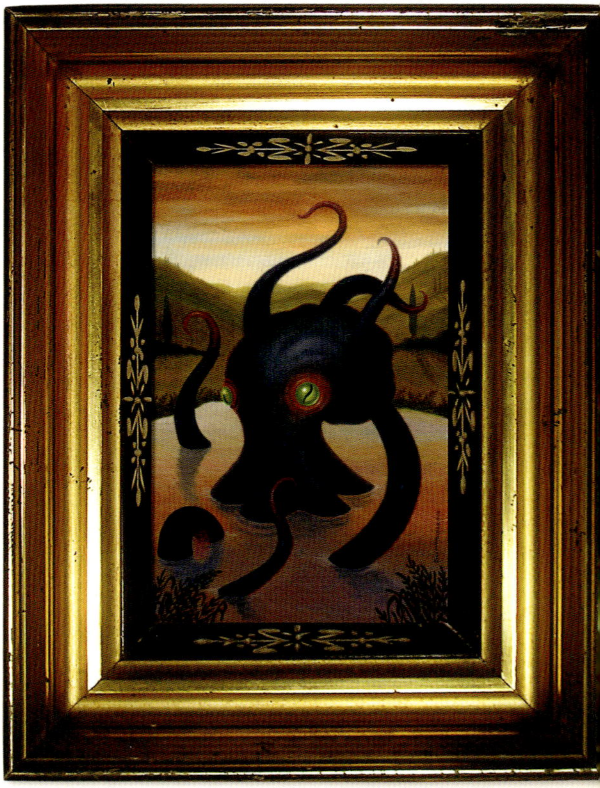

Acanthus Octossis
Extinct ~ ca. 1890

Great Prairie Squid
Extinct ~ ca. 1825

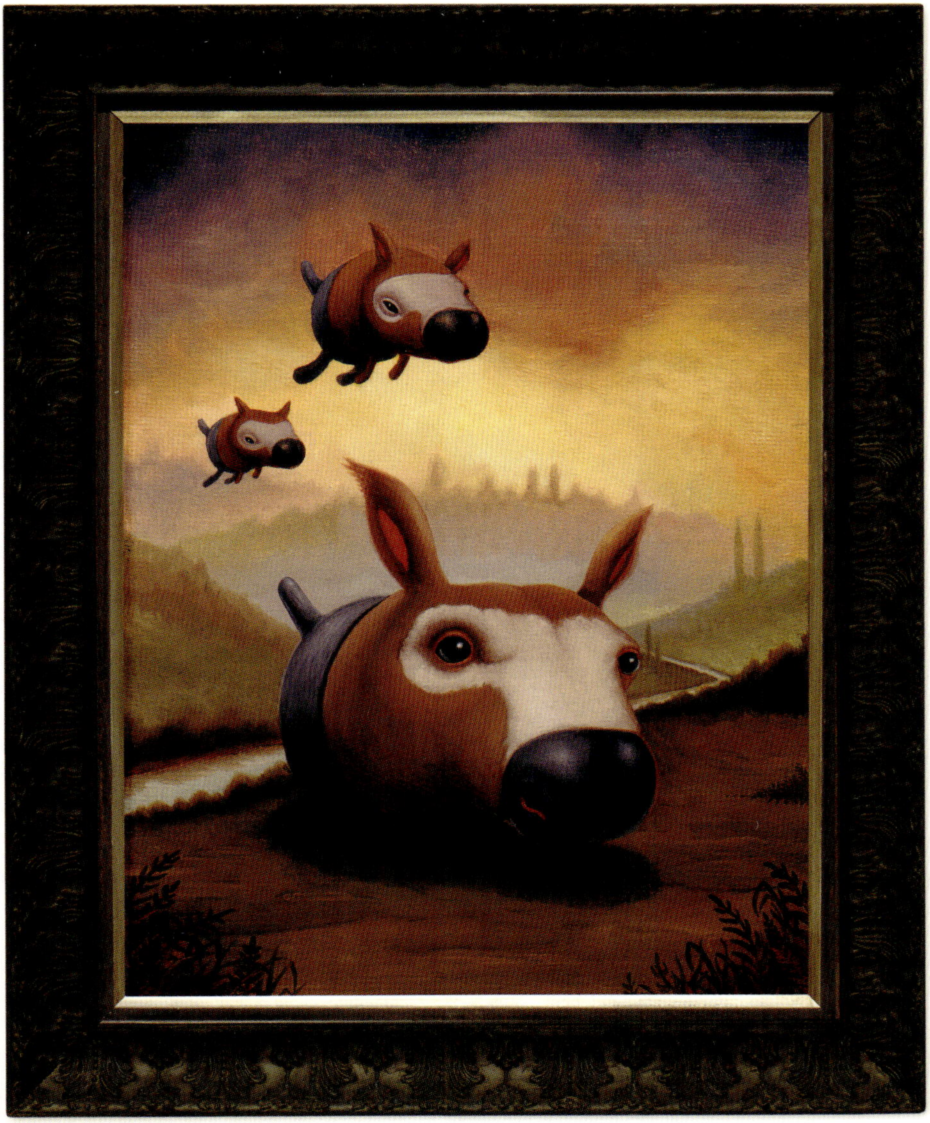

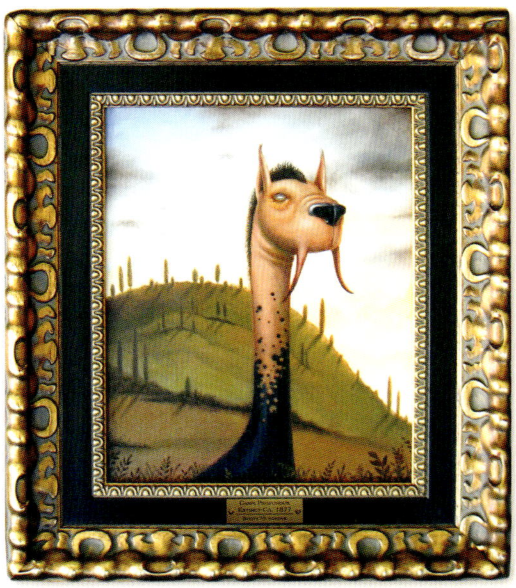

Fidgets
Extinct ~ ca. 1860

Canis Profundus
Extinct ~ ca. 1877

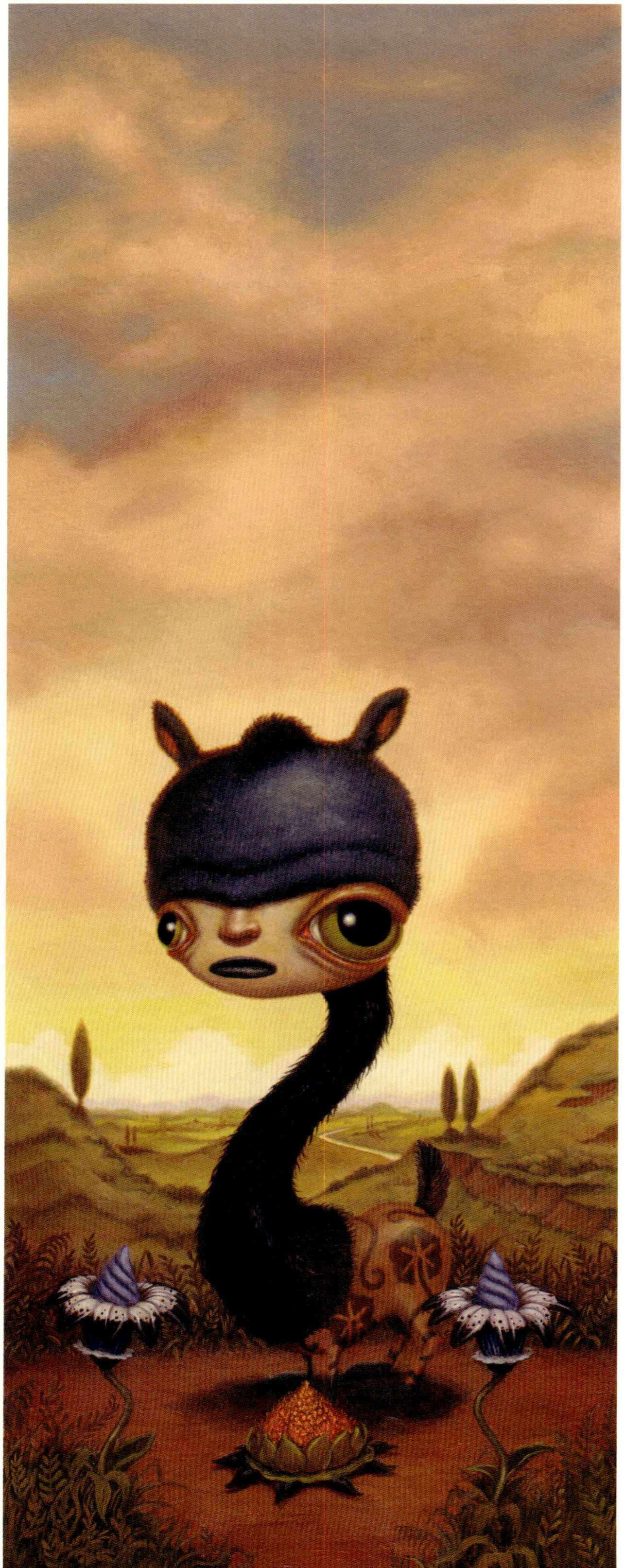

Shaggy Desert Llama
Extinct ~ ca. 1850

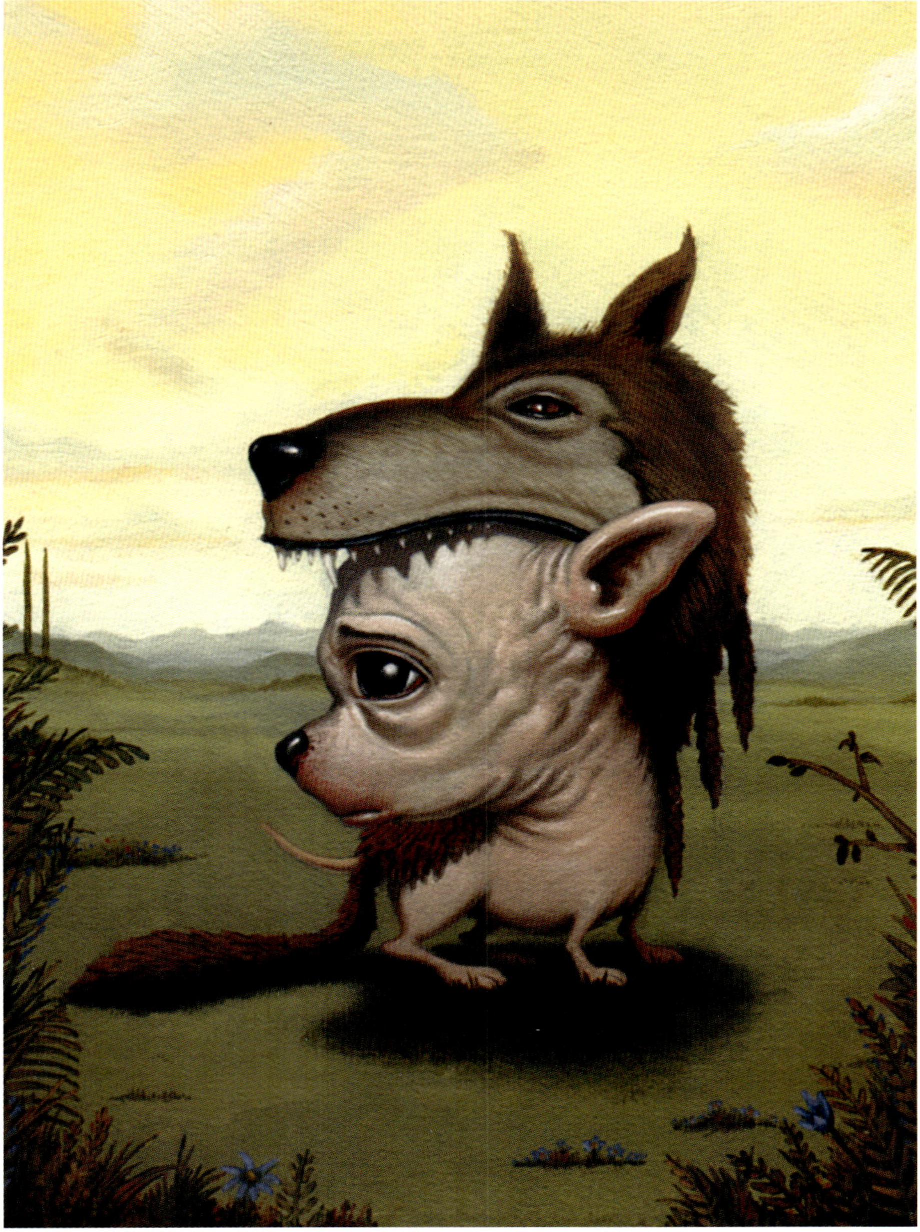

Canis Strategema

Extinct ~ ca. 1844

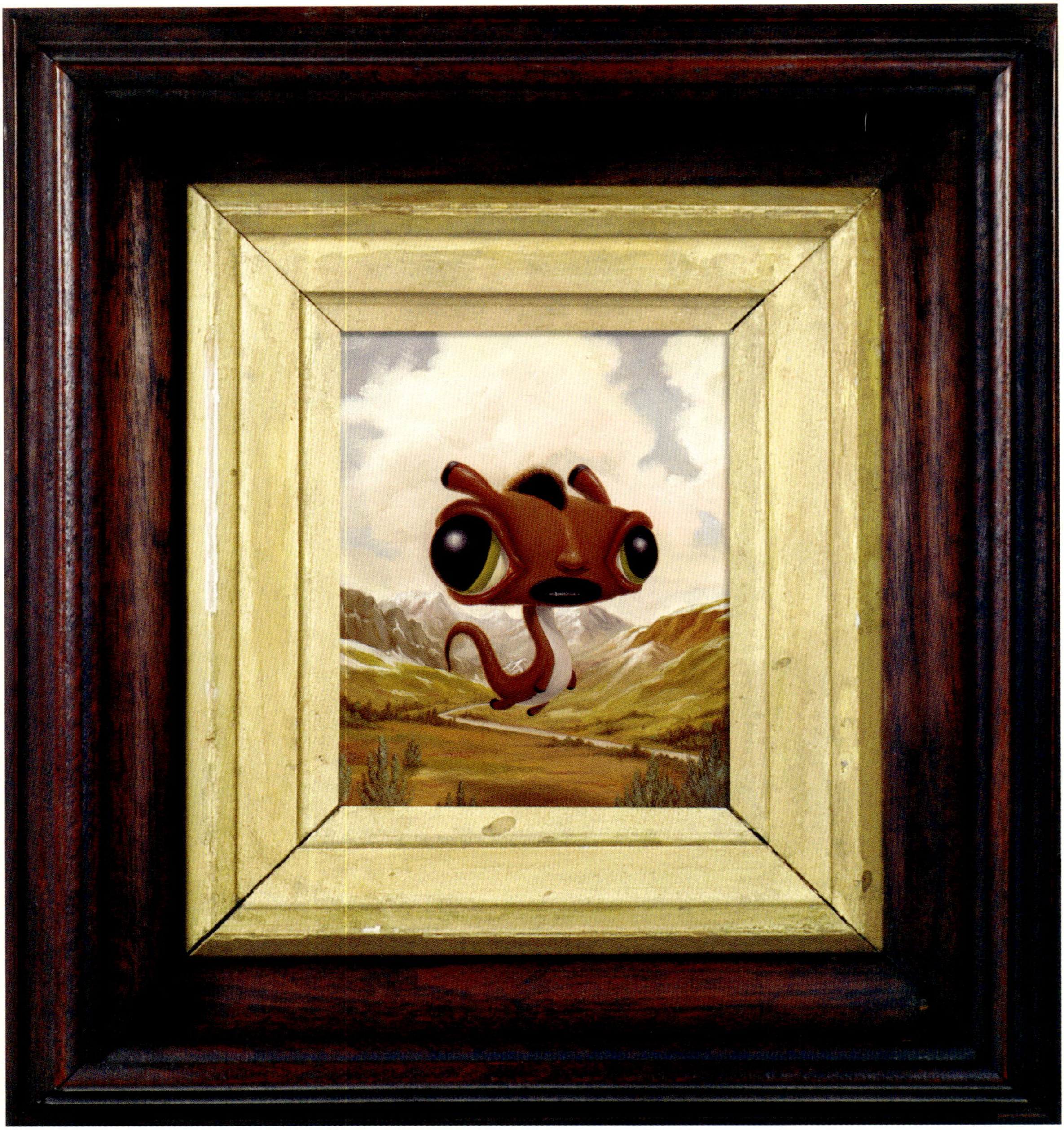

Junior Swamp Horse
Extinct ~ ca. 1805

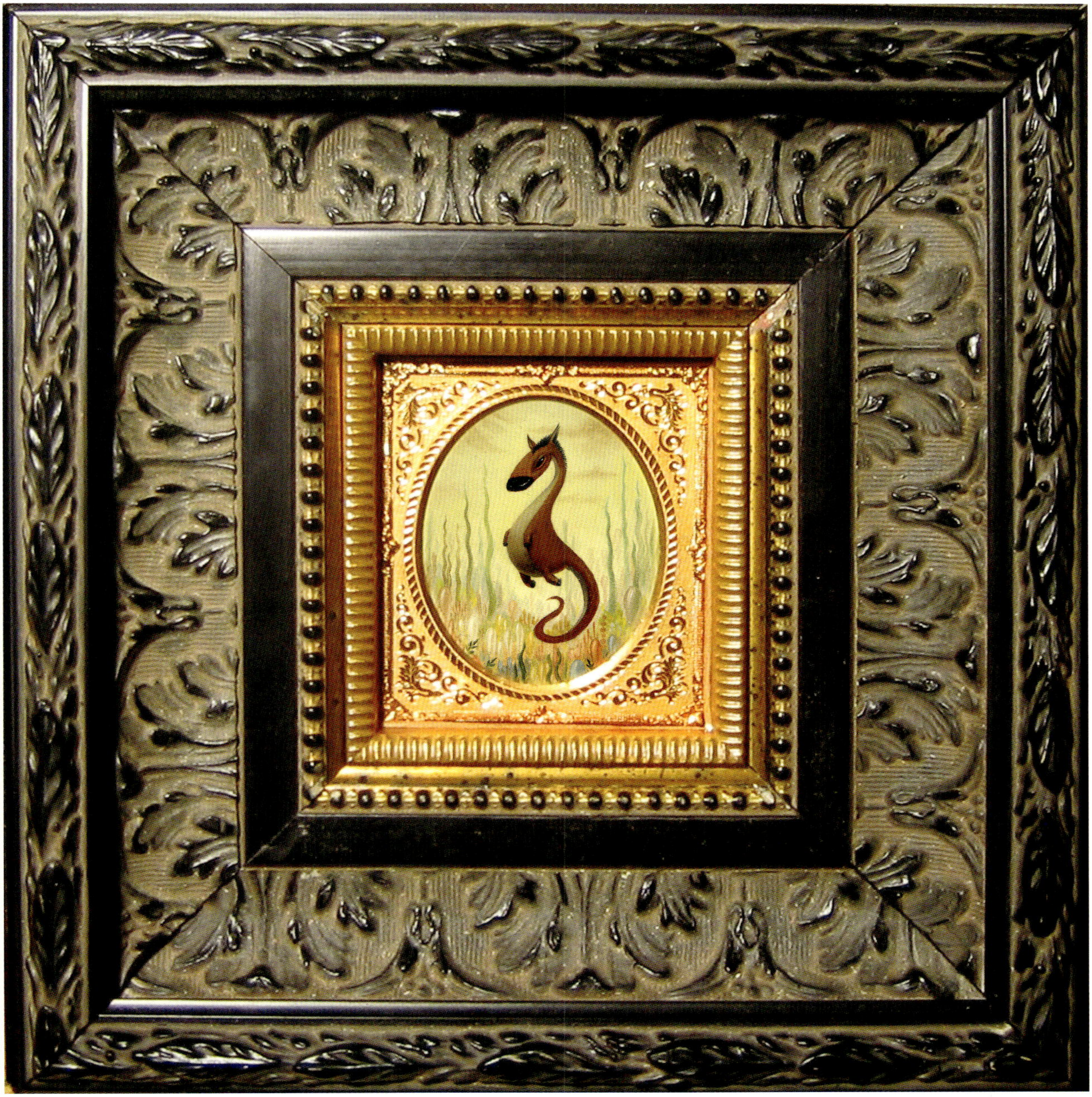

Dwarf Swamp Horse
Extinct ~ ca. 1805

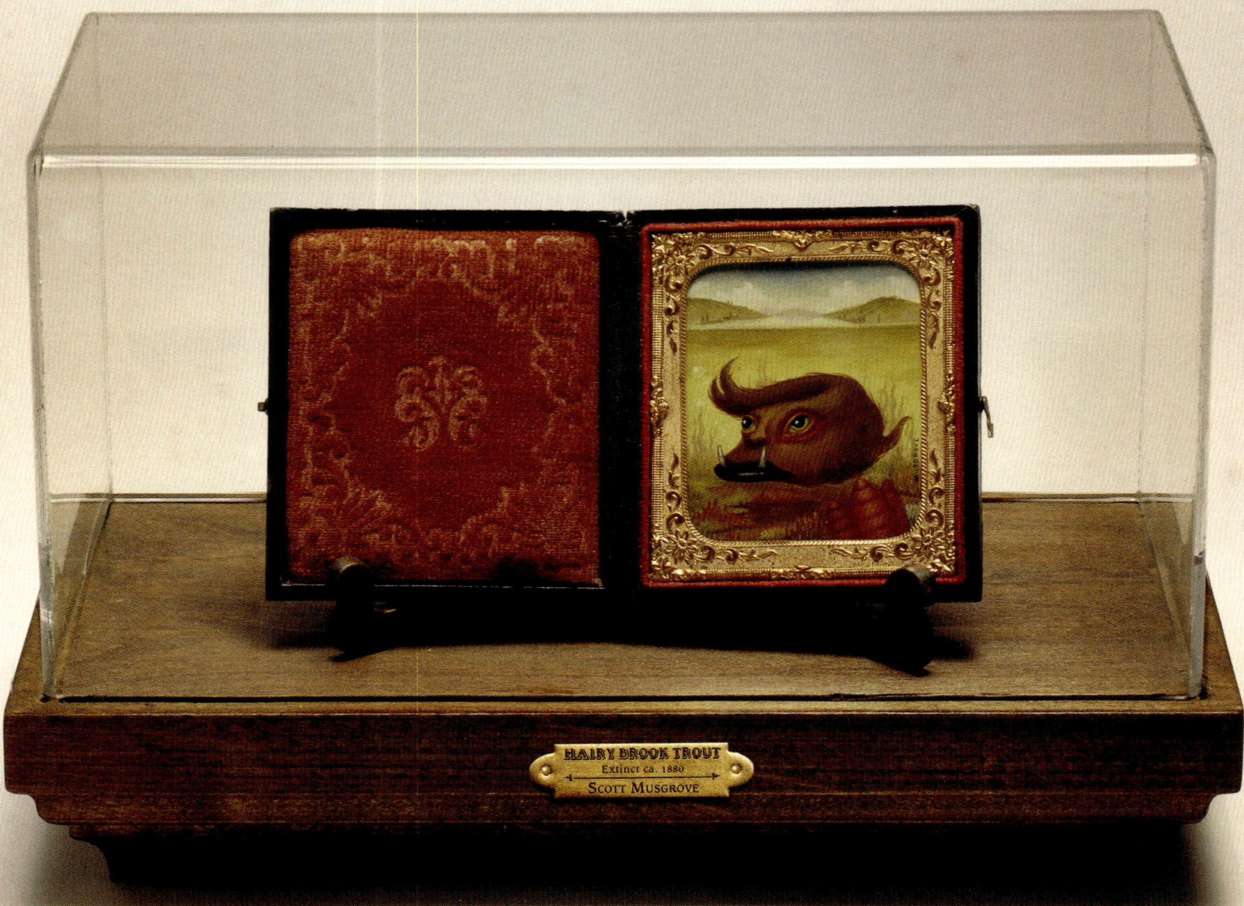

Hairy Brook Trout
Extinct ~ ca. 1880
IN UNION CASE ON CUSTOM SHELF

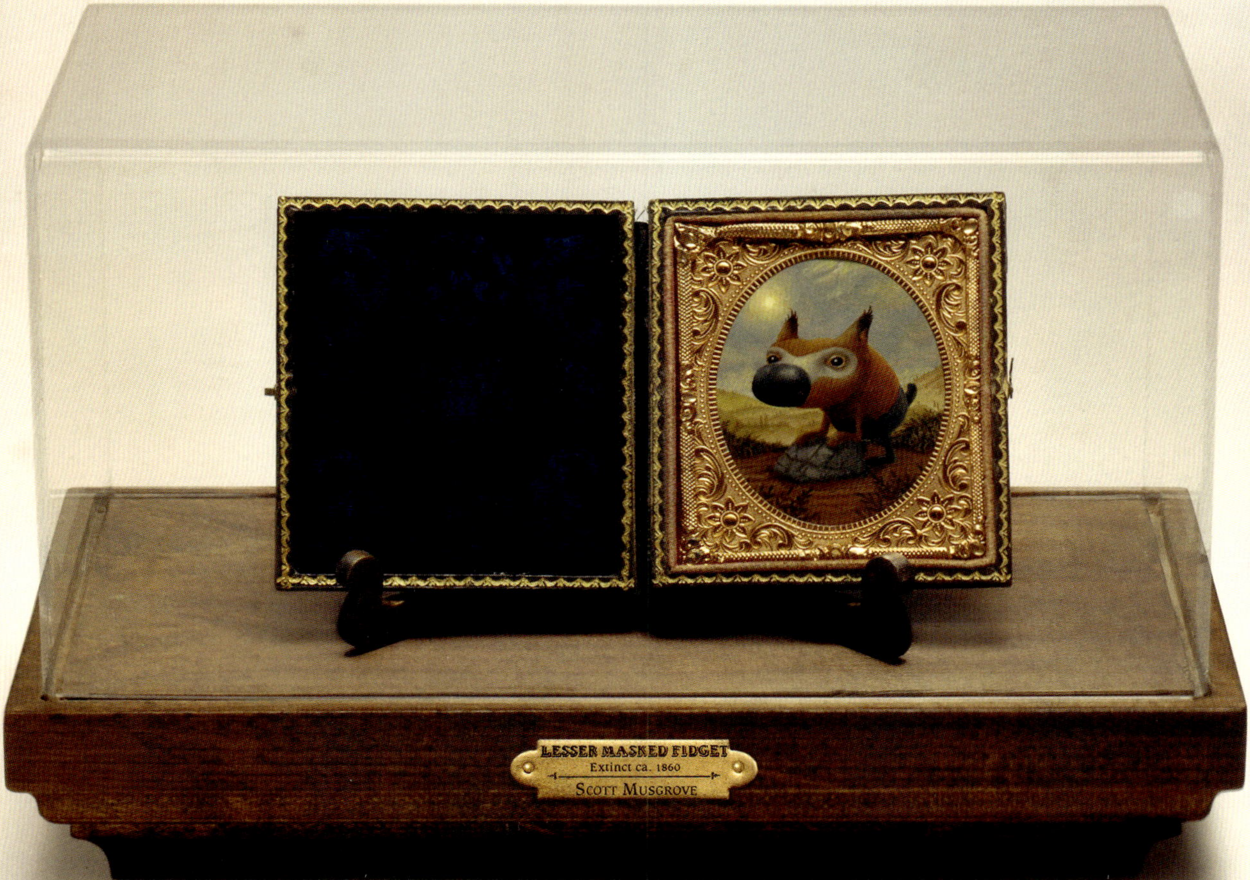

Lesser Masked Fidget

Extinct ~ ca. 1860

IN UNION CASE ON CUSTOM SHELF

Canis Calvus Demens

Extinct ~ ca. 1830

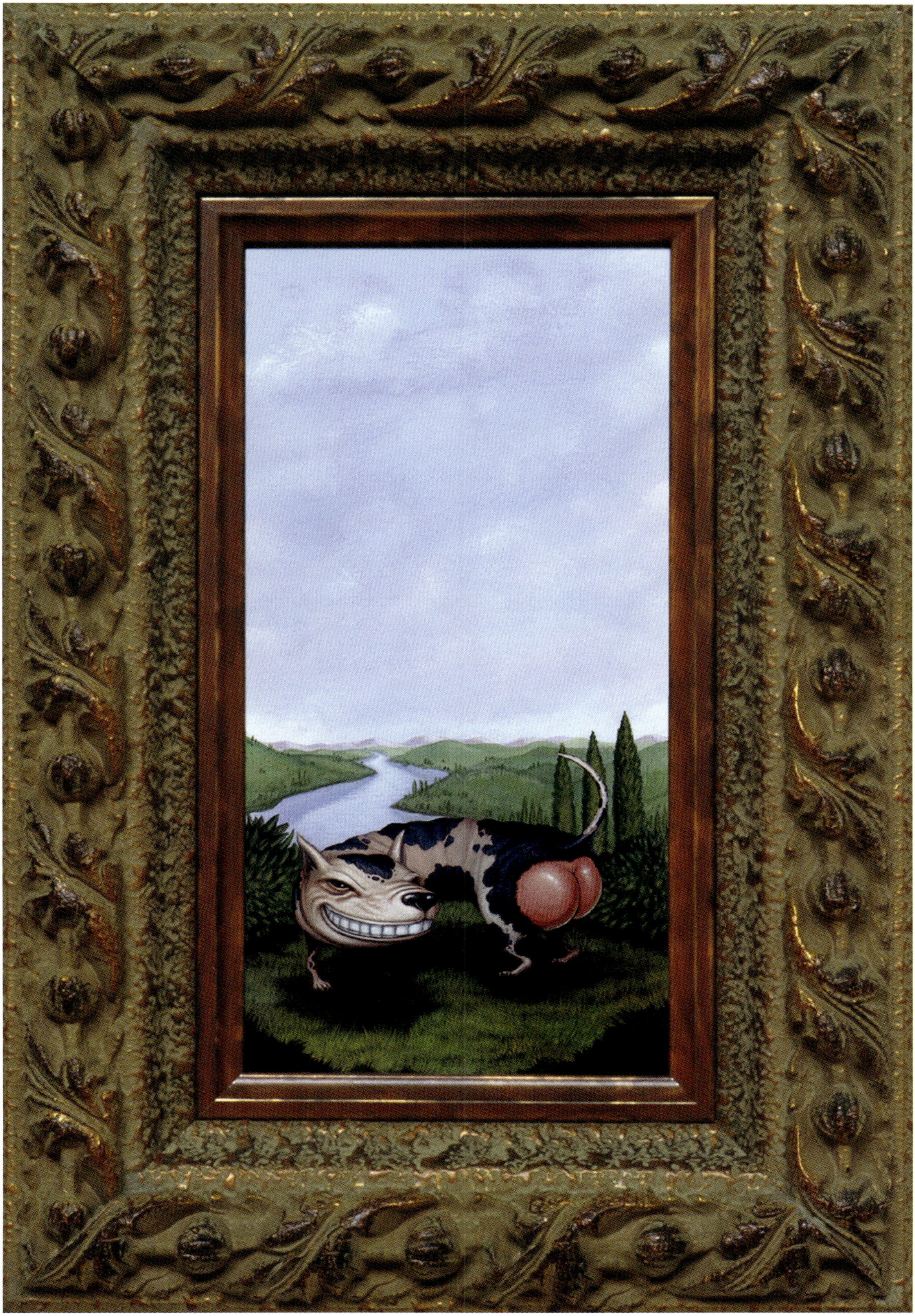

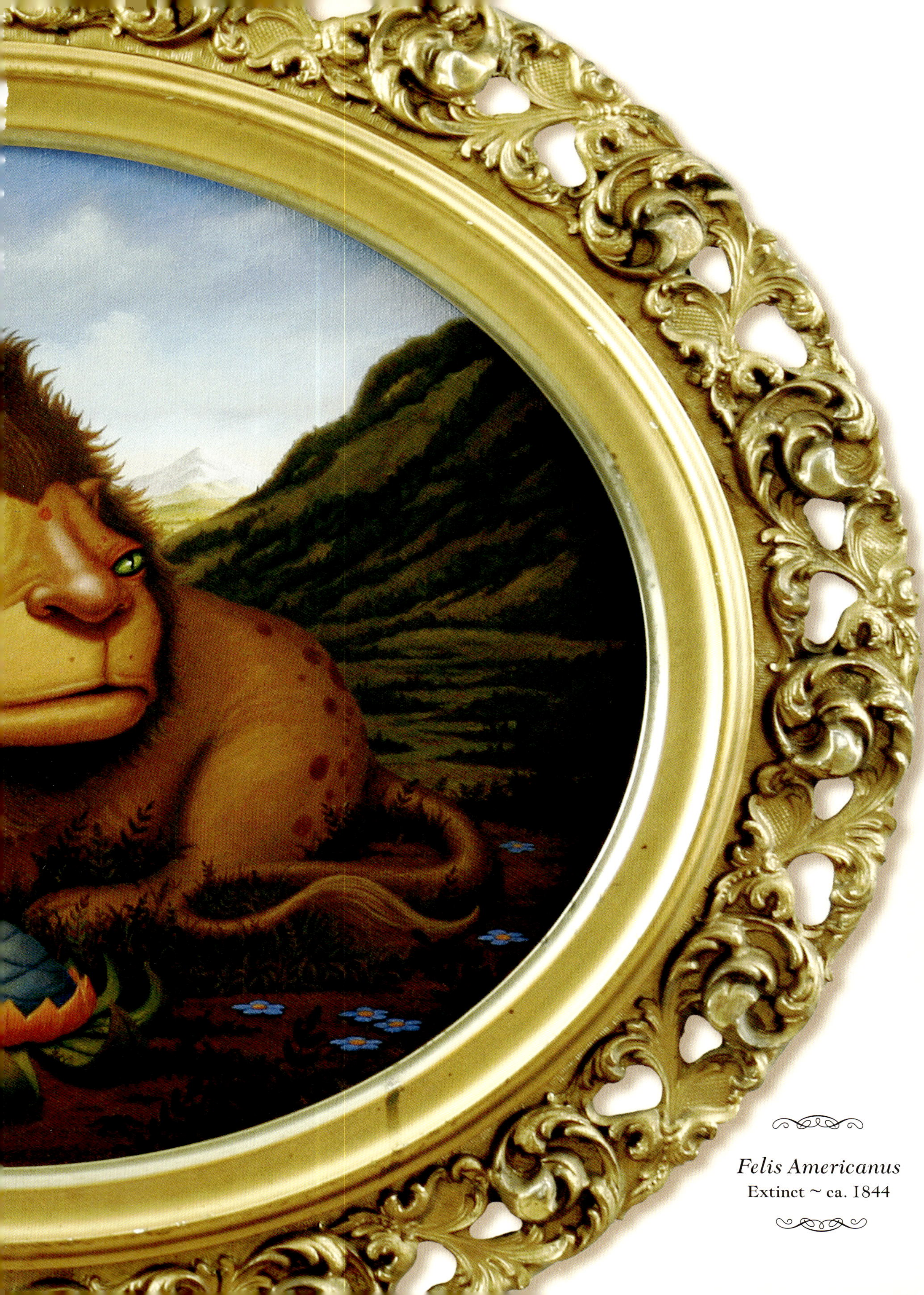

Felis Americanus
Extinct ~ ca. 1844

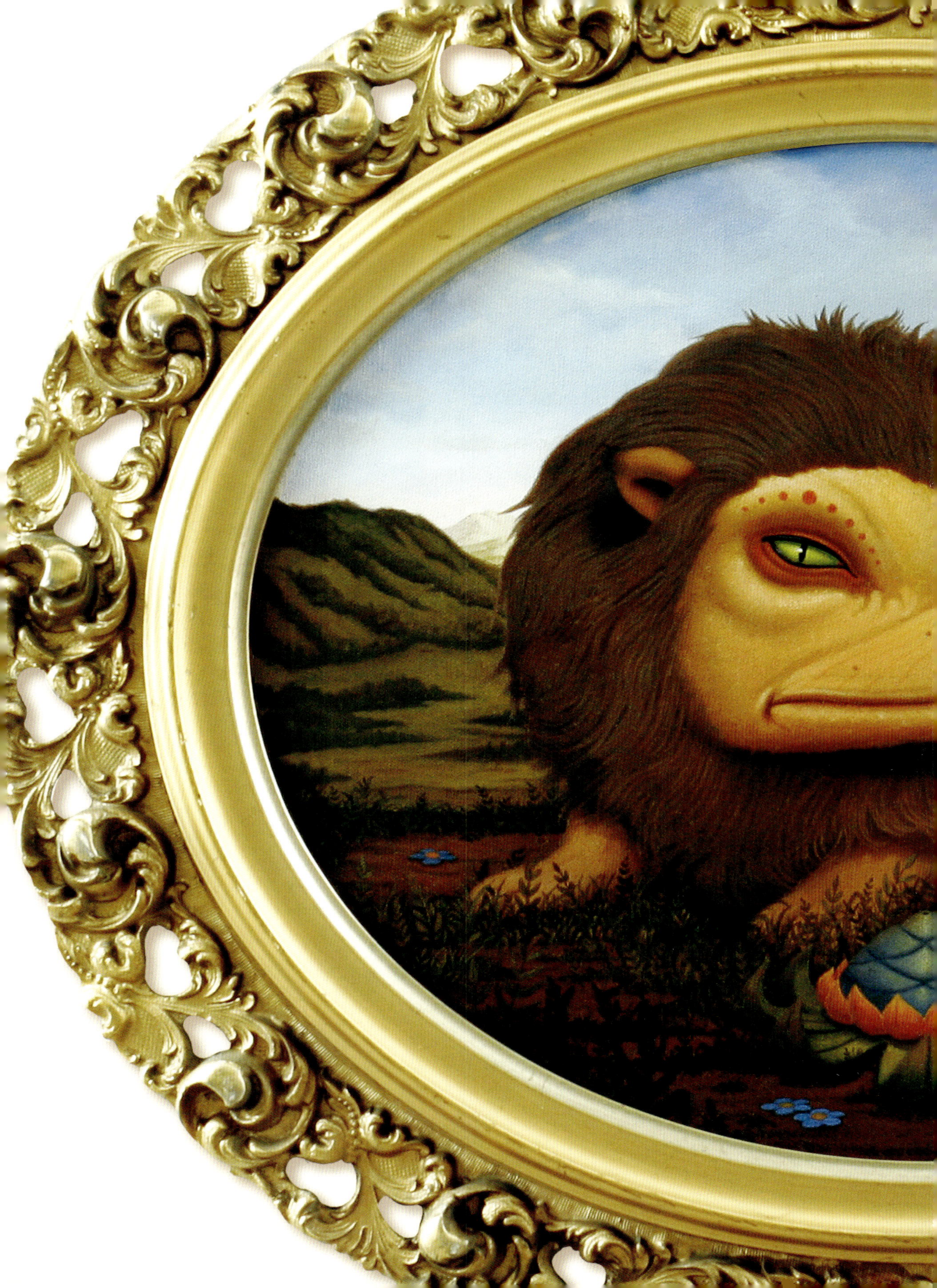

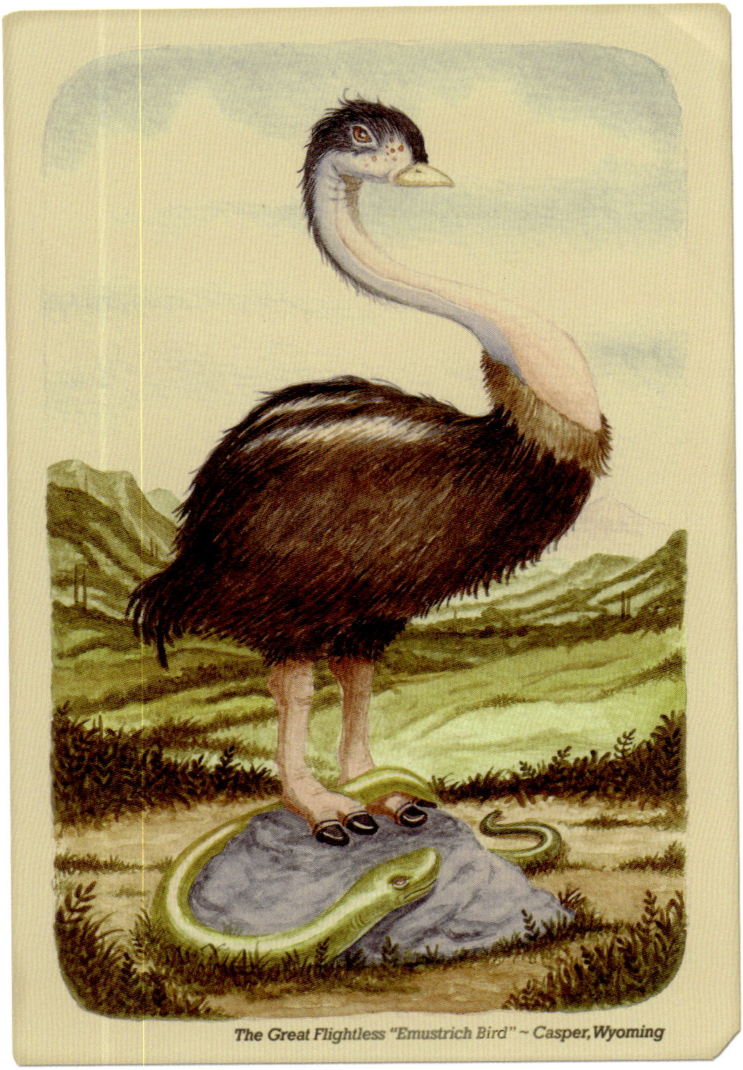

FACING PAGE

Great Emustrich

Extinct ~ ca. 1849

THIS PAGE: WATERCOLOR

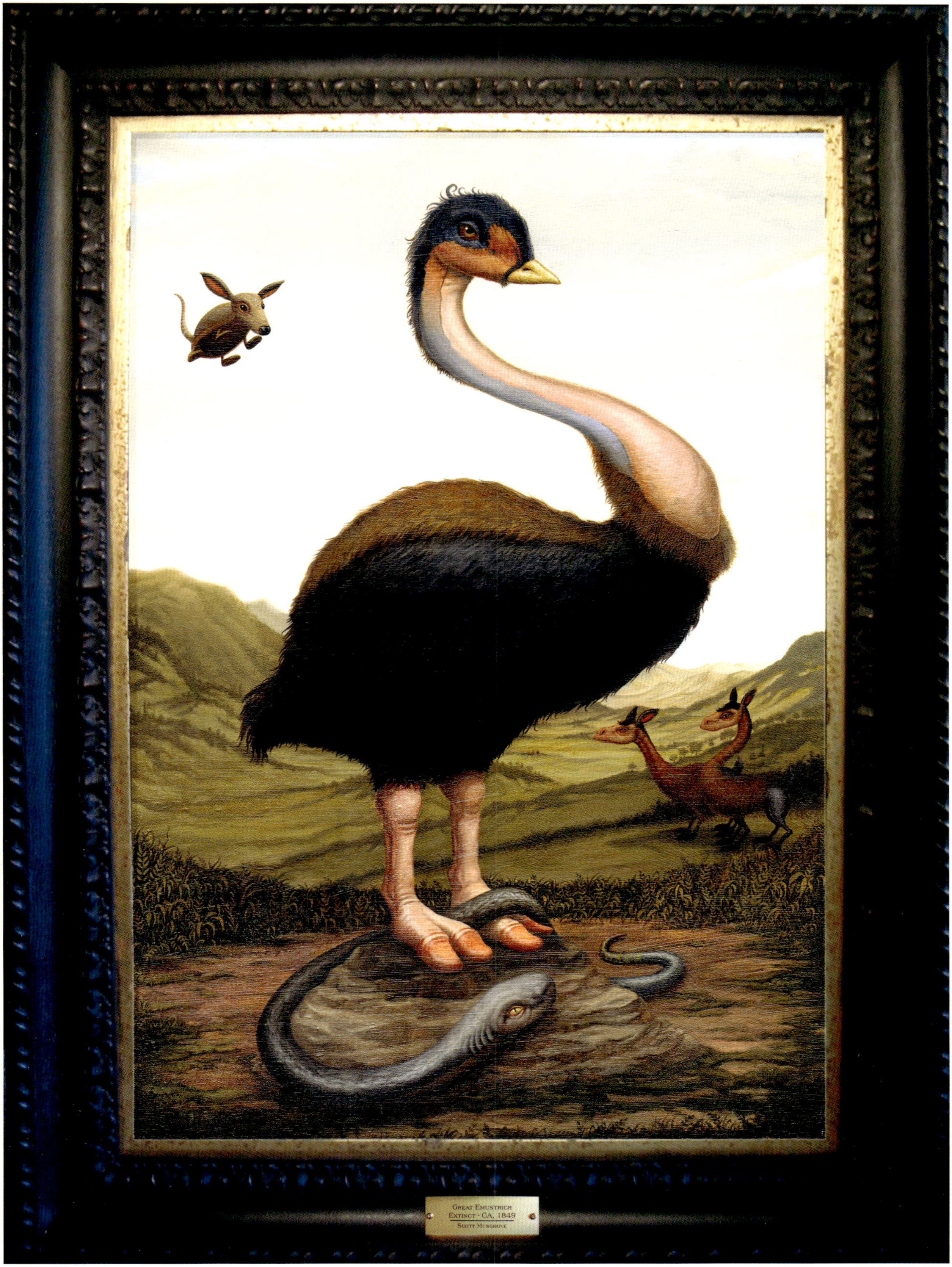
GREAT EMUSTRICH
EXTINCT - CA. 1849
SCOTT MUSGROVE

Venus Flower Lizard
Extinct ~ ca. 1845

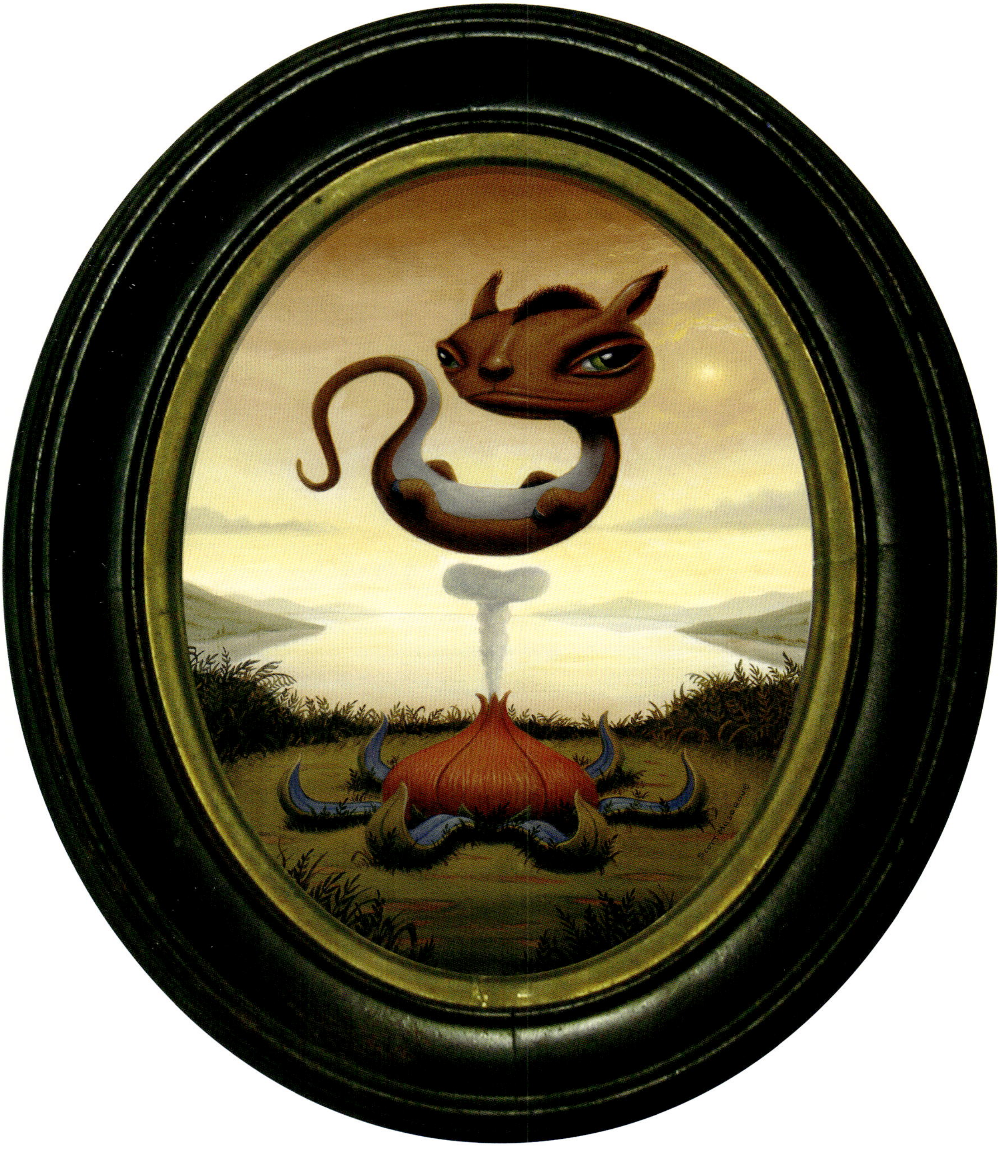

Great Lesser Plant Sampler

Extinct ~ ca. 1895

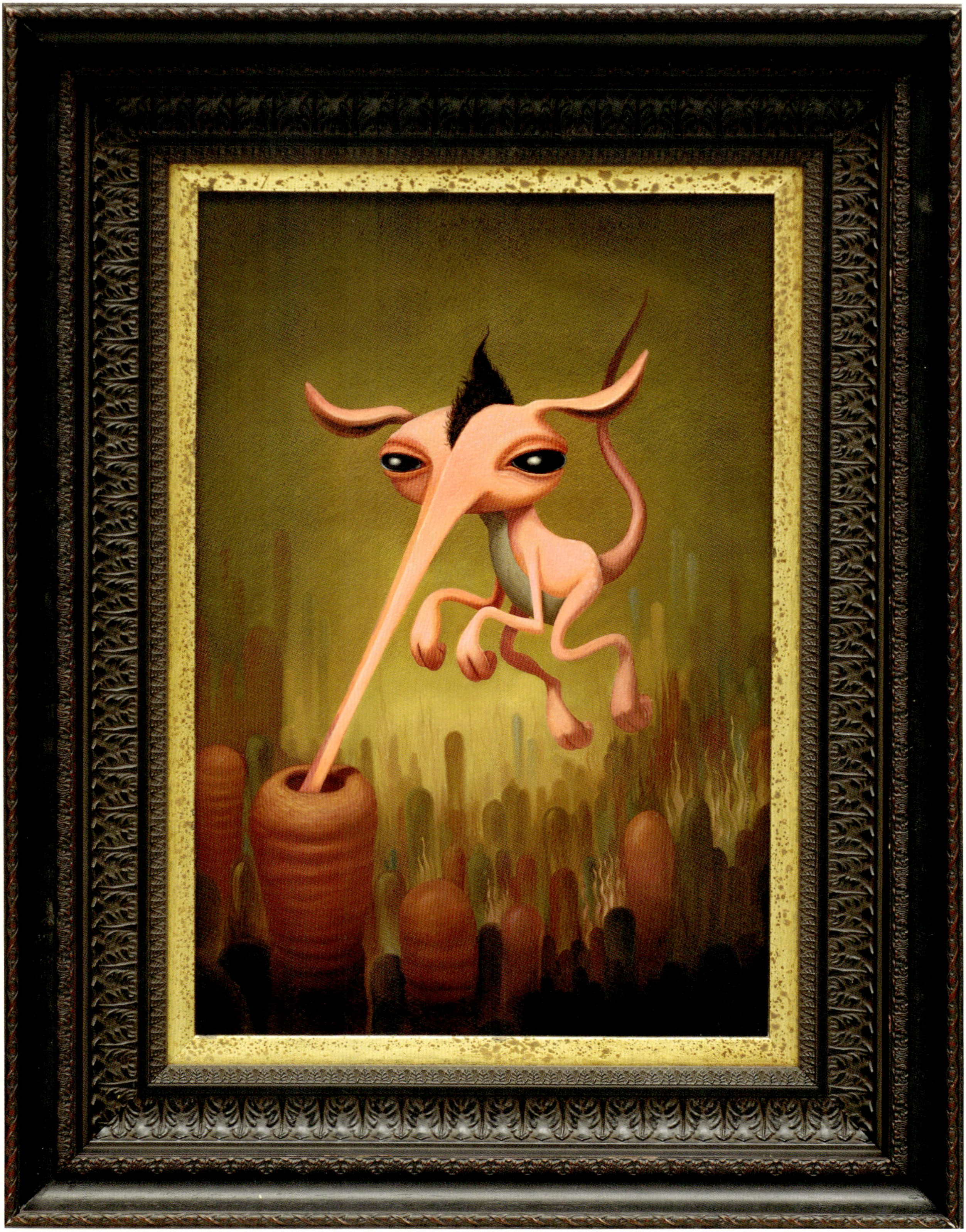

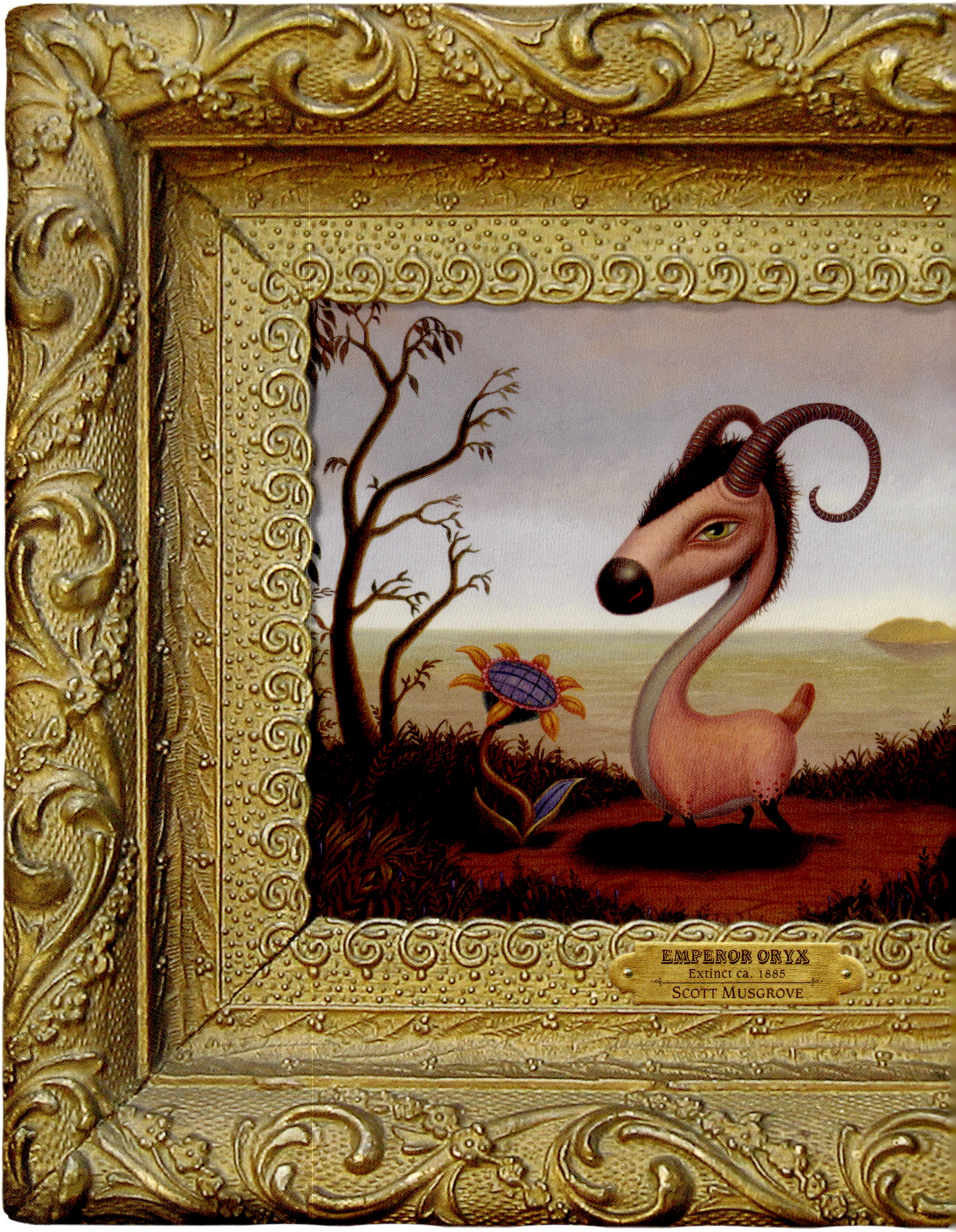
EMPEROR ORYX
Extinct ca. 1885
SCOTT MUSGROVE

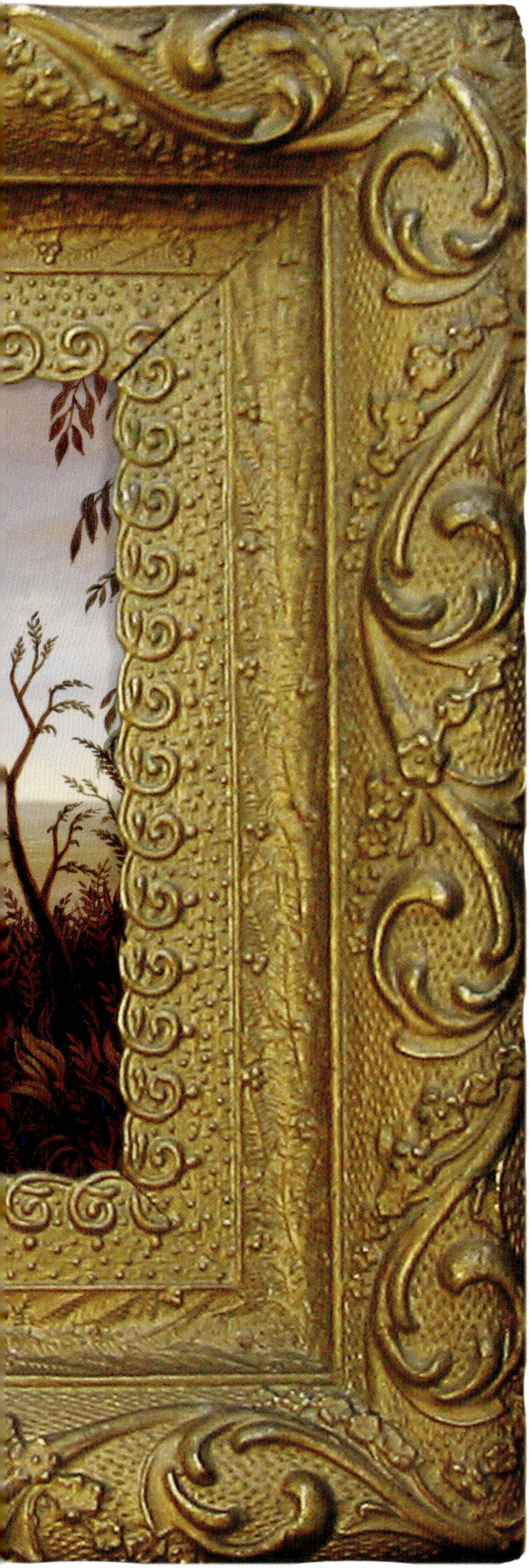

Emperor Oryx
Extinct ~ ca. 1885

Lesser Baffled Jackal

Extinct ~ ca. 1867

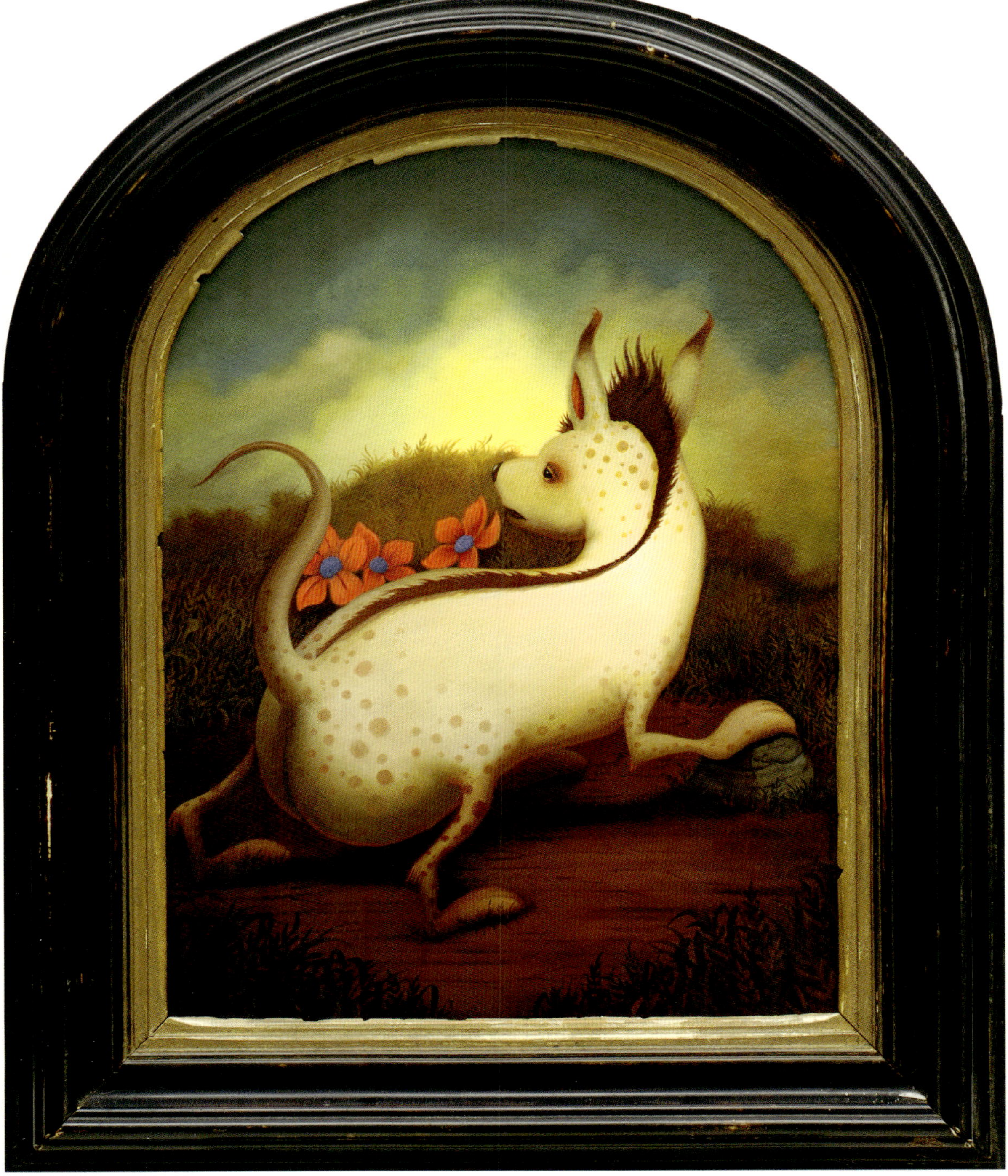

Guanicus Mater Matris
Extinct ~ ca. 1895

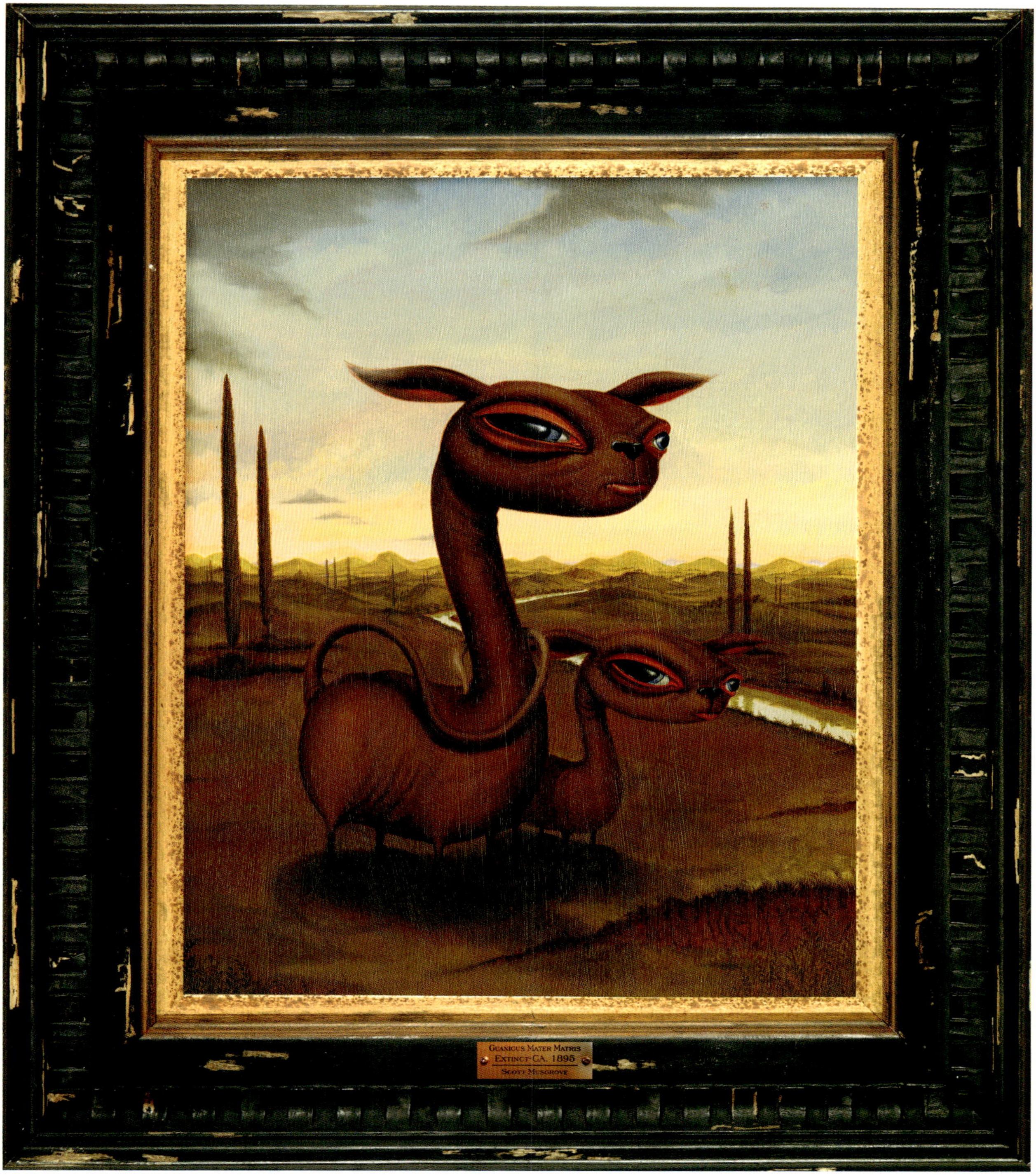
Guanicus Mater Matris
Extinct-CA. 1895
Scott Musgrove

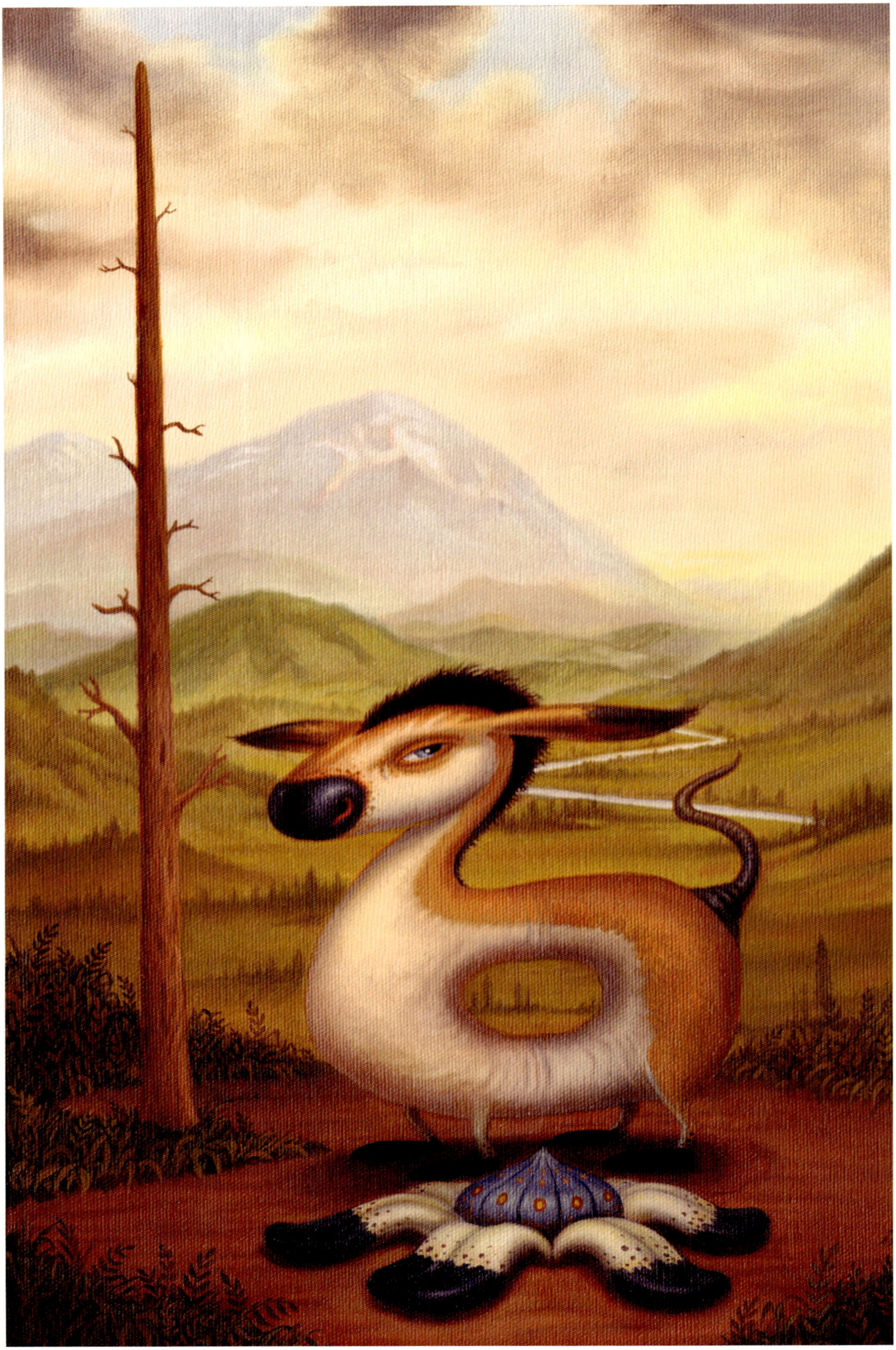

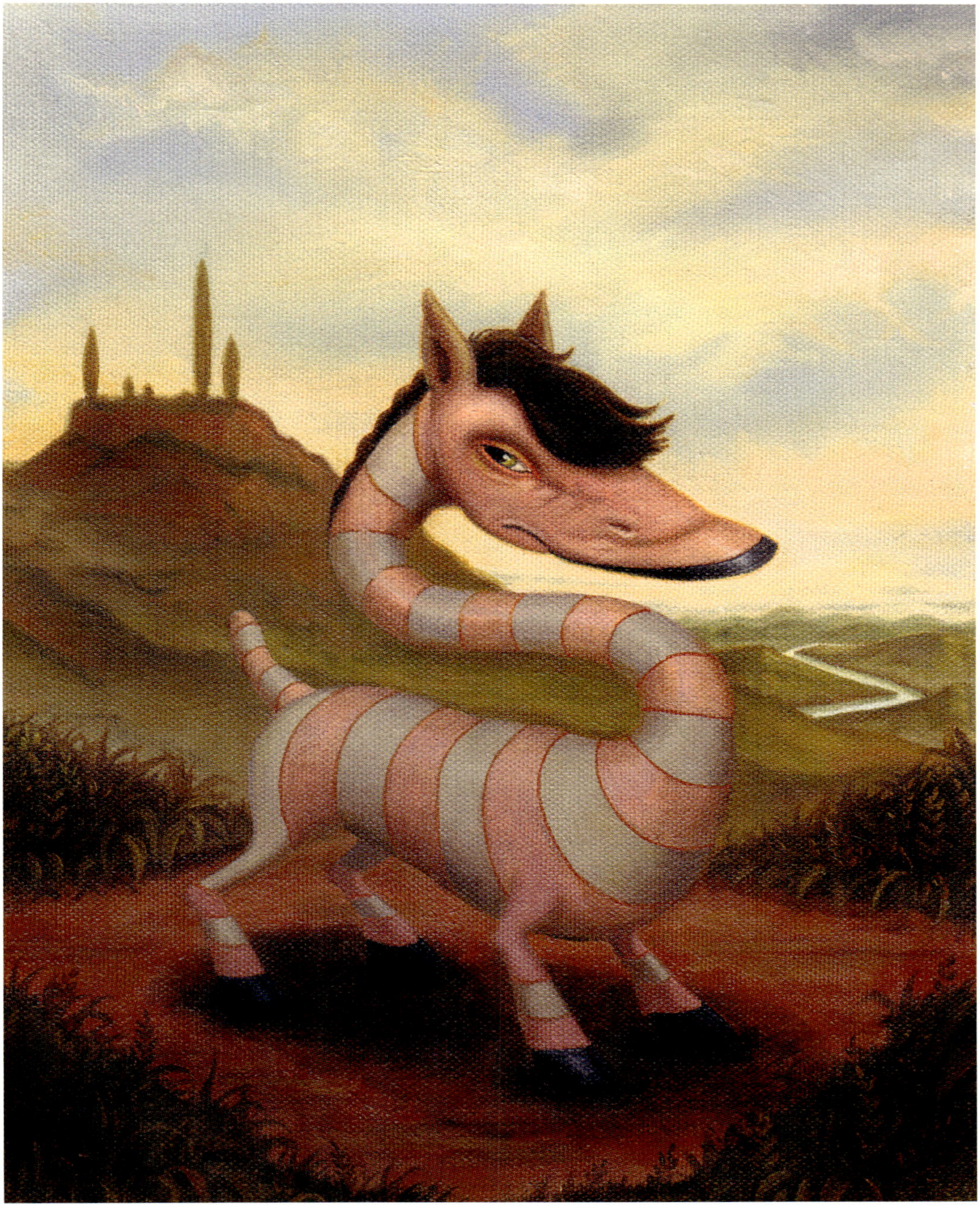

Crooked Pony
Extinct ~ ca. 1901

FACING PAGE
Elliptical Equine
Extinct ~ ca. 1864

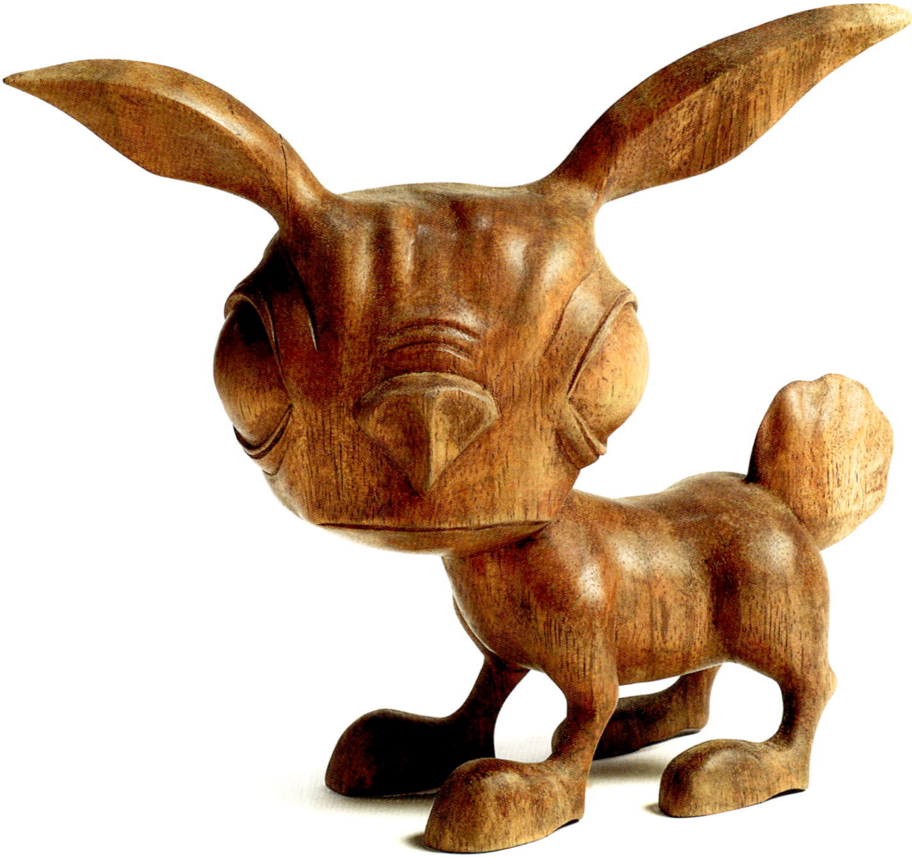

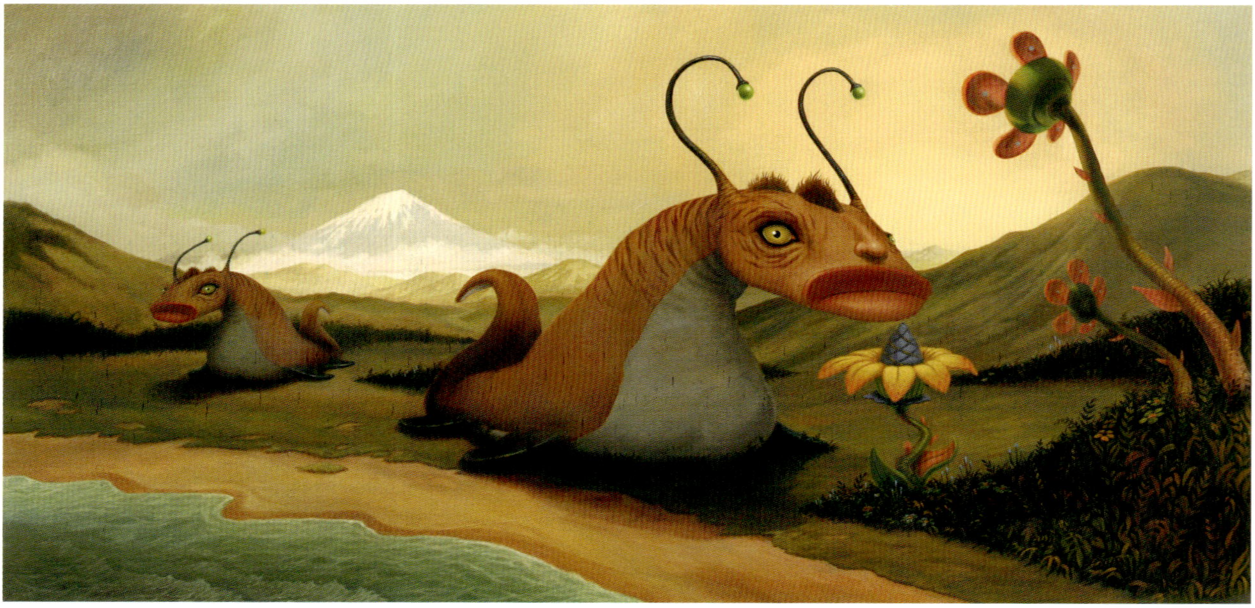

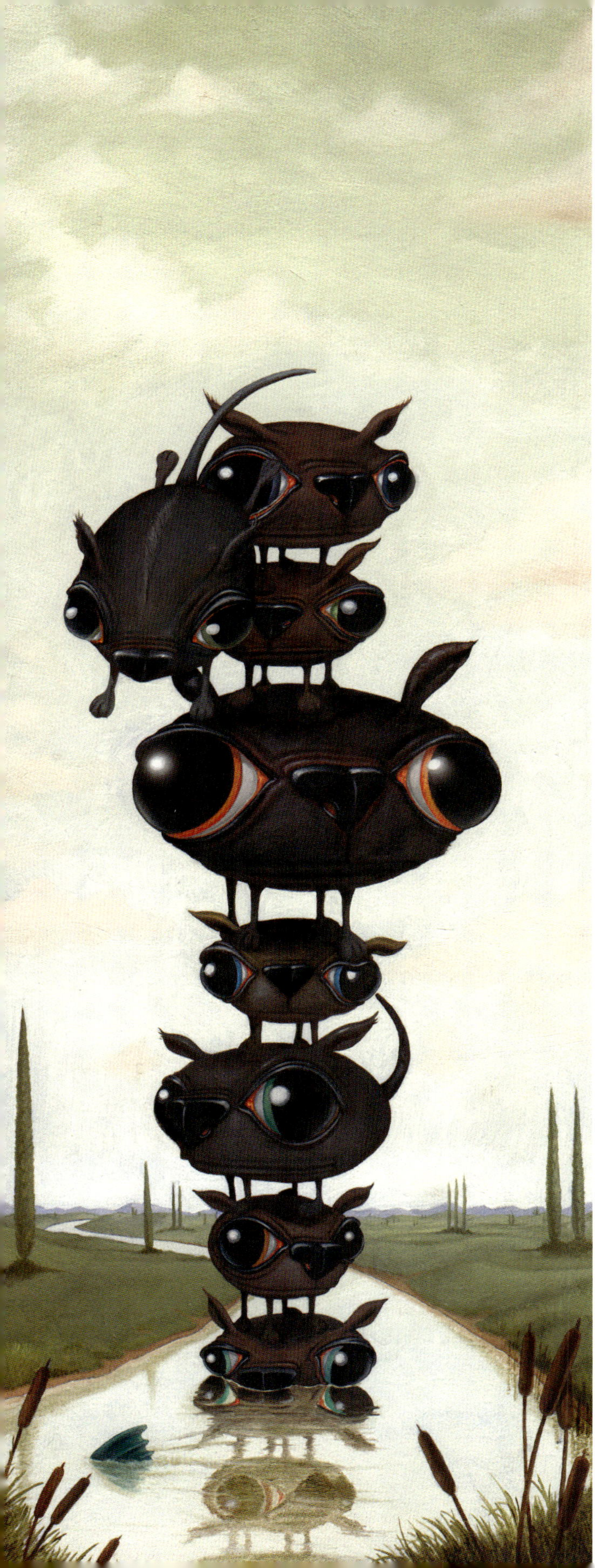

FROM LEFT TO RIGHT

Lepus Perilous
Extinct ~ ca. 1876
WOOD CARVING

Tubby Sea Tiger
Extinct ~ ca. 1823

Lupus Aquaticus
Extinct ~ ca. 1865

Swamp Island Ibex
Extinct ~ ca. 1883

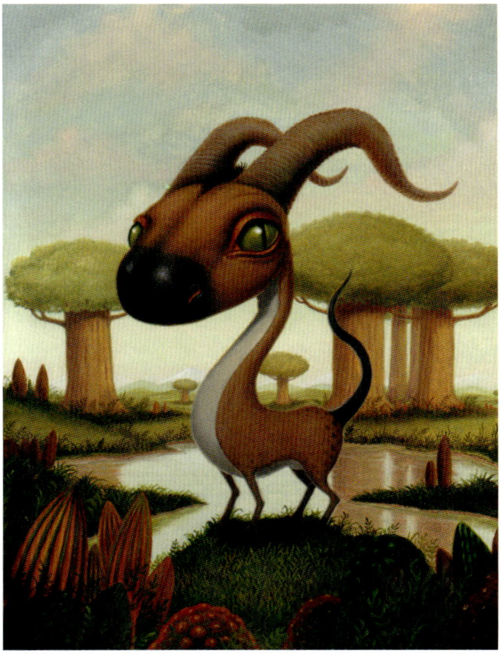

The Last Rhino
Extinct ~ ca. 1802
WOOD CARVING

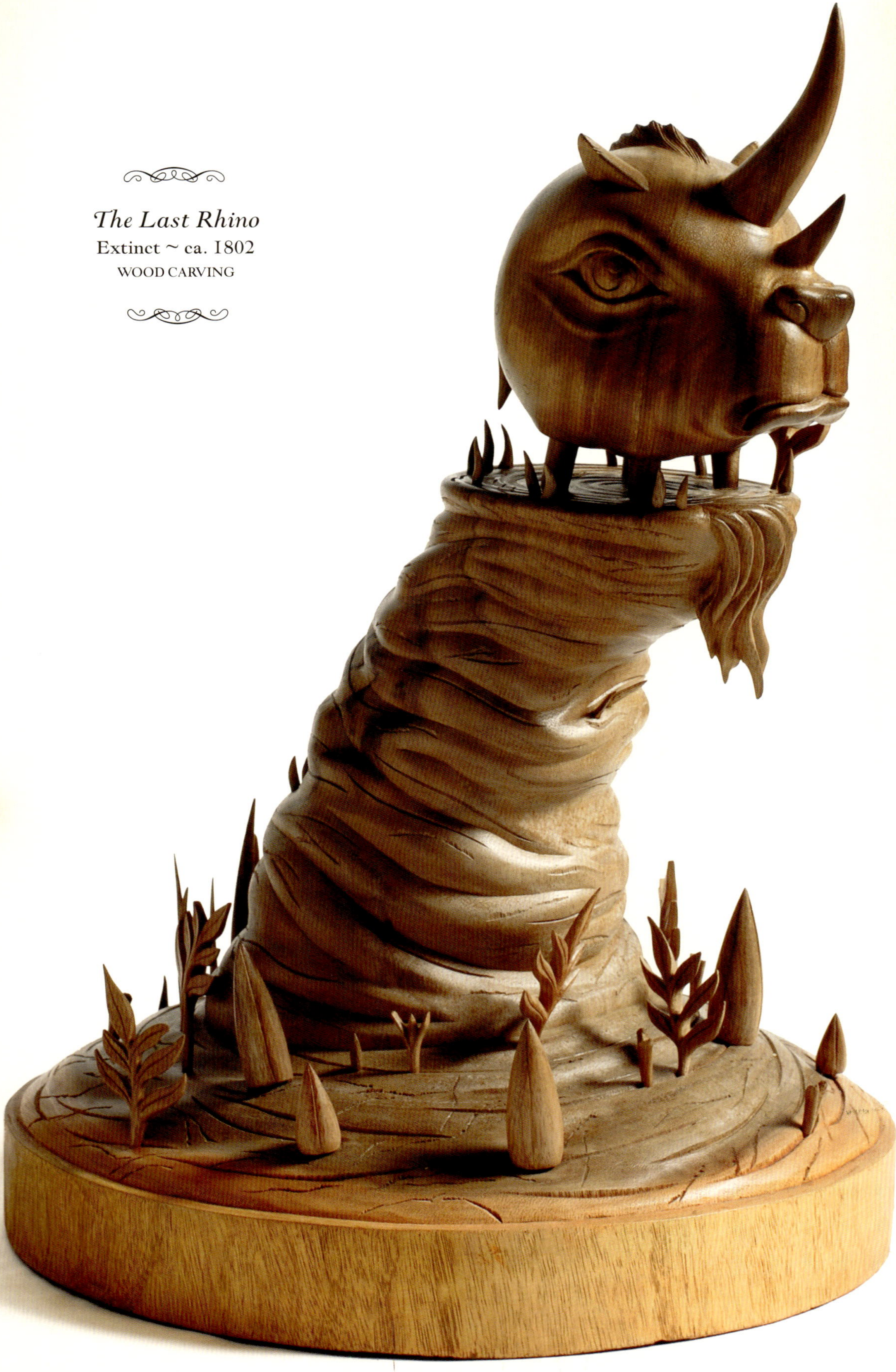

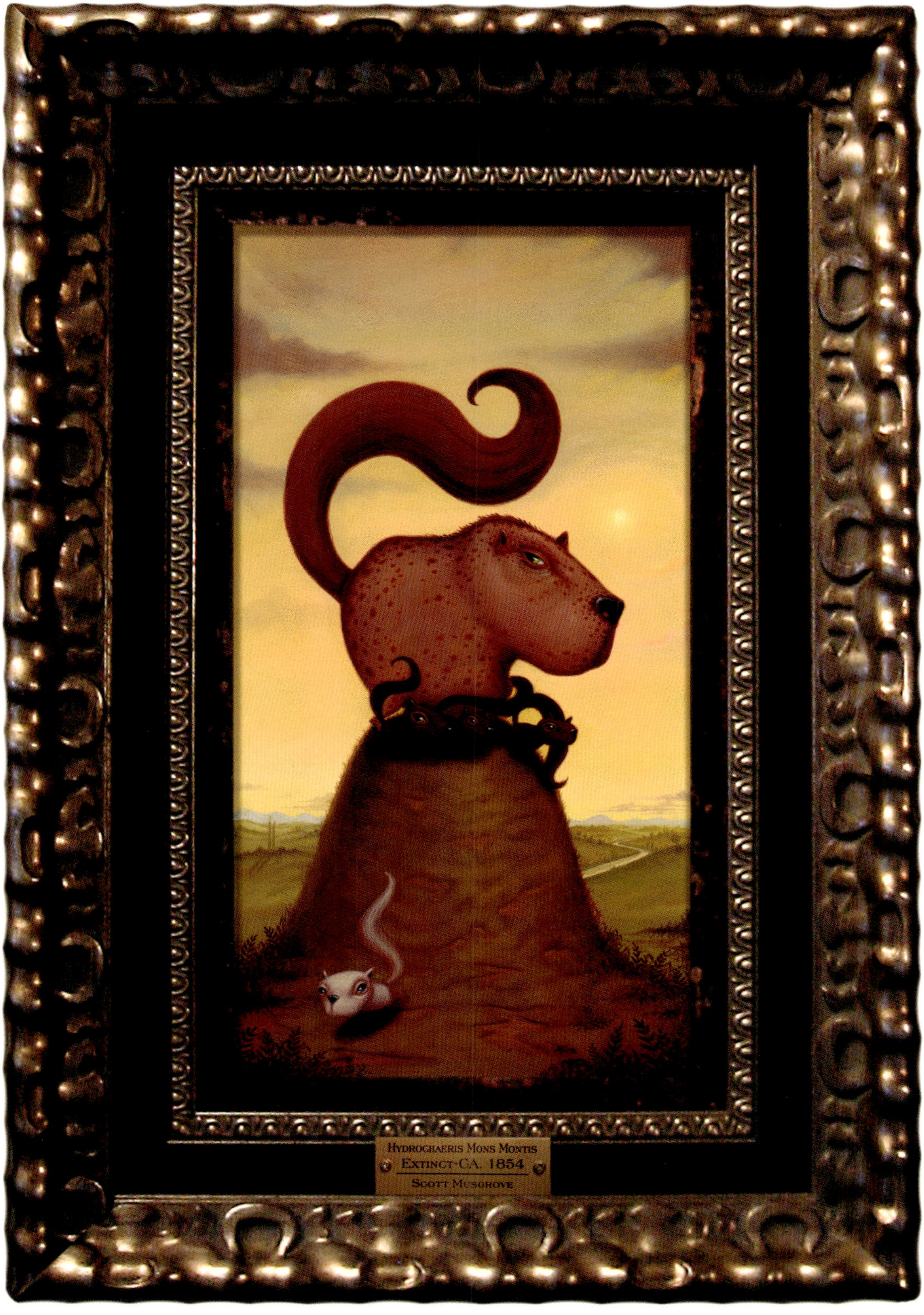
Hydrochaeris Mons Montis
Extinct-CA. 1854
Scott Musgrove

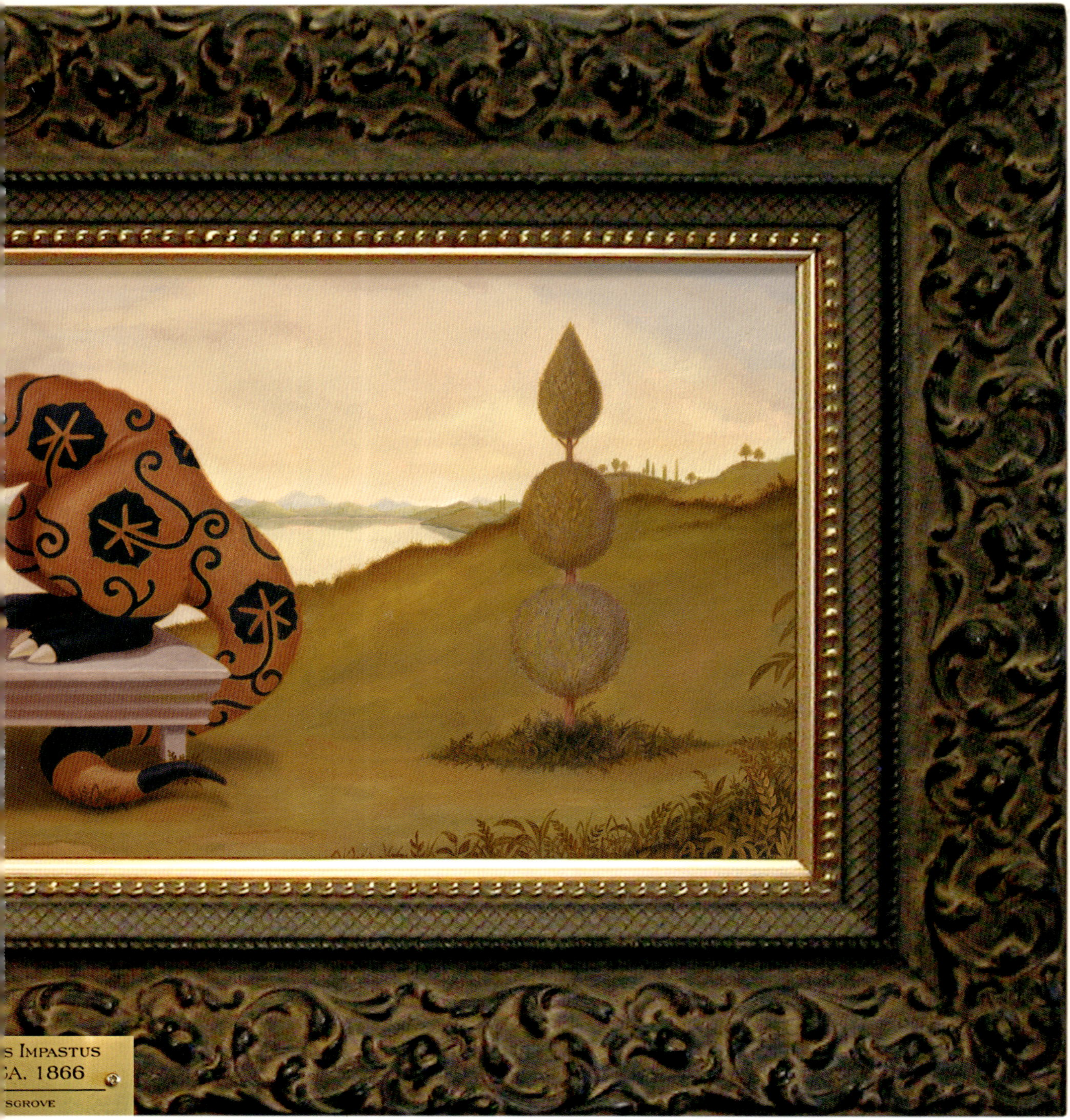
s Impastus
SA. 1866
SGROVE

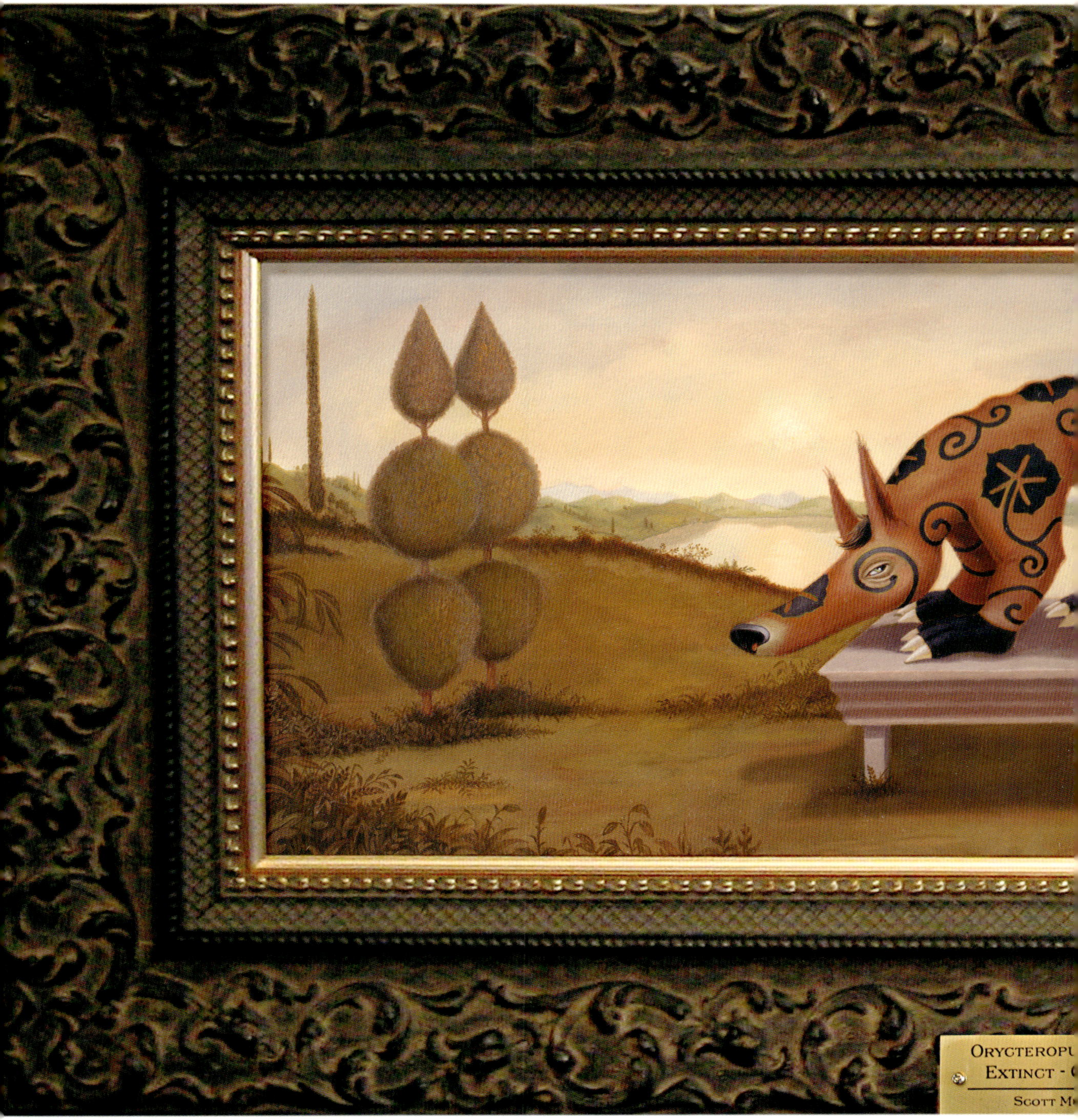
ORYCTEROPU
EXTINCT -
SCOTT M

Turpiculus Candidus
Extinct ~ ca. 1899

PREVIOUS PAGE
Hydrochaeris Mons Montis
Extinct ~ ca. 1899

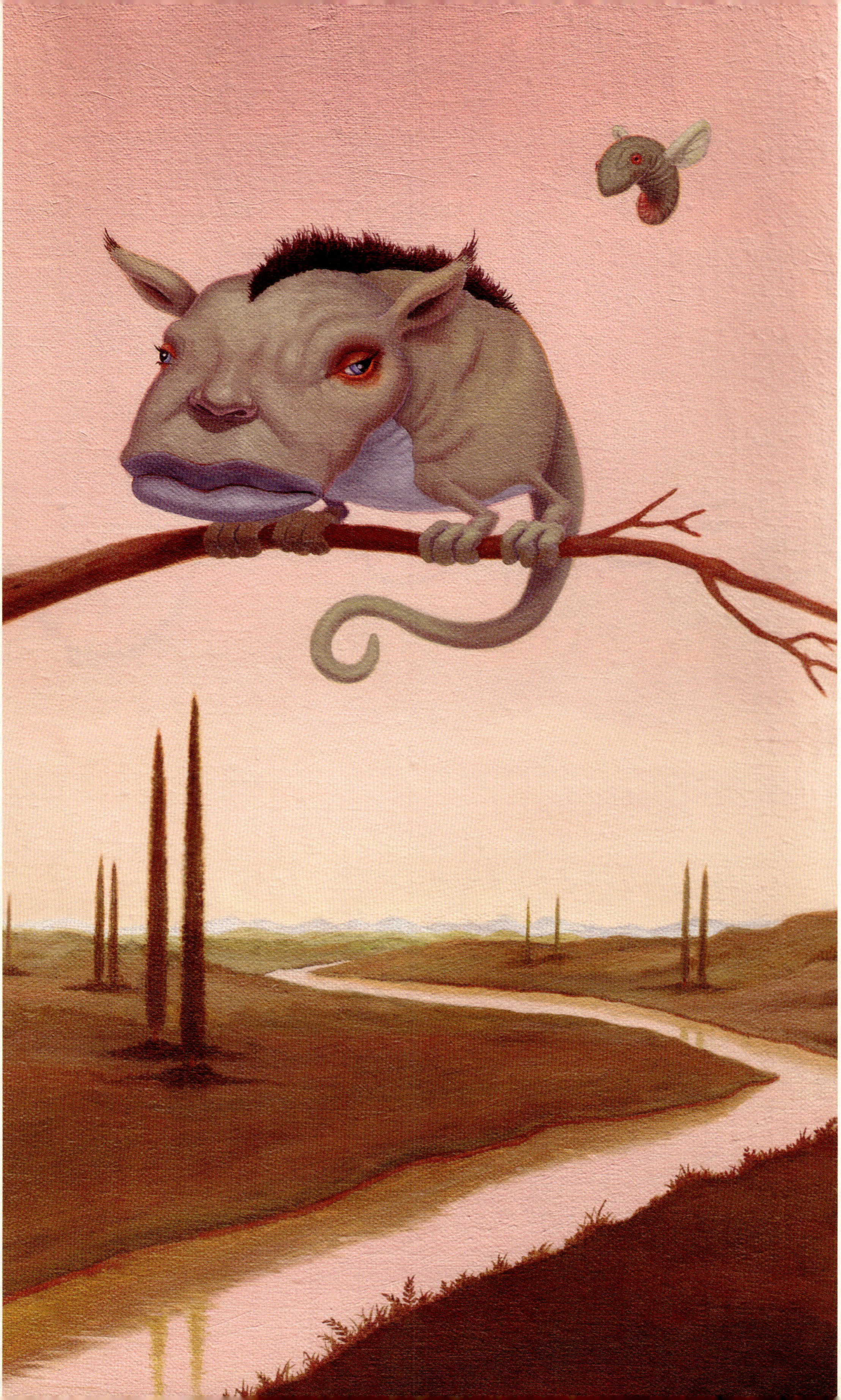

Lepus Perilous
Extinct ~ ca. 1876

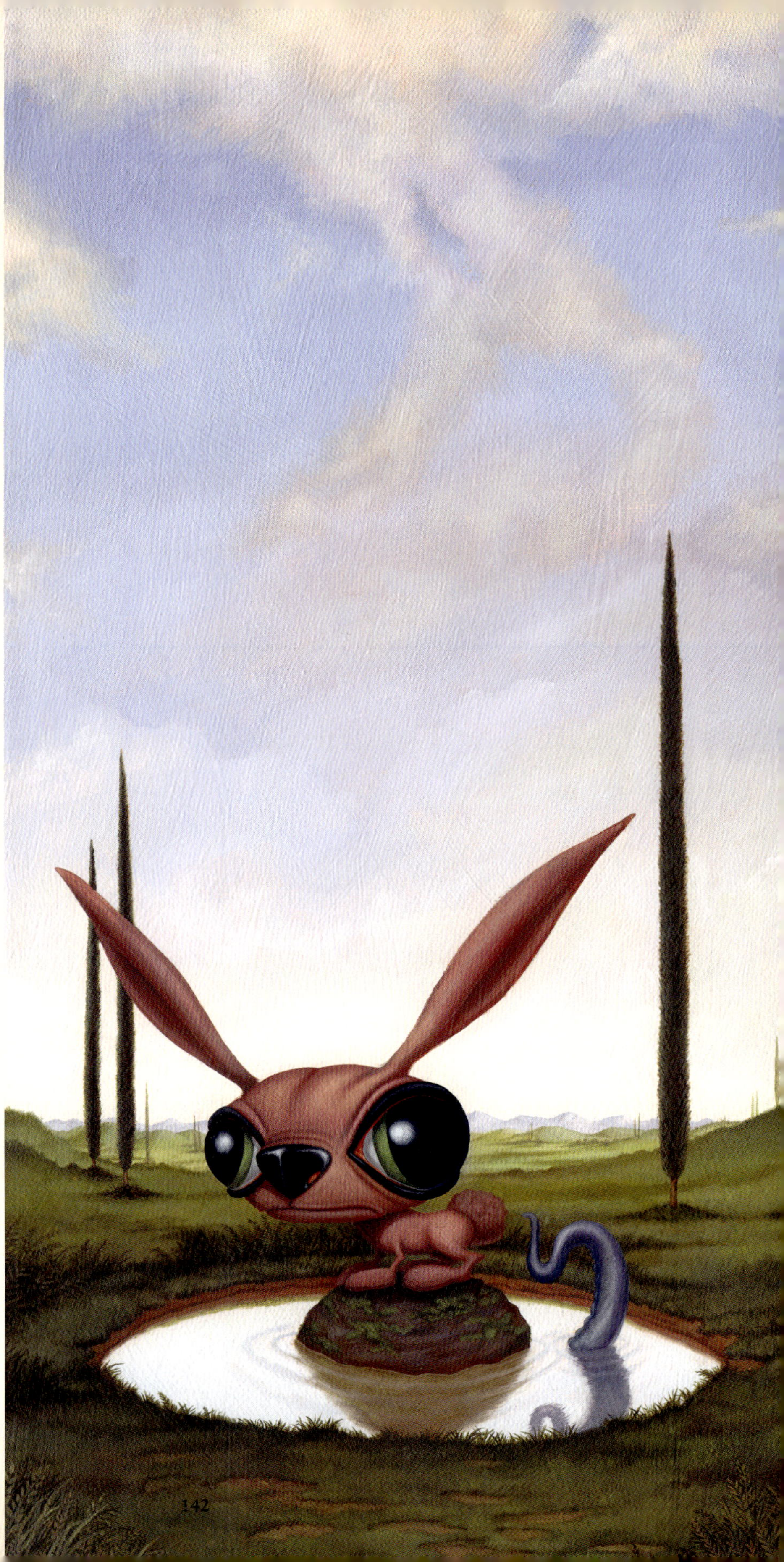

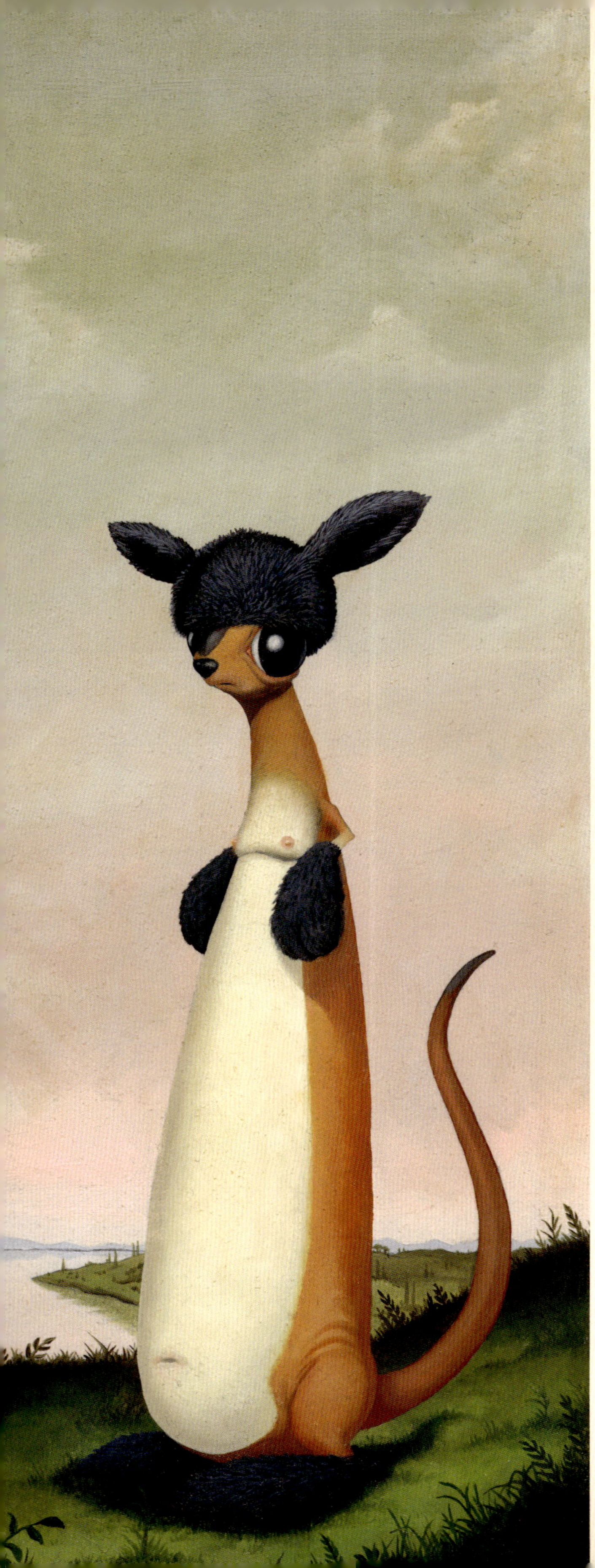

Prairie Boxer
Extinct ~ ca. 1862

Vegatatus Masticatus

Extinct ~ ca. 1814

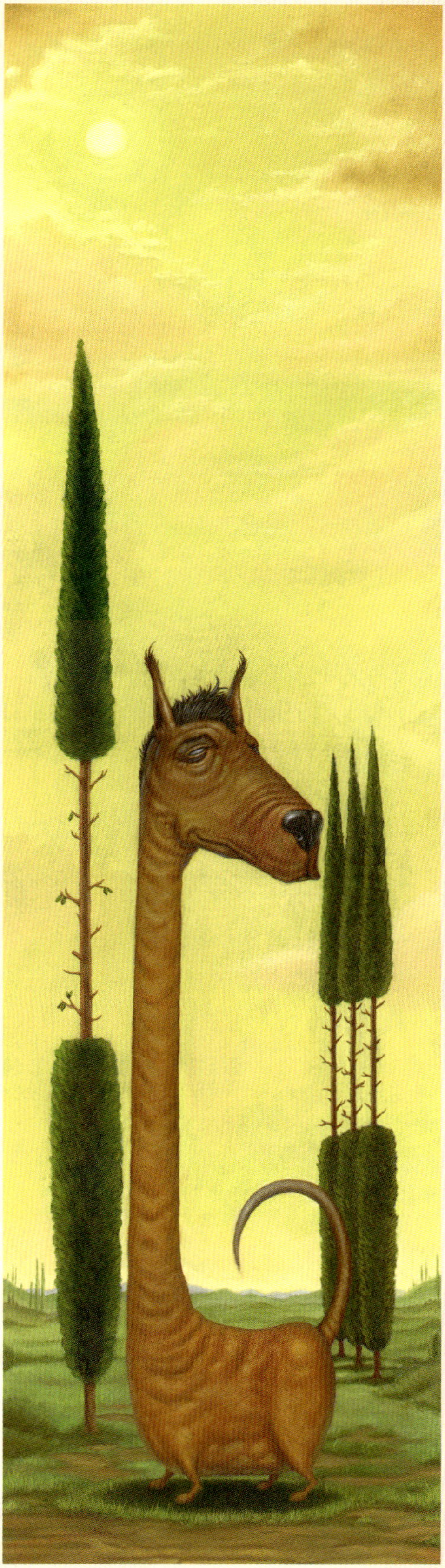

Harea Narcoleptus
Extinct ~ ca. 1821

Homus Destructus
Not Extinct Yet!

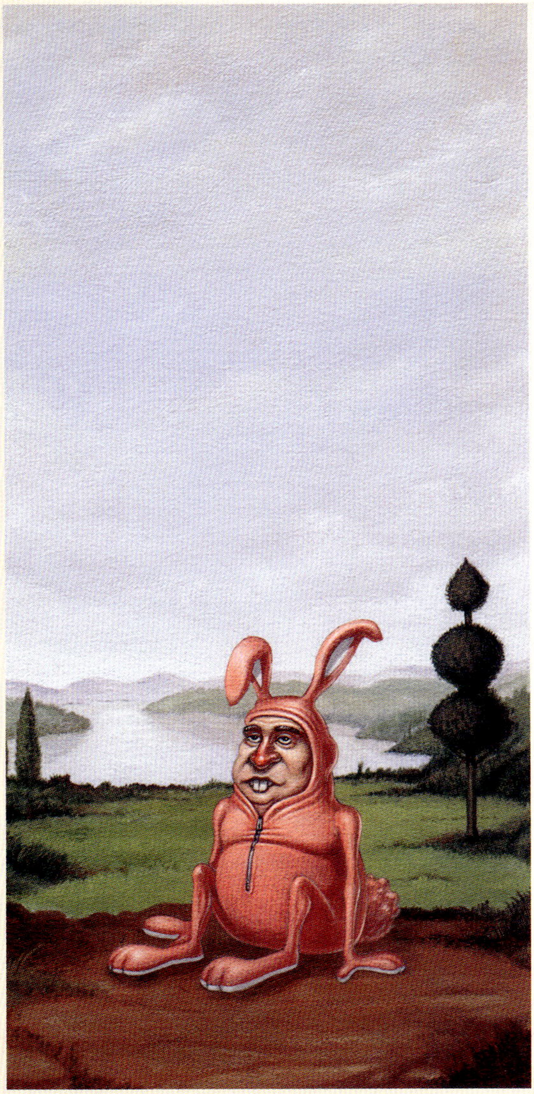

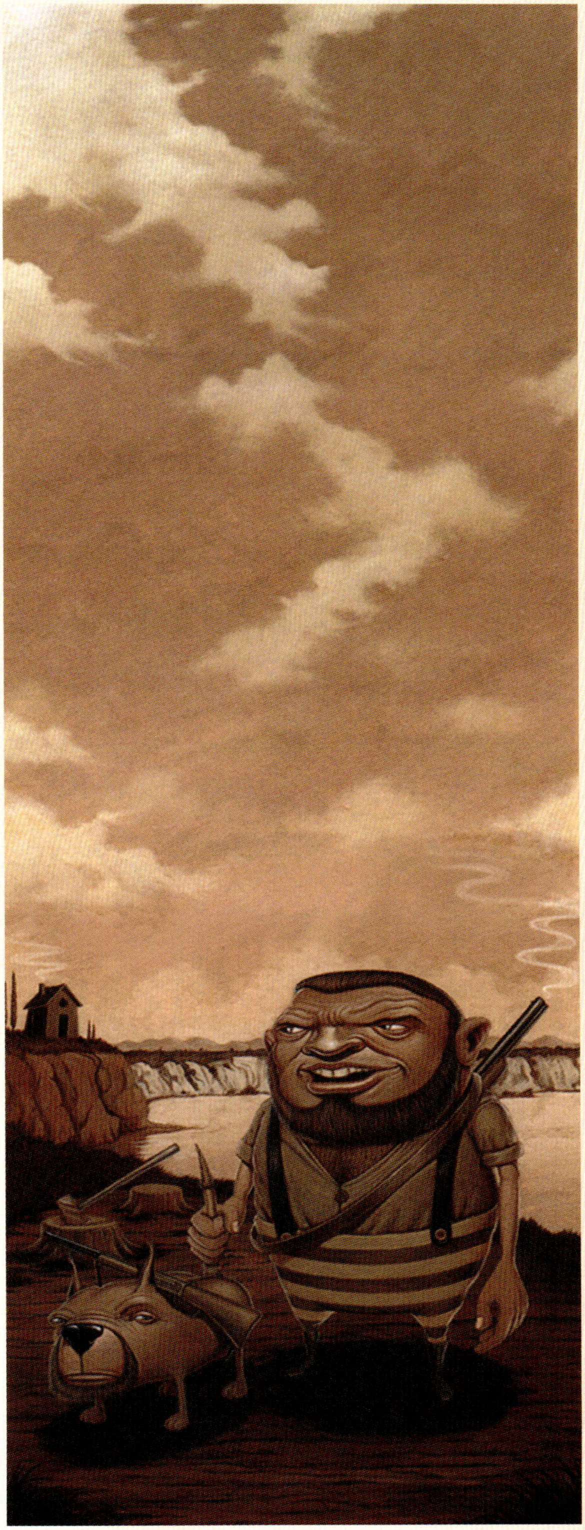

How The West Was Won

ca. 1803

The Great Hunt

Extinct ~ ca. 1830

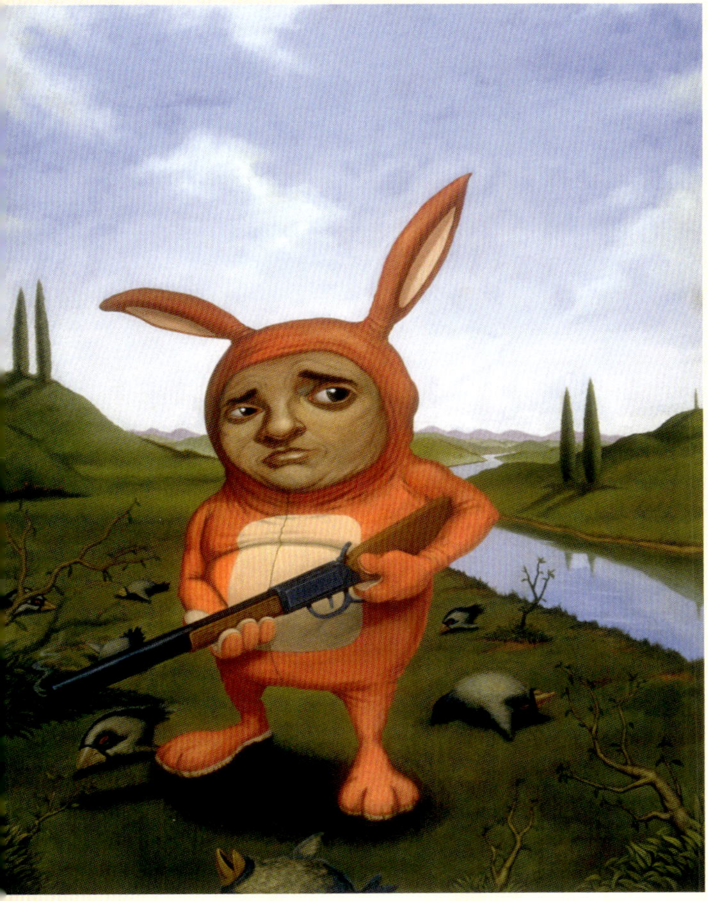
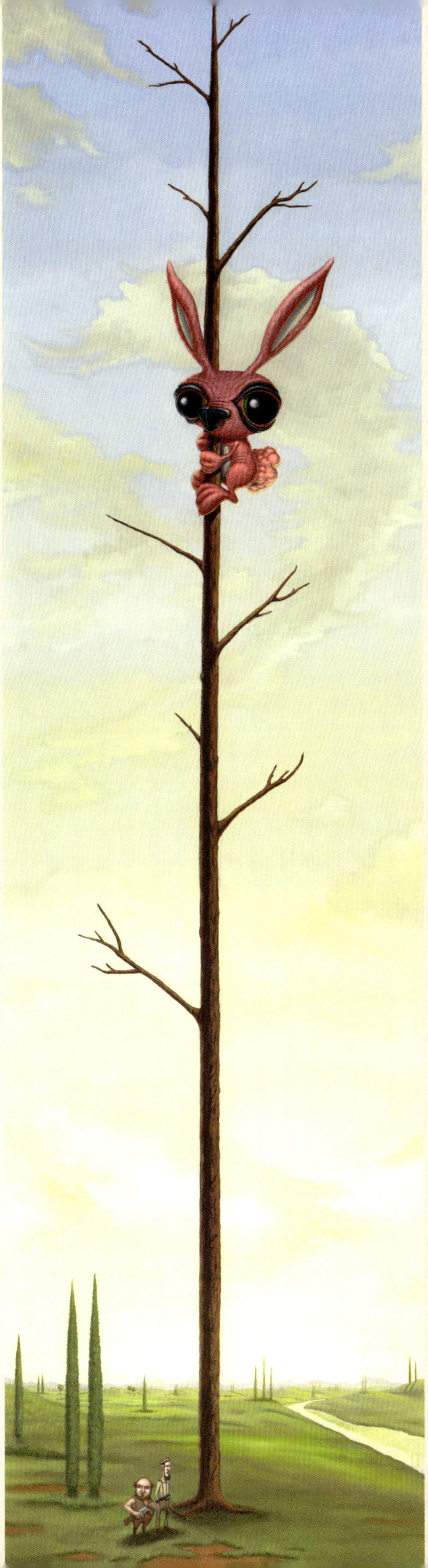

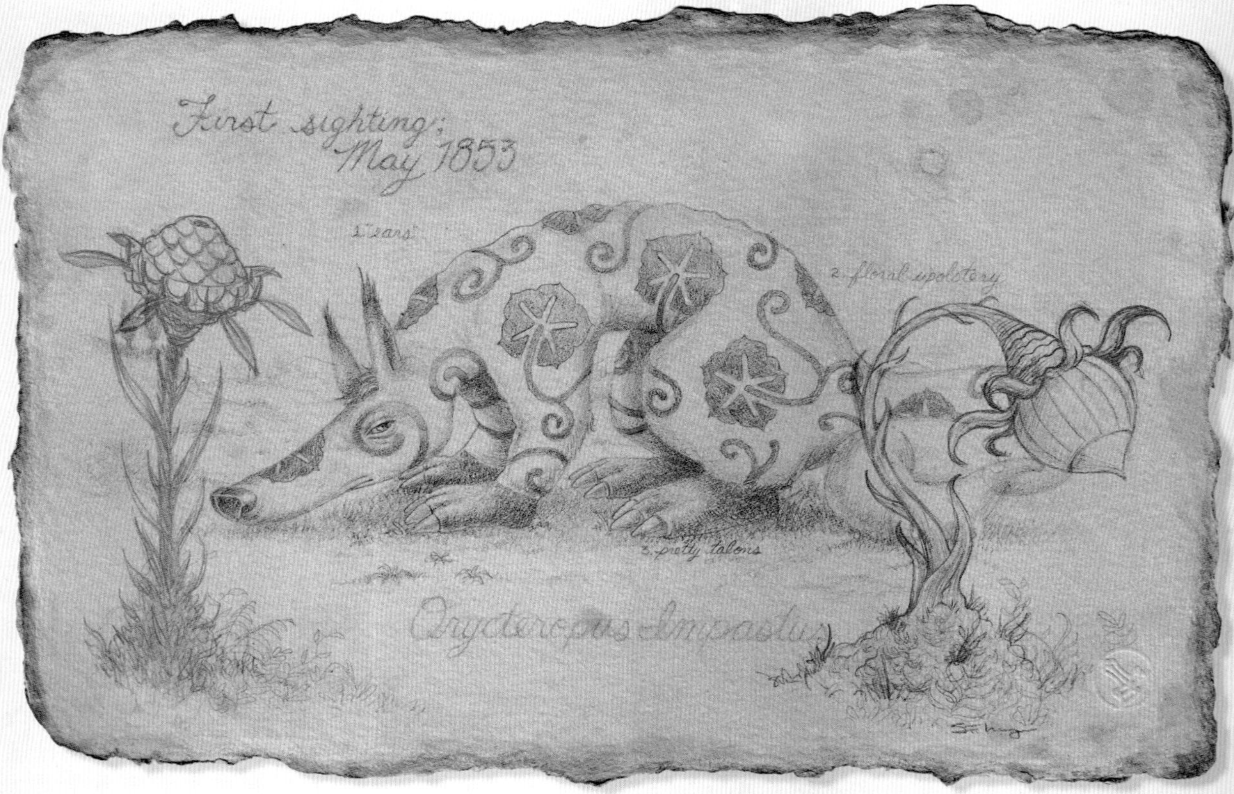
First sighting;
May 1853
1. ears
2. floral upolstery
3. pretty talons
Orycteropus Impastus

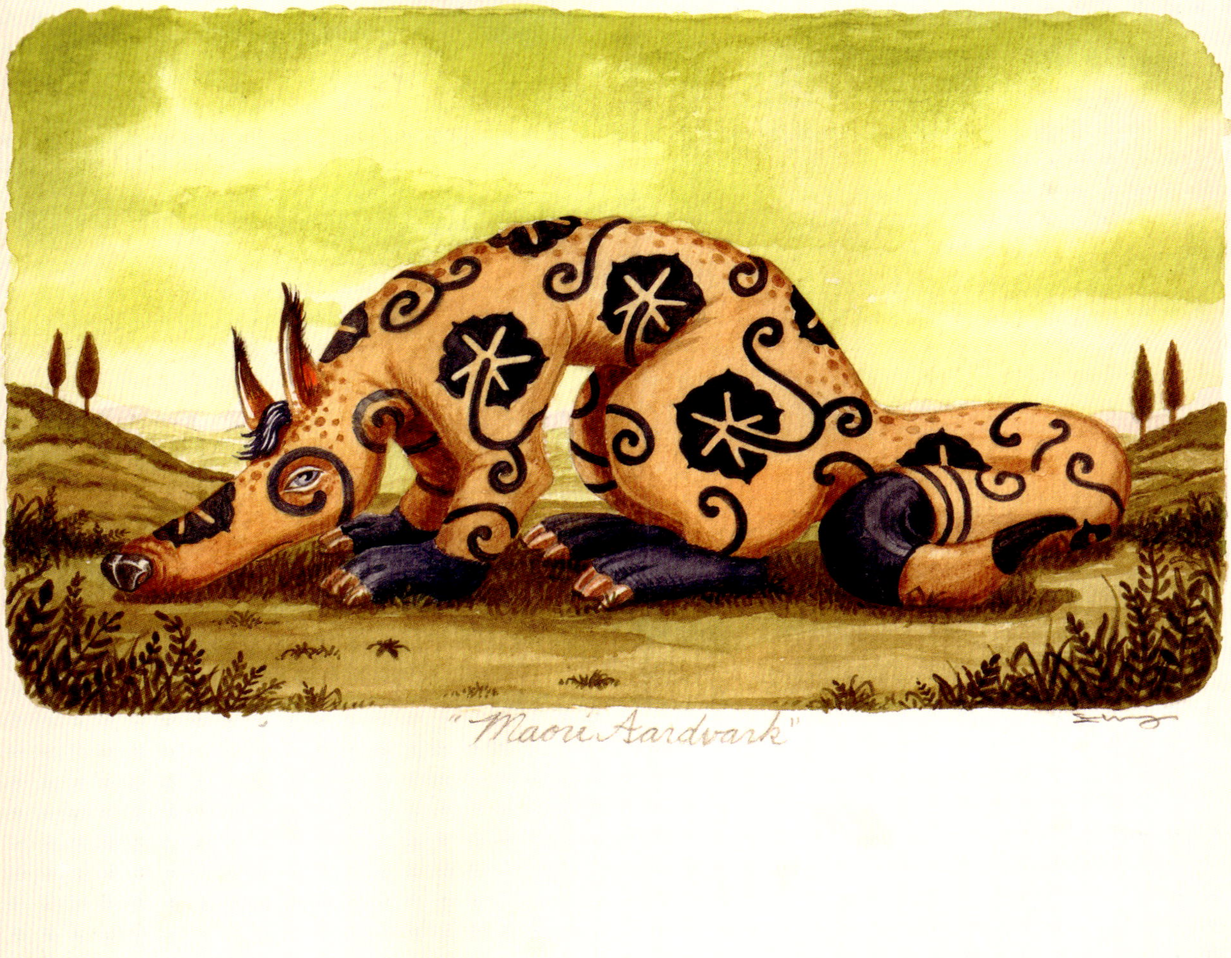

"Maori Aardvark"

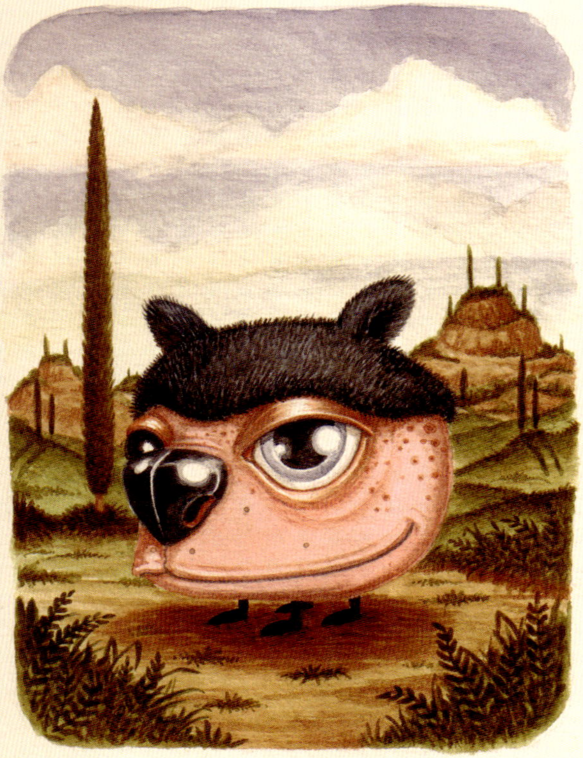
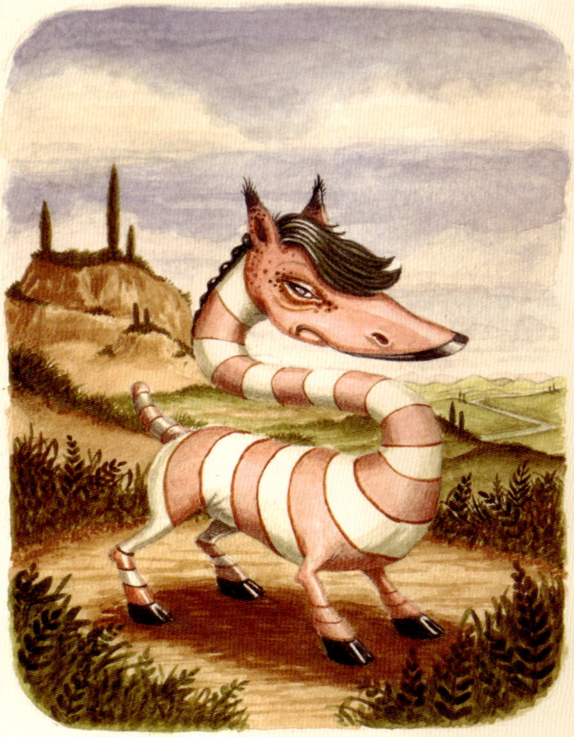
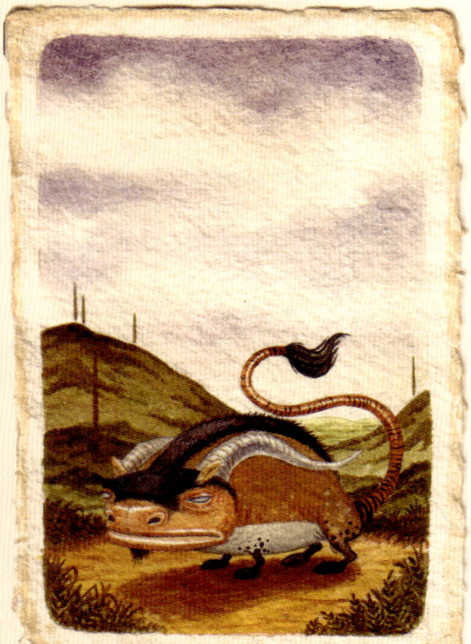
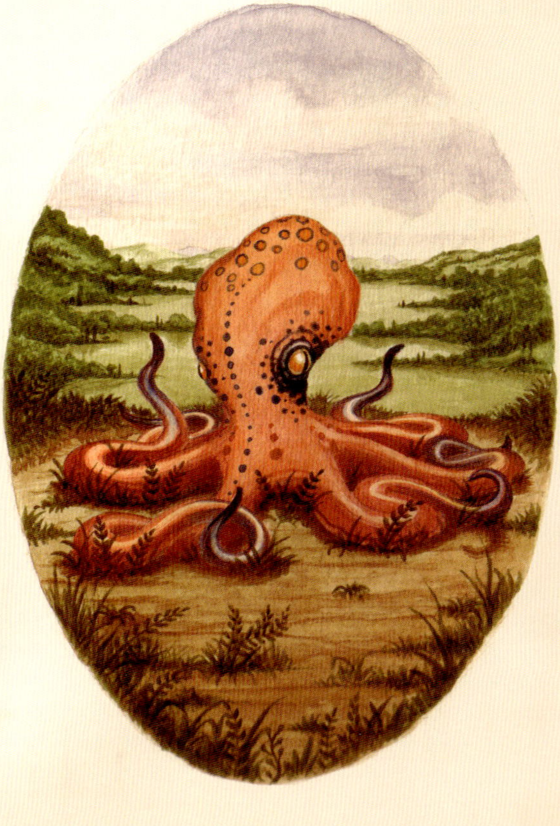

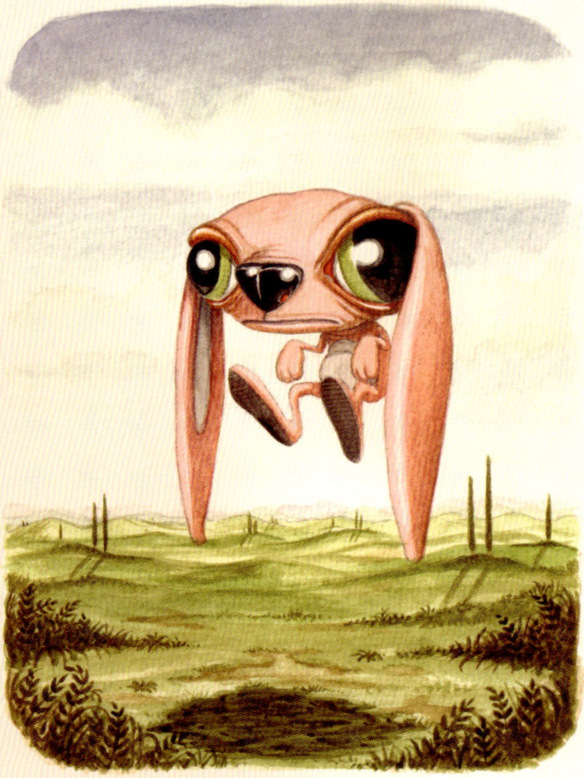

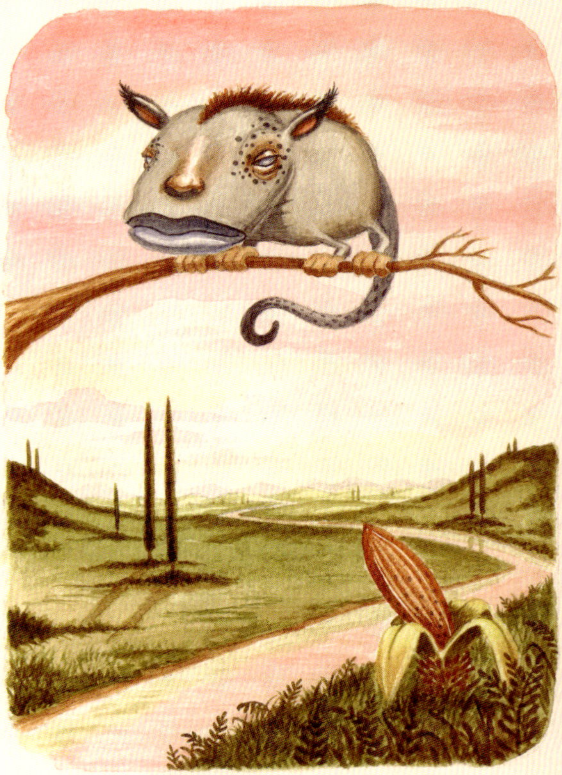

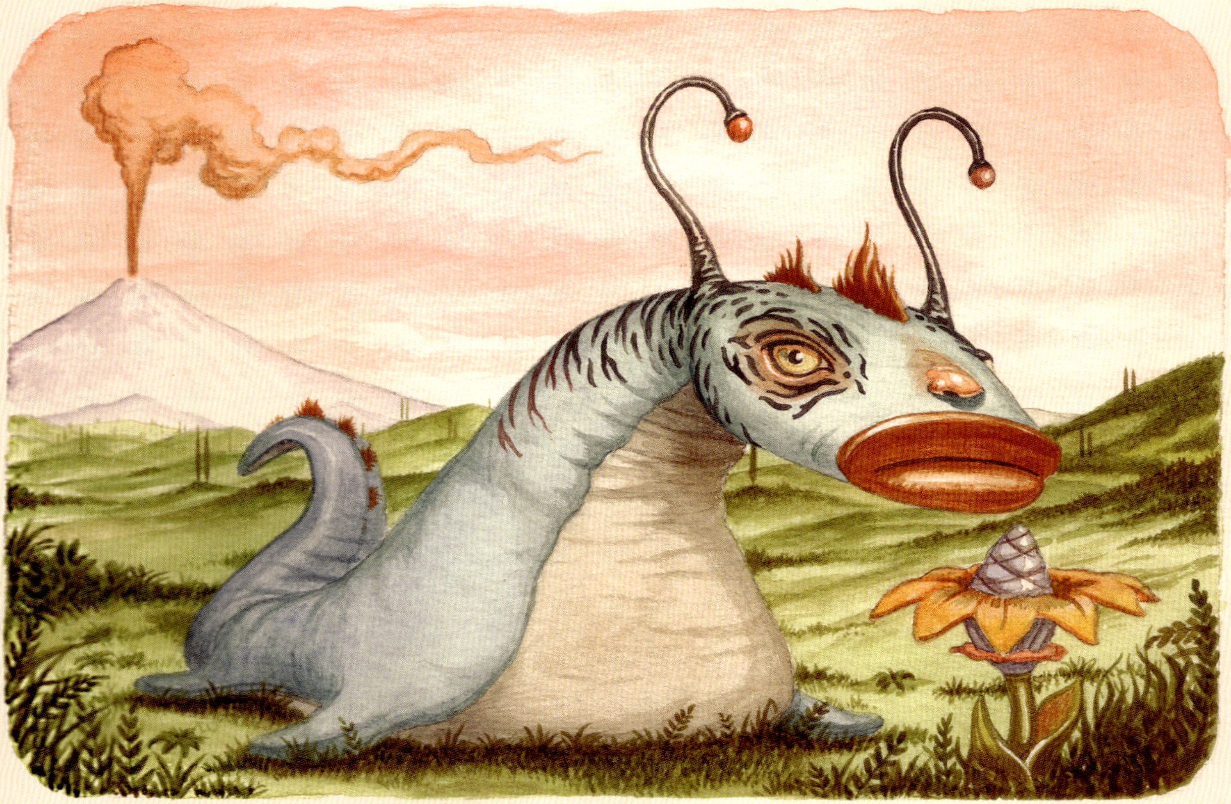

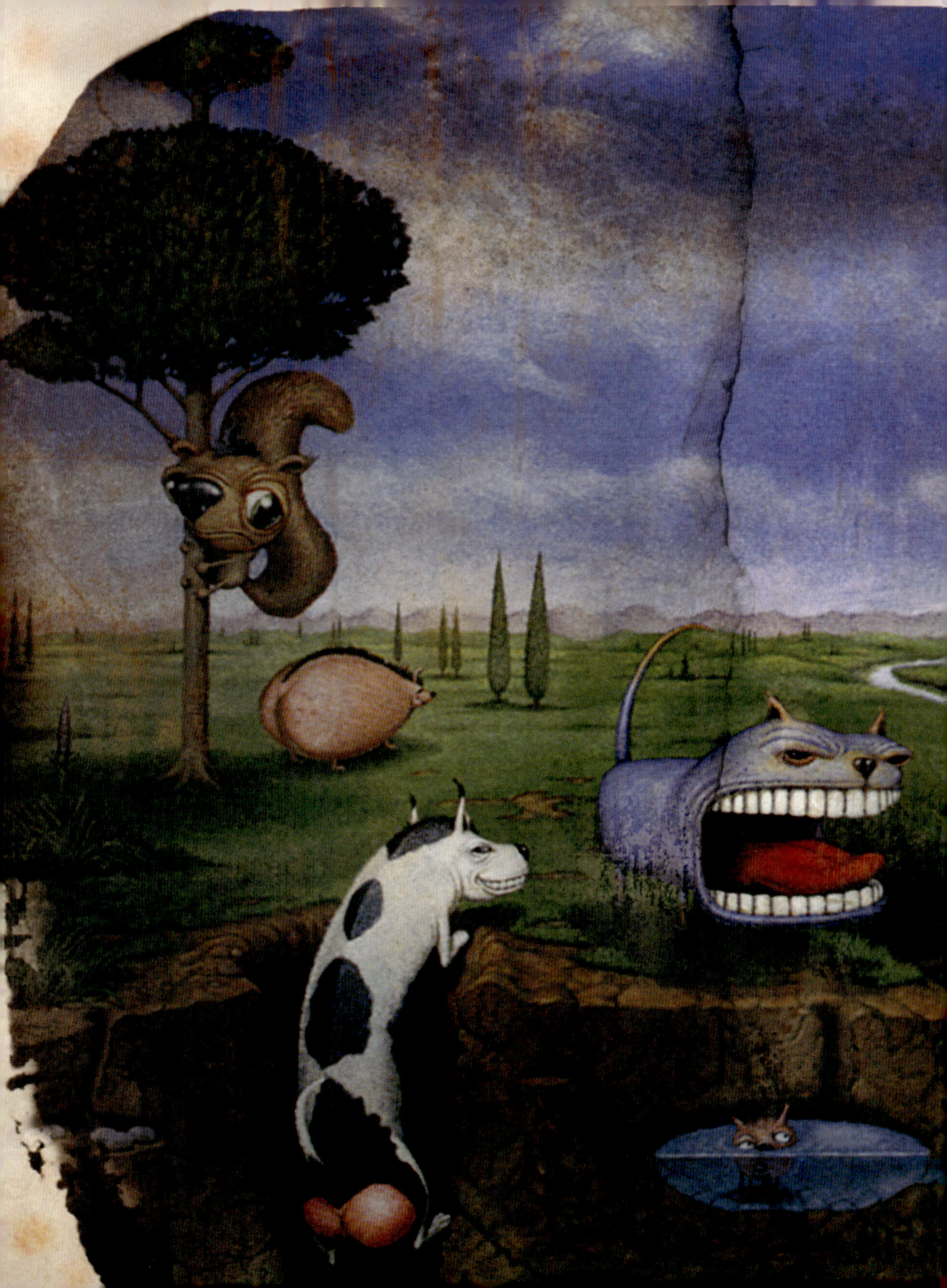

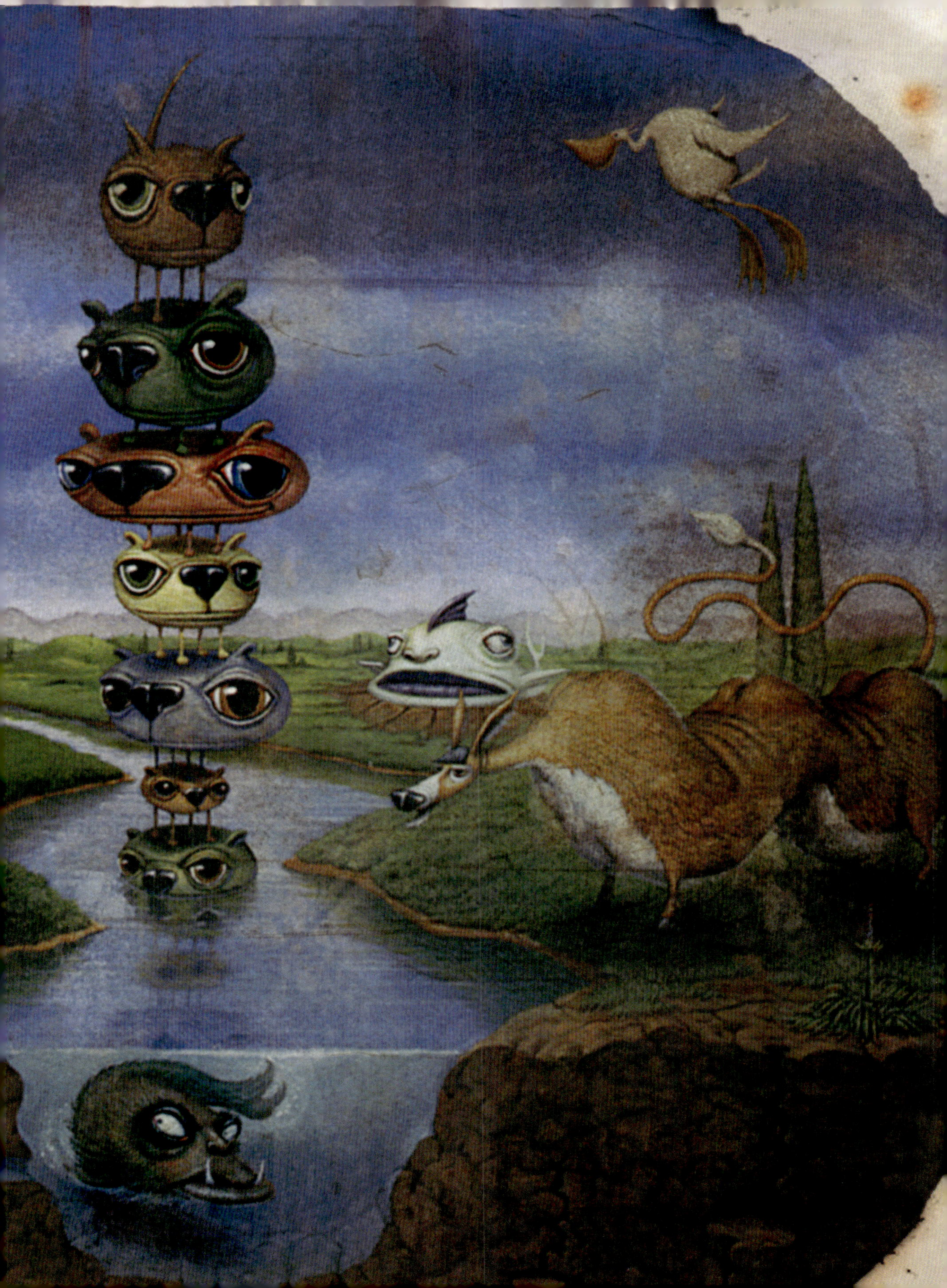

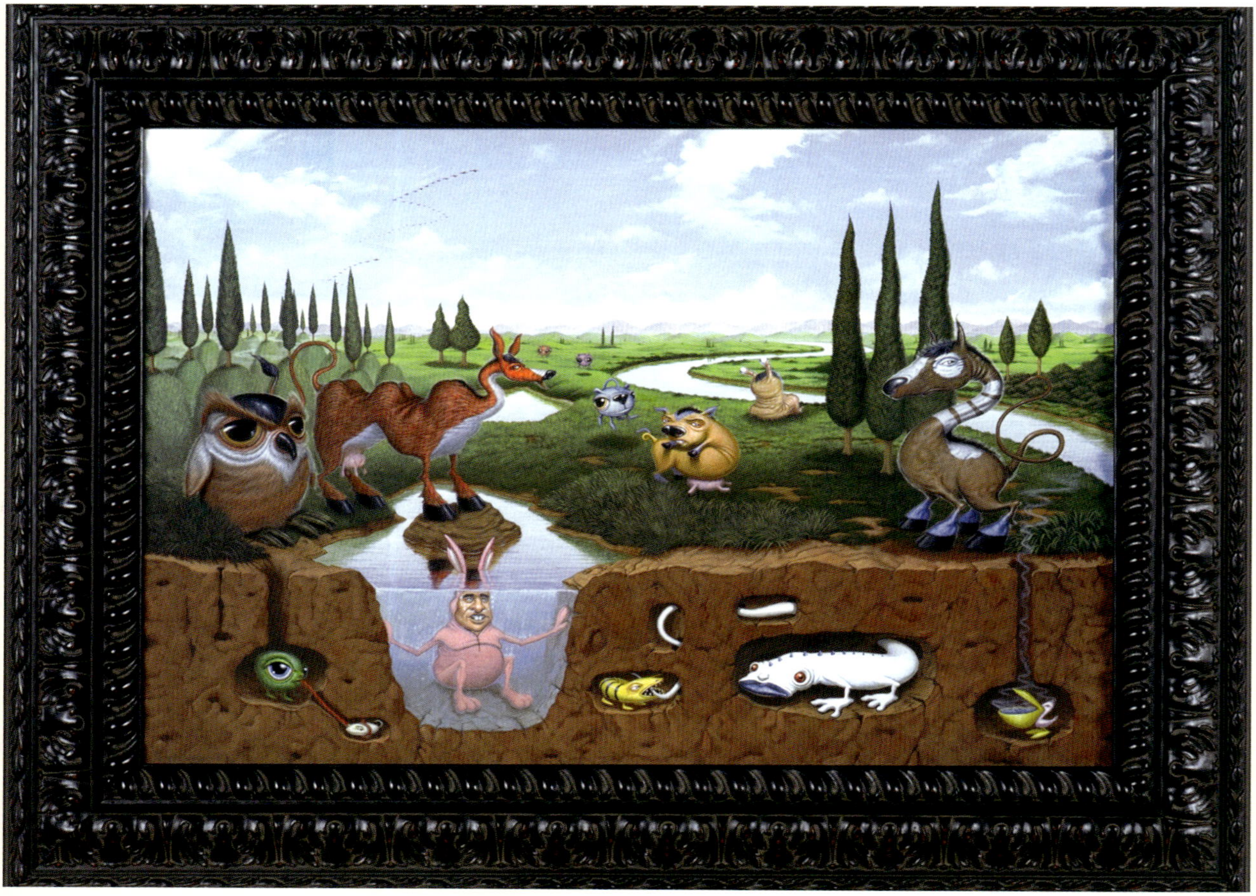

The Late Fauna of Middle America

MIDDLE AMERICA

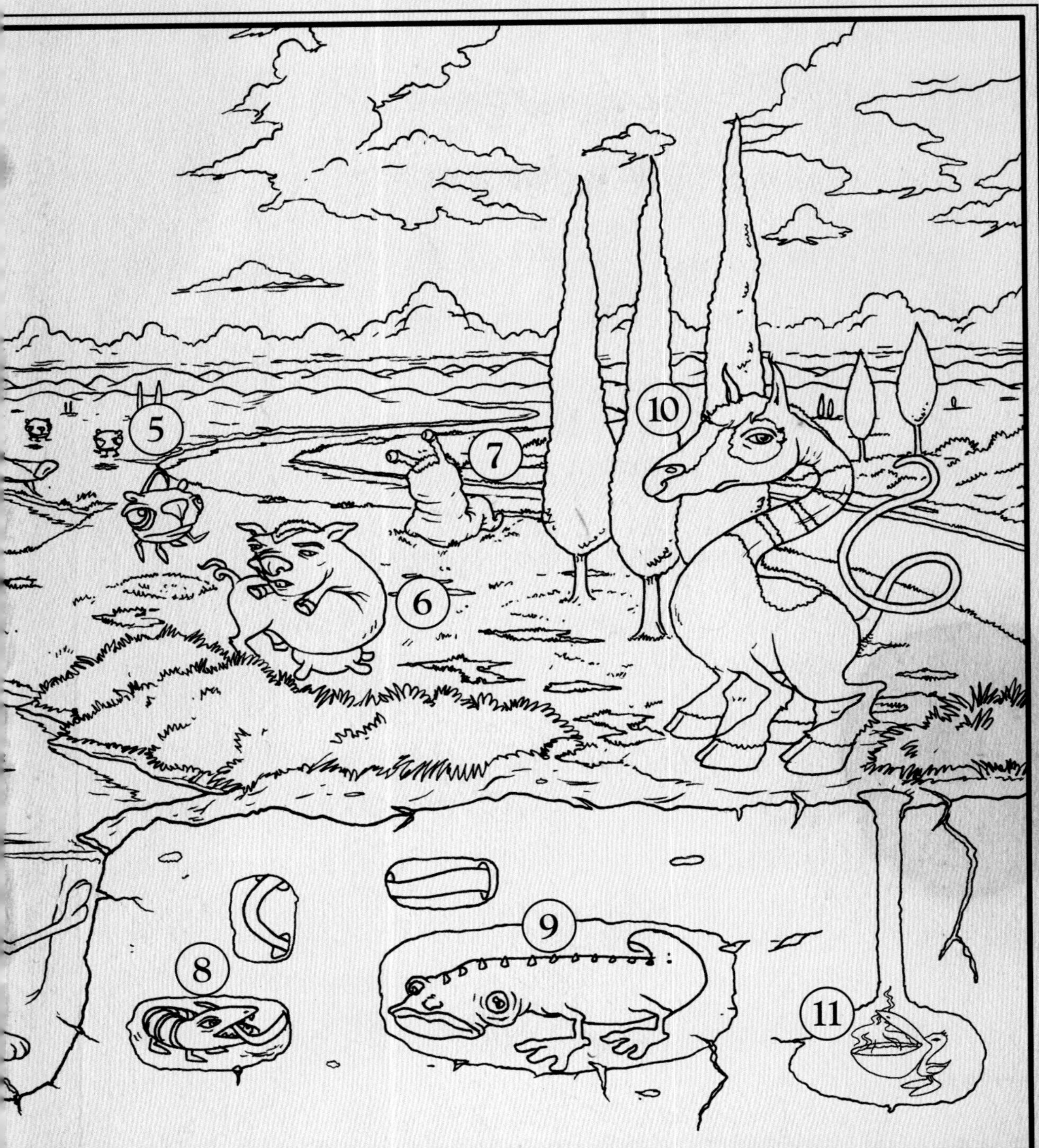

LATE FAUNA OF

INDIGENOUS ANIMAL *and* PLANT SPECIES *of* THE LOWER UPPER MIDDLE AMERICA REGION

Legend

1........... *SOMNUS CARNATUS OTUS*
(TORPID PUDGING OWL)

2........... *ASINUS DUAE*
(DOUBLE DONKEY)

3........... *FOSSA SCROTUS MORDERE*
(SUBTERRANEAN NUT-BITER)

4........... *HAREA NARCOLEPTUS*
(MILD RIVER RABBIT)

5........... *LUPUS AQUATICUS*
(MARSHY WEED WOLF)

6........... *LACTUS SUS SCROFA*
(MILKING BENT PIG)

7........... *CANIS CAECUS*
(SEEING EYE DOG)

8........... *CIMEX NIGROCINCTUS*
(STRIPED PRICK)

9........... *AMBYSTOMA ALBINUS*
(MALADROIT ALBINO CAVE NEWT)

10......... *HYDROPHIS CERVIX HOOVERUS*
(SNAKE NECKED HOOVER)

11......... *CICONIA TUMBA*
(GRAVE STORK)

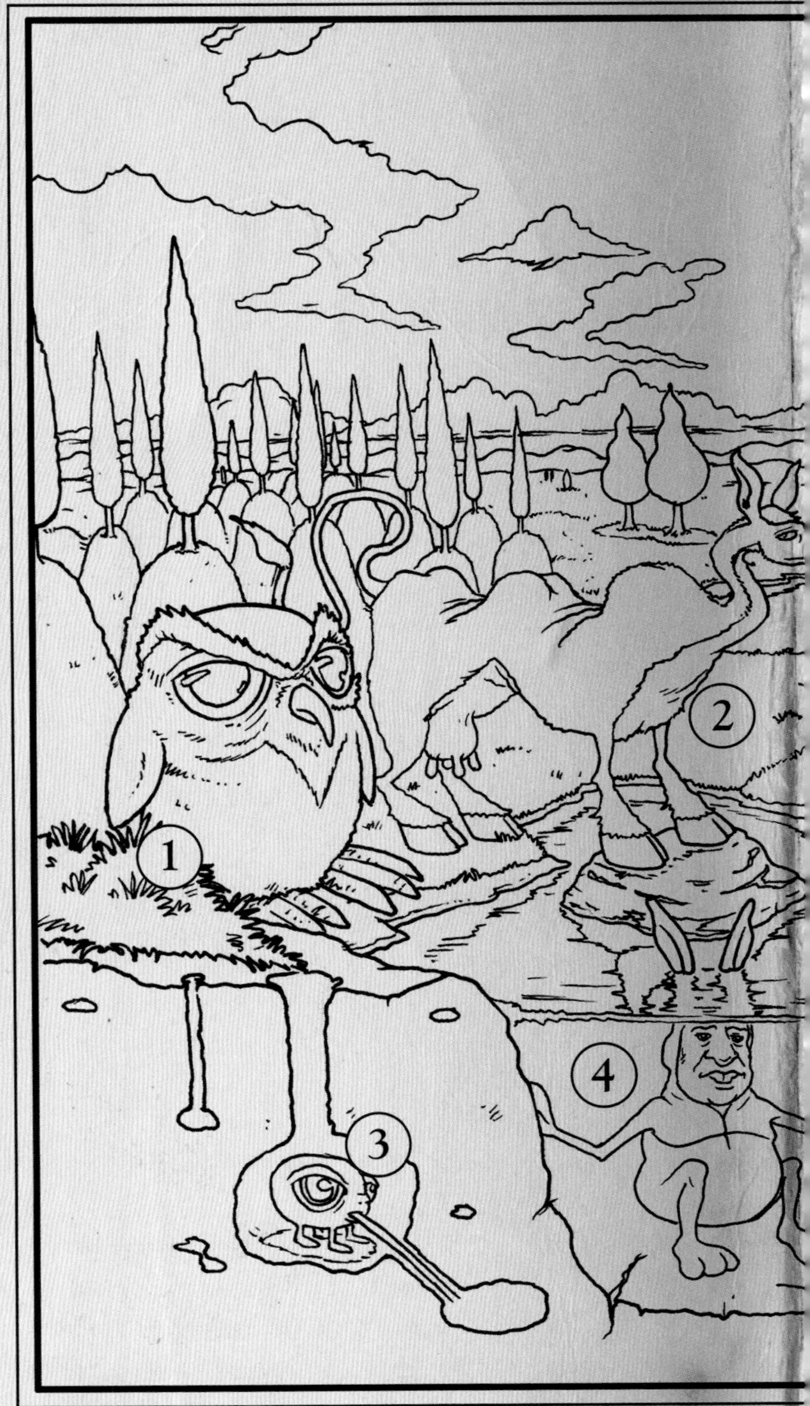

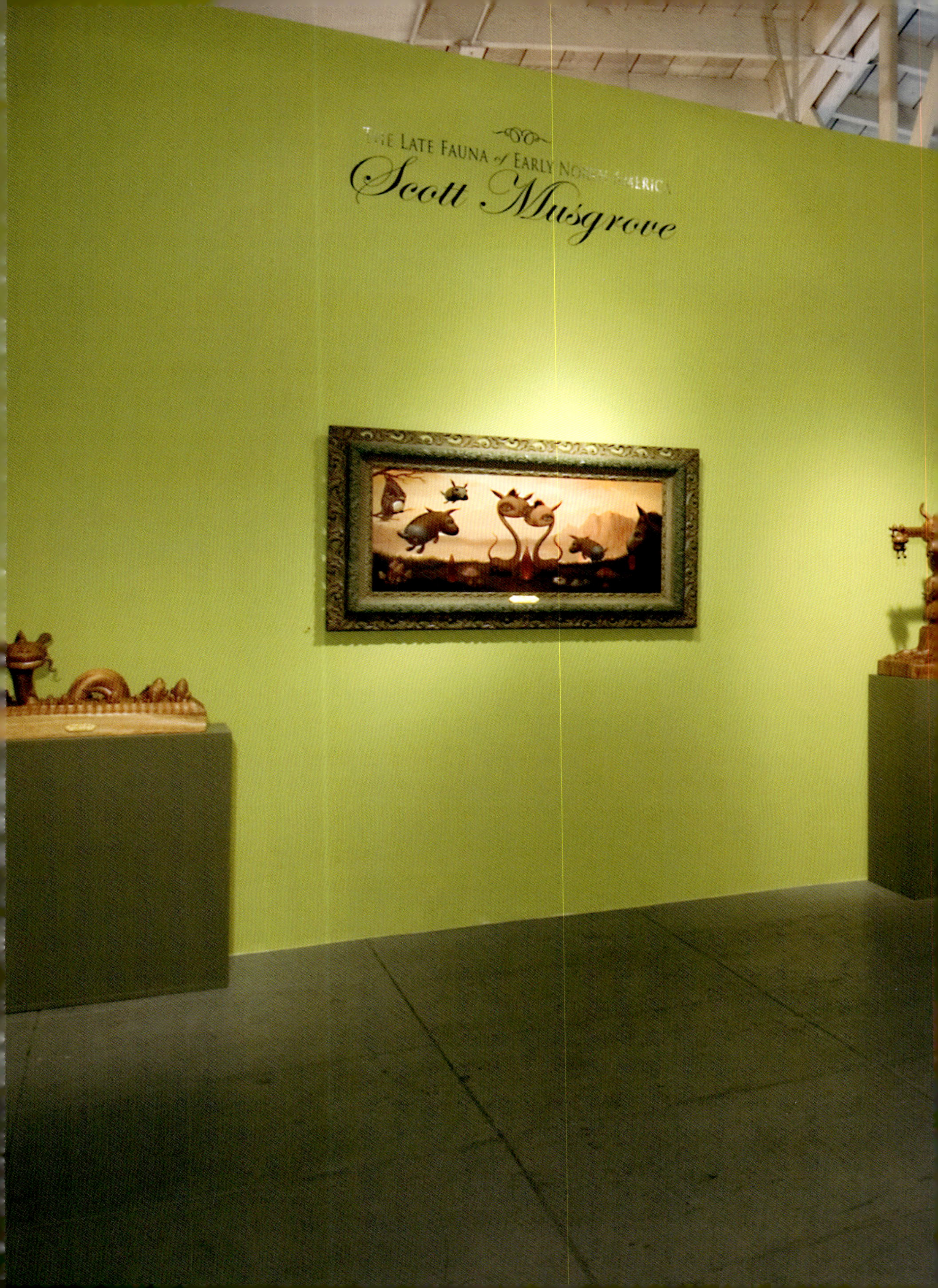
The Late Fauna of Early
Scott Musgrove

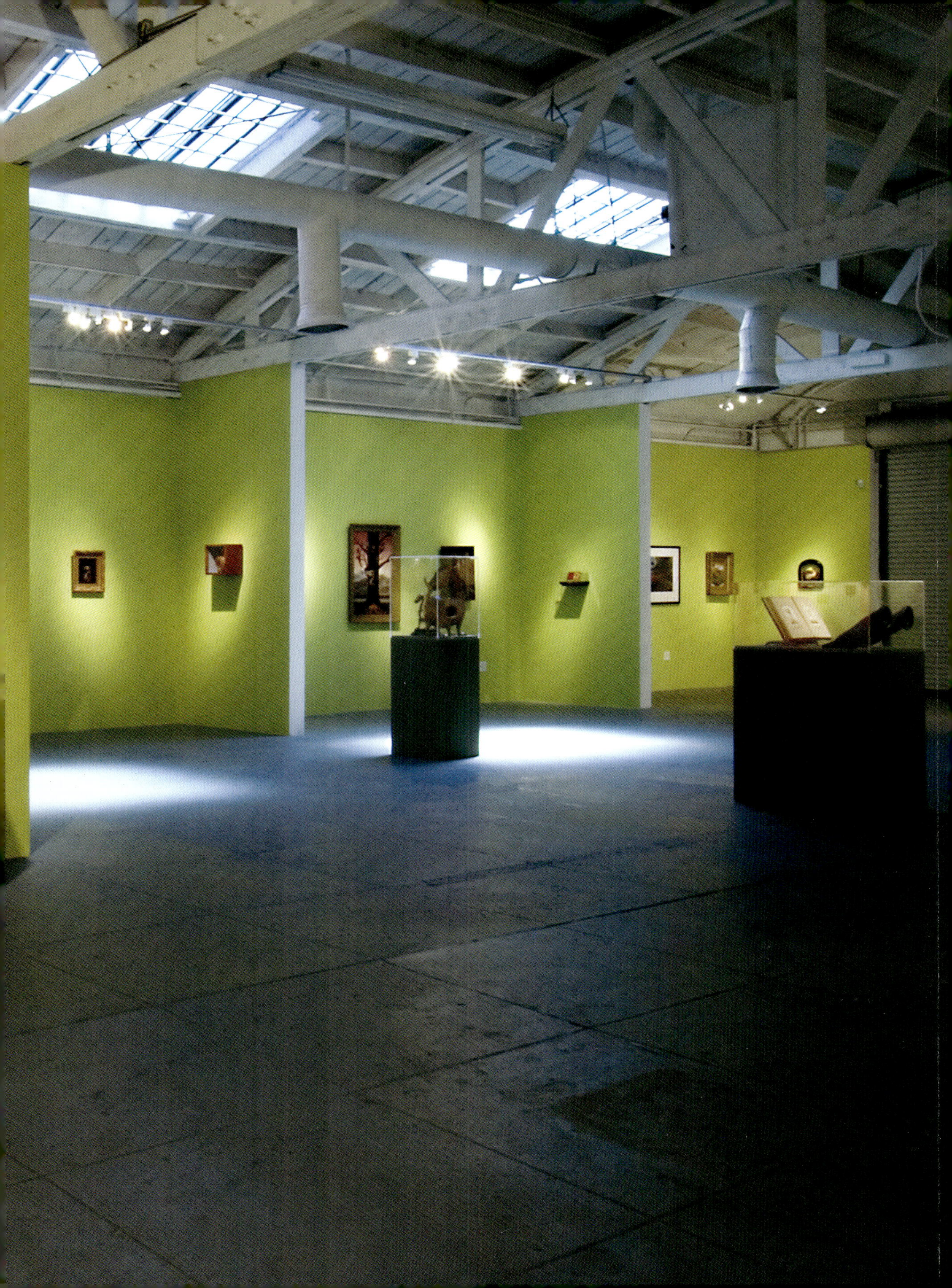

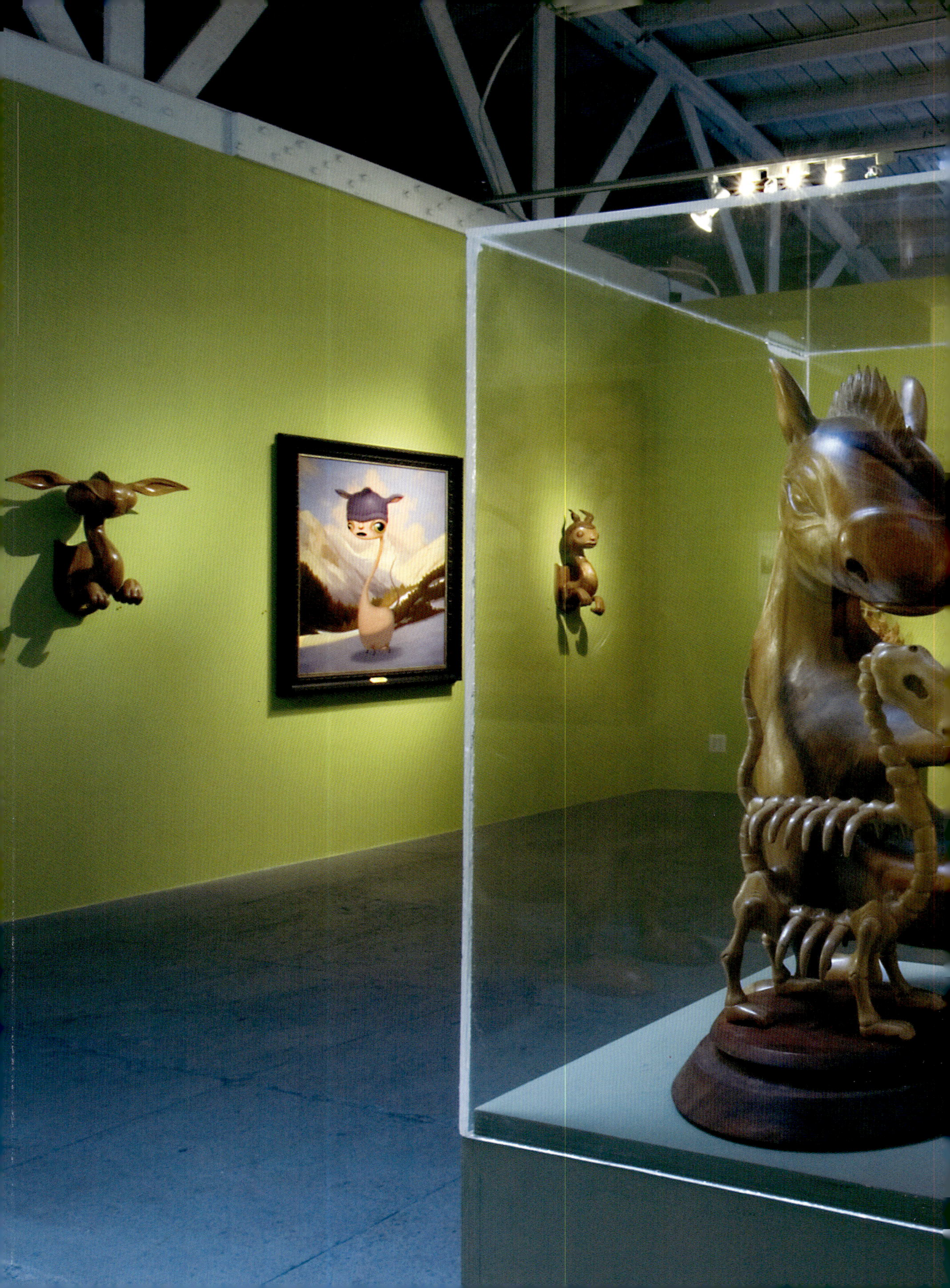

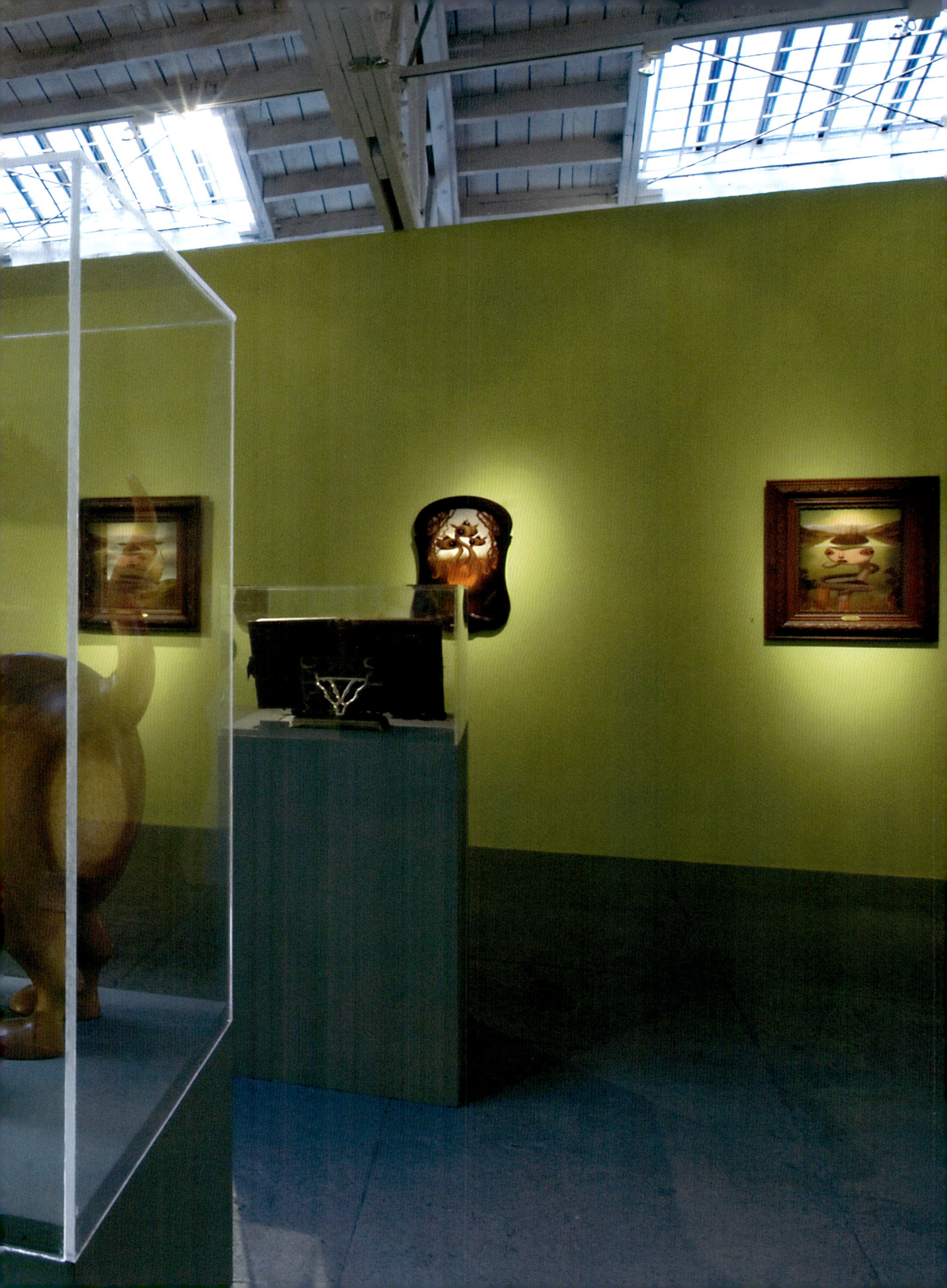

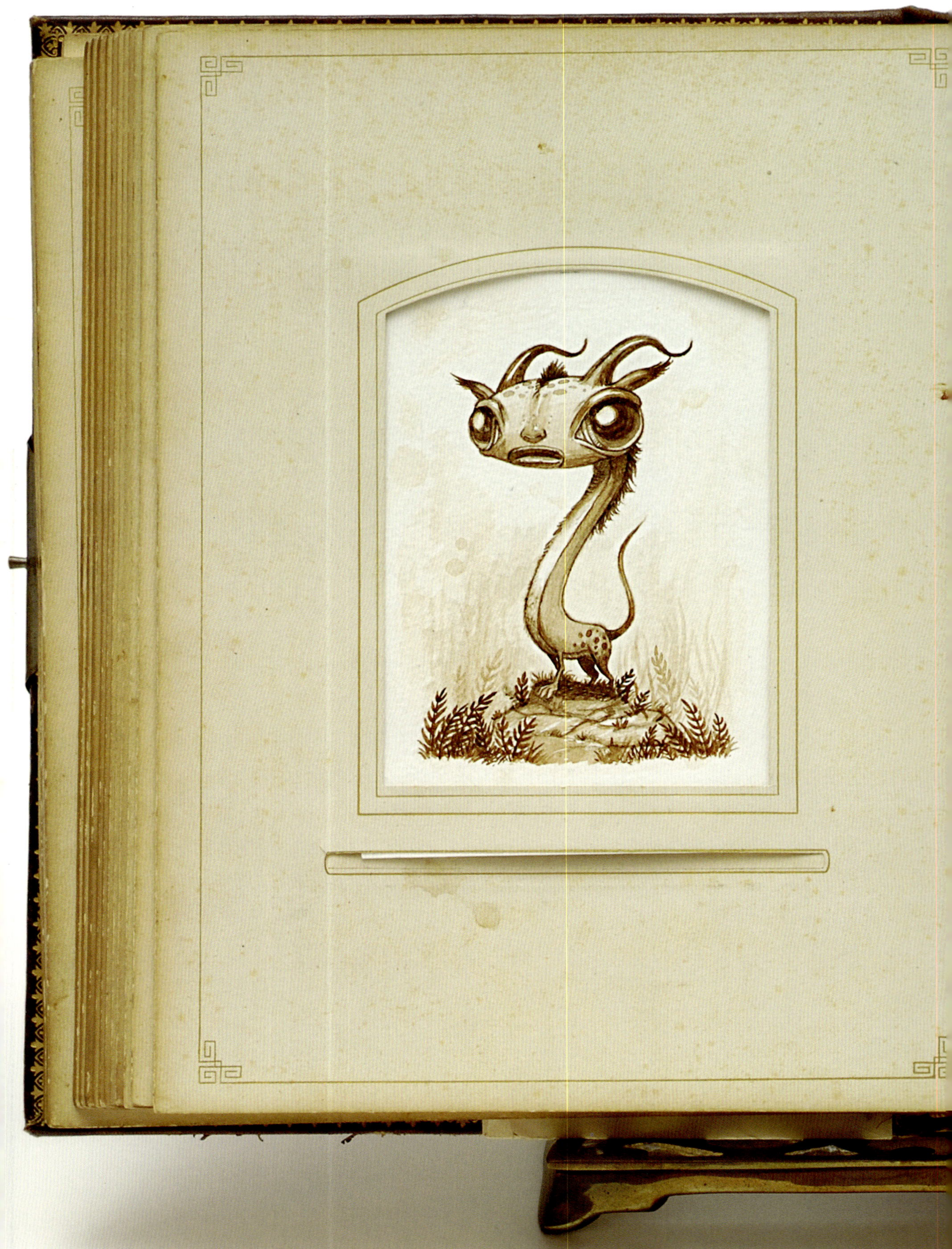

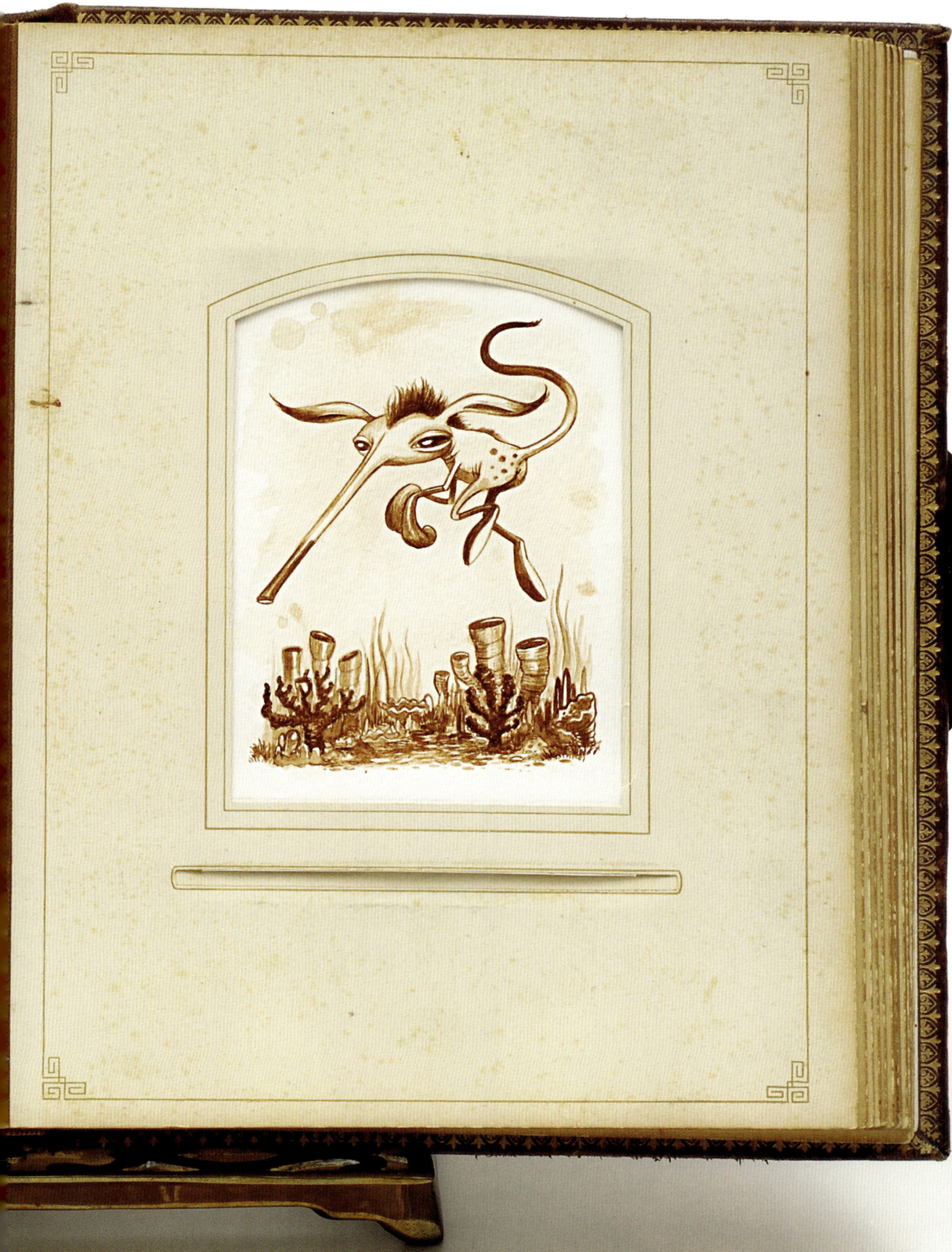

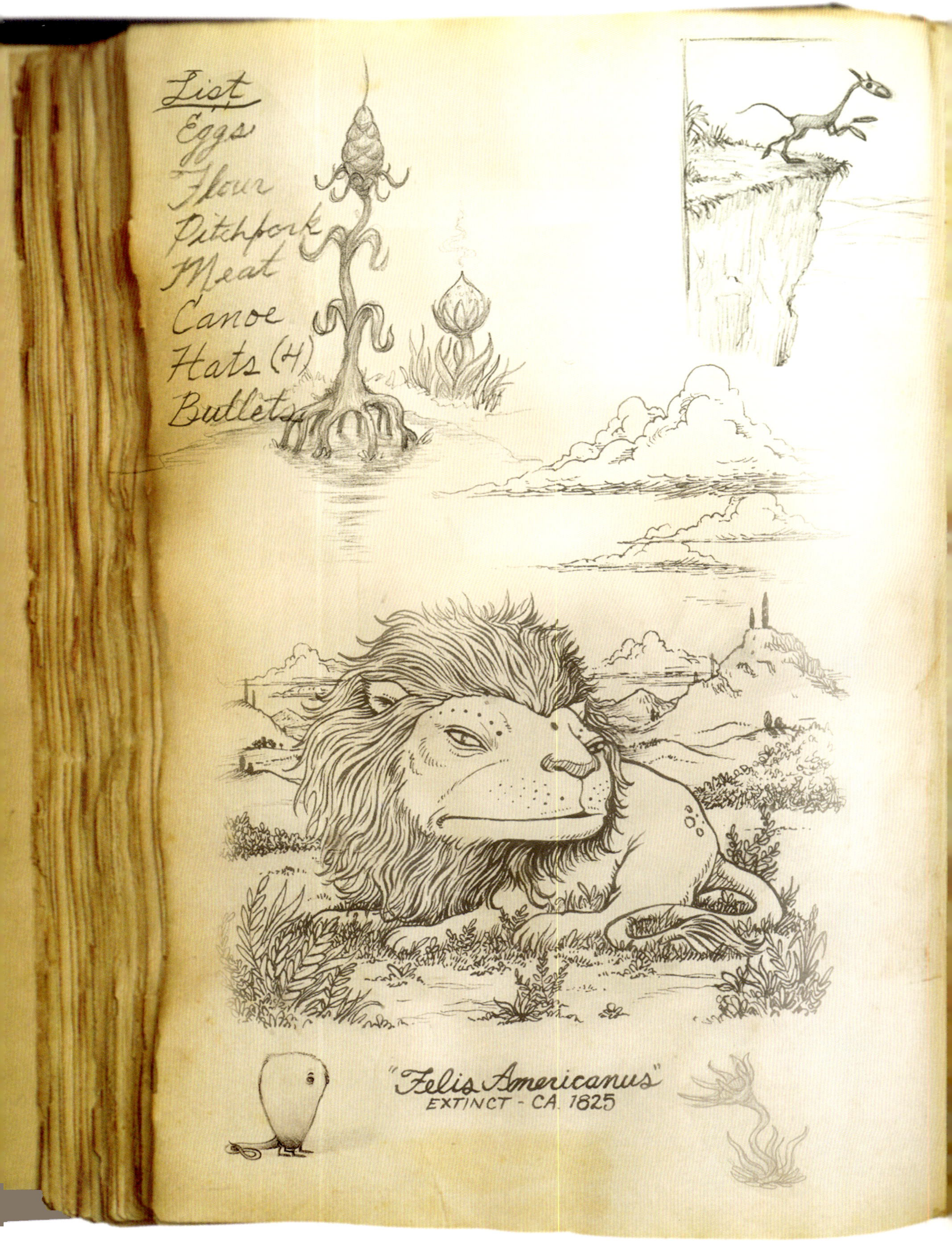
List
Eggs
Flour
Pitchfork
Meat
Canoe
Hats (4)
Bullets
"Felis Americanus"
EXTINCT - CA. 1825

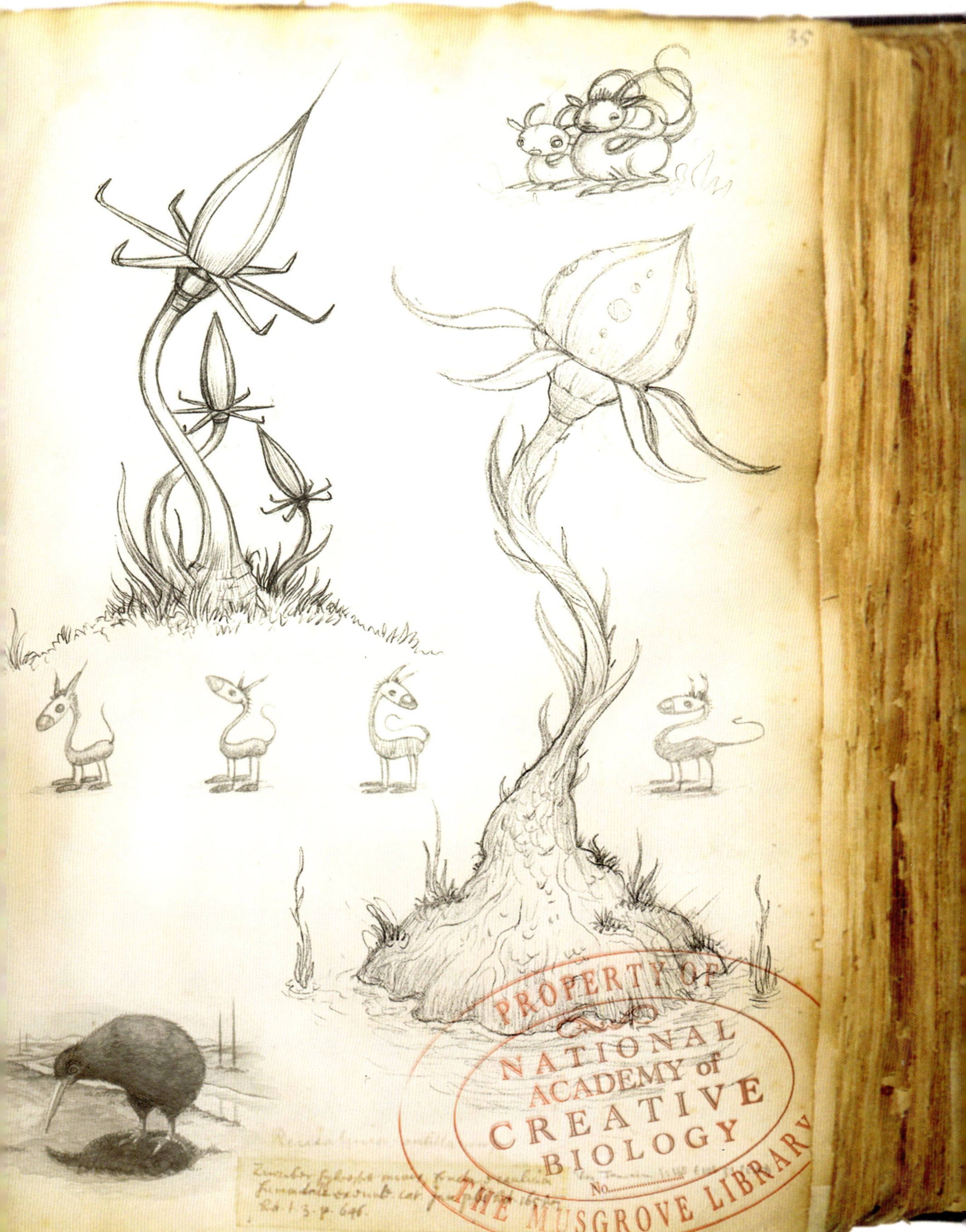
PROPERTY OF
NATIONAL
ACADEMY of
CREATIVE
BIOLOGY
No.
THE MUSGROVE LIBRARY

FAUNA VIABILITY TIMELINE & INDEX

EXTINCTED
PAGE NO.

1770 · 1810 · 1850 · 1890 · 1930

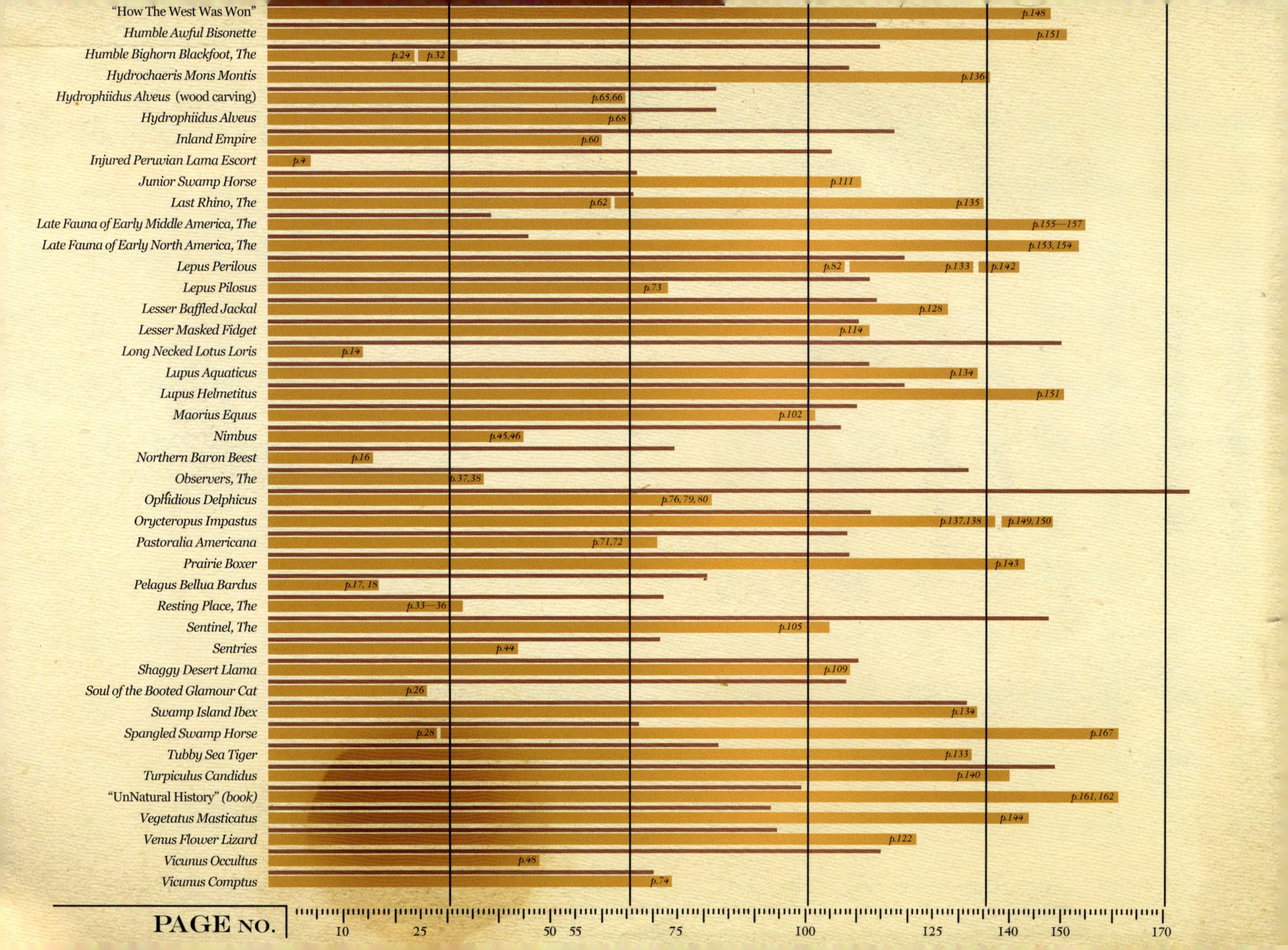
"How The West Was Won" p.148
Humble Awful Bisonette p.151
Humble Bighorn Blackfoot, The p.24 p.32
Hydrochaeris Mons Montis p.136
Hydrophiidus Alveus (wood carving) p.65,66
Hydrophiidus Alveus p.68
Inland Empire p.60
Injured Peruvian Lama Escort p.4
Junior Swamp Horse p.111
Last Rhino, The p.62 p.135
Late Fauna of Early Middle America, The p.155—157
Late Fauna of Early North America, The p.153,154
Lepus Perilous p.82 p.133 p.142
Lepus Pilosus p.73
Lesser Baffled Jackal p.128
Lesser Masked Fidget p.114
Long Necked Lotus Loris p.14
Lupus Aquaticus p.134
Lupus Helmetitus p.151
Maorius Equus p.102
Nimbus p.45,46
Northern Baron Beest p.16
Observers, The p.37,38
Ophidious Delphicus p.76,79,80
Orycteropus Impastus p.137,138 p.149,150
Pastoralia Americana p.71,72
Prairie Boxer p.143
Pelagus Bellua Bardus p.17,18
Resting Place, The p.33—36
Sentinel, The p.105
Sentries p.44
Shaggy Desert Llama p.109
Soul of the Booted Glamour Cat p.26
Swamp Island Ibex p.134
Spangled Swamp Horse p.28 p.167
Tubby Sea Tiger p.133
Turpiculus Candidus p.140
"UnNatural History" (book) p.161,162
Vegetatus Masticatus p.144
Venus Flower Lizard p.122
Vicunus Occultus p.48
Vicunus Comptus p.74
PAGE NO.
10 25 50 55 75 100 125 140 150 170

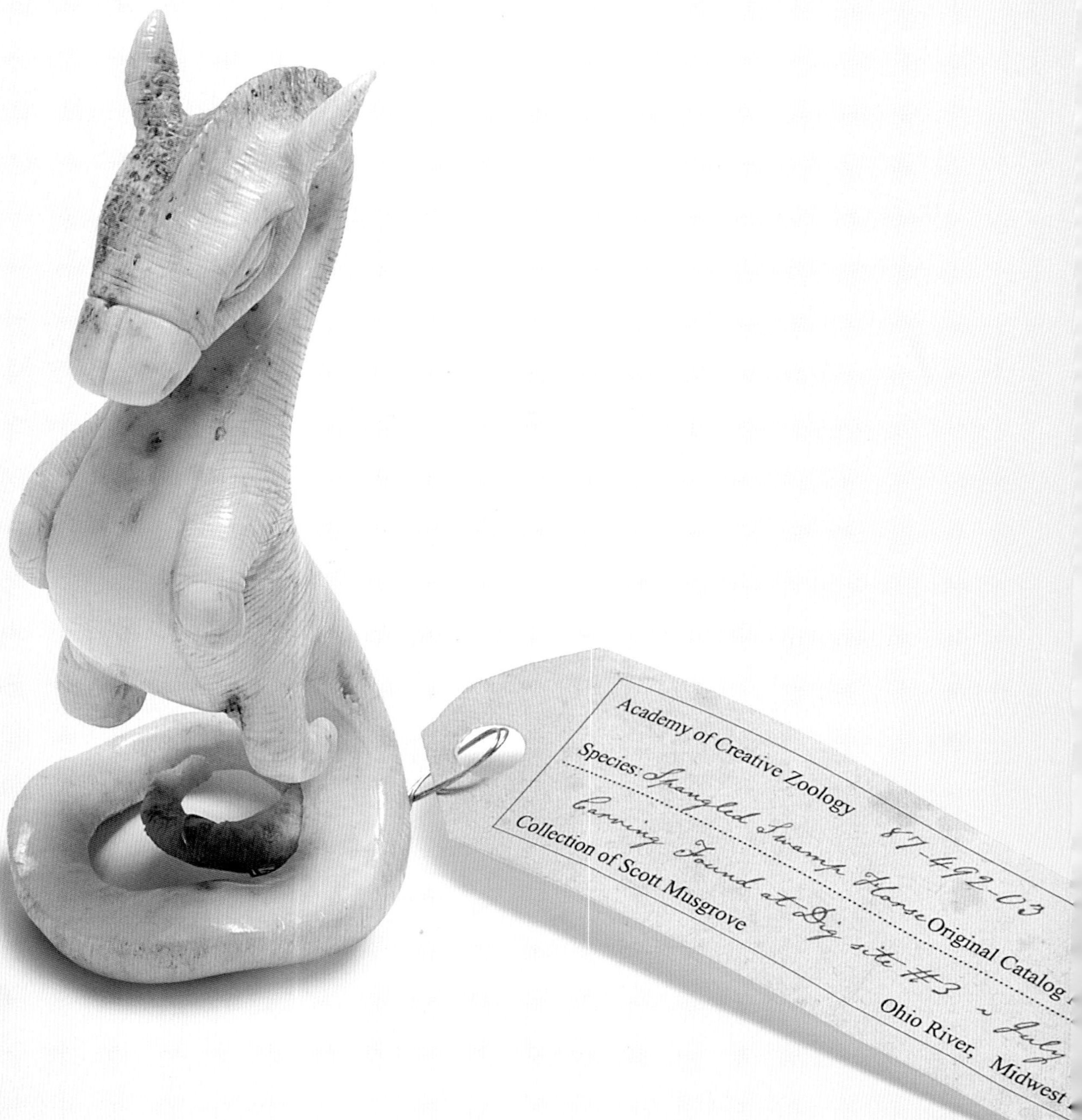
Academy of Creative Zoology
87-492-03
Species: Spangled Swamp Horse
Original Catalog
Carving Found at Dig site #3 ~ July
Collection of Scott Musgrove
Ohio River, Midwest

THANK YOU. . . . . Gretchen Sorrels-Musgrove, Sam and Mary Lynne Musgrove, Jim Sorrels, Tyler Sorrels and Mary Heller, Todd Musgrove , Trey, Linda and Samantha Musgrove , Wilda Musgrove, Shawn Wolfe, Brian Wallace, Randy Lewis, Billy Shire, Jonathan Levine, Joshua Liner, Annie Adjchavanich, Kirsten Anderson, Eric White, Joe Sorren, Brian Despain, Michael Leavitt, Jud Bergeron, John Arcudi, Shin Na, Laurel Ehrenfreund, John Roderick, Beau Hebert, Mike Minney, Mike Bianchi, Darick Chamberlin, John and Brenda Bush, Brian White, Eric, Dave and Carol Rea, Kevin Looker, Brad Keech and Pressure Printing, Ken Wagner Photography, Sally at The Gold Leaf, Barone Engraving

SPECIAL THANKS . . . . Chance and I Nyoman Sedayatana (wood carving, Bali)
Sculpture of *Great Lesser Plant Sampler* on pgs. 85, 86 is a collaboration with Michael Leavitt.
Photo Credit pgs. 159—162 Larry Underhill, for Billy Shire Fine Arts

BOOK DESIGN . . . . Shawn Wolfe

EDITED BY . . . . Janice S. Gore, Ph.D.

PRINTED BY . . . . Codra Enterprises ~ China
Forest Stewardship Council Certified Paper ~ New Growth Paper ~ Soy ink

PUBLISHED BY . . . . Billy Shire Fine Arts ~ 5790 Washington Blvd., Culver City, CA 90232
Last Gasp ~ 777 Florida St., San Francisco, CA 94110

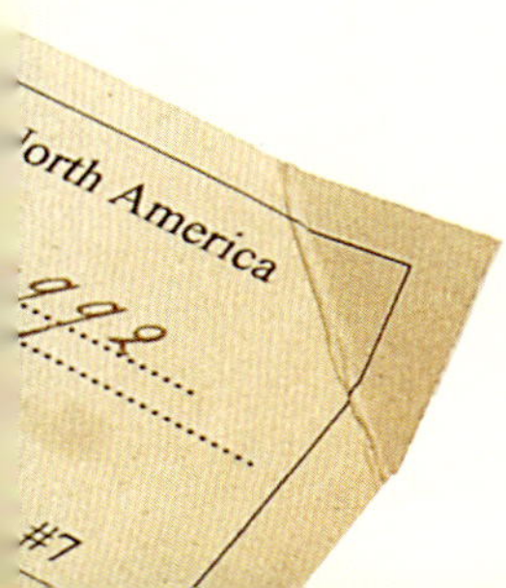

FSC
Mixed Sources
Product group from well-managed forests, controlled sources and recycled wood or fibre
Cert no. SGS-COC-003540
www.fsc.org
© 1996 Forest Stewardship Council

Recipe

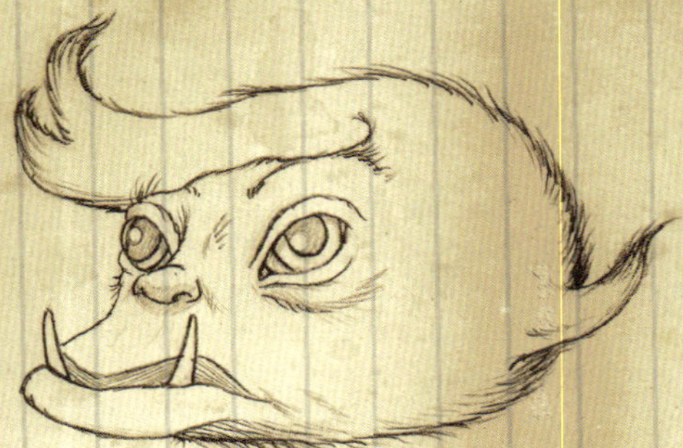

Hairy Brook Trout

Serves 70 people

~ Catch and Shave a 35lb. Hairy Brook Trout
~ Hold fish by the tail and Shake Vigourously until all the bones fall out.
~ Spoon out Musk Glands; 8–10 minutes.
~ Hack into bite-sized morsels.
~ Mix in Cast Iron Pot with 3 fistfuls of Donkey Lard.
~ Add Salt, Pepper and Gunpowder to suit taste.
~ Serve on a clean Horse Blanket
~ Enjoy!

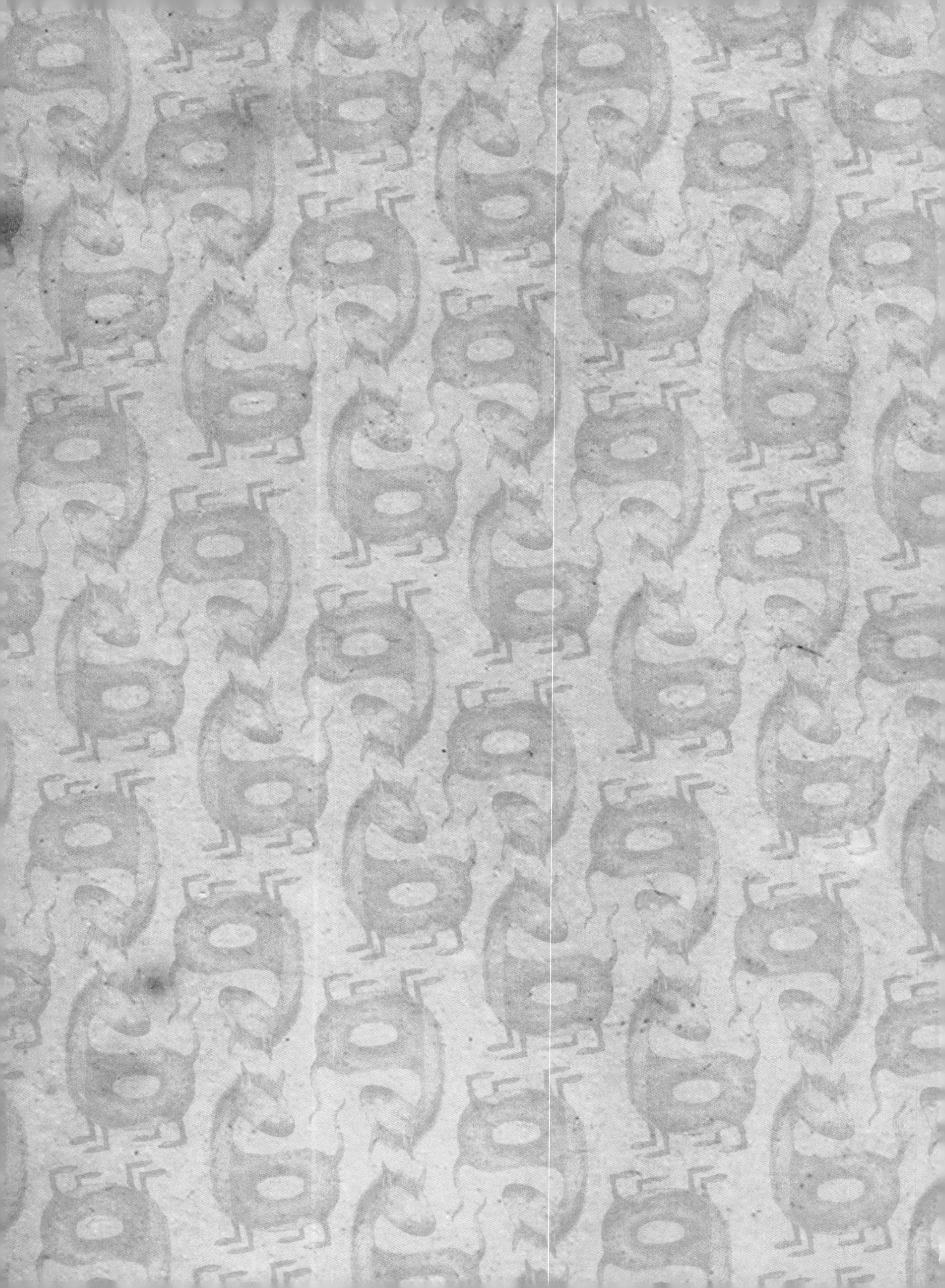